A Family Trust

Ward Just

A FAMILY TRUST

A NOVEL

PUBLICAFFAIRS
New York

Originally published in 1978 by Atlantic-Little Brown Books,
Little, Brown and Company in association with the Atlantic Monthly Press.

LIBRARY OF CONGRESS CATALOGING-IN-PUBLICATION DATA
Just, Ward S.
A family trust : a novel / Ward Just.
p. cm
ISBN 1-58648-034-0
1. Korean War, 1950–1953—Middle West—Fiction.
2. Family-owned business enterprises—Fiction.
3. Newspaper publishing—Fiction.
4. Middle West—Fiction.
I. Title.
PS3560.U75 F3 2001
813'.54—dc21   00-051788

FIRST PUBLICAFFAIRS EDITION 2001

1 3 5 7 9 10 8 6 4 2

As always, for Sarah

And for Joy Just Steiner

It is a strange thing to be an American.
                    . . . We dwell
On the half earth, on the open curve of a continent.
Sea is divided from sea by the day-fall. The dawn
Rides the low east with us many hours;
First are the capes, then are the shorelands, now
The blue Appalachians faint at the day rise;
The willows shudder with light on the long Ohio:
The Lakes scatter the low sun: the prairies
Slide out of dark . . .

—ARCHIBALD MACLEISH, "American Letter"

A Family Trust

Prologue

IN HIS LAST lucid moments he remembered it exactly. Capone's man was due at eight. Haight and Cavaretta arrived at seven-thirty. He put them out of sight in Charles's office. Haight was nervous and talkative but Cavaretta was mute. Haight never told him where Cavaretta had come from and he was glad not to know. He had no desire to know. When the man came he'd close the office door. Then Haight and Cavaretta were to leave Charles's office and station themselves on either side of the door, and listen. When they heard two thumps—he banged his big shoe against the desk leg twice, showing them—they were to enter without delay and show the man to the street, and they need not be in any way particular about how they did it.

Capone's man came at the appointed hour. He met the man in the lobby, as promised, and they went to his third-floor office. The man took the visitor's chair. Capone's man wore a pearl-gray fedora and a white linen suit, and he'd arrived in a black Packard. No chauffeur; he'd driven himself.

It was twenty-two years ago; he was sixty-three then. Capone's man looked to be in his middle thirties, though it was hard to tell; he was an Irishman with a quick smile. He'd taken his seat and begun to talk without delay. He said there were two ways they could go. He and his associates would buy fifty-one percent of the newspaper. Or they would start another newspaper. They had two men who were willing to do it: one man would be editor and the other would be publisher. Their capital was unlimited and they were willing to cut advertising rates to almost nothing—to a flat nothing, in fact, if that was what it took to drive the *Intelligencer* out of business. They'd give the paper away if necessary. Or everyone could be saved grief and anxiety not to mention money if you—he pointed at the editor—lay off our operations. He said, We're not bringing girls in here. We're not going to build a racetrack, contrary to any rumor you might've heard. It's just two clubs in the country, some dice, a wheel, half a dozen slots, a wire, and a gentlemanly card game or three. And of course refreshments will be served. These games of chance, and the refreshments, will be thoroughly supervised by Mr. Capone's people and I am here to personally assure you—he pointed his finger again—that the operation will be completely clean. We do not tolerate disorder, he said.

Where are the locations of the clubs?

The man in the fedora named them. Now, he said, we have been subject to harassment. Your sheriff, Haight, has harassed us. It has taken some time and trouble to find out who was behind Haight. And we have discovered that it is you. You own this town.

He looked at him, expressionless.

The man said, You're just like Mr. Capone in his town. Then he laughed, a high giggle. The man in the fedora was polite and fastidious in his language. What we want to do, the man said, is make a deal. Something fair and equitable to both sides. So that it will not be necessary to do the other.

His memory faded then. They talked for some time; or the man talked. The editor listened, occasionally interjecting a question. But while he listened, he weighed. This was a determined man and he had resources. He tried to calculate what the man in the fedora would settle for. Capone (assuming Capone was truly the principal) had obviously given him instructions and the editor wanted to know exactly what those instructions were. How much effort were they willing to put into Dement? The longer they talked, the less he liked the man. After thirty minutes his language became rough and his manner discourteous. He'd thought for a moment that an arrangement was possible, one club perhaps on the county line; local men involved. If the man in the fedora were trustworthy, they in Dement could live with that. His foot floated near the desk leg.

Finally the man jabbed a finger at him. "Amos, I can't fart around here all evening—"

And the editor had roared at him, "Don't you ever call me Amos!"

"—and this shitting little rag—"

The editor came out of his chair in a second and swept the fedora to the floor, Capone's man following. Haight and Cavaretta burst through the door and Cavaretta kicked him once in the head and Haight, swinging a billy, missed and cracked the editor on the arm. The man was on his feet then, dazed. He ducked one of Cavaretta's blows, side-stepped Haight, and swung wildly at the editor. Then he kneed Cavaretta and pushed Haight aside. The editor swung at him twice, missing both times. Cavaretta, grunting with pain, drove his head into the man's stomach. Haight, flailing, stumbled into the editor and they both went down. The man and Cavaretta were now in the outer office, beating on each other. By then the sheriff had his revolver in hand and was advancing slowly into the hall. But when he got there Cavaretta was slumped over a desk and the man had disappeared. Then they heard the crash of breaking glass and the engine of the Packard. The editor heard the horn, an insolent beep*beep*. And he was gone, having flung an inkpot through the front window of the *I* on the way out.

All in all, Amos Rising thought, a success.

Autumn, 1953

DEMENT, the town—

Forty miles north is a renowned spa, mineral baths and a golf course and a fine hotel and a lake; one great city lies a distance to the east and another to the south. The state capital lies farther still southeast. Dement the town is at the eastern edge of Dement County. In the county are a dozen smaller towns, ranging in size from a few hundred to a few thousand. Dement town, thirty thousands souls, is a county seat—containing the courthouse, the industries, the hospital, the Sears, the railroad station and the newspaper. It is a hard, thriving core surrounded by prairie. The highway skirts its eastern edge and a traveler from Chicago or St. Louis bound by road or rail to the spa would take no special notice of Dement. The town's character cannot be seen from the highway. In the manner of midwestern towns its features are plain, the business district low and compact, the streets narrow and regular. To the noiseless east lies a shallow river and the Reilly Bog. The town sits on a low bluff overlooking the bog, and the prairie beyond the bog. West, there are no impediments. An early traveler noted that Dement's situation, though remote, was agreeable and blessed with a climate "pure, bracing and healthful."

ELLIOTT TOWNSEND stretched, and moved heavily to the window, where he stood watching dusk. He threw up the sash and cold air caught him by surprise. The sun had disappeared behind the big oak, darkening the lawn and casting blurred shadows in the backyard cornfield. Townsend rested his fingernails on the sill and leaned out, shak-

ing his big shaggy head. Then he closed the window and stepped into
the narrow hall to fetch his hat and coat. He lit a cigar and marched
into the kitchen and through the back door. He was halfway down the
steps when the telephone rang. He paused for a moment, listening to
the ringing, then continued on his way, closing the door firmly behind
him. The ringing continued. Crows screamed at him and flew off into
the cornfield, circling the decrepit scarecrow.

He scuffed through the leaves, breathing heavily. "Bastards," he said
aloud. He pulled his fedora down over one eye and jammed his hands
in his overcoat pockets. Almost winter now and it seemed to him that
April was only yesterday. He measured the seasons in degrees of difficulty. Spring was difficult, winter was very difficult. He cocked his
head and listened; the telephone was fully silent now. He'd have to
hurry along; they'd try again in half an hour and if he didn't answer
then they'd send someone over to find out why. A deputy, hat in hand,
half expecting to find him face down in the bathtub. He grunted out
loud. Fat chance.

Townsend moved away from the house. He reckoned he had about
thirty minutes to collect himself, to put his private emotions behind
him. That was Amos Rising's boy on the telephone and he knew what
the message was. No other reason to call at five o'clock on a Sunday
afternoon. Townsend wanted time to think, because quite a lot would
depend on that first conversation, he and the three Rising boys together, probably at Charles Rising's house. Then the second confer-
ence in Amos's office. It was not just a simple matter of reading a
document and translating lawyer's language into family language. No,
that was the least of it.

He strolled on down to the cornfield. Hardly anyone left now, he
said to himself. Then aloud, "Except me." He'd outlasted everyone,
friends as well as enemies; Rising was the last one. The smoke from his
cigar smelled clean in the chill air, mingling with the aroma of dead
leaves and cold soil, as familiar to Townsend as his own sweat. He
paused at the barbecue pit, the pit black from fire; they'd had a fine
cornroast this year. The corn was good every year. This year it had

been very good, though Amos had not tended it properly. Couldn't. Townsend dipped his foot into the pit and kicked at an ember. Steppe and Tilberg and Harold ("Aces") Evans drunk, as usual; Tom Kerrigan sarcastic; the young ones nervous and careful with their smiles. And Amos not himself, nursing his brandy, distracted and irritable and, Townsend knew, in pain. No doubt this was the last of the cornroasts, the *real* cornroasts; damn thing was Amos's affair as much as it was his. More. For forty years the two of them had met the day after Labor Day to draw up the list. The cornroast was always held on the second of October, rain or shine. They'd begun with a dozen men and it had grown to fifty and then to a hundred and last month they'd fed and watered a hundred and fifty men and Marge Reilly, who came early and stayed only a short while. She felt, as she said, like a fish on dry land and it was true that she was an inhibiting influence. It was important to know what everyone was thinking. He and Amos, they wanted to be forearmed; they did not like surprises, so they worked the crowd like a couple of grifters, glad-handing, listening hard, lying a little . . . Well. They would do it again next year; same corn, same people. The boys would be there but the mood would be artificial. The thing was Amos's.

Townsend moved away from the barbecue pit and leaned unsteadily against the big oak. It was the only thing on the place that was older than he was. He'd built the house in 1910 and planted the cornfield the same year. Looking at the cornfield, fading now in the last light, he thought of the Indian Summer drawing in the Chicago *Tribune*, the *Trib*'s regular announcement of autumn. This was John T. McCutcheon's drawing, a man and a boy sitting before a fire, the old man relating stories of a frontier past in the Midwest. Indians rise from the flames; you can almost hear the war whoops. It was the heritage of the region, a swift dispatch of the Indians; no Sitting Bulls, no Cochises. In the Midwest the Indian leaders were faceless and quick to yield their lands. As a boy he himself had listened to the backwoodsmen talk of homesteading Birks' Prairie, fashioning cabins twenty-six by sixteen. One of them claimed to've known Lincoln, as a young man to have retained Lincoln in a suit against the government (and lost). Lincoln, he'd said, "was weird." But mostly they talked about the Indians—promiscuous, filthy, brutish, savage, citing the great Custer as evidence. Custer said the Indian was "a creature possessing the human form but divested of all other attributes of humanity, and whose traits of character, habits, modes of life, disposition, and savage customs disqualified him from the exercise of all rights and privileges, even those pertaining to life itself." He'd been that close to it; close enough to touch. Townsend remembered them becoming furious just talking about it, their voices loud and trailing off in obscenities. He remembered them so well, with their wide, unblinking eyes and lined foreheads. His father had told him that these backwoodsmen had good and sufficient reason for their hatreds. They'd been there after all, they were talking firsthand, men of strong prejudice. They didn't like bankers either, or the railroads or government officials, or land agents or attorneys. Townsend's lawyer father believed that it was the freedom guaranteed by the Constitution that restrained the murderous impulses of the people. He told his son, If this were Europe these men would be revolutionaries. We're lucky we live in the heartland of America. We're lucky we're where we are. These are good men, stubborn and hotheaded but not rebellious.

He tried to remember the circumstances of that particular conversation. It had begun with a reference to the martyred Custer. He thought it was probably when he was eight or thereabouts; in 1886, give or take a year. The man who hated Indians must have been about seventy. Elliott Townsend smiled to himself. It was a long link; his reach went back to the early nineteenth century. All that time in one location, what he didn't know about the region wasn't worth knowing. He and his father had practiced law continuously for eighty years, including the two bad years, 1887 and 1888. His father had got his wind up, God knows why; he'd pulled up stakes and taken his wife and young son to Nebraska. Elliott Townsend never knew why, had never been told; it had something to do with his mother, he was certain, but just what it was he never knew and never would know. When men died it wasn't just flesh and bone and soul that perished, or maybe not even mainly those things; it was veracity. His father thought he was going to bring law to western Nebraska. It was 1887. They acquired land with a cabin on it and his father made the rounds by horseback. The next year, as if in revenge for a decade of mild winters, the worst blizzard in the history of the West struck the region. This land, known then as "the great American desert," was occupied by new arrivals like the Townsends who did not understand the violence of the plains. That January morning in 1888 it was sixty-five degrees where they lived, men working the fields in shirtsleeves; in schoolhouses the stoves were cold and woodpiles neglected. By dusk that day it was ten below, the snow whirling in a frenzy; in two days there were some six hundred dead in Nebraska alone, west of the hundredth meridian. Forever after the hundredth meridian was the line of demarcation; beyond it was the great desert. The following summer his father packed up and they went back to the Mississippi Valley and settled in Dement. The blizzard wiped out a generation of homesteaders and stopped the westward movement dead, until memories dimmed. That beautiful day in January, the sun so high and milky; and the savagery that followed. His father never recovered; he was frightened for the rest of his life, haunted always by the sight of his wife frozen by the side of the road. She'd been caught only a mile or two from their cabin, had lost her way, and died. They did not find her for some time; drifting snow covered everything and a second storm followed the first. It was Elliott Townsend's earliest memory; that, and the backwoodsman talking of Indians, and General Custer.

He stared into the dead cornfield, his own, and wiped his eyes. He had lived seventy-five years but the memory of that January day had stayed with him, the canvas on which he'd painted his life. Nothing ever had been as bad as seeing his mother dead, and the cold silence before, his father mute with grief; he had known at the time that nothing ever again would be as bad. He forced his mind away from Nebraska and fastened on the backwoodsman. He was a primary source and not so different in his own way from Amos. Amos who was eighty-five, who'd heard the same stories, and whose reach went back even farther. He thought of Amos standing at the barbecue pit late at night, after the young men had gone. He and Amos and Tilberg and Steppe and Aces Evans and one or two others, talking quietly as the fire roared and spat. They talked of the young men, which ones were comers and which were not; they did not discuss the sons of those men who were present. There were always threats from the outside and it was important that a young man be reliable, "sound." Too often there was trouble of some kind, bottle trouble, women trouble, smart trouble—that last an Amos coinage meaning too smart or too dumb, depending on the inflection. A month before everyone had been subdued. Amos looked like death itself, gray and ponderous. He was the senior man and when he went it would rearrange the hierarchy, except unlike a pope or president no one could take his place. Every year one or two of them died and the town now was like an army with too few generals; restless foot soldiers everywhere and no one to command them. Law firms passed into younger hands; judges retired; the sheriff was old and ineffective. Now Amos. The end of the Korean War signaled something, though what it was seemed as ambiguous as the truce itself; they had not finished the war, they had ended it. Veterans returning to Dement seemed to Townsend a generation of pint-sized Insulls; they wanted to make their fortunes at once. In the past few years politics had moved off in unfamiliar directions, constituents to the east agitating for a highway, four lanes, to hook into the main road to Chicago and beyond. "Industrialists" from St. Louis and Chicago were negotiating for land and everywhere there was an abundance of loose money. All his life Amos Rising had feared the big cities, their turbulence and aggression, savagery, chaos, and surprise. He hated it when young men, the sons of old-line families, left Dement for the riotous cities, considering it a betrayal. The old man still had some of the backwoodsman in him. Dement wasn't a frontier anymore and the hatreds weren't so sharp-edged. The Indians were gone, replaced by a new and more formidable enemy. Amos called them aliens; by which he meant, outsiders.

Townsend rubbed his hands, rocking back and forth on his heels. *Amos,* he said aloud; and again, *Amos.* He understood the native-born restlessness and impatience that infected the times. Young men now had trouble locating their instincts; too much of what they saw and read and felt conflicted with the beat of life in Dement. *His* beat. He believed that the function of a newspaper was to supply a memory. The newspaper was not a check on government; it was a check on the passionate instincts of the people. Reliable instincts were nothing more than memories refined. A memory was a magnet attracting the filings of the present, and if the magnet were weak—well, it left a human being adrift and ill at ease on the surface of the earth. A man's memory could not function properly unless there were familiar things to see and touch. Amos Rising had made his newspaper magnetic, as familiar as a downtown street or the face of a daughter. Reading it, a soul was reassured. The newspaper offered consolation.

He spilled more smoke from his mouth, holding the cigar in front of him, regarding it with affection. He moved forward, lifting his head to look beyond the cornfield, the thick bogland lying ragged and dark against the horizon. *Amos.* Darkness closed around him now, and there were no lights between him and the horizon.

A breeze crossed the lawn and he pushed off from the oak. The cigar was now firmly between his teeth, an incongruous sight; a bowsprit on an ocean liner. It was time for hard thinking, no more reminiscence. It was time now to get the facts straight and arranged properly. He was obliged to separate money from power. He'd begin with that. Charles knew it all, the old man had explained it to him. So he, Townsend, would be addressing the other two boys. They were the ones whose understanding and support was vital. Speaking softly and slowly, so the three of them would have to lean forward to hear, he'd lay out the essentials. He'd say:

It would have been better if your dad had explained this to you himself. It's a complicated distribution. However, it is not ambiguous. He has divided the stock into two classes, preferred and common.

He would look first at Mitch, then Tony, then Charles.

The preferred is divided forty, forty, twenty. Forty to Mitch, forty to Tony, twenty to Charles. The preferred pays a fixed dividend. It is in first position, so to speak. But as you know, the preferred is nonvoting. (They didn't—how could they? The old man had told them nothing, and there had never been a stockholders' meeting.) *The common stock, the voting stock, is divided sixty, twenty, twenty. Sixty to Charles, twenty to Mitch, twenty to Tony.*

A pause, to allow them to digest the information.

Your father and I tried to reckon the distribution as evenly as we could on the basis of the profits of the newspaper. This is impossible to do with complete precision. But it is as close as we could get to it.

Another pause, too brief to permit questions.

It was intolerable to both of us, to your dad and to me, to see control of the paper split. Control must be in a single pair of hands. No successful newspaper was ever run by a committee.

He would look at them again, all three, to assure himself that they were following him, every word. Their reactions would determine how he would present the next point. He believed they would be silent, listening carefully; they would betray very little, with the exception of Mitch, who would be waiting for the hook.

Of course you boys are in harmony, you've always been in harmony. But unfortunately one cannot dictate the future, though God knows in the past your father and I have tried (ha-ha-ha). Who knows what might happen in a year or five years or ten. Illness, death, incapacitation; some other irregularity. No one knows the future. Of you three, your father believed that Charles was the better businessman. Therefore, he has been given control. Not, I hasten to say, control of the profits; he is in control of the policy. It was your father's wish that the present assignments continue. Mitch will continue as general manager, Tony as circulation director, and Charles will of course become editor and publisher. It was your father's wish that the two titles be joined. One cannot be an editor without being a publisher also; and of course the reverse is also true. The one authority strengthens the other. All of that is fairly straightforward.

He would pause again, and consult the document in his hand.

What follows, I'm afraid, is a bit more out of the ordinary. It's a codicil, and rather than read it, I'll try to explain it in nonlawyer's language. I'll explain what it means. It has to do with any eventual disposition of the newspaper stock. Your father has established a committee empowered to rule on any sale or transfer. It's a committee of three, Mitch, me, and Marge Reilly. It goes without saying that your father insists that the newspaper stay inside the family. As long as there is a family, this newspaper should belong to it. I am certain that the committee will never meet. However, it is there if needs be.

Then he would hand them the codicil.

How many hours had they spent together working on that provision? Hundreds of hours, literally hundreds, over twenty years' time. He'd brought in an outside counsel, and while everyone agreed there were legal problems, they also agreed it would take years to resolve them. It was uncertain if the codicil could extend to the next generation, Amos's grandchildren. They had created a device whereby all common stock was for practical purposes "in trust," in the sense that it could not be sold or transferred without committee approval and he and Marge Reilly would always vote to withhold that approval (if the buyer were an outsider). Among the brothers only Charles possessed a majority to sell, and Mitch would never stand for that. So the committee vote would most likely be unanimous. It had a kind of genius to it, this codicil; normally trusts were established to avoid taxes. Amos didn't care about money, all he wanted was the newspaper tied forever to the family (and vice versa). Specifically he wanted to tie to it Charles, whom he felt was best qualified to select a successor. Elliott Townsend tried to warn his friend that the boys wouldn't understand this will, *couldn't* understand it because they lived in different worlds; and because they were still young, all of them under fifty. It was just beginning to occur to them that they could be rich. Not as rich as Insull or McCormick but rich enough; very rich for Dement. Amos was indifferent to money, he was concerned only with the authority and influence of his newspaper, and he was determined to control its affairs from beyond the grave. He and the newspaper were the same thing; the soul of one was the soul of the other. Townsend didn't know how the boys would react, though he believed that the apparent equality of financial interest would quiet any objections. Until they began to think about it carefully, or hired a good lawyer to think about it for them; then the questions would begin. The fact was, Charles had control. He controlled the assets and was therefore empowered to choose his successor. It was the old man's property and he was entitled to distribute it in any way he saw fit. But Townsend did not want a family quarrel, and would do what was necessary to prevent one.

Trouble was, none of the boys understood or knew their father. He wasn't a father in the modern sense, he was a symbol, a progenitor, an ancestor more remote than a mere parent. He didn't take the boys into his confidence. He cared about them, they were his flesh and blood; he saw different parts of himself in each boy. But he didn't reveal himself to them, nor did he care to have them reveal themselves to him. He prepared for them an ethical sanctuary and supplied them with rules—what greater gift? Perhaps he felt that only in that way could he retain control. A single-minded man, he cared nothing for the role of paterfamilias; he had no interest in the personal lives of his children, any more than he cared for ornaments for himself—clothes or expensive vacations or yachts or women, except of course for Ella and Jo. His clothes came off the rack at Levay's downtown and he had never taken a vacation in his life. He and Jo had been married for fifty years, a union so thick it was impossible to think of one without thinking of the other. The boys did not know about Ella. Townsend shook his head and turned back, looking now at the old Ashcroft house next to his own, his eyes moving slowly upward from the first floor to the second, the deep-sloping roof with the belvedere at its crown. Other people lived there now, a young married couple. Amos'd said that when Ella died his desire died, too.

The cigar was dead and he threw it away. Of course Amos would be well today if she were still alive (either of them, in fact). If either

Ella or Jo were still with him, he'd live to be a hundred. (Townsend smiled at that: how many times in his office had he heard a client curse the dead? If only old Uh had not had the discourtesy to die, all would be well . . .) But it was true nevertheless, Amos had lived his life in compartments; and that one compartment, Ella's, linked all the others. He remembered Amos's labored breathing when they talked three days ago; pausing between sentences, shaking his head, muttering a little, then his signal on the buzzer to summon the nurse. Another injection; he was hurting. He wanted to talk it all out, as if the act of speech might bring it back fully. He said that in his whole life he'd only been with two women. He'd made love in only two beds, and those beds were scarcely a hundred yards from each other. They were second-floor beds, precisely the same height, both facing west.

Amos said, "She was a fine woman and shrewd. Ella took an interest, you know. Jo never cared much for the workings of things. Fine wife, fine mother; she was the one who raised the boys, kept the home fires. But Ella . . . Ah *God*, I hated it when she died. But anyhow the suddenness of it was a blessing. There was no suffering, and I know what I'm talking about. But when she passed on—" Amos turned away, finding no need to finish the thought.

Townsend, knowing the answer but irresistibly curious, had asked him: "Worse than Jo?" Ella was dead now five years; Jo three.

"Different," Amos replied.

Townsend smiled sadly. He looked again at the house, the severe gables, the second-floor bedroom, the belvedere. It had begun in the winter of 1913; Townsend could name the day if pressed. Ella's husband was ill and died in 1915. That year Amos bought the house without her knowledge and fixed an unreasonably low rent. He bought it because Jo asked him to—poor Ella, she'd said, Tom Ashcroft didn't leave her much. It would be nice for her, a dear friend living next to Elliott, maybe she and Elliott . . . Amos said he'd look into it, and then he bought the house. Years later, when it became necessary to explain to Ella Ashcroft what he'd done, he told her the house was hers for as long as she wanted it. And the rent she'd paid for decades, he'd saved that; it was hers now. She was not to think of the house as either gift or loan, she was to think of it as her own by right. By right of occupation. Then he handed her the deed. She'd told him, I've known for years. He looked at her, surprised. How? You, she said. It was obvious, you move around this house as if you owned it. As if it's yours as well as mine. You've got a particular look about you when you're around things you own, or think you own. Oh, he'd said, angry; he thought there'd been a betrayal. She'd laughed then; I don't mind. I like it. Why shouldn't I like it? She said this with a sparkle. And it's been fun for me, knowing you didn't know. There's so little that goes on that you don't know. It's been my secret, and I've loved keeping it.

I thought it was my secret, he said stiffly.

Well it isn't, she said. It never was.

She'd been right about that; not very much went on that Amos Rising didn't know about and approve. Next day he'd come to Townsend's office, blood in his eye, demanding an explanation as prelude to telling him that he was through as his lawyer and as his friend. An indiscreet lawyer was worse than useless, he was a positive menace. They'd argued back and forth for an hour, and Townsend finally convinced him that he'd said nothing, and that Ella had told the truth. She'd made an accurate guess (as women sometimes do).

He'd said to Amos, Women have intuition. She's known from the beginning. And truthfully, so what? It doesn't matter any in the fact. She's grateful. It's just your pride that's hurt.

Amos nodded noncommittally and Townsend answered the next, unspoken question. He said, And I suspect that Jo knows, too, about you and Ella. Or knew at one time. I expect that she both knows and doesn't know.

Impatient with lawyers' paradoxes, Rising had growled that he didn't think that was likely. Never, ever, had Jo so much as—

Townsend smiled his professional smile. Yes, he said. Do you really believe that? Do you think you married a nitwit? You live with someone as closely as you and Jo live. For Pete's sake, she's *got* to know. But she doesn't choose to make an issue of it. Perhaps she's forgotten now, she's pushed it off to one side for reasons of her own. That's hard for you to understand, but people do it all the while. In any event, don't you make an issue of it . . . He remembered Amos rising, and moving to the door. He thought then that he should go farther with his friend. He said, And let me tell you something else. *I* know, and have known all along.

Is that right? Amos said. Then, It's private. Turning away, he collected his hat from the rack in the corner. It's private, he said, and that's the way I like it.

That was the last time they'd spoken of it until three days before. When Ella died she willed the house to her sister. Amos instructed Townsend to quietly offer the sister five thousand dollars above the market price, buyer unknown. He wanted the house back. Coolly, the sister demanded ten. And coldly, without consulting Amos, Townsend had met her price.

He stepped around the barbecue pit and into the cornfield, his big head moving above the tassels. The air was still, and cold. The only sounds were the crunch of his shoes on the furrowed soil, and the rustle of the stalks as he shouldered by them. Ella dead five years, Jo dead three. Now Amos, today or tomorrow. It was hard to imagine life without Amos. He grunted and snapped one of the cornstalks between his fingers, and it made a *crack!* like a pistol shot.

HE PUSHED through the corn, stumbling a little in the furrow. He loved the look of it and the rough texture, though he had no desire to farm. Whatever desire he had, or might have had, died in Nebraska; that desire, among other desires. Nature did not interest him, or things either. He was truly interested only in human beings and the rules they lived by, and the preservation of his civilization. All his life Townsend had tried to think clearly and with realism. He was a conservator. That was what he did. He conserved things, as trustee or guardian or custodian; a curator of personal histories. He conserved people's estates, businesses, marriages; he held things together. Now he was obliged to hold things together for these sons: Charles, forty-three; Tony, forty-five; and Mitch, forty-nine. "The boys," mature in reverse order of their ages. But they would have to learn sometime. He could tender advice, but it was up to Charles to maintain for himself and his family the authority that Amos had so carefully accumulated over the years. He was not sure that Charles had an instinct for it, though he was very good in other ways. He was an excellent businessman. Amos had accumulated authority by creating illusions, and none of them understood it except Ella. Now he was eighty-five and everyone thought he was indestructible, they believed he'd go on forever. Townsend had mentioned that to him, along with the other things, when they'd spoken privately three days before. Amos had laughed loudly, it had hurt him to do so. Sure, he'd said. Indestructible. Dizzy spells, a prostate as big as a golf ball, insomnia, heart trouble, varicose veins and lately "this damnable thing" that had put him on the fourth floor of Mercy Memorial Hospital. And this for a man who had never been sick or in a hospital, ever. But he was lucky in his own way: Amos Rising was not a man preoccupied by pain, his own or anyone else's.

Well, all that was interesting in its way. A diverting digression. But it did not solve the problem at hand. The essence of the codicil was that a committee dominated by outsiders would rule on any transfers of stock. That was plain enough. But there was one other passage that would require an explanation. It was inserted in the codicil at Amos's insistence, despite his lawyer's objection that it was in no way enforceable. It was no better than idle talk but Amos demanded its inclusion. So Townsend knew that he would have to speak in Amos's voice, and convince them as if he were their father, because he himself despised unenforceable rules. It was his intention to insist that nothing had changed. Their father was dead but nothing had changed, the newspaper would go on as before. It was extremely important that the community understand the true situation.

Nothing has changed.

There would be continuity of management and of policy. The policy of the newspaper would not change. He would say that plainly, glancing obliquely at Mitch; he would let it settle, then go farther.

He meant the spirit. What the newspaper stands for, and has always stood for. That's his main concern, really his only concern.

Then, as smooth and offhand as he could make it, he'd tie the one to the other. He'd make the link explicit.

Of course we know that the paper will not be sold. No one has any intention of selling the newspaper, naturally we're all agreed on that. This newspaper belongs to the Rising family.

They'd nod; a sale at that time would be the farthest thing from their minds. He'd say:

In any case, times change. And God forbid sometimes people change with them. Your father was adamant that the newspaper remain in the family, supervised as he himself would supervise it, hence the establishment of the committee and the trust for purpose of sale. He understood you boys but of course he's less certain about the next generation down the line. Your father desired harmony and that is what we will have. There is no reason not to have it. We are all agreed here.

He would glance again at the document and say,

Your father was insistent that you boys remain at the newspaper to carry on its work.

Then he would tell them what to expect. There would be offers within the next few days. Certainly the proprietors of the Chicago newspapers would make offers, and they would be subtle because no one would want to cause offense. He, Townsend, would take responsibility for saying no in the most forceful terms. Of course the potential buyers would not quite believe him because his name was Townsend and not Rising. And they would not have knowledge of the codicil because while it would be filed as required by law with Marge Reilly, county clerk and friend of the family, it would be kept in the closed file.

So they will come to you boys and it is possible, indeed likely, that they will try to set you one against the other, these aliens, and that of course will be useless—

Townsend hesitated, lost in thought; then he shook his head. No, a bad idea. Too much loose talk and prediction. Even to raise the question was to admit of its possibility. And there was no possibility of a sale, none at all. There was no purpose therefore in getting into it. Instead he would speak of the newspaper's tradition and more than its tradition, its potential. That, he decided, was exactly the right note. At any event, it would work for the short term: follow the footsteps of the founder. Restraint. They'd have some help; everyone liked the boys. But at the courthouse and elsewhere they'd be waiting for signs of apostasy. The long dormant underground would waken and begin to probe. They would be waiting to see if Amos's commitments would be honored, and who would hold the balance of power.

Amos had given his instructions three days before. "Elliott, you've got to help out those boys, Charles in particular. You know the score, you've got to make your weight felt. If they bungle it, that's their own fault; but you've got to see to it that they know what's involved at all times. Who they can count on and who they can't, and what we've been doing all those years—" Easier said than done. There was no protocol or manifesto. In their own way they had tried to create utopia, a place secure and at ease, where a citizen could go about lawful business without interference. They'd worked to keep aliens out, the taxes low, and the law friendly. They'd worked to make Dement safe, and the power was in the hands of local men, men who were accountable. Amos Rising believed that the test of a society was not its size—neither census nor bank balance—but the kind of citizen who rose out of it, just that. His own life told him that each man had a location. It was a specific region from which one strayed at great risk to personal equilibrium; it was neither natural nor safe to live among strangers. He knew what others did not, namely, that the country was violent—violent beyond comprehension. Released from their moorings, Americans were murderous; that was the true meaning of the exploration and occupation of the continent. The government contained these impulses and by "government" he did not mean simply the superstructure of officials, elected and appointed, and the apparatus of law. He knew too many lawyers to have confidence in the rule of law. He believed in an almost mystical constellation of powers that be. Everyone knew who they were, the merchants and the bankers and the judges; landowners and the clergy and professional men generally. These men occupied positions as specific as the men on a chessboard. The men worked in harmony with the town; they understood its past and had a vision of its future. They had a reverence for the *look* of a place; its shape. They knew it as intimately as the palms of their own hands. Dement was no beauty, everyone knew that; but Dement was what they had and they all recognized the dangers of idealization. They were entirely aware of idealization because they had a canon, the newspaper, *The Dement Intelligencer,* Amos Rising editor & publisher. The *I* was the textbook; people read it for an understanding of the way life was, the way things were and would be—not everywhere in America, but in Dement for sure. It was to the town as a dictionary is to a language. The people, most of them, believed the newspaper because it did not surprise them; it was never extraordinary. They believed it because they had no cause not to believe it, and because it appeared to have the power of prediction. And of sanction. The secret was not to reveal facts but to withhold them. Elections became contests between men and ghosts. Unsuitable candidates for public office would look in vain for their names in the pages of the *I*. In any contest between a man and a ghost, the ghost would lose, and this experience led the editor to a hard conclusion: embarrassments were not disclosed, they were concealed. Embarrassments would be dealt with by men who knew the facts and were dependable. Dement in that way was an ossuary, skeletons sealed away in closets everywhere.

They, he and Amos, believed they were benevolent. This was not the Gothic South nor mercantile New England. It was not a place where a few rich men ran things to suit themselves. There were no rich in Dement. There were no mansions or slums or sweatshops either. Nor was there the cultural chaos of the northern cities or the thick offbeat religious traditions of the South. No family had been in the region longer than four generations, and there were only a few of those; arrival in Dement at the turn of the century was enough to establish a family as "old-line." And men had migrated to the Midwest to seek fortunes, not freedom; they required a house and land, a job, and political and social stability. Life therefore was even and regular, the contours of people's lives mirroring the landscape itself.

Townsend knew that he and Amos had done well enough for fifty years, but he also knew in his bones that night was falling; his era was nearly ended. It puzzled and depressed him because he could not analyze it. In his lifetime he'd been able to analyze to his satisfaction anything that truly interested him, but he couldn't analyze this. He and Amos were old farts, everyone knew that; *they* knew it. It was time for them to yield, and everyone knew that, too. But who were the successors? The question at issue was prosperity, a kind of lunatic prosperity whose sources were unclear. All of the towns ringing Chicago had a common identity, one no different from another; they were children of the big city. And they'd all be consumed sooner or later. Dement was different and had always been different. It was protected by the prairie itself, hundreds of square miles of the richest farmland in the world. The prairie was the sea and Dement an island fortress, remote and self-contained. Those other towns, they were like pilot fish following the shark. The cutting edge was Chicago's aggression, its heat and energy and money and the influence it bought. It worked as a magnet both ways, the towns attracting Chicago's money, Chicago sapping the towns' vitality. The towns looked to Chicago for a vision of the prosperous future. But turbulence would follow: opportunity, any opportunity, was blood in the water. He'd spent a good part of his life protecting the community, his town, and did not now intend to see it overrun. So he and Amos had blocked the highway and caused a strict zoning code to be written. They'd brought suit against a Chicago group seeking to establish a television station in Dement, and had won. He and Amos, they looked on themselves as regents of a principality under permanent siege from powerful neighbors. They had insulated Dement from the depredations of various gangsters (politicians, bankers and common criminals) and their armies of advance

men—leeches, they could suck a town dry. It wasn't a question of public morals; neither he nor Amos was a moralist. They left morals to
women and preachers. It was a question of control. They did not intend to stand by like peasants, embraced by the long arms of kings. An
outsider understood that if he wanted to do business in Dement he
would have to deal with the editor, Rising, and his mouthpiece,
Townsend, old bastards. They did not mind being so regarded.

But each year Dement's situation became more complicated because the encroachments had nothing to do with who was sheriff or
who was state's attorney, or even if there was a sheriff or state's attorney. The damnable problem was nothing less than the effects of prosperity itself, prosperity producing change and uncertainty and
unrealistic expectations. Somehow since the war, government had entered into an alliance with business. Local government had lost its grip
and the federals were indifferent to the effect of their programs, bureaucrats believing that it was all one country, each of the forty-eight
states identical. Perhaps that was one of the effects of the war, "the national effort." The war had seemed to give the country a fresh identity,
its face Washington, D.C. There was something grandiose and un-
American about it—as if, having displayed its prodigious energies
abroad, the country had to similarly prove itself at home: momentum
maintained, the war machine redirected. The dubious programs of
the New Deal could be (and were) contained, being primarily political.
But this was something else. It was an alliance between the government and the capitalists, by which one meant the bankers, builders, industrialists and their hired guns, the lawyers. These were lawyers who
had never seen the inside of a courtroom or pleaded a case before a
jury. And it was obvious where the new profits would come from.
They would come from the land itself.

An extraordinary thing was happening. Strangers were buying land
in Dement. No law could prevent them. Townsend believed there was
something metaphysical about the organization of a town. Which
things went where, and how it looked to the naked eye. On Blake
Street there was the *Intelligencer* and next to it the telephone company,

and then Woolworth's, Levay's, Steppe's, the cafeteria (whose proprietor made book), Walgreen's, the shoe store, and the courthouse in the square. The look of a town was no less important than the look of a human being. For as many years as he could remember, the Reilly Bog behind his own cornfield had been a topographical fact, part of the condition of life: it was a barrier to the east, and had always been a barrier. The bog was useless, too damp and thick to hike in, and inconvenient. The road east had to be detoured around it, a useful reminder of the preeminence of nature. Now they proposed to take part of this bog and turn it into a housing project and shopping center. They had bought it from the Reilly heirs through "nominees," no one understanding what was happening until all the parcels were put together. He, Townsend, was responsible for that failure; he had not identified the threat until it was too late. Now they had the land and intended to drain it and fill it, thereby "reclaiming" it, as if its highest and best use was not a bog but a parking lot. No outsider would ever understand: they would argue persuasively that this was progress, a thousand houses on two hundred acres of land; houses for families who had no place to live. And of course the broker was a Chicago man, a lawyer who had never seen the inside of a courtroom. So what? What did that prove? Some of the younger men (Charles Rising among them) argued that the project was good for everyone. The town would annex the land and that would give it political control, the taxes flowing to the town treasury. A thousand houses built over two years, a population growth of four or five thousand souls. The bog, a physical fact for millennia, would be drained and filled—the edges of it anyway; the part of it closest to downtown Dement—and who could argue that this was not beneficial? He and Amos were uncertain, that was the truth of it; and their objections sounded false and sentimental even to themselves. The younger men listened to them with elaborate courtesy and tolerance, and didn't believe a word. Why would they? But he knew he loved the place as it was, and remembered hunting it as a young man. He loved the Reilly Bog for the same reason he loved Amos, for its sanctuary and permanence. It was the way he felt about the region itself, no paradise unless you saw beauty in straight lines and flat vistas and slow-flowing muddy rivers; a place enclosed by its very openness. Approaching Dement from any direction, Townsend could name the owners of every farm and the number of acres under cultivation. He had searched their titles and drawn their wills for half a century. Their houses were set far back from the road, discouraging to visitors. In the beginning the road was important only as a way in. Now it was a way out. These were families who had spent their lives inside the boundaries of the county, cultivating the land and adhering closely to it and to each other. The farms would stay in the families; he'd written wills of such complexity as to tax the ingenuity of Mr. Justice Holmes. The truth was, they were a landlocked people.

The point he and Amos had tried to enforce was this. Open the town to development and speculation, and control would be lost. It did not take a Tiresias to imagine the day when everything, land, businesses, families, would be part of some other, larger complex. More outsiders, more blood in the water. The town would be occupied by foreigners and there would be no limit to their rapacity. Dement would be occupied as surely as any ignorant African "nation" had been occupied by French or British. It was money on a rampage and he guessed, after all, that that was it. That was what he didn't trust, though it sounded queer to say so. He and Amos had worried the problem for a year, to no satisfactory result. Through a surrogate, Townsend was fighting the housing project in circuit court, but his hopes were not high. Amos had said at last, "If the housing thing isn't settled before I die, you do what the boys want. I don't think they understand the consequences, but that's their lookout. But *you* watch it. And watch them."

Townsend agreed; they had no choice. How did you fight, and with what weapons? Charles Rising was a very different man from his father. He was a fine businessman and you needed one, God knows. Those two years, '35 and '36, the paper had almost gone under, thanks to the New Deal Depression. Amos had never understood how it was done, Charles's particular scheme of "refinance." And he had never bothered to explain it. Charles was single-minded and not inquisitive. He remembered once, it was years ago, he had taken Charles to the Field Museum in Chicago, where they'd lingered for many minutes over the suits of armor. The boy was restless and impatient, and later confessed to boredom. Townsend was unable to communicate his fascination with the armor, his admiration for the ingenuity and austere design. He tried to explain it to Charles, his fascination for armor— burgonets, breastplates, elbow gauntlets, cuirasses of all sorts. It amused him that the more invulnerable the armor became the more useless it was for any sort of warfare. Too heavy and clumsy, the infantry could not maneuver; it was impregnable but incapable of advance. Then of course with the invention of gunpowder the armor was suddenly worthless absolutely. Townsend was a man of deep-running pessimism, and he thought he saw a lesson in all that, and bought a burgonet for an absurd price and placed it atop his law library in the office. Charles saw no point to it at all . . .

Amos, he said aloud. Then Townsend murmured a short prayer, his head heavy and bowed, and turned to go home.

ELLIOTT TOWNSEND moved slowly through the cornfield. It was entirely dark now and the cold had a harsh bite to it. The scarecrow was swaying in the breeze, its tatters flapping. He pulled the greatcoat around him and lit a fresh cigar, the match warming his fingers. He looked then at his watch, squinting at it in the darkness, reading the numbers with difficulty, and then peered at the old Ashcroft house. He pulled his eyes away after a moment and moved past the big crooked oak, its branches creaking, black against the starless sky; ugly tree, so familiar. He climbed the back stairs leading to the kitchen and the warm light within. Inside, he shed his coat and put it in the closet and laid his hat on the kitchen table atop the newspaper. He wanted the hat handy. The newspaper headline read:

TRUMAN DEFENDS WHITE;
SCORES SEN. MCCARTHY

It was an account of the haberdasher's radio talk the night before, the former President undignified again in trying to justify his wretched regime and his cronies while denigrating American patriots, fierce men who understood menace, alien ideologies . . . Townsend glanced at the headline, then went to the refrigerator and took out the ice tray and gently placed two cubes in a glass. He stood very still for a moment, an old stooped man, momentarily puzzled by his surroundings. For an instant he thought Amos was there, the two of them preparing to go into the parlor for a visit. Then the image faded and he straightened and poured two fingers of brandy into his glass. He stood at the sideboard, sipping slowly, taking time to compose himself, emptying his mind of reminiscence and memory. Not so easy to do, he thought; a man left pieces of himself wherever he went. He'd turned on the other lights and the downstairs was now ablaze. He rubbed his hands together and did a little awkward shuffle, warming himself by the radiator.

The telephone rang and he dipped his head as if struck. *God, no.* He slumped against the sideboard, feeling his heart pound. He stood limp and still. Then he drained the brandy and coughed loudly, clearing his throat. The sound echoed in the empty house. He picked up the telephone after the third ring.

"Dad's gone," Charles Rising said.

"Yes," Townsend said. "I'll be right over."

"He passed away an hour ago. I tried to get you before, called twice. He just slept away, Elliott. But I was worried about you, you said you'd be home."

"Oh," he said, and thought for a moment that his voice would break. "I was just taking a little walk, walking out back. In his sleep?"

Charles said, "Thank God."

"Yes." He held the telephone tight against his ear and spoke with his eyes closed. "I'll come right over."

"Well," Charles said in his clear voice. "We're still at the hospital, but we're getting ready to go to my place. Really, there isn't anything—"

"I'd like to be there," Townsend said and added, unnecessarily, "If that's all right."

"Of course it's all right." Charles Rising spoke automatically, the voice clear and distinct; he was controlling it with effort. Townsend could hear bursts of conversation in the background, a confusion of sound in Amos's room. He saw the white walls and the high hospital bed and cylinders of oxygen; the buzzer on a frayed cord; the vials of medicine next to the latest edition of the *I*. The voices in the room rose and fell. Charles said, "We're through here now, we're leaving. Come to my place." He paused and put his hand over the mouthpiece and there was flat dead air between them. Then, "We'll have a drink and something to eat."

"I'll be right along," Townsend said. The background noise had stopped. "Is there anything I can bring? Anything at all?"

"I guess nothing," Charles said.

"Charles, do you want me to phone anyone?"

"Oh no." He paused. "No, not yet." Then, "No, we can do that later."

"Then I'll come along directly," Elliott Townsend said. And as he replaced the receiver he knew his own life was halved, diminished absolutely. A part of him was gone forever, he could never reclaim it. The old man silently toasted his friend, eyes up, looking beyond the ceiling to the invisible night. Mouth trembling, he nodded smartly. He and Amos, what a run they'd had together. He promised to carry on, vowed that in his heart, but for the first time in his adult life he could not embrace the future. There was nothing to embrace. Amos was dead, and there was only the remorseless spreading of the past.

2.

WHEN Townsend drove up the winding driveway the others were just alighting from their cars. All of them were quiet in the cold, their mouths pluming like fumaroles. Yellow porch lights threw grotesque shadows on the driveway. Townsend parked behind Mitch Rising's Buick, his headlights momentarily blinding the others. They all stood touching, cleaving together like stone figures in a sculpture; Rodin's men of Calais. They were reluctant to mount the front steps, as if they were the scaffold to a gallows. In the yellow light they all seemed physically connected, Charles and Lee Rising together, their shoulders touching as they swayed forward; Mitch and Tony walking arm in arm with their wives on either side. Tony's son was behind them, his head in silhouette, hands clasped behind his back. They moved up the porch in a pack, shadows undulating in the yellow light.

There was a low babble of voices when Townsend got out of his own car and joined them on the porch. He shook hands with the men and consoled each woman in turn. They muttered condolences to each other, Townsend brushing the cheeks of the women and putting his gloved hand into the gloved hands of the men. The women had been crying; the men looked solemn and embarrassed, though their eyes glittered.

"Let's get inside," Charles said, and they pressed forward on the porch. The door was locked and he fumbled for a key, cursing and patting his coat pockets. Then the door opened and light from the inside flooded the porch. It was Dana, Charles's daughter. She stood blinking in the doorway, then seeing her father and the others, all familiar faces, she took a startled step backward, her hands moving quickly to her chest, protecting herself. They were all of them unsmiling and when she looked at them their eyes refused to meet hers. From somewhere inside the house came the sound of jazz music, braying horns and a fast trap, riotous and hot in the silent cold sorrow of the occasion. She did not know what any of this meant, she had been listening to music and reading a book; she had not heard the cars and the doorbell had not rung. She had gone to the door for a breath of fresh air and had seen them, gray and massed and silent. Charles opened his eyes wide; she seemed to him for a moment a gorgeous and innocent dream inside his nightmare. Then he closed his eyes and put out his arms to her but she stood still as if frozen. Lee tried to edge past the others to reach her but Charles had already flung his arms around Dana and moved inside. He squeezed her against his chest, advancing both of them into the hallway, Dana's slender legs scissoring as she stumbled backward. Lee struggled to reach her but the others had come together silently in the doorway. The girl was propelled backward into the room by her father, huge and overpowering in his camel's hair coat and black scarf. His grief had at last spilled over and the others turned away in embarrassment as he wept, his voice breaking, explaining to his daughter that Grandpa was gone, they'd left him just now. Dana could not understand his cracked voice but felt his warmth and distress and love, and returned it. His tears frightened her; she had never seen him cry or imagined him crying. Finally Lee broke through and rushed to her husband and her daughter. The others watched as the girl stammered something and put her arms around Charles's neck. The music was very loud now and the others turned away from it. Charles released her finally and slumped against the wall, spent, his hands deep in his overcoat pockets. Dana moved close to him, at last understanding, and put one arm around his waist and said something. Lee hovered a foot away, her hands clasped in front of her. In her bright red sweater and Bermuda shorts Dana looked like an alien creature, gay and light as air, cheerful and beautiful and erotic at once; the rest of them were heavy and gray in suits and overcoats. Lee was already veiled. Dana was speaking seriously now but Charles had ceased to listen. He nodded impatiently and after a moment Dana was silent and demure. Then Charles turned to the others with a hard smile. It was like turning stage front to an audience; no one had moved from the doorway and the cold. Charles said, Close the door. Take off your coats. Dana was close against him now and the three of them moved

off into the den, Charles leading. Conversation resumed in the hallway. Charles turned to Dana and said, "Please." The girl disappeared
and the music stopped abruptly. When she returned she went straight
to her father and put her arm around his waist and kissed him on the
cheek. He smiled sadly, distracted, and patted her on the head.

Dana said, "I'll get the ice," and walked off into the kitchen. When
she returned with the ice bucket she was wearing a skirt and stockings
and a black cardigan sweater. The others were standing awkwardly
near the fireplace.

Charles said, "This family needs some refreshment." He turned to
Townsend, standing in the doorway. "Brandy for you, Elliott?"

He nodded. Fine.

The tension began to ease. Orders were requested and given. Tony
and his son Jake began to light a fire, each self-consciously polite to the
other. They seemed to move in slow motion.

Mitch excused himself.

Lee and Mitch's wife Sheila went into the kitchen to see about food.
Dana was about to follow but didn't. She stood watching her Uncle
Tony and her cousin arrange the fire in the grate. Tony's wife Jane
fussed with the room, patting cushions and arranging ashtrays. No
one spoke to Dana. In a moment the den was prim and a fire was sput-
tering in the fireplace.

Charles fixed himself a Scotch and motioned for Townsend to join
him on the davenport at the far end of the room. He said, "He wasn't
even conscious at the end. That was a blessing because I believe there
was a lot of . . . pain. This morning they operated again. They needed
my concurrence, which I gave. They thought it might have given him
a slim chance." Townsend nodded, not wanting to listen to any of this.
"A slim chance, they said, to hang on a little longer."

"Well, you do everything you can. Can't do more."

Charles said, "You saw him on Thursday. That was his last good
day. He got worse the next morning and a lot worse yesterday. Then
this morning—" Charles shrugged, slowly stirring his drink with his
middle finger. It was not a line of thought he was anxious to pursue.

"I'm glad you saw him Thursday." Townsend turned away, nodding in agreement. Suddenly he remembered years ago Amos describing his youngest son as "prematurely serious."

"You did the right thing."

Charles nodded. "I think so. I hope so. I'm not so sure whether they think so." He moved his hand, a gesture encompassing the room. He was speaking very quietly. "But for better or worse I was making the decisions and I decided to go the full route. *He* would've."

"Sure," Townsend said. "The doctors—"

"—yes, are great. Doc Green is great. But they don't know a damn thing, when you get down to it. They're very good, they say all the right things. They pretend to know all about it, but they don't. They do their best, I'm sure of that. When Mother died, bless her soul—" He looked away, distracted. He saw Dana standing by the fireplace and smiled at her. A shame she'd never really gotten to know the old man, though they did have a friendship of sorts. He lit a cigarette, exhaling with a rush. His finger still made circles in the drink.

"Was he conscious all day?"

Charles shook his head. "Woke up briefly around noon. They tried to feed him something but he wasn't hungry. I think he was half delirious. Talked a little about Mother and about Ella Ashcroft. That was the damnedest thing, Ella died—when? Ten years ago? I remember her well, a very nice woman, she'd sometimes take Christmas with us—"

"She died five years ago," Townsend said.

"Well, whenever. I couldn't make out what he was saying, mostly it was her name; then some other things I couldn't catch. He was just mumbling, it wasn't anything you could make sense of. I didn't really want to listen, it was like eavesdropping at a keyhole. Listening in on a private conversation. The thing is, you're used to seeing Dad—strong. Seeing him like that, it wasn't the old man you were looking at. It was a shadow." He sighed and took a long pull at his drink. "It was like a bad copy of the original."

"Can a man get a drink?"

Charles looked at Mitch and pointed to the drinks tray. "Help your-

self and come sit down." Mitch moved off and Charles looked back at
Townsend. "Anyway, it's a blessing. That's a hell of a thing to say, and
I hate to say it. I don't like saying it and wouldn't, except to you. How-
ever, it's true."

Townsend said, "He had a strong life. All a man could ask for.
More." Charles nodded slowly. "I know Doc Green did all he could.
You know, Charlie. There comes a time."

Charles had picked up a copy of *Town and Country* from the coffee
table and was leafing through it, idly turning the pages. His mouth
turned down in distaste as his eyes flitted from station wagons to
swimming pools to mink coats to diamonds, all of them pho-
tographed in expensive surroundings, Beverly Hills or Palm Beach or
New York City. The people were props for the goods. He said, "Place
won't ever be the same. No matter what we do or don't do. It won't be
the same. We won't be the same either . . . Jesus Christ!" Townsend
bent forward to look at the picture, two women reclining beside a
swimming pool in a Connecticut suburb; they were wearing two-piece
bathing suits. Charles looked at Dana, turning the magazine around so
she could see it. "This is the life, huh?"

She made a face. "No, Daddy."

He said, "That's my girl."

Mitch Rising joined them, sitting heavily on the arm of the davenport. He was a strong, heavy man, his white hair cut in a brush, Ma-
rine-style. The coat of his double-breasted suit hung in folds and an
evening stubble of beard covered his cheeks and lower jaw, giving him
a menacing appearance. The coat seemed two sizes too large for him.
Mitch's eyes were soft, almost feminine in their damp gaze. Charles excused himself, leaving the room, and Mitch gripped his drink with
both hands and looked at Townsend, smiling widely. He said softly,
"Charles tell you? He woke up briefly safternoon and started talking
about Miz Ashcroft." He shook his head, still smiling.

Townsend shrugged. "Old friends."

"Oh, great friends," Mitch said. "Lived a block away from each
other for forty years." Townsend nodded and looked away. "We

couldn't make out what he was saying. Which was just as well, I suppose."

"Mn," Townsend said.

"It hurt the hell out of Mother," Mitch said.

"I don't know about that."

"I'm telling you it did." He looked at Townsend, who was silent. "Not very many people know the story." His voice was rising now. "Charles doesn't know. Did you know that Charles doesn't know?"

"Yes," Townsend said. His eyes searched the room.

"Tony doesn't either." His voice was ugly now.

Townsend said, "No."

Dana watched them, her back to the fire. She could feel the heat on her thighs and calves and self-consciously smoothed her skirt. She felt the tension between these two men, men she had known all her life. She was as close to Elliott Townsend as she was to her uncle; and not very close to either of them. She listened to them now, Townsend typically monosyllabic. Mitch was tight. She'd watched him pour a tumbler full of whiskey, drain it, and as quickly refill it. She kept her eyes away from them, affecting disinterest. If they caught her listening they would stop and it would be lost to her. She had only to look away to be invisible. It was not difficult for her to detach herself. She felt terrible about her father but she didn't understand at first. She didn't understand why they were there, all of them so grim and unblinking; all of them in gray or black. Her father had not explained that her grandfather was expected to die so soon. He had not called (but of course he wouldn't); she'd had no warning. She thought it was something else, some other tragedy; an unexpected death like her brother's. She had recoiled out of fear, her father stumbling toward her and then in tears. And just as quickly out of tears. One moment she had been listening to Papa Celestin and reading *Tender Is the Night* and the next moment she was consoling her father; her mother coming close to them both, but not daring to touch. She glanced around the room. Tony and Jake were in a corner talking quietly. From the davenport she heard Elliott Townsend say:

"Get on some other subject, Mitch. You've exhausted this one."

Then Mitch's heavy voice, "He kept her for forty years."

She felt rather than saw Townsend turn toward her and measure her with his eyes. "Goddammit, Mitch. Be quiet."

She thought, oh hell. She turned farther away; she did not want them to notice her at all now. She moved a few steps from the fire.

Mitch said, "It killed my mother."

"A heart attack killed your mother, Mitch."

Mitch was rising now, still looking at Townsend. "A toas'. To Dad!" No one responded to the toast, or appeared to notice him at all. Mitch sat down again and Townsend whispered something to him. Then they were tête-à-tête, all words muffled. Muffled: the style of the family. She thought, Dick Diver and Tommy Barban, Rosemary and Nicole; she knew them better than the people in this room. Better than her parents and her aunts and uncles and her cousin. She was not like them, but she knew them. She knew what Rosemary would say even before she said it. She felt it in her heart and mind and blood. Some nights she was so hot she thought she could not endure it. She was hot in every pore of her, almost—she smiled—too hot to touch. The people around her, her family and the others, did not feel what she felt. If they did, they would behave differently. She believed that sometime she would fly out of control, and then what would happen to her? She believed that sometime she would truly act out the dreams that she had. She looked at Jake Rising, talking with his father. Jake, who had worked at the *Intelligencer* every summer of his life since he was twelve, in fierce competition with her brother. Now he was twenty, a tall, serious boy enrolled at the University of Michigan. Jake had been table conversation for as long as she could remember. He was doing well, doing badly, was a hard worker, was lazy, was "solid," was a "screwball." Once, it was several years ago just after Frank had died and her father was morose and unreachable, he'd turned to her and asked her opinion of Jake. She was surprised; her father never asked her opinion of anything. She'd waited a minute before replying and said, "He's conscientious." Her father had not let it drop there.

"What else?" he'd said. She'd shrugged. "Well, he's very mature for his age." She wanted to say that Jake behaved as if he were fifty years old, but did not. Yes, we know that, her father said. "But how smart is he?" Oh, she'd said, Jake's smart. Her father pressed again: "Don't hedge. Smart smart or book smart?" Then he'd grinned, teasing her. "Come on! How smart?" her father asked again. "Not as smart as me," she'd replied, furious, and left the table, mortifying her mother (bad manners) and confusing her father.

Her father returned. He looked at her and at Jake. "Jake, will you get me a drink?" He collected Charles's glass and Mitch's and Townsend's and moved to the liquor cabinet. Dana preceded him. Here, she said, let me. Jake shook his head and prepared the drinks himself.

Charles said, "Elliott, there's something you can help us with." He paused, as if the effort to go on was too great. But at that moment the telephone rang and Charles struggled to his feet. He swayed unsteadily a moment, then said, "The hell with it."

Dana said softly, "I can get it."

Her father appeared not to hear her, for he called to his wife in the kitchen. "Lee? Will you answer that? Then take the phone off the hook?" There was an answering murmur from the kitchen and the ringing stopped. But in a moment Lee Rising was in the doorway, looking from one to another of the men. She said, "It's the governor."

Townsend looked at Charles, "Why don't you take it? He'll just want to talk a minute. You'll have to do it sooner or later. There'll be plenty of those tomorrow. This one you ought to take now."

Mitch was on his feet. "I'll take it."

Charles waved him back. He moved into the hall and in a moment they could hear him, his voice unnaturally loud. *Yes . . . well, it's good of you to call. Yes, a shock to all of us.* Then a long pause and finally, *Yes, of course, as soon as we can get settled here. It'll be a pleasure. I'll call you as soon as . . .* Another pause, longer this time. *It'll be Tuesday, in the afternoon . . . Yes, I understand that and I appreciate the call.*

Mitch Rising looked at Townsend and smiled. "The press of business," he said with heavy sarcasm. "Wanted to make it on Tuesday but couldn't. Just couldn't manage it."

Dana asked, "Is that the *governor?*"

"None other," Mitch said.

"Is he coming to the funeral?"

"No, dear," Mitch said.

"I didn't know he knew Grandpa," Dana said.

"He didn't," Mitch said. "The governor's a much younger man but Dad supported him the last time out. Governor's grateful. As he damn well should be." Mitch grinned.

Townsend looked at the girl. "Amos—your grandfather—was the senior publisher in the state. And a very fine man, and there won't be another like him for a long time. *That's* why the governor called, to pay his respects." A glance at Mitch. "He was first on the line."

"Let's have those drinks, Jake." Charles took the three drinks from the boy and placed them carefully on the table. Dana smiled. Her father's expression was sour. She could tell that the drinks were weak, and her father did not care for weak cocktails. He picked up his drink and returned to the liquor cabinet with it. He did not look at Jake. He took a long swallow, then filled it to the brim with Scotch. "I've taken the phone off the hook. We've got some decisions to make." He was looking at Elliott Townsend but he was talking to Mitch. "We've got to decide about the pallbearers. Who. And how many."

The older man nodded, at ease finally in the role of counselor. He said what he always said at the beginning of business conversations. "What is it that you want to do?"

"I want to do it right," Charles said. "If it were me—" He caught himself and stopped. "But it isn't me. It's him. And the problem is that there aren't any old friends left. Just you and old Mr. Reilly and Reilly's in Florida and won't be making any trips back here. Someone ought to tell him, by the way, be a nice gesture, a family member calling him—" Charles smiled bleakly. "So that lets out old friends because there aren't any old friends, except you."

"Well," Townsend said tentatively. He stretched back on the couch, his fingers laced over his belly. "There are plenty of fellows around, not of your father's *age* perhaps, but good, close friends—"

"Compatriots," Mitch said.

"Compatriots," Townsend agreed. "Let me see. Just to . . . open the bidding. There would be myself and Haight, Steppe, Tilberg and Tiny Axelsen for sure. That's five."

Charles tonelessly identified them. "That's you, the sheriff, the chairman of the county board, the state's attorney and the circuit judge."

"Yes. And possibly Brandon. If Brandon can get back from Washington, Congress is in session—"

Mitch laughed. "Oh, I think he can."

"—and perhaps de Priest and Roth." He paused. "Judge Kerrigan."

Charles said, "The county chairman, the county treasurer, and the county judge."

Townsend nodded. "I think that would do it. If that's what you've got in mind."

Charles said, "I guess I would have to wonder why Kerrigan."

"An old friend. And the senior judge."

"He's a cynical bastard," Charles said.

Townsend steepled his fingers and looked up. "The law has nothing to say on that point."

"Um," Charles said. "And if we're having Elmer Tilberg, why not what's his name—Aces Evans. He's the senior state rep. And an old friend or compatriot or whatever term you're using. Why not Aces?"

Townsend nodded slowly, and said nothing.

Mitch looked at his brother and smiled. "Charles, Aces and Dad were feuding."

"I didn't know that."

"Well, they were."

"Mitch is correct," Townsend said. "There was some turbulence. Amos thought that Aces had gotten a bit big for his britches. He was spending quite a lot of time in Springfield. Spending time and making money. He'd acquired quite a taste for poker—again."

"Oh," Charles said, puzzled.

"Yes, he was winning. Your father had the exact amounts. I don't remember what they were, but they were substantial."

Charles nodded, understanding now. "If Acres was winning, who
was losing?"

"Apparently there were three or four losers. But the big loser was
the contractors' association. And I believe the bankers' association, or
anyway that was the scuttlebutt that your father heard. And, I might
add, believed."

Mitch said, "It's true. I checked."

Charles said, "Do you know it for a fact?"

"I talked to Dad about it. He confirmed it, in an oblique sort of
way."

"How oblique?"

"Well," Mitch said. "It was a funny kind of poker game. It was a
game where Aces' two pair always beat the bankers' full house or the
contractors' three of a kind. And the games were always held the
night before an important vote—"

Townsend turned to Charles. "Your father spoke to Aces. In his office, and very firmly. Aces denied it at first, then he admitted it. Oh,
there were extenuating circumstances. There always are. His wife is
very ill, you know, and Aces is getting on. I think he's fifty-seven years
old and hasn't managed to put much away. But your father told him to
stop and of course Aces promised he would. According to Amos, he
was ashamed of himself. But he didn't stop. Or hadn't, as of a couple
of months ago. As recently as September he was still in the poker
game, to which a number of *other,* ah, interested parties were added.
The doctors, the highway people, and the oilmen." Townsend leaned
forward, looking first at Charles and then at Mitch, and then at Dana
standing silently by the fireplace. Jake had remained near the liquor
cabinet but he was listening, too. Townsend thought it was as good a
time as any for the children to have their first civics lesson, though he
wished Dana was not there. A sixteen-year-old girl would not understand these facts; she'd have no context in which to put them. "That

was quite a game, usually five or six fellows and it lasted only ten minutes. It only lasted as long as it took to cut the cards and deal." He lowered his voice. "Charles, I do not think it would be appropriate for
Aces Evans to be your father's pallbearer. It would rehabilitate him.
The story is out. Not the details, who and how much, but the broad
outlines. It is known by a number of men who are waiting to see what
your father would've done. They are assuming that something will be
done. Your father was not a man to sit idly by—" Townsend paused
and put his drink on the table. "No one knew what, uh, obligations
Aces had acquired. But your father was going to cause him to retire at
the end of the next session. Retire gracefully and for good."

"I always liked Aces Evans," Charles said. "The goddamned fool."

"Everybody likes Aces. That's part of the trouble, and it's true he
was a fool; a fool to do it and a fool to get caught." Townsend said, "It
appears that someone in the game was doing double duty."

"Well, Dad was always wary of him." Mitch leaned forward, nodding at his brother. The three heads were only inches from each other.
"We can't do it, Charlie. It's too damned awkward."

Charles threw up his hands. "Hell, it isn't *my* idea—" He turned to
Townsend.

"Trouble is," the old lawyer said smoothly. "Trouble is, that's not
the really tough question. No one gives a damn about Aces, in the final analysis. The really tough one is Kerrigan."

She was listening carefully now. Jake had moved from the liquor
cabinet to the fireplace and was now standing next to her. He asked
her, whispering, if she was following the conversation. Partly, she said;
she was following it partly. He said, "It's criminal stuff." She clucked
twice and shook her head. "How awful." Jake looked at her a long moment, trying to decide whether she was being sarcastic. Dana was
standing aslant, smiling, her eyes bright and wide open. He thought
she was really wonderful looking with a spectacular body, though she
was reserved and sometimes sharp-tongued. Sometimes she was a
stuck-up little bitch, an embarrassment to her parents; impetuous. She
was known in the family as impetuous, inhabiting a different world

from the rest of them. He said, "You don't have to be sarcastic." She said, "Sorry, Jake," and meant it. She had no desire to bait him; his uncles did that better than she could. He looked at her and wondered if she was a virgin. It would be exactly like her to purposely set out to lose her virginity. She would plan it the way Eisenhower planned D-day, with nothing left to chance; she'd have the weather reports and the estimates of enemy resistance on the beaches. Dana's trouble was that she was too smart for her own good. It would get her into trouble someday, if it had not yet gotten her into trouble. He turned away from her then and stood listening to the men.

". . . so what's the problem with Kerrigan, except that he's a cynical bastard. What the hell," Mitch said. "Was he in the poker game, too?"

"No, no, nothing of that sort at all. My God." Townsend laughed. "Tom Kerrigan!" The older man kneaded his hands together, dipped his head, and waited. It was inconceivable that Mitch did not appreciate the situation between Kerrigan and Amos.

"Oh, of course," Mitch said at last. "I didn't connect it. I didn't connect that with this."

Dana nudged Jake. What was all this about? Jake shook his head and put a finger to his lips. She nudged him again. Then he looked sheepishly at her, and said he didn't know what it was about.

Townsend said, "The thing's before Judge Kerrigan now, on the docket next week, I believe. It was something your father took very seriously. It was one of the last things he mentioned to me. We talked about it quite a little."

"The zoning," Charles said, wanting it in the open.

"Oh, yes," Mitch said.

"Yes," Charles said. He glanced at his daughter and at Tony's boy Jake. It would be awkward to send them away now, but neither of them had the experience to appreciate the subtlety of the situation. They would surely get the wrong impression. Charles said, "I argued with him about it, to the extent that anyone actually argued with Dad. I don't want to go into details"—he nodded almost imperceptibly toward the fireplace—"but Dad was dead set against. I don't know, he had some damn sentimental feeling about the bog. He'd dug in his heels and that was the end of it. He simply refused to deal with it in any realistic way. He didn't understand that it was on the track and there was nothing to be done—"

"Not exactly," Townsend said. "He was dealing with it. He was against it and proposed to fight it. And things that are on the track sometimes fall off. Happens all the time," he said mildly.

"So you delay it for a year, so what?"

Townsend smiled. "You delay it for a year, that's what. And then another year and another if need be and you'd be surprised how soon folks just seem to forget about it."

"I don't buy that reasoning," Charles said.

Townsend began to explain it, laboriously, point by point. Dana tried to follow him but she had no real interest in Kerrigan or the bog or the lawsuit. She was thinking about Nicole Diver and Tommy Barban at Nice. She was supplying the details that the author had omitted. She felt her face redden, and her body begin to fill. Oh God, she thought, if just once . . . Jake turned to her. Are you hot? he whispered. She began to laugh but stopped at a look from her father. Oh no, she said. It's so cozy, the fire. It's warm all right, Jake agreed. Her face not quite straight, she turned back to listen to Elliott Townsend, droning:

". . . he thought it would create problems, more problems than it would solve. He didn't think the country was ready for it, a thousand houses, new people . . . a drunk loose in a saloon . . . "

She thought of drunks loose in the saloons of the Riviera. Loose in their clothing, nothing clinging, then a long run on the moonlit beach, yachts anchored offshore, and laughter, unending laughter in the night.

Her father said, "There are cross-controls . . . "

Townsend: "Too many twists and turns . . . "

She moved closer to the fire. She wasn't listening to them at all anymore. Day and night she thought about sex, her own sexuality, an expectation of—excitement. It was always with her now, her knowledge of herself giving her strange gratification when boys called her "cold."

Well, she would wait. She was very good at waiting and she could wait
a while longer, until one fine day a *man* would step into her life. She
believed she was too old for awkward boys—

". . . now your man Eurich is apparently a crackerjack," Townsend
said. "But there's a problem he's got to solve and he hasn't solved it
yet. He's got to get the zoning variation and he's got to get past the
suit in Kerrigan's court. He's got to establish there won't be a health
hazard and then he's got to prove that the houses won't be ticktack."

Charles smiled. "Now you've gone too far, counselor. I don't recall
that 'ticktack' is a phrase in our building code. Maybe you could find
that for me, refresh my memory."

Townsend smiled back. "Look it up. You'll find a similar word. And
maybe you'd better get your friend Eurich to look it up, too. It's an old
code but it's a good code. It's very stringent and I'd be the first to admit that it hasn't been used much in recent years. It's a code that's
been more honored in the breach, as you might say. But it covers a
multitude of sins. And I ought to know. I wrote it."

Charles shook his head. "Okay, I give up. Or, rather, I don't give up.
I'll just give up arguing about it tonight. And anyway, you're the one
who brought up Kerrigan's name, Kerrigan as a pallbearer—"

Townsend shrugged. "Just exploring all the possibilities."

"Well, I gather that one isn't, then."

"Depends," Townsend said. "Depends on your relationship with
Tom. From your point of view, I suppose it'd make some sense. Bring
him under the tent right away." He smiled thinly and reached for his
glass. "But if you have Tom, you've got to have the others. You can't
have one without having them all."

Charles said, "Very foxy."

"Accurate," Townsend said.

Charles looked at the older man affectionately. "You and Dad. How
long—"

"Just about forty years. Forty-five, if you stretch it."

"Times are going to change, Elliott."

"I expect that they will. They usually do."

"We aren't going to be able to run it the way you and Dad ran it."

"Why the hell not?" It was Mitch. "Why not? Same paper, same family. Nothing has changed except Dad's gone. We're going to carry on exactly as he would've. *Nothing has changed*—" Townsend was nodding vigorously.

Charles looked at his brother, expressionless. Inside he was angry. That idiot. Everything has changed. Every single thing. "Perhaps," he said mildly. "But we're different people." He was speaking to both men. "It's a different world, or going to be. It's beyond politics, it's business. The guy on top isn't the guy who spends his life obstructing—"

"Jesus, Charles," Mitch said. "Jesus Christ, can't you wait a week?" He looked at his brother, and then at Townsend. "Dad's gone."

"Well, Christ—"

"We have to live with things as they are."

"We can wait till after the funeral," Mitch said.

"Sure, Mitch."

"If Dad was against it, then—"

"Dad didn't understand it," Charles said. "You don't either."

Townsend intervened. "Amos was told that most of the financing, the real financing, would come from Chicago."

"True. It's a complicated arrangement."

"I reckon it is," Townsend said. "Now the boys in the legislature—"

Charles held up his hand. "Elliott, that's part of the problem between us. No offense, but you don't understand how it's being done. It doesn't have anything to do with the state. And that's why they're angry as hell down there. We bypassed the capital entirely, there isn't one dime of state money or state control, either. It's *federal*. It's FHA. And it's the first goddamned thing that Dick Brandon has ever done for us." He wagged his fingers, expecting Townsend's protest. "I know Dick did a hell of a job on the Committee. It's a great committee, he and Velde and the others. I take my hat off to them. But between some pinko movie star and a federal loan guarantee, I'll take the guarantee.

Dick finally got off his ass and started paying attention to his constituents, in addition to the Reds."

Townsend looked directly at him. "Better the crook you know than the crook you don't. You think I'm kidding. But I mean it."

Dana was listening carefully now. They had forgotten all about her and Jake. She was fascinated with their language, so hard-edged and practical. The room was abruptly still, the three men lost in thought. She imagined the old man, lifeless in a mortuary, his skin going to gray, his eyes glazed over, his muscles and tendons stiffening, his life's blood inert and congealed. But the force of his personality continued, was continuing; she felt his presence in the room. She realized then that she had never seen a dead man, though she'd read scores of descriptions in Tolstoy and Faulkner . . .

Townsend said, "It's for Kerrigan to decide. The suit's in his court. I b'lieve, by the way, that he'd reached an accommodation with Amos."

"Is that right?"

"So I believe," Townsend said.

"It would be hard to enforce that agreement," Charles said.

Townsend replied, "That would depend on the nature of the agreement. What was promised. And by whom. And in return for what." He turned to Charles. "You know, Amos wasn't always wrong."

Charles returned his look, hurt. What kind of remark was that? It seemed to him sometimes that all his life people had tried to move him into a niche, to fit him into their own puzzle; to place him where they thought he belonged, at the right hand of the father. He said, "Of course not." Then, brusquely: "I guess, Elliott, I ought to have some expression from you, which side you're on. Now that Dad's dead. If push comes to shove, who you'll be working for. Because this is likely to drag on for a little."

"If Dad made a deal, we'll keep it," Mitch said.

Townsend ignored him. "You shouldn't have to ask that, Charles. I'm with you boys on everything and anything. But you'll get my opinion, full and without editing, just as your father did. We'll thrash out whatever it is and reach an agreement and then I'll go do whatever it is that you want done. That's the way we worked it. But he'd know where I stood, first. However, when the decision was made there wasn't any doubt in my mind, or in his either. About loyalty."

Charles held up his hand. He apologized, he hadn't meant that the way it sounded. They'd talk about the housing project later, they'd already spent too much time on it. Now it was time for a refill. He motioned to Jake, standing next to Dana. "Stoke us up, Jake." Then, to Dana: "How are you feeling, honey?"

She nodded. "Fine."

"Not bedtime yet?"

She shook her head. No. It was only eight o'clock.

"You look a little tired."

"It's only eight o'clock, Daddy."

"Seems like three in the morning to me," he said.

Mitch turned to Charles. "You ought to offer the kid a drink." He meant Jake, but then he turned and nodded at Dana. "Both of them. Let 'em join us." Charles muttered something Dana could not hear. "Hell, Charlie. They're listening to every word we say anyway."

"They're kids," Charles said.

"They're not going to be kids forever," Mitch said.

Charles said, "Is that a promise?"

The three of them turned to watch the boy self-consciously making the drinks. Charles saw that he was going heavy on the ice and water and light on the whiskey. He sighed. Then he said, "Get yourself a beer, son. Join us if you want. You too, Dana. We're just talking family business, one way or another." He said, "You might as well listen to it. But it's private, understand that. Confidential."

Jake smiled and nodded, evidently pleased. He brought them the drinks and then went into the kitchen to fetch himself a beer. Returning, he said, "Aunt Lee wants to know when to put the phone on the hook. She says the buzzing's driving her crazy."

"Tell her ten minutes."

"Ten minutes!" he yelled and sat down on the floor. Jake sat just apart from the three of them, and took rapid sips from a bottle of Miller's. Dana had not moved.

Charles turned to her and to Jake. "We're trying to figure out pallbearers for Grandpa's funeral." Suddenly and unexpectedly his voice caught and tears came to his eyes. He looked away, biting his lip. Then he took a long drink, swallowing in huge gulps. When he finished the tears had vanished. "Goddam drink hasn't any whiskey in it," he said roughly, not looking at anyone. He lifted himself slowly off the davenport and walked to the drinks tray and poured an additional finger of whiskey into his glass. The others were sitting silently. He said, "What do you think, Elliott?"

"Well, we've just described the political route."

"Yeah," Charles said without enthusiasm.

"And there are damn few old *friends* left. There's just me." He smiled mechanically. "And I'm too old to lift a casket all by myself." Then, "Of course you could go to the paper."

There was something in Townsend's voice. Charles felt outmaneuvered. He understood then that they had been negotiating and the old fox had put it over on him. Charles surrendered gracefully. He said, "Well, that's it of course. The other way, it's a damned political convention. Just like the cornroast, no different. I don't think that's what we want."

"Well, it's a family matter," Townsend said smoothly.

"What do you think?"

"I think it solves a lot of problems."

"I had a feeling that you might," Charles said. They were talking to each other now. "Perhaps you could spell it out."

"I meant that you could have the department heads of the newspaper. You three, me, and the department heads. That would be about twelve men. That way you avoid any . . . political considerations, hurt feelings, misunderstandings. You simply don't get into them."

"Um," Charles said.

"That avoids the politics of it."

"The politics of what?" Jake asked.

Charles said, "You've got a point, there are advantages—"

But Townsend was turning to the boy. "Your grandfather was an important man, in many ways the most important man in town p'litically. He had many friends who were, are, in the political game. These friends would expect to be pallbearers at his funeral and would be hurt if they were not chosen. But there were many, many friends. To select one over another is difficult. Many of them were . . . business friends rather than personal friends. There might be hurt feelings and misunderstandings. That's what we're thrashing out here." The lawyer smiled, his words closing over them like cotton wool.

"Can I get in on this?" It was Tony Rising, the middle son, Jake's father. He had been at the window, motionless, staring into the night. Mitch thumbed him to a chair.

"We're talking about the politics of funerals," Mitch said.

"That isn't funny," said Tony.

"Wasn't meant to be," Mitch said.

Charles looked at Mitch. He was unsteady himself but could see that Mitch was worse. He had never been able to hold his liquor. Charles said, "We're trying to figure out the pallbearers. Elliott had a pretty good suggestion. What do you think about having the three of us, Elliott, and the department heads? That would make about twelve."

"Not us," Tony said.

"Why not?"

"We should be with our families, not carrying . . ." He paused and bit his lip. "We can be honorary pallbearers, if that's what you want."

The telephone rang then and they were silent. Lee appeared at the door and turned toward her husband. She said that a Mr. Irish was on the telephone, he only wanted a minute . . .

"That's Bill Eurich," Charles said. "I'll take that one."

"Who's Bill Eurich?" Tony asked.

Townsend watched Charles disappear into the hall. "That's the Chicago fellow who's putting together the housing project out by the bog." Tony Rising followed his brother to the telephone. They could hear his voice, thin and querulous. Didn't Charles think they ought to take the phone off the hook? What the hell, it was only eight-thirty, couldn't they have a drink in peace . . . Charles said it didn't make any difference to him. But the calls had to be taken sometime. There was no avoiding them. Tony returned to the den where the others were sitting silently.

"How the hell did this Eurich find out?"

"Tom-toms," Mitch said. "The jungle telegraph."

Then the women were in the room, bearing trays of food. There was a cold turkey and a ham and potato salad and potato chips. The women hunted for clear surfaces to put the platters on. Ashtrays and table lamps were moved to one side or placed on the floor out of sight. The men stayed out of the way, standing awkwardly in the doorway, drinks in their hands.

Charles put his hand on Mitch's shoulder. "Bill Eurich sent condolences to all. A hell of a guy," Charles said, shaking his head. "He was gracious about it. More gracious than the governor—" Mitch moved away when the telephone rang again. Tony said he didn't want to answer the phone and Charles said that was all right, he'd take the next one. The food and silverware were placed on the coffee table and everyone remarked how good it looked, particularly the cold turkey, the breast meat white and ragged, looking like freshly split wood. It was time for conversation to become general. It was time now to tell old stories and reminisce and allow emotions to work their way to the surface. They all helped themselves to small portions, then resumed drinking. The conversation became louder. Dana excused herself and went upstairs, to her own room.

Charles found himself alone on the couch, staring at a photograph in a silver frame. It was stuck in the bookshelf between two of John Gunther's "Inside" books, a faded snapshot of himself and his father and Dana, Elliott Townsend's dark cornfield in the background. Dana was in the middle, much smaller than either of the men. His father had his arm around Dana's shoulders, pulling her close, his big hand enveloping the little girl's bicep. She looked off-balance, as if she might fall. Dana looked straight into the camera, a wide, pleased smile on her face. Amos stood with one hand on his hip, looking down at the girl. It was a photograph taken five years before, the second of October, 1948. He remembered, the first few guests had already arrived. A spectacular year for the cornroast. They had all expected Truman to lose. They hated Dewey but they hated Truman more. Dana, so delicate in white organdy; she looked like a flower between two thorns, his father eighty and looking sixty and he, Charles, not yet forty and looking fifty. The family resemblance, the nose and the set of the shoulders, was striking. No mistaking grandfather and granddaughter in that picture. Yet no part of Dana now reminded him of the old man, though of course why should it? It was Frank who had taken after Amos; Frank the spitting image. He shook his head sadly and the tears began again. However, he fought them back and joined the others standing around the fireplace. They were telling the Capone story, family legend. Two of Capone's lieutenants thrown on their asses into Blake Street by the hick newspaper editor in Dement who'd refused their offer of "cooperation." Amos and Sheriff Tommy Haight and that gorilla Haight had hired—what was his name? Cavaretta— standing in the doorway of the *I*, arms folded, ". . . and don't come back!" Charles moved closer to the roaring fire, smiling at the mix of fact and legend, a Roquefort of a story. Then someone handed him a knife to carve the bird again.

Dana, upstairs, smoked a cigarette and stared at her bookcase. The titles blurred into one another, the Nancy Drew mysteries with her brother's Hardy Boys and the newer books, the Modern Libraries and paperbacks, *Opus 21, Dodsworth, The Amboy Dukes, The Stories of F. Scott Fitzgerald, Light in August,* and the book she was reading now, *Lie Down in Darkness,* a story that spoke to her with an intensity more fierce than the others. The story of Peyton Loftis was more real than her own life. The emotions were. She herself could not always separate what she felt from what she was supposed to feel. Sometimes she did not feel anything. She turned to the photograph in the bookcase. She was eleven when it was taken. She remembered the cornroast but she could not connect to her younger self, wrapped in organdy. Her

grandfather: it had never occurred to her that he could die. Her grandfather was like a great house on a hill, one of Tolstoy's mansions,
dominating everything around it, dwarfing the countryside. Beside
him, every other natural landmark was in miniature. But the old man's
interior was always in shadows. Dana looked again at herself, standing
between her father and her grandfather, these kin. A lock of hair hung
over her forehead. She was a bit closer to the camera than the others
were, leaning into the lens. She remembered her mother telling them
to move closer together and her grandfather's huge hand on her upper
arm. But she was apart, definitely apart, her smile frozen and her arms
stiff at her sides. They had made copies of the picture; one was downstairs in the den and another was in the old man's office. The year was
1948. Now her grandfather was dead and she could already see something of the older man in the younger; the younger as he was now, not
then. This evening she had seen her grandfather in her father; did
death transfer his spirit? There was nothing similar about them in 1948,
they were utterly unalike in look and gesture. She could see nothing of
her father in herself. She supposed she would in time. She bent closer
to the picture, running her finger along its edge, wondering what it
was that a father transmitted to a daughter. It was obvious what he
transmitted to a son, but what about a daughter? Freud talked of images, archetypes, exemplars, and various sources of envy. Were these
legacies that could be refused? She stared at the books. Nicole Diver
hadn't known either; Peyton Loftis knew but was helpless. Her
brother had known and waited for it with open arms, an eager lover.
He wanted it more than anything and knew moreover that he could
get it, seeing himself "in a line." But her brother was dead and there
were no remains. No, she would not be helpless. These legacies, of
course they could be refused—refused or ignored, whatever they
were, however they were defined. Suddenly she felt elated. Perhaps
she was lucky after all; it was possible that legacies did not apply to
women. Looking at the photograph again, she smiled—confident that
she was consciously standing apart. She remembered now that the old
man's grip was tight and how she struggled against it. Of course he

had relaxed his dry fingers when he felt the pressure. Who would want to bring distress to a little girl? Not him, her grandfather. He was gentle as a light rain to women. Now in two days she would attend his funeral, this apparently political ceremony. Well, there were ways and ways to honor the dead. She would find her own way. Dana turned then to her record player and stacked six of her best: old, dark music; the blues.

3.

THEY all awakened late. Her mother and father had coffee in their bedroom, as was their custom. Dana breakfasted alone, the house completely silent at ten o'clock. She was excused from school for the day and spent the morning reading. At eleven she knocked on her parents' door and found them still in robes and pajamas, drinking coffee and talking. They changed the subject when she walked in. Evidently it was family business; adult business. Her mother explained to her about the funeral, what would be said and done and where they would sit. She told her what to wear and what to say. The family would be in the front pew, entering from the side of the church. Her father said nothing, just sat on the edge of his bed sipping coffee and staring into space. Then he went into the bathroom and presently she heard the shower.

"Dad's very upset," her mother said. "We must do . . . everything we can." Dana nodded. "Sunday night was a trial for him." Dana nodded again. "It was difficult."

"Uncle Mitch?"

Her mother shrugged. "Mitch wears his heart on his sleeve sometimes. So we'll stick close to Dad today."

"What did he do?"

"I don't think he knew what he was doing," her mother said. "He was upset. All of us were."

Dana said, "Who was Mrs. Ashcroft?"

"You remember her, don't you? A friend of the family, a dear friend of your grandfather's."

"Uncle Mitch didn't like her."

"No, dear. He didn't. Let's get dressed now, Luther will be here at twelve-thirty."

Luther Roberts, Amos Rising's hired man, was driving a Cadillac limousine. The three of them climbed into the rear seat and at a few minutes after one began the journey to the church. Luther drove very slowly and none of them spoke. The car was redolent of old men. Cigar smoke clung to the seats and roof, and a pair of battered black rubbers was on the carpeted floor. When they crossed the narrow bridge into Dement proper and saw the courthouse looming ahead her father murmured, "Dad's kitchen cabinet. They'll all be here today."

THE COURTHOUSE was Dement's landmark, its dome and spire visible from the state highway. Strangers were uncertain at first whether it was the silhouette of a courthouse or a church. This courthouse, less old than the town, was guarded by a bronze infantryman, symbol of the Union. Its formidable steps led to a navelike lobby where a blind man sold chewing gum and coffee under a portrait of Elmer Tilberg, Sr., first chairman of the county board of supervisors. The building had always functioned as the political center of the region. Nine to five the lobby was crowded with men in groups, overcoats slung over their forearms, fists tight against their hips. The men collected along the walls of the lobby, their padded shoulders polishing the marble. These were lawyers and their agents, assessors, township supervisors, office-holders and office seekers, and in every group an older man who had no official business at all but was there by virtue of seniority. Their conversations related to power and paper. Certificates of births, deaths, marriages and divorces, deeds, titles, suits in chancery, tax rolls, civil proceedings, all of the raw material of the public memory and the men who processed it: the county clerk and the judges (county, circuit, juvenile and probate), the recorder of deeds, the treasurer, the state's attorney, and the twenty-eight members of the county board of supervisors—administrators of the various colonies and baronies that comprise the dark continent of American government. In a low-slung building attached to but not part of the main structure were the sheriff's office and county jail, a separate hemisphere, emphatic and visible evidence of independent status. The jail, six cells and a bull pen, was barely adequate to the needs of the county.

The unmoving bronze infantryman stood rifle aloft, one fist pointed east, bandages binding his temples, eyes bold and cast upward the better to see Missionary Ridge. From the monument one gazed down Blake Street to the river, a long slope ending in low river buildings, brick warehouses, and the narrow ribbon of gray water. On summer and fall mornings a mist hung over the river until midday, obscuring the bog and the prairie beyond. On those days it appeared that the town was an island, its borderlands obscure, unknown and unknowable. Then when the mist cleared the fields of corn and wheat materialized as if by magic, extending beyond the limits of eyesight, an infinite sea under a limitless sky.

Townspeople were bound now for the Presbyterian church. In the courthouse, trials were recessed and offices left in the hands of subordinates. Appointments were cancelled and lunch dates cut short. Everyone in the courthouse wore a dark suit and conservative tie. It was a ten-block walk from the courthouse to the church and most of the mourners walked the distance. They began leaving the building at one-thirty in groups of two and three and as they walked down Blake Street to Elm the ranks began to swell. Businessmen and lawyers emerged from their stores and offices and soon there was a steady flow, almost a procession, of mourners moving to the church. Two city policemen were at every corner, astride their idling motorcycles. It was understood that at the church the crowd would be handled by sheriff's deputies. Sheriff Haight himself was there on the curb, dressed in a sober blue suit and observing the conduct of his men.

Naturally enough the courthouse had talked of little else for two days. Amos Rising's death was a political event of the first magnitude. At first the talk centered on the details of death, the length and depth of the suffering, the condition of the corpse, and the extraordinary (and costly) measures taken by the doctors. But that was only a prelude to rich and fantastic speculations concerning the succession. No one could remember the last time Amos Rising had set foot in the courthouse, but his newspaper was read with the care and attention normally reserved for railroad schedules or tide tables; the *I* set the day's agenda. It was understood absolutely that the *Intelligencer* represented the official view of events in Dement. With the old man gone and his three sons in charge it was obvious that that view would change, and reality therefore change. The old mirror was smashed and the new one not yet in place. But which son would take charge? The clerk of the county court, Marge Reilly, arrived early on Tuesday morning and when the doors opened at nine she found herself the most popular official in the building. It was the most unusual day of her twenty-one-year tenure as clerk of the county court, a jurisdiction that included the probate court as well. These visitors who arrived outside her office door, what did they want? They wanted a look at the will.

She hunched over her desk and stared at them, four men in huge suits, cigars in their mouths or rancid in the ashtray, round blowsy men with sparse hair and pink cheeks and pouches under their eyes. (Wasn't it strange, none of the courthouse hangers-on was thin; some were short and some were tall, but all of them were overweight.) They sat poised in front of her, still wearing their heavy coats, hats in their laps.

A terrible thing, they'd chorused. Horrible, shocking, a tragedy. But not, the spokesman Earl amended, unexpected.

No, she said, not unexpected.

Earl sighed heavily. Old Amos, a thorough man. Of course—thank God!—he would have his affairs in order. He was not a man to allow the future to take care of itself . . .

She nodded, waiting.

Yes indeed, Earl said, wagging his head. Amos Rising and I were like *that*. He held up two thick fingers, rubbing them together, smiling sadly. Then he cleared his throat.

It isn't here, she said finally.

Earl nodded. Now they could begin. Well, *when*—

That isn't for me to say, she said.

His manner became grave and he clucked once. Now Marge, he said, there's a law—

One of them produced an envelope from an inside pocket, the lines from the appropriate statute scribbled on the back, and handed it to Earl. He carefully raised his eyeglasses to his forehead with one hand, holding the envelope two feet from his face with the other.

Here, he said, I'll read it for you . . .

"A will may be inspected by the public . . ." This, from the one sipping from a container of coffee; he was a township supervisor lately on the outs with the old man.

Now this statute, the third one began.

And she'd laughed in their faces. She'd said, Earl. Earl, Earl, Earl. I know the statute. I know it by heart and can recite it, all of it, not just the lines you have there. But that's only one statute among many. There's another which contains quite a different meaning. If you'll read *all* the statutes (she knew he never would; these clowns had the attention span of adolescents). If you'll read all the statutes pertaining to a will in probate you'll see that much is within the purview of the clerk, in consultation with the court and with the state's attorney and, of course, with decedent's attorney.

The clerk, Earl said. You.

Me, she said.

So it hasn't been filed.

Didn't say that.

Then it *has* been filed.

Didn't say that either. Of course in due time you could sue for a writ of mandamus . . . She watched the one with the coffee container knit his brow and begin the laborious process of searching his vocabu-

lary for mandamus. It was a search through a thicket of moots, sub-
poenas, pari passus, affidavits, habeas corpuses, and mortis causas. She
said, And I don't think you'd want to do that. Might make some folks
angry.

Earl replaced the cigar in his mouth and leaned across her desk and
smiled, disclosing a row of even, stained teeth. He touched her on the
forearm, his finger making a red mark on her white skin. He said,
Come on, Marge. Everyone's interested. We're friends, we're all of us
friends here. Give a little.

Sorry, Earl, she said. Then she stood up and turned over the papers
on her desk, the ones they'd been trying to read upside down. These
men were like schoolboys. She said, It's time to go to work. Don't you
boys have anything better to do? She watched them as they rose in a
foursome to return to the foyer. They would remain there for fifteen
minutes, polishing the marble with their camel's hair shoulders, and
then they would be back for another series of questions. They'd bring
a retired bailiff with them to give their mission a sense of legitimacy.
They had to have something to report: some small fact, any fact at all
would do. But they would find her door closed and her assistants un-
helpful. When they returned she would have the will and the codicil
out of her top drawer and into her private safe. That was the arrangement she'd made with Elliott Townsend and she intended to fulfill it
to the letter. There was a time when blood was thicker than the law,
and this was it. Her father had been one of Amos Rising's closest
friends (indeed, she had not told him of the old man's death, fearing
that the shock would break his fragile health). She'd known Amos all
her life and had known Elliott Townsend for more than thirty years.
Come on, Marge, she mimicked Earl, *give a little.* She laughed out loud,
shaking her head. The will and the codicil would remain in her safe for
as long as Elliott wanted. She believed it was possible to keep the codicil a secret forever, or for as long as they needed to keep it a secret. It
had been done before in extraordinary circumstances. A strange codicil, no question about that, and subject to misinterpretation unless you
knew the family. If you knew Amos and his relation to the boys then it

was absolutely in character. In any event, these were private matters between the deceased and the family and the public had no true right to pry into them, whatever the law said.

At one-thirty Marge Reilly looked into a hand mirror and touched up her cheeks with rouge, applied her lipstick, smoothed her dress and touched her hair and put on her hat. Thus prepared, she checked the safe, left her deputy in charge of the office, and joined the judge and the state's attorney on the front steps of the courthouse for the ten-block walk to the First Presbyterian Church.

Elmer Tilberg suggested they take his black DeSoto, the sedan the county supplied the state's attorney. Haight's men would see to it at the church. But Tom Kerrigan thought not; a mild day, he said, let's walk instead. And Kerrigan in the lead, the three of them moved off down Blake Street.

They were silent a moment, then Tilberg turned to Kerrigan. "Who are the pallbearers?"

Marge answered him. "People from the newspaper. And Elliott, of course."

"Any honoraries?"

"No."

Elmer lifted his eyebrows but said nothing.

"Logical, when you think about it," the judge said.

"Too many of *us,* Lord knows," Marge said.

"I loved that old man," Elmer said.

Tom Kerrigan looked at him sideways. "It's okay, Elmer. He can't hear you now."

"Well, it's true," Elmer said stubbornly.

"No doubt," said Kerrigan. "There'll be an outpouring of love this afternoon. Oceans of it."

"That's right," Marge said. Tom Kerrigan's sarcasm was something they all had to live with. It went with being Irish.

Kerrigan lowered his voice. "Have you told your dad yet?"

She shook her head. "I talked to him yesterday and I didn't have the heart to say a darned thing."

"I can call him if you like," Tom Kerrigan said. "Your dad and I—"

"No," she said firmly. "It would have to come from me." She touched him on the arm and added, "I appreciate the thought."

Now they were halfway down Blake Street, in the center of the shopping district, moving slowly through the noontime crowds, the two men and Marge Reilly conspicuous in their dark clothes and formal hats and overcoats. They passed a television repair shop and the cafeteria and the department store, its serene plastic mannequins gazing round-eyed through wide windows. The three of them were preoccupied and did not notice the shoppers: robust women in cloth coats with children and packages and wallets in their palms. The merchants called them the lunch mob, lookers more than buyers. These were women from the old neighborhoods on the south side of town, their English labored and rough and amusing to the merchants with whom they did business; women of the old world, they always paid cash. On the street they were quiet and hesitant, as if visiting; the children were well-behaved, solemn almost, as they accompanied Mother in search of goods. The windows reflected the images of the women, speculation bounced back: their heads cocked, heavy fingers tapping chins. When one of the children got out of line and began to skylark on the sidewalk the women would snap *stopthat* and cuff the child if he were within reach. And the child would return meekly to the fold, staring into the window at the shoes or cameras or greeting cards or nylon hose or saxophones.

Elmer said, "Did you see the editorial today?"

Kerrigan looked at him. "Of course."

"Well written," Elmer said.

"They said what they had to say with clarity."

"I didn't," Marge said. "I didn't see it. I spent the morning with Earl and the boys. Thought I'd never get away. Boy and brother, they'd keep you all morning."

Tom Kerrigan grinned. "What did they want, the will?"

"You guessed it."

"The codicil, too, I suppose."

"Word does get around," she said dryly.

"What codicil?" Elmer asked. He turned around to face them, stumbling a little over his feet.

She said, "Over to you, Judge."

"Amos wrote a codicil to his will," Kerrigan said slowly. He turned toward Elmer but he was really talking to the woman. "It has to do with distribution of stock. There are certain conditions pertaining to its eventual disposition." He paused and added, "If, whether, when or who—any of those four."

Elmer said, "Oh."

"Isn't that about right, Marge?"

"Don't ask me," she said cheerfully, wondering how much he really knew as opposed to what he was pretending to know.

"The point is," Kerrigan said mildly, "the paper will go on as it always has. Except that instead of dealing with the old man face to face we'll be dealing with the boys, mainly Charles. And they'll be dealing with a ghost. On the whole, I prefer our position to theirs."

Elmer said, "Mitch is the oldest. I figured Mitch—"

"No," Kerrigan said. "The old man was shrewd about that. Mitch is too involved. I think Amos understood that the paper had to move ahead, even though that wasn't his favorite direction. And of the three of them Charles has the best shot at *keeping* it. I mean protecting it." He knew he had lost Elmer. Now he was speaking for the benefit of the woman only, letting her know that he knew the situation. "But Charles is a very different man, I'm not sure the old man knew how different. But he's a wizard with the books and I think the old man understood finally how important that was. And would become." He glanced again at the woman, knowing now that he was about to lose her, too. "When the center doesn't hold . . ." He said, "That's an Irish idea."

Marge looked at Tom Kerrigan. He was staring straight ahead, his wide mouth arranged in its customary half smile, one end up and the other down. A brilliant mind, she thought, not for the first time. But his tongue was too sharp. He angered the powers that be. Years ago, when her father was still active, she'd listened to him give Tom advice. Don't be so damned quick off the mark, her father had said; impatience is not a virtue. And it isn't necessary for you to inquire into everything that goes on around here, *and comment on it.* Be a good thing if you stayed away from Mason's at noontime, too. That place— she remembered her father scowling into Tom Kerrigan's implacable smile—is wired for sound. And she remembered Tom draining his glass and looking at her father with that smile and saying, That's not my metabolism. Then, cheerfully: We are who we are, and the way he said it indicated he would do nothing about it. He would not change. It was Irish stubbornness; the powers that be had selected him and the powers that be would have to suffer the consequences. No, her father replied, *you'll* suffer the consequences. And Tom nodding and agreeing. In that, he'd said, you're absolutely right.

"Of course they would never sell the newspaper," he said. "Why the hell should they? It's a damn good living and I suppose it's in their blood. If you believe that sort of thing. I don't."

"You've lost me," Elmer said.

Not for the first time, she thought.

"They look on it as a public service, no doubt," Kerrigan said.

She flared. "And why not?"

"It's quite a codicil," he said. "It reads like wool against marble, I should imagine."

She laughed in spite of herself. They were talking now in low tones, approaching the newspaper building. A knot of black crepe hung on the door. Marge waved to the switchboard girl, whom she knew, and got a sad gesture in return. That day's editorial, titled simply *AMOS RISING,* was Scotch-taped to the glass. A small group of men, all dressed in dark suits, was gathered in front of the building, reading it.

She said casually, "See much of him lately?"

He pursed his lips. "A little. Before he went into the hospital. And once after."

"Seemed alert," she said.

"Very."

She said, "He was vigorous until the end."

"Well," he said, raising his eyebrows. "Yes and no."

Now she knew they were talking about the same thing. She hated to do this to Elmer but she wanted to find out before the close of business that day. She wanted to know the state of relations between Tom Kerrigan and Amos Rising, and if Tom had made a deal.

"There was talk he was weakening even before he went into the hospital." She paused, wondering what she would say next. Elmer was dumb, but sometimes he surprised you. "A little uncertain."

"I think that's fair to say."

"I'd heard it both ways," she said. "That he was strong as ever and that he'd been—weakening."

"Well, he knew the situation. And he didn't like it." Tom Kerrigan looked at her over the top of his eyeglasses. Elmer was staring pensively ahead. "He wondered whether he was analyzing it correctly. His health."

"Did you talk for a long time?"

"Long enough."

She hesitated, wondering who had been present at the meeting; whether it was private or not. She said, "I suppose the boys were there. Charles."

"No," Kerrigan said. "Actually, they weren't there."

"So you saw him alone."

"Oh, I didn't say we were alone." He looked sideways at Elmer. "People were in and out," he said vaguely. "Elliott came by, stayed for a minute."

"You reached a meeting of minds—?"

Then Elmer Tilberg skipped ahead of them, full of energy, turning to face them both. "He was against the project. Against the zoning and would have fought it to the bitter end. Everyone knew that and if you're going to try to disprove it you're going to have to have evidence. You're going to have to have evidence of some kind." He stood obdurately in their path, waving his forefinger.

They both smiled and shrugged. It was true after all, what everyone had said about Elmer for years. Dumb, dumb as a post; but sometimes he surprised you.

They were passing the Elks Club and others had caught up with them. She looked left, across the narrow lawn and through a picture window into the bar. The bar was crowded. She noticed that everyone at the bar was seated on a stool, hunched over. The place was dark. On the wall back of the bar was an enormous elk's head, the rack flared in a bony fan. The bartender moved back and forth with a bottle in his hand. None of the men appeared to be talking. Then several of them turned and watched the others on the sidewalk. In a moment all of them at the bar were facing the sidewalk. One of them said something and the men at the bar laughed. Presently they turned on their stools and faced front again, so many heavy black birds on a fence rail. The bartender resumed his rounds with the bottle. She quickly averted her eyes and they moved along.

There were six of them now and they walked in a bunch toward the church. It was a narrow structure and high, though surprisingly spacious inside and plain, except for the carving around the choir and pulpit. The lawn and the steps leading to the arched door were crowded with people. A hearse and three limousines were idling at the curb, the people on the sidewalk self-consciously turning away from them; the back of the hearse was stuffed with flowers. Tom Kerrigan took her arm to lead her up the steps. Elmer had dropped back.

She said quietly, "What's going to happen, then?"

He said, "The old man was angry. He wanted this last thing. And he wanted me to get it for him." Kerrigan lowered his voice. "But he was aware that it would be tough and there would be plenty of opposition. He didn't want to strangle Charles but he believed the thing was no good. He told me a little about the arrangements he'd made . . . about the *I*."

"And are you going to get it for him?"

Kerrigan shrugged. "He's dead. I made no promises to him. It irritated him but he accepted it. The truth is, Marge, the opponents have a lousy case. The only heavyweight in this town against it is Elliott Townsend—"

"And me," she said quietly.

They were interrupted by friends, and separated. At this service Marge Reilly preferred to sit with strangers, so she edged quietly away and sought one of the ushers. She was escorted down the aisle by a man she did not know. This one looked uncomfortable and when her hand inadvertently touched his, she knew he was a workingman, his fingers thick and ridged to the touch. His suit was electric blue and his shirt a dazzling, fuzzy white; obviously a new shirt, and he moved uneasily in it. He mumbled something to her as she sat in a pew in the middle of the church on the left side. He seemed to want her to sit elsewhere, he was so nervous and awkward in his movements. When she turned to thank him she saw he was sweating, and his eyes could not meet hers. Then she remembered: he would be one of the men from the plant, doubtless the superintendent of one of the mechanical departments. She smiled encouragingly at him and he fled down the aisle. She turned to greet the man on her left and saw it was Luther Roberts, Amos's hired man. But Luther Roberts did not notice her, so intently was he staring at the coffin and its bank of flowers at the front of the church, under the plain cross.

The coffin was open. The old man's bullet head, white, fringed with wispy white hair, was barely visible against the polished bronze and white satin. She wished they hadn't done that, there was no necessity for it. She felt the man beside her stiffen, and she wondered what it was that he stared at so. Then she saw the family, waiting in the wings. She listened to the rumble of the organ and watched the people file in. It was probably the biggest funeral that Dement had ever seen or ever would see. Everyone from the courthouse and Blake Street and some out-of-towners as well. There were representatives from many of the state's largest newspapers. Kerrigan had told her to expect that, remarking that it was exactly similar to the death of a head of state. Other governments, those that were friendly as well as those that were not, always sent official mourners.

The family filed in from an anteroom to the right. Mitch and his wife first, then Tony and his wife, finally Charles and Lee. They stood awkwardly, pivoting; then Charles made a brusque motion with his hand and Dana and Jake filed in. There was confusion as they arranged themselves around their parents. Then they all sat, the heavily veiled women instantly dipping their heads. The rumble of the organ sent shivers through the quiet of the church, and the Reverend Horace Greismann moved slowly to the pulpit. Marge lapsed into reverie, lulled by the organ's echo. She loved listening to her father and Amos, so secure with each other. Her father was not what anyone would call a conspicuous success; he'd read law and opened an office but mainly he managed the family farms. He'd done well enough, better than he might have, not so well as he could have. He and Amos, they were two of a kind. They liked to reminisce about the land, just that. How it had been, what it had become. Who owned which parcels and how the parcels had come to be acquired, the reasons for the success of one family and the failure of another. Who was down on his luck and why, and solutions—a job to be found for this man, a loan for that. Between them, they knew everyone who mattered. She could hear them now in the parlor, their heads almost touching, their voices low, a vibrating timbre, punctuated now and again by scornful laughter. Once, she'd been thrilled to hear them talking about her— Amos leaning over in his chair and tapping her father on the knee. That's a fine daughter you're got. That Marge, she's entirely reliable and aboveboard. Then a few words she could not hear and finally, You're a lucky man, you rascal. When she'd come to him years ago to discuss a job in the courthouse he'd listened and arranged for her to work in the clerk's office. Skeptical, he said he couldn't understand why a fine girl would want to bury herself away in that marble zoo— but if that was what she wanted, he'd see what he could do. She was twenty-five then and it was evident to her that she would not marry. She was attached to her father, caring for him when he was ill, cooking for him, and managing the family homestead near the bog. She did not feel put-upon or cheated in any way. She was happy looking after him. It was not a perfect life but no lives were perfect and she was satisfied in other ways. She felt a tug when she saw children like Jake and Dana Rising but of course if she'd had a husband and children she could not have gone into politics, or devoted herself to her father. And she liked politics. She liked the courthouse milieu and she liked to campaign, not that there was ever any danger of her losing an election. When she was thirty, indeed it was her thirtieth birthday, Amos called her into his office and suggested that she run for county clerk. She protested that she had no backing. The present clerk, everyone knew he had family problems, but he was an able clerk. No, Amos said, you'll have all the backing you'll need. "The incumbent will not be renominated." So she ran and won and that was twenty-one years ago. Now she was a fixture in the courthouse, a familiar face in the building and on the ballot. If only she could keep her health; the job sustained her, the quadrennial victory at the polls a validation (in part) of the path she had chosen. And it was a path taken by choice, nothing had been forced upon her. Now Amos had brought her into the *I* itself, she and Elliott Townsend empowered to rule on any sale or transfer of stock. Her father would be pleased. He believed the Reillys had special responsibilities as a pioneer family . . . She felt movement beside her; Luther Roberts was standing; they were all standing for the hymn. Horace Greismann was ascending the pulpit very slowly; he looked so frail and worn, his skin like parchment, his long face grim as death itself, his fingernails scraping the rail as he rose step by step.

The family: Charles on the outside, then Mitch, then Tony. Their children and wives were between them, all squeezed into one long row. But it was the boys who commanded attention. Dana was between her father and mother, turning the pages of the hymnal, her head bowed. She joined the congregation as it sang, Pastor Greismann's reedy voice leading the way. *A mighty fortress is our God, a bulwark never failing.* Her voice was barely audible. The last time Dana had witnessed a funeral was two years ago, when they had brought her brother home from Korea in a pine box wrapped in an American

flag, two soldiers as escort. The box was sealed and until last year her
mother had held out hope that Frank was still alive, wandering somewhere in Korea, or in a prison camp. She remembered the slow ca-
dence of the eulogy; everyone was weeping. The church was crowded
then too, and she remembered her grandfather's hard, ravaged face.
Greismann had given Frank's eulogy and it had seemed to her that
he'd gotten everything wrong. She remembered listening to it, believing that she would go to pieces. ". . . a gallant soldier in our gallant
army . . ." Then some reference to MacArthur, then mercifully he was
done. Her legs had begun to tremble uncontrollably and she had to
lean against her grandfather for support. He'd held her tight at his side
for the remainder of the service, none of which she remembered now.
She had bawled without shame. There was just the coffin and the flag
and the two soldiers on either side of it. It was a nightmare to her now,
the memory of her legs shaking and out of control; her mind and
body out of control. She had feared the same reaction today but it had
not happened. She moved closer to her father, taking his arm.

Then Horace Greismann was speaking. His slender voice carried to
the center of the church and then died. Dana caught only a few words,
"eternal rest . . . a triumphant life . . ." and one or two other words and
phrases, heard and forgotten at once. She felt the tension inside her
mother and father, particularly her father; she sensed the fire inside
him. And behind her, a thousand eyes boring into the backs of their
heads—the rifles of a firing squad. She realized then that she hated the
public nature of this; it was as if they were all onstage. It was a public
ceremony. She wished she were incognito in the back of the church.
She would have liked to have sat with Marge Reilly, inconspicuous,
anonymous among the mourners. They thought she didn't understand it, this funeral; but she understood all of it, every single thing. It
was as if Dement were a firmament, the sphere containing the fixed
stars. The polestar was now extinguished and all navigation therefore
chaotic. For forty years Amos Rising had been the polestar, all other
lights measured in relation to his. Now he was gone and the family

would have to readjust no less than the town. There was already a subtle change in her father. His tone of voice was different, and his manner had become suddenly heavy.

Her mother whispered to her, "A lovely eulogy."

She nodded. Yes. She had not heard a word, save those few which she had no use for, and did not believe. She gave her father's arm a squeeze, but he did not respond.

Her mother whispered, "It's almost over."

She nodded again. "I know."

Now they were standing. The organ thundered and light suddenly burst into the church, painting the walls a vivid white. The family shuddered as if struck. From her seat Marge saw Charles put his hand to his cheek, his gaze never leaving the dead man; Tony swayed and was steadied by his wife. A few rows ahead she noticed Tom Kerrigan, one eyebrow raised in God knew what cynical speculation. He was seated with Elmer Tilberg, Judge Axelsen, and Aces Evans. As she sang her eyes wandered front again and she saw Elliott Townsend, both hands gripping the rail in front of him. Tears were streaming down his cheeks, though his body did not move. He was still as stone. And ahead of him Dana, looking almost indecently lovely, her long auburn hair curling over her shoulders, her slender body bent slightly forward. Marge saw her hand touch her father's elbow, and fall away.

The hymn was ending. She shifted her feet and accidentally bumped the man on her left, Luther Roberts. When her arm touched his she felt him tremble. Looking left, she saw that he was crying and it shocked her; she'd not expected it, he seemed so impassive. Huge tears stood in the corners of his red eyes, and he had ceased singing. Her glance was swift and she immediately looked away, not wanting to interfere. She had a fierce desire to put her hand on his arm and say something comforting, but did not. Something about him discouraged that. He stood, massive and stooped, staring at the flower-laden coffin.

The family wobbled down the aisle, Lee in the lead, then Charles and Dana. The sunlight was blinding and Lee walked straight into it, head high, though Marge could see she was unconfident; she was not comfortable leading this procession. Marge tried to catch Dana's eye but the girl was avoiding all contact, her face grave and cast down. She smiled weakly as the other members of the family passed by, Mitch tight-lipped and Tony slack and worn-out. She heard Luther Roberts mutter *amen* as the pallbearers began their long walk, struggling with the bronze coffin. Desmond, the managing editor, and the man in the electric blue suit were in the lead, gripping the coffin rails with both hands. Elliott Townsend was the last man on the right side, his hand laid flat on the shoulder of the coffin, an escort providing safe conduct. Horace Greismann followed, clutching his Bible to his chest like a nosegay, his face gaunt as a mule's and his eyes shining. He nodded to her as he strode stiffly by. Counting the house, she thought.

Now they were all moving down the aisle and out of the church. Conversation began in a murmur and grew to a low roar. She stepped out of the pew, looking around to smile at the colored man behind her. He returned her smile, entirely composed now. Outside in the sunlight, pressed up against the others who'd gathered on the steps, she felt a hand at her elbow.

Dana said shyly, "I wanted to say hello . . ."

"Oh Dana," Marge said, pleased, "I'm—"

"How are things at the courthouse?"

"I'm *so* sorry."

"Keeping you busy?"

"About the same."

Dana looked around her. "They're all present and accounted for, it looks like."

"Of course there's terrible shock just now," Marge said, keeping her voice low. "Your grandfather, you know, he was . . ." She said, "There was no one like him. Never will be." Dana did not respond and she said, "Wasn't it a lovely service?"

Dana looked at her, her eyes narrowing. "They never tell the truth. They didn't tell the truth about Frank, either."

Marge Reilly smiled sympathetically at Dana, this girl she'd watched grow up. Dana Rising had never been reluctant to speak her mind, ever. And she was Amos's favorite, in the two years since her brother's death. Marge said, "Well." Horace Greismann was—Horace Greismann. You took him and you knew what you were getting. She said, "We'll all miss him," meaning Amos.

"It was the same with Frank."

"I know, dear," she said.

"Grandpa didn't think dying was a triumph. As a matter of fact, he hated it. That's what he told me. He told me he was dying and he hated it. Why couldn't the service've been private?"

"Oh, Dana!" The older woman was truly shocked. "He had so many friends, he knew everyone in the county. There were so many people in the church, so many standing in the rear—"

Dana said, "I saw them."

"They wanted a chance—"

Dana smiled sadly at her, making words unnecessary.

"—to pay their respects," she ended lamely.

"I wish it had been different," Dana said. Then, "I've got to go now. At least the burial is private, or mostly private, and we're through with the eulogies." She smiled hesitantly and hurried down the steps, eyes lowered. Marge watched her go, watched the crowd in front of the church make a path for her as she hurried to the limousine at the curb. Dana's manner bothered Marge Reilly. It was—superior. She thought Dana was too young to put herself at such a distance from people. She saw in Dana qualities that distressed her in other young people, a silent stubbornness and refusal to—what? Be "nice." They were difficult to satisfy . . . Marge turned to find Tom Kerrigan at her side, grinning.

"Come over here," Kerrigan whispered, steering her to a vacant place on the sidewalk. "I've got a bet with Axelsen. I'll make the same bet with you, even odds on a fin." He looked at her, suppressing laughter. "Even odds that Aces will be the first one over there. The first one to express his condolences and deepest regrets *personally.*" He pointed to the three black limousines idling at the curb, one car for each brother and his family. There was a problem with the coffin; the pall-bearers were struggling to get it inside the hearse. Meanwhile, the families waited impatiently in the limousines, all of them staring straight ahead, silent. Those on the sidewalk were collected in small groups, talking quietly and maintaining a respectful distance from the cars. The eyes of the mourners darted to the cars and back again.

"Oh, Tom," she began, exasperated.

"No, watch! There he is, look at him. He's trying to make up his mind."

It was true. Harold ("Aces") Evans was rocking back and forth on his heels, a sprinter in the blocks. He was talking fitfully with Judge Axelsen and a township supervisor. Suddenly he made up his mind and broke, lurching over to the first of the limousines, the one containing Charles Rising and his wife and daughter. Aces Evans tapped loudly on the window glass but Dana waited a moment before she pushed the button that brought it down.

"Thank you, young lady." He looked past her into the interior of the car.

Dana stared at him blankly. "What do you want?" The question so took him aback that he was speechless, his mouth forming O's like a fish. Very calmly the girl asked again, "What do you want here?" and gave a little toss of her head.

"Dana!" Charles said sharply.

Aces Evans smiled warmly and looked past the girl to Charles and Lee. He knew she was still looking at him. "It was a beautiful service, simply beautiful," he said, "and I want to take this opportunity to say how sorry I am—"

"Thank you, Mr. Evans," Lee said.

Dana was staring at him. He moved away slowly, backing up, but not before he heard Dana ask her mother, "Can I roll the window up now?" It was the coldest voice he'd ever heard in his life.

Kerrigan and Marge Reilly had heard none of this. Kerrigan said, "A fin, you owe me."

"Tom, you're going to get in trouble one of these days."

"I've got an eye for it," he said. "Look at Aces, he's got the look of a kid who got away with the cookies. Got his hand in the jar and got it out again. Barely." That was true, too. Aces Evans was sauntering back to the de Priest–Axelsen group, his demeanor signaling his concern for the bereaved—though if anyone had looked closely they would have seen something else in his face, too. He shook his head sadly, though confidently. He was confident they'd pull through, as he'd just spoken to the principal son; offered his condolences in person. He was in a position to say that they'd pull through all right, they were a tough family. Now others moved up to the limousine. Marge saw that Lee Rising had a look of horror on her face; Charles was speaking sternly to Dana. Then to everyone's surprise Charles got out of the car. The pallbearers were still struggling with the coffin. He shook hands with those near the car. Horace Greismann put his hand on Charles's shoulder. The coffin was now inside the hearse and they were ready to go. Charles moved back to the car, then hesitated and turned and walked up the steps of the church.

He took Marge Reilly's hand and kissed her on the cheek. He shook hands with Kerrigan, accepting condolences. He said, "The burial is private. But I ought to be back in my office by five-thirty. Why don't you and Tom come by for a drink and we'll talk a little."

She nodded and said, "Of course," without thinking. Tom Kerrigan just nodded.

"There'll be two or three others there," he said, backing down the steps. The others on the sidewalk were looking at them.

She said, "Fine, Charles."

"I'll see you then," he said, moving down the steps.

She watched the first of the cars go, then something jogged her memory. She said to Kerrigan, "I don't know if you noticed, but I was sitting next to Luth Roberts—"

"Who's Luth Roberts?"

"Worked for Amos," she said. "For years. Sort of a gardener, though there weren't many gardens to speak of around the house. Luth looked after things, mostly Amos, drove him around sometimes. He cared for Amos when the family wasn't there, which they nearly always were."

"Of course," he said. The Robertses were an old family in Dement, and he'd heard Amos speak the name. They were said to be the oldest colored family in town.

"Well," she said. "He was certainly moved by the service. He was *weeping*."

"That figures," Kerrigan said.

She sighed; really, Tom was hopeless sometimes. "*What* figures, Tom?"

Kerrigan laughed and lit a cigarette. "Trust that old bastard to be a hero to his valet."

4.

THE CEREMONY was brief and all of them lingered at graveside a moment, thanking the pallbearers and repeating endlessly what a beautiful service it had been. Elliott Townsend stood a little apart from the family, staring dully at the bronze casket. His hat was at its familiar rakish angle and his hands were deep in his overcoat pockets. He did not move at all when Charles walked over to him and put a hand on his arm and asked him to stop by the office at five-thirty. When he told Townsend who would be there the lawyer's eyebrows went up a fraction. Charles said crisply, "No time like the present." Then he climbed wearily into the car and drove home with his wife and daughter.

He told Luth Roberts to wait, that he'd be out again in thirty minutes. The three of them went inside and sat in the library. Lee asked him if he wanted a drink and he said no, and his daughter asked him if he wanted to take a nap and he said no, and for the moment they all sat and looked at each other.

"It's all over now," he said at last.

Lee said, "The church was certainly full. It was a lovely tribute."

"Four hundred," Dana said. "Someone said."

He was half listening. Yes, it had been a full house. Then he remembered, feeling the anger rise in him. He looked at Dana. "You were extremely rude to Mr. Evans."

She nodded. "Yes."

"We do not behave in that way in this family." He leaned forward in his chair, staring at the girl.

"Charles—" Lee began.

"He is a man twice, three times your age."

Dana pulled her legs up under her on the sofa and tossed her head. "I apologize," she said.

Charles said, "It was embarrassing to your mother and me."

"We were surprised and disappointed," Lee said. "That was not your normal behavior."

"I want to know one thing," Charles said. "Why?"

Dana had been silent, almost dreamy as she sat poised on the yellow sofa. Normally she would say nothing, just agree and agree for as long as it took for the conversation to die. But this was something else. Her father was making it into something else. "It's so hypocritical."

"What's hypocritical?"

"You know." When her father said nothing, just stared at her with his hard eyes, she continued. "He's the man in the poker game, isn't he? Grandpa didn't like him, wouldn't have anything to do with him—"

"That's enough," Charles said.

"—but it's *true*." She uncurled her legs and rose, all in one smooth motion. "He just wanted to be the *first*. And him of all people. Did you see the way he looked?" She giggled, remembering his watery eyes and red face, and off-balance Gable mustache.

Charles said stiffly, "I have known Harold Evans for thirty years. He and my father, your grandfather, were close friends for most of those years. But whether we were, are, friends or not—" He caught himself. What was he doing, explaining—making explanations to this teenager? A teenage girl. His father had never explained, never apologized; things of this kind were understood without explanations, or ought to be. He looked at his daughter's impassive face. "He's an older man and therefore entitled to some respect. He hasn't had the advantages you've had, though I suppose that wouldn't make any difference to you—" He felt he was being dragged into something against his will.

Dana smiled with as much sincerity as she could muster and replied, "I'm sorry. It just seemed to me—hypocritical."

"I don't think you've had enough experience to know what is hypocritical, as you call it, and what isn't."

She said again, "I'm sorry."

"It was very embarrassing for us," her mother said.

Dana said, "I had no idea, and I'm sorry."

Charles shook his head then and began to talk of good manners and politeness. She listened but her mind was elsewhere. Her father had been hurt by what she'd said. It was as if she'd attacked him, and that was a mystery to her. He'd made no secret of his contempt for the politician but when she'd brought it into the open he resisted, and it was more than simple resistance. He seemed to be saying, Insult Aces Evans and you insult me. Question his motives and you question mine. She'd been—outspoken, and girls of her age and position were never outspoken. She was nodding now, listening to her father. He was talking about hypocrisy, her favorite word; her least favorite quality. The one bad quality that could destroy any good one. He said, "Good manners have nothing to do with hypocrisy." Finally, "Of course I will have to apologize myself to Mr. Evans." She moved forward then, an expression of incredulity on her face. But she said nothing. She'd learned long ago that in her family it was always wiser to let things go. Gone, they would slip from memory. Or slip from the foreground; they would never slip from memory. She stood over her father, waiting for him to finish. When he did, she excused herself to go upstairs. She apologized again, though all of them knew now that the apology was not genuine. However, it was enough that it be tendered and the old order thereby respected. She hurried to her bedroom, grateful that her father had not lost his temper. The truth was, they had both been wrong. But he took it so personally. Aces Evans was not sinister, he was ludicrous. Why had no one laughed?

Watching her go, Charles felt suddenly drained. He'd made no headway, she'd not yielded an inch. He supposed it was something he'd have to accept, a phase no doubt; she lived in a different world. His world and his father's world were more or less identical, at least the values were identical, and he never dared challenge it; it had never occurred to him to challenge it. But Dana had a dark internal life that he didn't comprehend. He felt defied but could not identify the source or cause of it. He turned to his wife, lowering his voice. Dana was impetuous, it was something they would both have to watch, often she didn't seem to show respect . . .

"I'm more than ever convinced—"

"Oh, Lee," he said.

"—that another school, in another part of the country, is exactly what the girl needs."

He sighed. That was no solution at all. That would only aggravate the problem. Lee had first brought it up a year ago and he'd refused to discuss it. A *prep* school. There was no need for it. But she'd persisted and worn him down. Their daughter's education was important to her; it was something she understood better than he did. Charles had finally ceased his objections though he'd never agreed in so many words. It was not something he could explain to his wife but he was afraid that if Dana went away she would never return, and she was all he had now. It was something he knew in his heart. He knew it by listening to her and watching her, and what he heard and saw and was fearful of was not anything that could be helped by another education. She was being pulled away and the solution was not to let go; it was to hang on.

He said, "We can talk about it later. I've got a meeting at the office now."

CLIMBING INTO the front seat of his father's car he nodded at Luth Roberts and they drove downtown in silence. Charles needed to think;

it occurred to him after talking to Townsend that he had no real plan. He had to put Dana out of his mind and concentrate on the present moment. He asked Luth to drop him by the side entrance. It was unlikely that anyone would be in the lobby or the editorial department on the second floor, but he didn't want to take chances; he didn't want to meet anybody. He was tired of condolences; the funeral was over. Luth said he was glad to wait for him, but Charles said there was no need. He was half out of the car when he paused.

"Luth, did Elliott Townsend get in touch with you?"

"He did."

"Well, it was something that Dad wanted to do." Luth Roberts nodded. He was not looking at Charles. "Well," Charles said. It was awkward; Charles thought that his father had shown a strange lapse of judgment. But he and Luther were close in their own way.

"I was surprised," Luth said.

"You were with Dad a long time."

"I was still surprised."

Charles hesitated, irritated by the tone in the black man's voice. What did he want? Charles said, "I'll be glad to buy it back from you. Blue-book value—"

"No, thank you," Luth Roberts said.

"As you wish," Charles said stiffly.

He looked directly at Charles for the first time. "It was written in the will?"

"Of course," Charles said. "You can go get it anytime."

Luth nodded. "I'll get it tomorrow, if that's all right."

"It's in the garage," Charles said.

Luther looked at him with a flicker of a smile. "I know," he said.

"There's one other thing." Something about the man made Charles nervous. He was so still, his face immobile, his eyes as hard as onyx. "With Dad gone, we'd—the family would—be glad if you'd stay on. There's work to be done at my place, and at Mitch's and Tony's."

"I'm sixty-five years old, Mr. Rising."

"Sixty-five," Charles said. Of course he was sixty-five; Charles remembered having the Social Security forms filled out when he was transferred to the company payroll. "Well, even so—"

"I'm going to retire now on my Social Security and what I've got saved. Take care of my mama, who's old. My house is paid for." He glanced at his hands, resting at ten and two on the steering wheel. "Time to relax."

"Wish I could," Charles said. Then, "But whatever you say." He leaned over and patted the other's shoulder. Whatever his faults, Luther Roberts had been good to his father. And had been repaid, the black Cadillac bequeathed to him. What the hell was in his father's mind? What would Luther Roberts do with a Cadillac sedan? That was the trouble, they all drove around in expensive automobiles . . . And he'd probably want the license number that went with the car, license number 1893 that Amos Rising had for thirty years; 1893, the year he'd founded the *I*.

"Does the license number come with the car?" Luth Roberts asked.

"No," Charles said.

Luth looked at him a long second, his eyes burning. Then he smiled. "Too bad."

"But I think I can fix it."

"I'd be pleased if you'd do that."

"Be happy to." Charles got out of the car and closed the door. He hadn't wanted to do that, surrender the number. It was a number that belonged to the family. Mitch and Sheila would be furious. But he was challenged by the look in Luth Roberts's eyes and felt obliged in other ways.

Luth, sitting perfectly still in the driver's seat, pressed the button that brought down the side window. "Your father and I talked about that car for many years." He was staring straight ahead, talking into the windshield. "That car, and the one before it, and the one before that. I wasn't sure—"

Charles was distracted, irritated with himself. He said, "Well, it was something that Dad wanted to do."

"—that it would actually happen."

Charles nodded and walked away. Luth looked after him, his features softening a little now. He said aloud, "I thought somebody would stop it. A colored man driving a black Cadillac sedan, license number eighteen ninety-three. The big black boat. *Amos Rising's* big black boat. I'm damned if I didn't think you'd find a way," he said to Charles's retreating back. But Charles did not hear him, he was well out of earshot. Charles Rising was always out of earshot, Luth thought. Out of mine, out of his father's. A man who wanted to do the right thing, and often did, but a man out of earshot. He watched Charles open the heavy steel door and disappear into the pressroom.

THE PRESSROOM was deserted and Charles paused to look at the great silent machine, his father's pride, a six-unit Goss press sunk in concrete. It was capable of printing twenty thousand newspapers an hour. There were two color decks, used twice a week. He smiled. That had been a struggle. The old man believed that newspapers should be printed in black and white, like books; newspapers were for reading, not looking. A subscriber paid three cents for the newspaper and *read* it. He'd said, If you want to publish *Life* magazine, go to New York City. But Charles had prevailed, it was after all an advertising matter; the advertisers wanted color (or would, once Charles explained to them the advantages of ROP color display). The editorial content would not be affected, though the old man was impressed with Charles's argument that with the color decks they could print the American flag in red, white and blue on Tuesdays and Thursdays. The flag was displayed next to the nameplate on page one. Charles stared at the press, so heavy and dangerous. The rolls of paper, almost as big as coupés, were slung under the press itself, feeding it from below, the paper snaking into the machine at sixty miles an hour, the tension adjusted to a point barely short of fracture. Ink fed downward by means of a succession of rollers. The newsprint ran over lead castings distributed on the six units: page one, the editorial page, society, sports, classified, and all the pages in between. Razors chopped and trimmed the newspaper, sculpturing it for arrival on the conveyor belt.

Charles stood looking at it, dwarfed by it, this visible symbol of his father's authority. The printing press, surrounded by the sweet smell of ink and oil, and cream-colored newsprint blank as an infant's memory. At ten-thirty and again at noon and at one-thirty the building trembled. You could feel it in your gut and through the soles of your shoes and hear it in the distance, like the thunder of an approaching storm, the sound and motion fusing until they were difficult to separate, what you heard and what you felt. The dozen men in the pressroom communicated by high sign, the foreman nodding and wigwagging and one of the men correcting the speed of the press or adjusting the oil level or the ink flow. A sheet ripped and there was a breakdown, the press roaring in anger. The Goss moved every bolt in the building and when it commenced its run, a low throb at first and bursting into a high whine and then a scream and at last a heavy rhythm, all of it was reminiscent of the humming of engines belowdecks on an ocean liner. And at least twice a week the old man would be there in person, watching the run in vest and shirtsleeves, standing near the conveyor belt to snatch the sixth paper from it, checking for typos and tombstones, pied type and bungled headlines, to admire the antique design of page one, and to inspect the editorial page and glance at the masthead:

The Dement Intelligencer
AMOS RISING, EDITOR AND PUBLISHER
FOUNDED 1893
"Lord, I believe; help thou mine unbelief." MARK 9:24.

The biblical quotation was the contribution of his wife, Jo, and it pleased him to have it there. He read the paper methodically, a heavy eraserless pencil in his hand. He believed the newspaper was alive, a living thing with soul and heart and mind. Charles looked around the big silent room and could see his father standing, legs apart on the

throbbing floor, a ship's captain at the wheel, his head buried in the *I*.
He called himself editor. His title was Editor and Publisher but when
he was obliged to identify himself he said "editor." That was one thing
that would change. Charles would call himself publisher. That was
what he did, *publish*. Someone else could edit. People could be paid to
edit, though he would leave the title vacant for a while, perhaps retire
it altogether.

He remembered the first time he took little Frank to watch the run.
That was ten years ago, the middle of the war; the other war, not
Frank's war. Frank pushed the button to start the Goss and he recalled
the boy's wide smile as the noise gathered. His father had appeared
then and the three of them watched the run, the old man snatching
the first paper off the belt to give it to Frank, then taking the sixth for
himself. Charles had watched them both read the *I*, the boy unconsciously imitating the old man, head back, legs wide apart, holding the
newspaper open in front of him as if the sheets were wings. It broke
his heart to remember this but he never stepped into the pressroom
without some fragment coming to mind. The old man had taken the
boy by the hand and led him through all the departments of the newspaper, introducing him to every employee in the plant, explaining to
him what they did—or letting them explain. Charles tagged along, as-
tonished at the boy's questions: Frank took it in by instinct, and nothing had to be explained twice. Thereafter he spent all available time in
the back shop of the *I* and later, when he was older, working as an apprentice printer. Everyone liked him and on his eighteenth birthday his
grandfather gave in a brass nameplate that read *Frank F. Rising, assis-
tant to the editor,* and wrote a note: "You can have the desk that goes
with the title any time you want." Charles explained that Frank would
go to college, wanted to go to college, and the old man replied that
that would be all right. He had never been to college and Charles,
Mitch and Tony had never been to college but it would probably do no
positive harm, depending on the college. It would be a midwestern
college, of course. Oh yes, Charles had said hastily, no question of
that. But Frank enlisted in the Marine Corps in June of 1951 and was

dead before the end of the year. Charles and Lee had tried to stop him; it made no sense. But the boy was stubborn and there was no string Charles could pull to keep him out of Korea. Identification was made by fingerprints; there wasn't anything else. Charles missed his son more than he could say. From that first tour of the building he had seen himself as a link between his father and his son. He knew exactly what he wanted: to consolidate the financial strength of the paper and when he was sixty-five to hand it, intact, to the boy. Charles knew himself well enough to know that he was not a printer or an editor. He was a publisher and counting-house man, a creative accountant and modern businessman who understood the town and where it was going, and knew that the *I* could be the leading edge. Had Frank lived, the line would have been continuous; but when he was killed, Charles told his father bluntly, Give me control. Let me pick the successor. Divide the money so there's no ill feeling there, but give me passing-on rights. So the three of them, he and his father and Elliott Townsend, had drawn the will. And his father had insisted on the committee. And insisted that Mitch be the family representative. Grotesque, he thought; simply grotesque.

Charles turned away and moved up the iron stairs. The others were due any moment. He hurried through the circulation department on the second floor and through the rabbit warren of desks that comprised display advertising. His and Mitch's and Tony's offices were on the third floor. His father had the small corner office and Tony had the office next door. Mitch was down the hall. Charles's office was the largest of the four, but it faced an alley and a blank wall. This office by rights should have been Amos's but the old man preferred the corner—where he could watch the street and talk undisturbed. His office was approached through Tony's, Tony acting as gatekeeper. At five o'-clock no one was visible on the third floor. But Charles's secretary was there, as she promised she would be. He asked her to go to the tavern across the street and buy a bottle of Scotch and one of bourbon and a bag of ice, and borrow half a dozen glasses. He handed her twenty dollars and she left the building.

When she returned, Townsend and Bill Eurich were there. She put the bottles and the glasses on her own desk and the bag of ice in the wastebasket. Then she said good night and left.

Charles told the others to help themselves. He'd have a weak Scotch. Eurich prepared it, using a heavy hand as always. Waiting for the others, he and Townsend were talking politics. Townsend was lamenting Taft's death and Eurich was nodding. Then Townsend asked Eurich what he did and the younger man began an explanation. He was a lawyer but he did not litigate. "What I do is try to get people together. A man owns an option on some land somewhere. Another man has got a piece of a construction company. Someone else has got a connection in Madison or Indianapolis or Springfield. Or Washington. And the fourth man has an idea. He knows where a highway's going or a military base. A public building. A housing development, shopping center. These fellas come to us and we put them together and take a broker's fee . . ." Townsend listened, his face betraying nothing.

Charles sat heavily in his own chair. Eurich was explaining to Townsend how it worked. A lawyer was indispensable because only a lawyer could understand the regulations and write a contract to conform to them . . .

Charles thought that Bill Eurich—"Irish" to his friends, "Bill" to his acquaintances—could convince Townsend if anyone could. They'd met a year before and made it a point now to lunch every six weeks. It was Bill Eurich's opinion that Dement was on the edge of a boom, but needed a push. Get in early, he said, and you control it yourself. Get in late and you've lost control. He described a project near the Indiana line. It had all been done locally. They forced the city council to annex the land and finance a new sewer line. All local: local builders, local attorneys; local real-estate outfit was given an exclusive rental contract. Of course as a matter of courtesy they'd cut in one of the Chicago firms that happened to have a connection to one of the big retailers. The work was spread around, everyone was happy; everyone benefited. Most important of all, the financing was handled by the largest of the two local banks, in association with Eurich's bank in the city. Part of that was federally guaranteed so the risk was minimal and the return on investment a sure thing (as much as anything was a sure thing). They'd only deal with top people; there was no room for fly-by-nights or heisters in operations like this one. The thing was, Irish said, you got everyone in tight. Each guy depended on his partner. He'd laughed then. "My friend, it's like the buddy system in the army. You ever been in combat? You watch out for your buddy and your buddy watches out for you. You see a guy not holding up his end, you talk to him. Makes for efficiency, you bet."

This was a month ago, and they were having drinks at the Chicago Athletic Club. Irish had flown in from Madison. Charles said, "Irish, it sounds dandy. But what bends?"

And Irish had laughed loudly, and signaled the barman for another round. "That's the point," he said. "Nothing bends. Nothing has to bend. No bend in the law, no juice for the local pols. Oh, there's chicken feed here and there but nothing out of line. The point is, you go into a town where there's some control already. Where you can put a few guys in a room and make decisions and have those decisions stick. Where the territory's been staked out, you understand? The particular hook to this—" He took a long swallow and smiled. "I'll tell you a secret because I like you." He laughed again. "And because you'll figure it out anyway. The catch is that there aren't half a dozen guys in our three states who know how to put these deals together. They haven't begun to understand the new connections between the towns and the counties and the state and the federals. The war changed it, at least that's what I believe happened. And it's still too early to see where it'll lead but whatever it is the federals'll be at the head of the parade. And it's guys your age and mine that understand this. Take this town. They think you lay some moola on a precinct committeeman, get a curb cut, talk to the assessor, and that's the end of it." He shook his head in sympathy with those out of step with the times. "Hell, that's just the beginning. Before you get into any of that you've got your tax lawyer in place, your bank, and whatever politicians you need. You

have your *group* and each guy is responsible for his own sector. Now
the other thing is obvious when you think about it and these other
guys are getting smarter all the time and they'll see it, too. You'll see
deals all over the place in the Loop. And that will be great, and a lot of
guys will get rich, but they still haven't discovered the underlying principle. They want to control the buildings. And those aren't what's going to be important. What's going to be important is the *land*. Control
the land and sell the buildings; or control the land and lease the buildings. That's where the money's going to be made for the next—hell,
pick a number. Thirty, forty years; long enough anyway. It's a very
simple law of economics. There's going to be more of everything,
more goods, more services, more money, more people." He looked
around the room, smiling slightly; then, confidentially, as if he were
sharing military secrets, he extended his fist and began to tick off statistics on his fingers. He spoke of population trends, bank deposits, estimates of industrial growth north and west, estimates of capital
investment, probable trends in transportation and land use. And the
gradual expansion of government services, state and federal. These
were precise, often a number and a decimal point, and each fact was
related to the others and all of them spelled growth. "There's going to
be more of everything except land, and there's going to be less of land.
Land: that's the goose and the golden eggs. Control it and you control
the growth. Five guys in a room can shape an entire town. *Own* it, for
the matter of that. And it goes like dominoes, or did near the Indiana
line. You have a shopping center. Next you throw up a housing development convenient to it. Then you sell some land for an industrial
park convenient to *that*. Click, click, click. Gas stations, restaurants, an
outdoor movie, an office building. In three or four years you're going
to see money come out of Washington like the Johnstown Flood. And
the government is friendly, for a change. This government is going to
see that the businessman gets his fair share. And let me tell you something else, friend. The boom, when it comes, isn't going to happen
here"—he gestured out the window, in the direction of the Outer
Drive—"because this place is going to be black as the ace of spades in

twenty years. A dying asset. No, it's going to be out there on the periphery. Everything is, Charlie. The periphery." He drew the word out,
parry-furry. "It's not at the center anymore but the edges. That's
where the opportunity is. The center is a mine that's played out because we've been digging at it too long. The smart guy tomorrow is
the guy who runs his business like they run the government. Borrow
on your assets and expand. It's like printing money." He was silent for
a moment, brooding, then went on in a low voice. "Nothing's going to
be done the way you're used to doing it or I'm used to doing it. You've
got to watch the government with a hawk's eye because that's where
it all is. Watch the edges, they're always in shadows. The periphery.
The thing I like about your town, and the thing my partners like about
your town and the reason we're spending time and energy on this
project, is that it's under control. It's like an old-fashioned family, close-
knit. Everyone knows who's in charge, you don't have to go to the
Supreme Court to get a sewer line extended or a few hundred acres
annexed to the town in order to get the fire and police and thereby
knock down the insurance rates—" He paused to draw breath. "Guys
like to be under the umbrella of a close-knit town. Where the people
are friendly."

Irish had continued in a blizzard of facts and figures in the quiet bar
of the Chicago Athletic Club. Charles understood at once that the
lawyer was talking a different language from his friends in Dement,
and it seemed impossible that he would not succeed. Confidence bred
confidence. It took time for new ideas to trickle down to places like
Dement, and having Bill Eurich was like having a key to the future.
He'd watched his face, the direct blue eyes and the strong chin and the
mouth that always seemed poised on the edge of a joke. His ebul-
lience was infectious, a native-born optimism and an entirely different
style from the dour conservatism of his father and Elliott Townsend
and the other Dement old-timers. Charles was in no way worried. Bill
Eurich was a different breed of man, a man in motion, not landlocked;
a man who worked the edges.

"It's going to go all right," Charles said finally. "It's good for everybody and you couldn't kill it with an ax. But Dement's different. Understand that. It'll take some effort, getting everyone in line."

"I'm relying on your advice and good counsel absolutely."

Charles reached across the table and they clinked glasses. "Tell me one thing. Where did you get those statistics? That was all new to me."

"It's private, I can't get into that." He looked at Charles, whose eyes had narrowed. There was a sudden chill between the two men. What could be "private" about facts? "What the hell," Irish said. "This is between us, right?" He motioned for the waiter to bring them another round of drinks. "I get them from my kid."

"What do you mean, your kid?"

"My kid's at the university. They have all that stuff there. They have teams of students gathering data. 'Sociology.' My kid funnels the stuff to me and it's pure gold. What the hell, I'm paying the university for his education." Irish laughed then, as the waiter put down their drinks. "And the university is paying me back. With interest."

"You're the only guy I know who's actually gotten anything back from the bastards."

"Let me tell you something," he said. "There's nothing that can beat good information. And this stuff is solid, rock hard."

Charles laughed out loud: a true partnership, father and son. Unorthodox, but a partnership nonetheless. Later that night, over a steak at the Blackhawk, Charles told Bill Eurich about Frank, his promise as a newspaperman and his cruel death in Korea. The other man, hearing the story, put his knife and fork on his plate and turned away, genuinely moved. "Oh Christ," he said. "That's the worst luck a man can have. I'm sorry as hell to hear about it." Charles shrugged. He was tight and trying to appear nonchalant. "And Frank was your only son?" Charles nodded. "Any other kids?" Charles put up his forefinger: "One daughter." Eurich said, "I'll bet she's lovely." Yes, Charles said; yes she was. She was beautiful and smart in the bargain and impetuous as hell but a good girl, growing up too fast. "But it's not like having Frank," Charles said. "A son, particularly when there's a family business involved." Eurich nodded in agreement. "Of course not." Charles looked across the table at the other man, a more experienced, more worldly man. He said, "It's not something that I can explain very well. But she's growing away from us already. She's"—he laughed gruffly—"very sophisticated. I guess that's the word. She doesn't seem to like Dement, I wouldn't be surprised if she moved away, when she grows up and gets married. I don't know what to do about it," he said thickly. Eurich nodded; he understood that. Thank God he and Bill, Jr., had an understanding. "They get those ideas," Eurich said. "Just try to ride with it." Charles said, "That's what I'm doing." What the girl didn't understand, Eurich said, was that the Dement of today wasn't going to bear any relation to the Dement of tomorrow. It would be a different place altogether. "You're lucky as hell, you're tapping into it right at the start. All the towns are going to change sooner or later because all the money and most of the talent is outside. But you're coming in on your own terms, and at the beginning of it. And if you're like the rest of us"—he smiled triumphantly—"you'll be doing it mainly for your kids, and their kids . . ." Charles looked up, surprised. He had not thought of it in that way, and was pleased.

But that was a month ago. Now they were in his office, all assembled, drinks in their hands; it was time to do business. Charles said he was glad they could come on short notice and nodded at each one, Eurich, Elliott Townsend, Marge Reilly, Tom Kerrigan, and the newcomers, Joe Steppe, chairman of the county board, and Harry Bohn, the banker. Charles said he'd thought of delaying the meeting but decided against it because there was a certain amount of agitation in the county and if it were possible to reach a meeting of minds *here*, that was in every way preferable to a drawn-out controversy, with the risk always that the project would be lost altogether. He knew that several of those present had doubts. But he thought that once his friend Bill Eurich explained it those doubts would dissolve. The point, after all, was what was good for the community: housing and jobs. He stepped aside and Eurich rose and moved behind Charles's desk. He wanted to be able to look directly at the woman and at the judge, Kerrigan. He began with a joke, and then spoke in earnest.

First he dealt facts, the changing nature of the county from rural to urban. Overcrowded housing, a decaying downtown. "In ten years your downtown will look like Nagasaki." He deftly compared Dement to similar towns, similar distances from large cities. Then he described to them the details of the housing project and the shopping center to come. A thousand houses, four point two thousand people. But in many cases, most cases, they would not be new people; they would be Dement people. The new houses would be built as fast as it was possible to build them, but to begin next spring they would need the zoning variation now. Nodding at Kerrigan. And an annexation. Nodding at Steppe. He did not understand the objections. The Reilly Bog was now a bog; reclaim it, and it was prime land.

Marge Reilly was listening intently, almost painfully, very nearly mesmerized by the rhythm of Bill Eurich's voice. She was nervous and disconcerted; this was her first meeting of this kind. She'd watched Joe Steppe, the most powerful politician in the county, first nodding in agreement with Eurich, then openly smiling as he disclosed his facts. Eurich was so practical, his facts so well collected; she felt a little stupid. And she felt it was all happening very quickly.

"I don't quite understand . . ." she began. Eurich leaned forward, perched on the edge of Charles's desk, encouraging her. "You say it doesn't matter what we do, the town is going to grow by leaps and bounds anyway."

"That's essentially correct."

Well, she thought, they might as well get right down to it. "There are people here who are worried about the colored. This project would be a magnet to them."

"I can understand the concern," Eurich said. "And it's shared, believe me. I can assure you absolutely"—he clapped his hands together—"that this project will not be a Little Ivory Coast. Or a Little Italy or a Little Ireland. In the first place"—he looked up, smiling at the ceiling—"the mortgages will be federally guaranteed and of course they will have to have assurances . . . No, this is not a project that will collide in any way with the values of the community—"

"A little United Nations," Kerrigan said under his breath.

"—and I think that Charles and the paper can be helpful in that regard." He looked at Charles and Charles nodded.

"I have another question," Marge said. "Hard to put into words." She picked up her handbag and put it in her lap, fussing with the clasp. Then she laughed hesitantly. "It's so much. All at once." She glanced at Eurich, who was nodding sympathetically, waiting for her to finish. "Four thousand people. You know, that land used to be owned by my family." She described the contours and history of the land, and told an anecdote about the various Reillys who had lived on it. Then, "You bought that land through nominees, a parcel at a time." She went on, her voice hard now. "If I had owned it, I never would've sold. But my cousins had different ideas. Because you bought the land through nominees you got it for less than you might've if you'd bought it— aboveboard. In your own name."

"Correct on all counts," Eurich said. "But your cousins drove hard bargains. Understand, as it is the land is almost valueless. It only has value if someone is willing to finance the drainage. We couldn't afford to do that if we'd paid inflated prices for the land. As it was, we *did* pay top dollar; for the land as it is now. We were not out to shyster anyone. My partners and I do not do business that way. We are"—he looked at her but she avoided his eyes, and he knew he'd won—"businessmen."

"It seems to me that we've got an opportunity here to grab hold of the future," Charles said, speaking for the first time. "I think it's time we recognize a break with the past—"

She said, "I know your father was against this project." She looked at them all in turn, these men in their dark suits and polished shoes.

Charles said, "I think that's too strong, Marge. I don't think he was against it as much as he was . . . unconvinced." He smiled. "My father was . . . skeptical of change. He didn't like it a whole lot."

"No," she said. "He had a certain idea of Dement." She paused, aware that she was sounding sentimental. She felt like a minority of one, arrayed against determined men. "I'm sure that Mr. Eurich has the best of intentions," she said, though the truth was she was not sure of that at all. She felt helpless against Eurich's logic, the sheer force and plausibility of it. Against this logic, her only weapon was sentiment; her understanding of history. And it wasn't enough and she knew that, too.

"I guess we've got to face the fact that Amos's world is a thing of the past." Townsend's voice was slow and deliberate; she recognized it as his courtroom voice. This was the first time he'd spoken and she was eager to hear him. "Mine, too, when you come right down to it. I think what you're getting at, Marge, is a way of life. But my goodness"—his voice rose indignantly—"we're not living in a museum. For myself, I want to see the town be a part of things. The truth is, the town has to grow or it'll die. That's what happens to towns in this part of the world. They grow or they die."

Marge looked at Kerrigan, wondering if she had an ally there; it was clear to her that Townsend had thrown in with Charles. Her own thoughts were so muddled. But she saw Kerrigan's half smile and she knew he'd come out somewhere else, somewhere in front of her and in back of Eurich. Kerrigan waited for Townsend to finish and then asked quietly, "How much profit? And who?" He was looking at Charles.

Charles said, "Obviously, it is a business venture. Everyone involved will make a profit." He stared blankly at Kerrigan, as if he didn't understand the question.

"Who? Who'll make the profit?"

"Everybody," Eurich said. "That's the beauty of the deal. Everyone involved will make a profit and a handsome profit at that, but it's truly the *town* that will benefit." He looked around the room, a wide smile on his face. "Anyone out there who doesn't like a profit?" Harry Bohn and Joe Steppe laughed. Steppe shook his head and nudged Elliott Townsend. Only Tom Kerrigan could've asked a question like that. Steppe thought that sometimes there was something Socialistic about Kerrigan.

Eurich leaned forward, clasping his hands; his expression disclosed concern and sympathy. He wanted very much to win over the woman, sensing that her support would be invaluable. The project would go without her, of course; but his first principle was harmony. "Marge, I want to make sure that I've answered your questions. I don't want to be in any way evasive, because there's nothing to be evasive about."

"No, no," she said.

Too quickly, he thought. "I understand your doubts. It's a big step for the town. But it's also true that I've got to know the decision fairly soon, one way or another. This is only one of several projects my partners and I . . ." Eurich smiled and let the sentence hang. Then he reached for the briefcase lying on the floor beside him. The threat was so subtle, she thought; it was more nudge than threat. "Well," he said. "If there's nothing else, I think it would be appropriate for me to leave now. You good people can talk about it among yourselves. I've left a sheaf of stuff with Charles, all the facts and figures. Every fact we've got, also some designs of the houses themselves . . ." He turned pleasantly to Kerrigan. "There is a suit of some kind, is there not?" The judge nodded. "Presumably a decision will be forthcoming quickly?"

"Presumably," Kerrigan said.

"Time is always of the essence," Eurich said.

Charles came around the end of his desk, thanking Eurich for coming. Excellent presentation, he said. Eurich put his arm around Charles's shoulder and they spoke about a golf game; his club's course was open until the end of the month.

Marge Reilly listened to them, aware of something new. Suddenly she felt like a guest in a stranger's house. Somehow, subtly, it was clear that Charles and this Eurich were very much on the same side. Of course she knew that but this was different; she'd known it in the concrete and this was abstract. The two men were friends, and she had not known that. This went beyond any financial interest. She felt an instant of irrational resentment. It was suddenly clear to her that Charles had moved a step away from his old friends. She wasn't sure what that meant, or if it meant anything. But he'd allied himself with an outsider. A few days earlier she'd seen Eurich's name mentioned in the *Tribune*. The *Tribune* had described him as an "industrialist," whatever that meant. What was an "industrialist"? He owned no industries that she knew of. This outsider and Charles Rising were transmitting the same signals, in the way that her father and Amos had transmitted the same signals.

Eurich was at the door now, shaking hands with all of them; he was particularly courteous to her. He was charming, there was no doubt of that; and as tough as he was charming. And, she supposed, as smart as he was tough.

Charles walked down the hall with him, indicating that the others should stay and mix themselves a fresh drink. She watched them go, their voices receding. It was clear to her that Charles admired this Eurich. And she would have to agree that there was much to admire, the polish and the shrewdness and the ambition, and the charm. So far as she could tell he'd been level with them. There was nothing concealed—as he'd said, why should there be? The "deal" was perfectly straightforward, and did it matter so much that it came from the outside? She was suddenly weary and sad, uncomfortably aware of her minority. She was not a loner by nature, in fact she distrusted those who made a point of going against the grain; it was one of her complaints about Tom Kerrigan. But her instinct told her this meeting was important, and it went beyond the simple question of rezoning a tract of land; a bog, a useless swamp. It wasn't as if they were going to remake the county. This was just one small parcel of land on the edge of town. A piece of property on the periphery. But my goodness, she thought, they're going to jam those houses in there like rows of sardines. Well, she wouldn't have to live in them. And no doubt they were correct in assuming the houses would be bought like hotcakes. Eurich was no doubt correct, there was a crying need. And a crying need must be satisfied. And no doubt he was correct that this project would act as a magnet for other projects. Of course there would be other projects and she imagined that in ten years the town would have a new face. *A damned fine thing for Dement,* Eurich'd said, and he ought to know, this industrialist with his surveys chockablock with statistics. But it was a new kind of deal. No one took a risk; it was a riskless venture.

Charles returned, all smiles. He mixed himself a drink and then went behind his desk, standing where Eurich had stood. "A hell of a guy," he said. Steppe and Bohn and Townsend nodded and finally Marge Reilly nodded, too. Then Charles turned to Kerrigan. "Tom, what do you think?"

Kerrigan shrugged. "Smart. Lucid." Then, "What's his cut?"

Charles said, "I don't know. I imagine it would be a percentage plus a broker's fee. Hell, he's the linchpin. Without him, it never would've got off the ground. And of course he has partners, too."

"Who are they?"

Charles named Eurich's partners, his associates in the law firm. He said, "These are quality people." Then he turned to Bohn. "And of course Harry here is going to handle the financing from this end. All the accounts are funneled through him; loans, too. Harry's the bank of record. The point I'm trying to make is that it's a local deal, exactly as Eurich said."

Kerrigan turned to the banker. "How do your people feel about it?"

Bohn said, "Solid gold."

Kerrigan said, "Um."

"Look, Tom." Harry Bohn leaned forward. "A banker friend of mine, a good friend and a reliable friend, worked with Eurich on the deal he put together at the Indiana line. It was clean. There were"—he paused to clear his throat—"no problems whatsoever. No problems with the financing, the performance bonds, the construction, the legal work. There were"—he paused again—"no strikes. Work began on time and ended on time and everyone was satisfied. There's a file a mile long on Bill Eurich and not one mark of red ink on it. He's solid gold. That's another thing to bear in mind. Not all of them are. Eurich's a cut above that crowd. A good cut."

"Um," Kerrigan said.

"And, entirely confidentially and not to leave this room, but we're making Bill a member of our board of directors."

"Why?" Kerrigan asked.

"Because he's damn valuable, that's why. He understands the business, and he has contacts all over the state."

Marge was listening carefully to all of this and nodding. The truth was, it all came from outside; the ideas, the money. It was a little clearer to her now, how these men were linked. Someone had introduced Eurich to Charles. Charles had introduced Eurich to Bohn. Now Eurich would sit on Harry Bohn's board and have a voice in Dement's bank.

Kerrigan said, "What do you suppose made him think of Dement for this project?"

Charles Rising smiled. "Bill Eurich has done more research than you can imagine. He's got the facts. When he put them together, they spelled Dement."

Marge had one question, but she didn't know how to put it. "Charles," she said finally. "It doesn't make any difference to me. But do you have a financial interest?" She added quickly, "I'd feel better about the whole thing if you did."

"No," he said. "Eurich and I may go partners in another thing he's got cooking. Nothing in Dement, this is a thing near Saint Louis. Eurich and I and Harry may do something there. But believe me, I'll keep my eyes open. Both as publisher here and as a member of Harry's board. We all want this done right. But I confess I don't see." He shrugged. "The cause for concern."

She said, "It's so abrupt, is all." Then, "I don't suppose there would be any point to a referendum."

"Oh, Marge," Charles said. He was trying to keep the exasperation from his voice. "My God, that's a can of worms. And how much would it cost? Thousands. That's a lot of taxpayer money to decide what can be decided by the people in this room, the way we've always decided things. And you never know what's going to happen in a referendum. This is a private business deal, after all. I mean, hell, you wouldn't have a referendum to decide whether a new auto assembly plant would be located here. You'd say, Come on in, the water's fine." He shook his head vigorously. "There's a last thing, I wouldn't mention it at all because it isn't completely wrapped up. But there are three firms, nationally known firms, ready to sign up for the center right now." He named them. "That's how eager businessmen are to locate here."

"Let's let the court decide the issue of law first," Kerrigan said.

"And when would that be?" Charles asked.

"Late next week," Kerrigan said. "I would imagine."

She said vaguely, "It was just a thought." Chain stores, they had an allure, no question of that. Local merchants were so often behind the times. She looked at Elliott Townsend, and then at Joe Steppe; no support there. Their faces were turned away from her. Elliott had said very little and Joe nothing at all. She sighed and smiled at Charles. Her opposition was ended.

Townsend said, "The suit may be withdrawn."

They were all silent a moment. "One or two of the plaintiffs sound determined," Kerrigan said.

Townsend smiled. "I've read the briefs. I don't believe there's much of a case there. It's hard to argue that the highest and best use of a bog is as a—bog. Wouldn't you agree with that, Tom?"

"The code is ambiguous," Kerrigan said. "As you well know, as the author of it. However, if the proper appeals are filed it is a case that could drag on quite some little while."

"I don't think anyone wants that," Townsend said quietly. "Do you?"

"I don't believe they do," Kerrigan said.

"I don't either," Townsend said. "Though it might be different—" He let the sentence hang.

"Yes," Kerrigan said.

"—if Amos were still alive." Townsend wanted that on the table, in plain view, where everyone could see it. He was sending a signal to

Kerrigan, and to Steppe and Marge Reilly, notifying them formally of his shift of allegiance from the father to the son. The project would go forward because Charles Rising wanted it to go forward. The transfer of authority was complete.

Kerrigan rose. "I've got to go." He offered Marge a ride and she accepted. They finished their drinks and promised to meet again before the end of the week. They shook hands all around and the judge and the county clerk left the newspaper office. In Kerrigan's car, silent, they began to drive up Blake Street. The lamps were dim and the dome of the courthouse and the Civil War monument were blurred against the night sky. She thought of Earl and the others in her office that morning, the funeral, and the meeting just ended; it had all gone so quickly, as if it had happened to someone else. She glanced at Kerrigan, pensive, driving cautiously through the uncrowded streets. She did not care to express all her doubts to him; there was no way of knowing what he'd make of them. He took a cigarette package out of his pocket, offered her one, and lit them both. He said, "It's going to happen. It was true, the opponents didn't have much of a case. They could've tied it up for a time, but that was about all. Too bad in a way because it's an interesting case." He looked at her and smiled. "*They* want it," he said. "And it'll go through and we'll have four thousand new people and a shopping center. But hell, people have to live somewhere. In this life, everything's a trade-off." He eased up on the accelerator as they slid by the courthouse, its interior lights gleaming yellowly, casting shadows on the lawn. Across the street from the courthouse a neon sign flickered, TAVERN. Kerrigan pointed to it. A few figures could be seen leaning over the bar watching television. He said, "This is all going to hell, in twenty years the downtown will be deserted and all the action will be on the outskirts—"

"Action?"

"Money," Kerrigan said. He braked for a red light and laughed. "That's all this place'll be good for. But by God, it'll be good for that. Under the direction of our new publisher."

She looked out the window. "A boom town. *Dement*."

"It isn't going to be a closed corporation anymore, Marge."

"No, it isn't."

"Marge," he said. "I don't know Charles very well. Tell me about Charles."

"Well. As you no doubt know by now, Charles will manage the paper. He'll do very well at it. Trouble is, he has no liking for politics. And of course that was the one thing Amos was a genius at. So it'll be different."

Kerrigan looked over at her, surprised. He had not expected her to say so much.

"Charles understood as a little boy that he could not compete with his father on that ground. The political ground. So he acquired an understanding of business, and let me tell you he does understand it. Of course business was something that Amos always considered beneath him. But he came to know soon enough that it was Charles who saved his paper for him, in the thirties when times were hard. And he knew that he didn't have to understand the balance sheet as long as Charles did. Charles was blood and could be trusted. Now Mitch could have been the heir and God knows he has a taste for politics but he has no imagination. He'd simply try to imitate Amos and Amos knew that and knew also that it wouldn't work. Trouble with Mitch, he discovered his taste for politics in the army, and that's not the best place to discover it." She paused but Kerrigan was silent, listening. "Mitch doesn't like people, it's as simple as that. And Tony—Tony is Tony. We all know Tony. And that's the greatest irony of all because the old man liked Tony best of all. Really *liked* him. They lunched together every week of their lives for thirty years."

"But Charles—"

"—shares one characteristic with the old man. Charles wants his way. He believes he knows what's best, just like Amos did. He'll go about getting it in a different way. It won't be Amos's way. It'll be some other way. I guess we got a hint today. I don't know," she said. "I think it was too bad about his boy, Frank."

"Yes," Kerrigan said.

"It changed him," she said.

Kerrigan asked, "How?"

"He felt—betrayed, I think. I'm not sure of my facts," Marge said wearily. She realized she'd said too much. She was tired now.

He was silent a moment. Then, "I have a theory, too—"

"I don't want to hear it," Marge said.

"All right," said Kerrigan.

Elliott Townsend left shortly after the other two. He and Charles agreed to meet for lunch on Friday; he wanted to satisfy himself that Eurich's project was entirely checked out according to law. They knew now that Kerrigan would not pose any threat. He was free to rule for the defendants. They did not mention the meeting the next afternoon with Mitch and Tony; that was family business. Joe Steppe left with Townsend and Charles prepared a last drink for Harry Bohn.

Bohn said, "Congratulations." Charles Rising smiled broadly and dipped his glass in acknowledgment. "Just so you know, my people are very enthusiastic. This is going to be a hell of a profitable adventure all the way around. And I think Irish is going to be able to make a real contribution on the board. He's new blood. He's got angles I never heard of. We've already laid off part of this loan to two banks downstate that he's done business with before—"

"Absolutely," Charles said.

"And I owe you a vote of thanks," Bohn said.

"You're damn lucky, you know that?" Charles said suddenly.

"Why?"

"In your bank there's just you. No family, no stockholders to speak of. I mean no stockholders that you don't control lock, stock and barrel. There's just you and your kid."

"You're unhappy with what your dad did?"

"No," Charles said. "I came out all right. It's just that there're all these bodies around, members of the family. He had a problem. He didn't want to hurt Mitch and Tony but he knew damn well that the cart couldn't be pulled by three horses. Not these three anyway. He wanted to cut them in on the dough, but not on the control. He un-

derstood control better'n any man I know. He understood that completely."

"Tony wouldn't've wanted it anyway."

"Hell, no," Charles said.

"But Mitch wanted it."

"Mitch wanted it," Charles said. "Wanted it so bad he could taste it.
Mitch wants to play Prendergast in Dement." Charles was silent for a
moment. "I don't think Mitch understands that that period has come
to an end. A full stop. Shit, Joe Steppe didn't say a word tonight. Who
did the talking? I did. You did. Eurich did."

"Marge did. Tom Kerrigan did."

"Well." Charles smiled. "There's no way in hell we're going to get
anything done around here without lawyers and judges and Marge
Reilly. Kerrigan's bad news but he'll pass by this one. And Elliott was
damned skillful, I'll give him that. Tom knows now that you want this
thing and I do and so does Blake Street and anyone who has a *stake* in
this town, and why go up against that when you don't have to?"

"I agree with that," Bohn said. "But listen to this. This deal was
damn near derailed because of the uncertainty. The Berlin guys didn't
like it, that it was in court. It made them nervous and at first they
wanted to heave some money around, dumb bastards, and I told them
it wouldn't work. I went down there with Eurich to tell them that it
wouldn't work. Not in this instance. Tom Kerrigan's no Aces Evans. I
told them they had to be a little bit patient. And they said to me, 'Can't
you control your town?' I had to let them get that speech out of their
system. Then Eurich took over and told them it would be all right because he had your assurances, and we both knew what we were doing.
They didn't like it but they came back on board. But it almost went off
the track, Charlie, and that's the thing I wanted to convey to you, a
thing we've got to consider in the future—"

"You're satisfied with your end?"

Bohn nodded. "More than satisfied." Harry Bohn had a boyish face
with a dimple on each cheek and when he smiled he looked like an
overweight choirboy. "This is the best thing that ever happened to me.

It puts the bank in a position to really take off. It's extremely profitable for everyone. All around."

"The meeting went all right," Charles said.

"Perfect," Bohn said.

"Poor Marge."

"With her, it's sentiment."

"And you have to sympathize," Charles said. "The damn bog means something to her in a personal way."

Bohn said, "We moved ahead ten years today." He looked closely at Charles, and then asked a question. "What do you really think your old man thought?"

"I know what he thought," Charles said. "He didn't want it but he knew he'd have to fight a delaying action. He would've delayed and delayed but Eurich's people wouldn't've lost interest. He would have taken Bill Eurich into that little office of his and had a talk. Just to indicate how tough he could be. There was no chance he could delay it forever but he could've tied them in knots and forced them to commit a bundle in lawyer's fees, which they wouldn't want to commit. Until next year or the year after. Then they would've been back and the terms wouldn't be as favorable and the town would've lost, ultimately. You wouldn't be in the deal. Steppe wouldn't be. I wouldn't be. To tell the truth, I think he didn't like to think about it because it depressed him. But you're right about the other thing. We moved ahead ten years today."

"And it's just the beginning," Bohn said. He finished his drink and stood up and the two men shook hands. They laughed together a moment, then Bohn left and Charles was alone in his office. He leaned back in the chair and put his feet on the desk. The room was still filled with the smell of the others, Eurich's Cuban cigar, Marge Reilly's neutral perfume. Smiling, he offered a silent toast to the ceiling. Then another to the photographs, the ones of his father and of Lee and of Frank and Dana as children, the boy in a cowboy suit and the girl in a party dress.

My God, he thought; what luck. What luck to be at the controls in this town—the town he was born in and grew up in, familiar with it as he was with his own skin. Every street corner and building held a memory and no name was mysterious. He'd carry on in his father's tradition except by a different path. His father was one who liked to be visible in all ways; he ruled by force of personality, his authority almost ecclesiastical. Charles was not like that, he didn't have the physical dimensions for it. He liked to move behind the scenes, sitting in a room with half a dozen other men, asking questions and making decisions; reaching a consensus and acting on the consensus. They were together now, he and Bill Eurich and Harry Bohn and Joe Steppe and old Elliott, Elliott a link to the past; Elliott a necessary part of it, though he had to acquire a younger man for a partner. That was one thing he had to have, a young man who knew the score or could be taught the score, because Elliott's responsibilities would grow. Of course he was like Amos, he didn't think anyone could tell him anything. And he believed that towns grew in isolation, compartmentalized and removed from the world, each town its own sanctuary or asylum. It might have been true at the turn of the century but it was true no longer. The Midwest was a single body and the cities were its lifeblood: you took the blood or you died. Elliott and Amos did not understand that money was health, it was salubrious. They did not know how to use it, and that was the trouble. In their day there was no requirement to know the similarities between assets and liabilities, and the differences between stock offerings, debentures and bonds. When Charles described to his father the manner in which he'd saved the newspaper from bankruptcy in 1936, his father was indifferent; when he'd described it to Eurich, Eurich had been quick in his admiration. Then he, Eurich, told him how it might have been done faster and cheaper. "You bring in an outside partner in a minority position." And Charles had nodded and said nothing, keeping to himself the knowledge that it was murderous to surrender any slice of control, no matter how small; even partial outside control meant boards of directors. Meetings and a record of those meetings and outside board members and their lawyers. Then it was no longer a family business; it was public.

Oh, he thought; this town, it was complicated and you had to know the people. You had to know their parents and their children and where they went to church and what they wanted for themselves. What was absolutely necessary for the Rising family was not necessarily so for the Bohns, bankers for four generations. Harry Bohn ran his bank like a private checking account. He and his wife and children and two aunts and six of his oldest employees held a hundred percent of the stock. He was accountable to no one, and for twenty years had managed the bank like a corner grocery. He'd been lenient with his debtors and had survived the depression but the bank had not grown. It had not moved an inch and would not move an inch because Harry Bohn's father had very nearly lost the bank in 1919 and had died in 1925, a suicide. He'd overextended, and it killed him, or so his son believed. Charles, himself a member of the bank's board of directors, had urged Harry Bohn to consider Bill Eurich for the board, and Bohn had finally agreed. It was essential that the bank grow with the town, and they in Dement retain practical control of their own capital; their own blood. If they didn't, someone else would. There would be a new bank controlled by outsiders and when that happened Amos Rising's nightmare would come true. It might still be necessary for Harry Bohn to sell off partial control to one of the large city banks. A bank was not a newspaper. If Bill Eurich was right the town was on the edge of a furious expansion, and you could not expand without money. But that was a problem for the future. Just now it was enough that Harry have the benefit of Eurich's experience and insight.

The truth was, Harry Bohn did not truly understand his business. He did not understand balance sheets, they were no more than dictionaries; certain numbers defined certain concepts. There was a grammar to it, a syntax and structure, a left-hand side and a right-hand side and it was not always advantageous to draw hard-and-fast distinctions between the two. A man always looked at the right-hand side first; liabilities disclosed more than assets if you knew what to look for. It was where the assets were concealed. But you had to know yourself which was which. You had to invent your own grammar and interpret your books in your own way. From time to time his father had complained; he did not understand what he was reading. Where am I? What does this mean? He didn't understand any of it and Charles tried to explain and then gave up. At the end of each year he was able to demonstrate that the net worth of the newspaper was greater than the year before, even though "net worth" was a relative concept. Depreciation was an asset or a liability, depending on the point you were trying to make, and with whom. The future was an asset if you calculated it properly, though it was nowhere indicated on the balance sheet or on the P and L either. An outsider would not be able to find it, or the profits.

Damn, he said aloud. He walked into the hall, through Tony's office and into his father's. The spirit of the old man was still there, buried deep in the leather desk chair and the shabby rug and the squat mahogany desk and the hat rack, with that damned hat hanging on it as it had for twenty years ... He put his drink on the desk and took the old silver key ring out of his pocket and opened the top drawer and drew it toward him. You could read a man's life from the contents of his desk, this one filled with old things, papers, business cards, pencils; the detritus of a lifetime. He would have to sort it out sometime. Or let Mitch do it; it would keep Mitch busy. He pulled the drawer all the way out and gave a sudden wheeze, *Good Christ*. The old man's revolver, loaded, safety off. He broke the breech and extracted the cartridges and aimed through the window at a streetlamp. *Click!* Then he returned the revolver and loose slugs to the drawer and closed and locked it. That damned gun, it dated from the time of the troubles with Capone's people. If they really were Capone's people. His father had never known for certain; he assumed that they were. That was twenty years ago and the old man had kept the gun in the desk, loaded, ever since. Charles Rising turned off the desk lamp and sat awhile in the unfamiliar leather chair, the room dark and the building silent. He was a lucky man; he knew absolutely what he wanted to do and was in a position to do it. And it was a very near thing; he could as easily not be a newspaperman at all. Charles remained only a moment. The office was small and gave him claustrophobia.

5.

SHE SAID, "You're sweet, but no."

"Well, then—"

She knew he was disappointed. "I can't."

"Shoot. I knew I was calling too late."

"I'm not going with anybody else."

"Then." She heard his voice brighten; no telephone line could disguise it. "Then come on, what the heck. We'll have a ball. It's dumb and probably won't be any fun, but."

"Can't," Dana said.

A long sigh of disappointment. "Come on, Jeez Crise, it isn't as if—"

"You ought to take Janie. I'll fix you up."

"Janie who?"

"Janie Cockran, you know her. She's really good-looking, you'll like her. I know you'll like her and I'm going to fix you up. I'll talk to her tomorrow."

"Jeez Crise," he said. "How old is she?"

She said, "She's fifteen. But that's all right." She thought a minute, searching for points in Janie Cockran's favor. "I don't think she drinks. But she smokes." Dana was lying on the floor with her legs raised flat against the wall. She wiggled her toes and put the telephone to her other ear. Downstairs she could hear men's voices. "She's very old for her age, I promise you'll like her. I know it, give me a chance—"

"Where are you going Saturday?" His voice was hesitant; she guessed he both wanted to know and didn't want to know. "You're serious, you're not going to the dance? With anyone?"

"I'll be in New York," she said casually. The voices downstairs grew louder, and she could hear the clink of ice and glasses. She knew that in another five minutes she would be asked to get off the telephone. She wiggled her toes again, and beat a little tattoo on the wall.

"New *York?*"

"With my mother," she said. "We're staying at the Biltmore." She knew he had never heard of the Biltmore and was immediately sorry for having mentioned it. But she had been thinking of the clock for days, imagining herself under it.

"What's happening in New York?"

She said, "We're looking at schools. They've decided to put me in a school in the East." She forced disappointment into her voice. "Or *she's* decided. He doesn't like the idea at all." She giggled again. "He thinks it's about the worst thing that ever happened, or I think he does. He doesn't say much about it. He just nods and grumbles a little and says, 'Well, if you think that's best.'"

"Well, why? I mean, what's wrong with here? Everybody's here, not there. The East? I don't understand that at all, not one bit."

She said, "They want me to go to college." That, she thought, was at least part of the truth; not a lie, anyway. "They are not too excited about my grades here." That was definitely not a lie, except for English and history. "And she wants me to be under good influences." Dana laughed out loud, she knew that would confuse him. "She means you. The Sen-Sen didn't cover you up the other night."

"It didn't?"

"You smelled like a brewery."

"Oh Crise," he said.

"Hey, Bobby?" She listened to his breathing a minute. "I'm kidding. Really, I'm kidding. Reeeel-y, no kidding I'm kidding."

"Yeah," he said.

"They didn't suspect anything. They like you."

"I'm really not too anxious to itch off your old man." None of them were. And when she was at their houses their parents always asked after her parents, though in many cases they'd never met. Once, she and a girl friend were walking downtown to the movie and she

suddenly turned and said, I'm just as good as you are. Dana was embarrassed. Why would she say that? The girl said, My father said that
just because your family . . . Of course, Dana said; of course. But she
felt that the girl didn't believe her own words, or the words her father
had supplied her. She was the smartest girl in the class, and one of the
nicest, and chronically overweight; and her father was a milkman.

She said, "I'll be back next Wednesday." She felt his bewilderment
over the telephone. "She's promised to take me to a couple of shows.
But listen," she said. "How about Janie Cockran? I can fix it up, no kidding. She knows who you are, knows you're a friend of mine and so
on."

Bobby said, "Is she hot?"

Dana laughed. "How would I know?"

"Can you find out?"

"*You* find out," she said.

"You can find out easier'n me and it'll save a lot of trouble for
everybody."

"Well, she's a freshman—"

"A *freshman?*"

"But I'll do my best. How hot do you want?"

"Very hot," he said.

"Well, I don't know how hot she is. I suppose she's medium-hot."

"Dana!" It was her father, standing at the foot of the stairs. "Dana,
time's up! There are other people in this house who might want to
make a call or receive one. Cut it short, please." He stared at her a
minute, then turned away.

She nodded at her father and said into the telephone, "I've got to go
now. Let me know tomorrow."

"I'll come over after dinner."

"All right. Call first. And don't forget the Sen-Sen."

"Oh Jeez," he said.

"I'm joking, Bobby." She hung up, reaching to cradle the receiver.
The truth was, Janie Cockran was not hot. Not cold, but not hot either. But neither was Bobby. She decided it was the perfect date, if

Bobby did not get polluted. Or act as if he were polluted, which was the same thing. Worse. She rose and went to the banister and leaned over it, trying to catch her father's eye. She signaled that the phone was clear and he nodded. She remained at the banister a moment, watching them; her father, her two uncles, and Mr. Townsend. Mr. Townsend was reading from a pile of documents. Legal language of some kind. From time to time he'd put the paper to one side and smile and talk conversationally. She listened for a moment.

". . . knows what might happen in a year or five years or ten. Illness, death. No one knows the future. Of you three, your father believed that Charles was the businessman. Therefore he has been given control . . ."

She watched her father light a cigarette very deliberately. The expressions on the faces of her uncles did not change. She was lulled by Elliott Townsend's voice. It seemed to her to resemble the voice of a family doctor; soothing, reassuring. Her Uncle Tony seemed the most distracted of the four, as if he wanted this over and done with as quickly as possible. He fidgeted with his drink and kept glancing at his shoes, as if some message were to be found there. Then she saw her father look at her and she moved away from the banister. The look said, This is private. As she moved away, the lawyer's voice rose.

"Not, I hasten to add, control of the profits. It was Amos's wish that those be divided equally among the three of you. Amos believed that a great enterprise could not be run by a committee. So Charles has been given control of the policy, but not the profits. Those will be divided, as I'll demonstrate in a minute . . ."

Taking one last look, she saw Mitch Rising's jaw tighten; he always looked fierce to her, and she did not know if he was feeling less fierce or more fierce than normal. But that was a tense room. She felt that words were being withheld. In that room, words and phrases were hidden everywhere. Feelings were hidden, and no doubt would remain hidden. One would hunt for them in vain. She heard her mother working in the kitchen; a pot clattered, a door slammed.

Dana walked down the hall to her own room and closed the door.

The kitchen sounds were beginning sounds, not ending sounds; she knew her mother would be there for some time. She went to the window and opened it an inch, feeling the cold air. The light was failing. Past the wide lawn and the oaks that framed it was the prairie, extending as far as she could see. It was interrupted by a single stand of woods in the middle distance. Her room was stuffy and she waited a moment, considering. The faint drone of men's voices disconcerted her. Abruptly she closed the window and went to her clothes closet and rummaged on the top shelf, where her stuffed animals and games and old magazines were kept. She fished until she found the thin silver case containing her Lucky Strikes. She put it in her shirt pocket and left the room, closing the door and hurrying down the stairs, taking the stairs two steps at a time. The men looked briefly at her but did not stop talking. Tony Rising gave her a small smile and a wave. She fetched her heavy coat and a long scarf from the closet and was almost out the door when she heard her father's voice.

"Sweetheart, where are you going?"

"Out," she said.

"You mean to someone's house?" The four men were looking at her with solemn faces.

"Just for a walk, Daddy."

"Be careful," he said.

She nodded. "I will."

He said, "It's dark out."

Her mother, from the kitchen: "Don't forget your coat."

Her father said, "It's cold out, don't catch cold."

She said, "Yes," and closed the door firmly and marched off down the lawn to the trees, the cigarette case friendly in her pocket. She pulled up the collar of her coat and did a little dance, the brittle dead grass crunching under her feet. She thought, I will be very careful. Very. It is cold and it is dangerous. Very. There is no telling what evil lurks upon the prairie. When the dapper man in the Jaguar draws near and asks me to go to West Egg with him, I'll tell him no thank you. Dangerous. And when he asks me if I'd like to share his magnum of champagne and brings it dripping from the cooler in the backseat, I'll tell him no thank you. Hazardous. And when he asks me to share his stateroom on the *Ile de France*, I'll tell him no thank you. Perilous. Paris in the spring? No thank you. Dinner at the Ritz? No thank you. And when he suggests that I go to bed with him—that his crowded life will not be complete until that glorious event—I'll tell him. She laughed out loud. *Yes!* But not right away, not until we get to know each other better, in the car and on the deck of the ocean liner and over cocktails in the hotel bar . . . She flung her arms wide and did a reel down the lawn, dodging the birdbath and the cast-iron love seat. She played jazz music in her head, imagining that somewhere on that lawn Kid Ory was concealed, blowing his sweet trombone, and dancers whirled in the shadows. She wrapped the scarf around her neck and ran the final few yards to the woods at the end of the lawn. Out of breath, she crept around the largest of the trees and peeked back at the house. Her mother was at the kitchen window, her hands clasped in front of her, staring alone into the blackness. She waved and saluted, knowing her mother could see nothing. Then, as Dana watched, her mother's hands went to her face and stayed there; then she turned and moved slowly away from the window.

Dana opened the cigarette box and took out a Lucky Strike, tapping it against her thumb before she put it in her mouth. She brought out two kitchen matches, striking one against the other. The cigarette lit, she coughed once and leaned against the tree, letting the Lucky dangle from the corner of her mouth. She scuffed the earth happily, caressing the worn silver case between her fingers, looking at the stars and humming to herself. The blues repeated in her head, fragments of "Rampart Street Parade" and "Basin Street Blues" and "Milenberg Joys." So happy, so sad. The blues touched her soul, releasing emotions that burned and excited her and made her want to shout with the sheer power of what she felt. She wanted to talk about it, to explain what it was that she felt; but there was no one to tell. No girl she knew was interested. Only two boys she knew had any interest in the blues and they refused to talk about it with her. They were older boys, of course. Once or twice she had joined their conversations and they had changed the subject, uncomfortable at her intervention. It was as if she were intruding on them, discussing a subject that was theirs and theirs alone. They appeared to be offended that she'd put herself on an equal footing with them, competing in some unfair way; but it was not a matter of competition, no one was keeping score. What was so masculine, so exclusive, about jazz music? Other than the unfortunate truth that women were no musicians. There were no female sidemen, other than—she thought a moment—Lil Armstrong and Marian Mc-Partland, and they were married to jazzmen so they didn't count. She supposed that was why they didn't. There were the singers, Bessie Smith and the others, but they were *singers*, not cornet players or drummers or clarinetists. Perhaps it was the passion of the blues, an energy and emotional force that women were not supposed to understand. Or acknowledge that they understood. It was all right if they understood it as a member of the audience. Idiotic, but perhaps true. She smiled then, thinking of herself as a vast undiscovered continent. Dana the dark continent. She was a native in her own country, similar to an African savage. Livingstone would discover her someday and then Stanley would discover Livingstone and before long Dana the dark continent would be mapped, "discovered" and publicized. But until then she would have to keep her knowledge to herself. She thought that as a rule boys were less mysterious. Those two jazz connoisseurs, they had not been rude or insulting to her; they had been courteous in their own way. She was too good-looking for any boy to be rude to, or want to be rude to. So they listened to her politely and tolerantly and then they changed the subject.

She blew a smoke ring and the wind took it away.

Saturday morning, she thought. I cannot *wait*. I cannot wait to be on that airplane, Midway to Idlewild. I cannot wait to see New York from the air, and sally into the Biltmore lobby. That was truly an undiscovered country. She could not imagine herself living away from home, living with a strange girl in a dormitory filled with other strange girls. Except they did not call it a dormitory; they called it a "house." "Nice girls," her mother called them. She knew that her mother was worried; she suspected the smoking and was very critical of Bobby and her other friends. She had heard them talking, or rather heard her mother talking; her father said very little. Her mother surprised her. She'd said, "Dana is a superior child . . ." Then their voices lowered and she knew they'd returned to poor Esther. Esther the scarlet woman, a genuine scandal. That had happened two years ago and everywhere in Dement there were discussions behind closed doors. These led to a reform of the school curriculum, specifically the teaching of biology. Poor Esther had become pregnant and her parents and the boy's parents forced them to marry; it was a mutual embarrassment too profound to conceal. The embarrassment was greater because no one talked about it out loud. Esther and the boy disappeared in their senior year and were married out of state, with the families bravely in attendance. The boy went to work in his father's hardware store, which suffered an immediate loss of business because the women customers could not bear, they said, to chat casually with Sonny at the cash register. It was mortifying. What was there to say to him? How's Esther? How's the baby? By their presence, the women thought, they were bearing witness and therefore approval. Neither Sonny nor Esther held up well. The father's business faltered and he and the mother suffered for the sins of their son. The hardware store was now for sale, but it would be many years before the town forgot, if it ever did forget. In the event, Esther delivered twin boys; and of course that was regarded as a rebuke. Esther's Revenge.

She stubbed out her cigarette and began to stroll back to the house. Esther and her Sonny; the story was not unusual. At school they were very casual about it, after the first week of gossip and rumor. When they saw how upset the adults were, they became themselves studiously nonchalant. It was no big deal, people had babies all the time. But the truth was, the ferocity of the adults frightened the children; it frightened them the more because none of it was in the open. No child would admit this; they kept their heads high. But they thought, One mistake and such terrible retribution; lives closed off and cursed

before they had begun. They thought, There but for the grace of God
. . . She had written Frank a long letter describing the scandal, and the
town's reaction to it. He was then in Korea and his letter back began
with a long description of the progress of the war, a strangely pes-
simistic account. Then he said she should not be surprised at the reaction of "the powers that be" to Esther's "sin." He'd known both Sonny
and Esther and it was obvious from the beginning that they were
headed for trouble of one sort or another, either separately or together. He wrote, "Live by the sword, die by the sword." The letter
ended with instructions for her own moral safekeeping. She'd cried
when she finished the letter; it was the sort of message that she'd expect from the school principal or old Greismann. Its tone was harsh
and supercilious and she found hints that Frank believed "rotten behavior" damaged the morale of the troops, fighting Communists a
world away in Korea. Reading it again the day after the funeral she
reached another conclusion. He was scared to death. Reading it a second time, it made no sense; Frank was simply repeating fragments of
the various sermons he'd been read in his lifetime. Vicious, Dana concluded finally; Dement was more narrow and more vicious than anything conceived by Sinclair Lewis. But she understood it; she did
understand it. She fingered the cigarette case in her pocket and
thought she would understand it even better when she was eighteen,
and went away to school.

She approached the house, moving around it to the back door. She
would slip in unnoticed, and return to her room and listen to Kid Ory
and finish *Lie Down in Darkness*. She paused a moment, looking again
at the stars against the night sky, then eased the door open and stepped
through it. She was assailed immediately by loud voices, and moved
off into the shadows of the coatroom. The men all seemed to be talking at once. Then Elliott Townsend's voice, droning heavily and finally
overwhelming the others.

". . . times change. People change with them. Your father was
adamant that nothing interfere with the distribution of control as he
established it. Hence the committee, and the trust it supervises. Of

course he had complete faith in you boys. Total and complete faith. But he was not certain about the next generation down the line. And there should be nothing surprising about that. No one is certain of the next generation. Generations differ, one from another. Codes of conduct change . . . "

"A committee of outsiders," Mitch said contemptuously.

"I don't look on myself as an outsider in this family," Townsend said. "You shouldn't either."

"But I do," Mitch said. "No offense. This is not personal. Not personal with you or with Marge Reilly either. But the *I* is a Rising property. It's Charles's and Tony's and mine. And our family's. I just find it goddamned insulting to have a committee of . . . non-family members ruling on what we can or cannot do with the stock. As if anyone *intended* to do anything with it—"

Townsend said, "Well, what do you intend?"

"Nothing," Mitch said. "Not a goddamned thing. But I don't have to be advised of that fact by you or anyone else."

Townsend nodded slowly and looked again at the document before him. He waited a moment before resuming his lawyer's explanation.

"Your father desired harmony. And that of course is what we will have. There is no reason not to have it. We are all agreed here. Your father was insistent that you boys all remain at the newspaper to carry on its work. The codicil obviously has no implications for the present moment. Because you boys don't intend any distributions. Transfers or sales or whatever. We are talking for the future only. A future that none of us can foresee."

"It's not right," Mitch said.

"It's apparently what Dad wanted," Tony said in a low voice. "I think we ought to honor that. We ought to take him at face value. Dad always knew what he was doing. Elliott has a point, too, that this has nothing to do with the situation now. It is for the future only."

Mitch said, "Crap. Elliott, whose idea was it really?"

Townsend looked at him steadily, eyes narrowing. "What do you mean by that?"

"Your idea or Dad's?"

"Your father's," Townsend said coldly. "That is what I said in the first place, and I'm not in a habit of lying to clients. Who also happen to be the sons of my oldest friend."

Charles said, "Mitch, you are a member of the committee."

"A minority of one," Mitch said.

Townsend said, "What makes you think that my interest is any different than yours? What possible reason can you have for that view? What the hell is wrong with you anyway?"

"What the hell," Mitch said. "What the hell." He reached for his glass and drained it. His face was flushed and his eyes red. "You," he said to Charles. "You're the one who's got control. You don't care, what difference does it make to you? The I, all of it that matters, is now in your hands." Mitch made a show of cold anger, but it didn't work. His voice was a whine now. "You're running the outfit and Tony and me are the spear carriers. We're locked in. We're locked in in all ways."

"That was not what your father intended," Townsend said smoothly. "And I do not believe that Charles will operate in that way."

"What way?" Mitch demanded.

"With a lone hand."

"Of course he will. He's just like *him*. Just like the old man, he's a replica of the old man, he'll never—"

"Mitch," Charles began.

"This is all fucked up," Mitch said. He stood and lurched to the liquor cabinet, shouldering Tony aside. He muttered something, then began to pour Scotch into his glass. Charles nodded at Elliott Townsend, who shrugged. "It's just the way it always was," Mitch said, his back to them. "Charles gets what he wants, always. Tony—hell, Tony never cared. Charles was always the right man in the right place. You never gave a damn, did you Tony?"

Tony looked away, embarrassed at this.

"Tony!" Mitch roared, turning suddenly and staring at all of them. Charles said, "Mitch, for Christ's sake."

"I am satisfied with whatever it was Dad wanted," Tony said slowly. He looked at his two brothers, knowing that of the three of them he knew his father best; loved him best, and was loved in return. He supposed he had paid a price but did not know or care whether it was high or low. He said, "I don't care what it is, I intend to follow his instructions to the letter."

Mitch moved to the window and stood looking out. "Should've stayed in the goddamned army. Liked the army; army liked me. Goddamnedest biggest mistake I ever made in my life. A lifetime of mistakes; that was the biggest." He was silent a moment. Then, "What happens when I want to write a will. Leave my stock to—that whore who waits table at Mason's. What happens then?"

"All wills have to be cleared by the committee, so far as *I* stock is concerned," Townsend said. "The assumption of course is that the stock will stay in the immediate family. Your father assumed it; I do. Won't it?"

"Shit," Mitch said.

Tony turned and looked at him through his wire-rimmed spectacles. His small hands had tightened into fists. "Don't talk nonsense, Mitch."

"And what happens when I die? Or you do. Or Marge Reilly does. Who fills the vacancy on your 'committee'? Who decides?"

Townsend pursed his lips and glanced to one side. "Charles does," he said softly. "One member of the committee will always be a member of the family. One of you three. The other two will always be outsiders. But in the event of death, Charles chooses the successor."

"Charles chooses the successor," Mitch repeated, his voice old and worn-out.

"That's right."

"And if Charles is dead?" Mitch turned from the window and began to pace. "Our Charles is dead. What then?"

"Charles's heir decides," Tony said.

Mitch turned on him. "How the hell would you know?"

"Because it's logical," Tony said. "And—" He was going to explain that their father had told him about this will, had described its various provisions and the codicil. But he looked at Mitch and concluded that that would be too cruel. What purpose would it serve? He said, "I understand what Dad was doing. And I don't see what the problem is. Elliott, explain it again."

"Yes." Mitch mimicked Tony's soft voice. "Explain it again, Elliott."

"The point is—"

"As if it made any damned difference," Mitch went on. "Charles has got the controlling shares of the common. That's what's important. It doesn't matter what Tony does or what I do. It's what Charles does."

"Mitch," Townsend said. He paused for emphasis. The conversation was beginning to unravel and he didn't like it. "Nothing has changed."

"Jesus, Elliott," Charles said. He couldn't let Townsend go down that road. He hated this; hated every part of it. He loathed disharmony. He had sat quietly by, permitting Mitch to have his say; but he couldn't allow this. "Jesus Christ, everything has changed. Don't do the nothing-has-changed routine. It has. We all know it has. *Dad is dead.* We all have to come to terms with the new . . . situation. We're not going to get anywhere by pretending everything is as it was. It isn't." He looked with kindness at the old lawyer. "It's not, Elliott."

"In the essentials nothing has changed," Townsend said stubbornly.

"All right," Mitch said. He pointed at Charles with his glass. "Just tell me this. You're editor and publisher now. Where do I fit in? What's my role here? What do I do with my days at the *I?*"

"What you've always done," Charles said patiently. "And done damn well."

"That won't do, brother. You said it just then. Dad is gone. I operated with him. That was what I did. There was a race for sheriff or state's attorney, I went down and checked out the available guys. I spent a lot of time talking to people and a lot of time listening, too. Talking for him. I was his right-hand man p'litically and everyone knew that." He paused and looked away. "Of course, I could do for you what I used to do. Is that what you want? Maybe you want that. Is that what you want me to do? Maybe that's *my* highest and best use."

Charles stared at him a long minute, then turned away. When they were schoolboys, Mitch Rising, larger and more combative than his younger brother, was a protector. The slender and more vulnerable Charles was saved from beatings by fear of Mitch's retribution. The dependency ceased when Mitch ran away to join the army in 1923, and had never resumed. When he returned home in 1926 Charles was in high school, and it was a different Charles. He'd grown remote, not the least interested in stories of the army life at Fort Riley. But every time Mitch looked at him he saw a fifth grader, books under his arm, in flight from a gang of other fifth graders. A bright boy, popular with teachers. Mitch had never been popular with teachers. Charles said calmly, "I don't think that's necessary, Mitch." He paused to light a cig-arette, feeling the past collapse into the present. "But the other is still important. Very important. Why wouldn't it be?"

"It's not the same," Mitch said.

"I know that. But it means you're more valuable than ever. You're the only one of the three of us who *knows*—"

"That's right," Tony said.

"Really, Mitch. More than ever."

"Oh Christ," Mitch said, turning again. He wasn't looking at any-thing now. "I don't want him to be gone."

The three men moved forward in their chairs. The lawyer saw his opportunity. He said, "The spirit, we can keep that alive. That's what Amos wanted. I wish I could remember everything he said, the last time I saw him. He was a happy man, knowing he had you three. He wanted the spirit to live. His. Yours, now. All of you three—"

"Tony, you, me," Charles began.

"We'll make it the best paper," Tony said.

"It already is," Mitch said. He was waiting to be convinced. "That damned committee—"

"It's a committee that'll never meet," Townsend said.

Tony said, "Elliott's right."

"Dad should've had confidence—"

"He did," Charles said, looking angrily at Townsend. "That's why he put you on the committee. Put you there to watch out for Tony and me, God knows what Tony would do in a pinch. Sell the *I* to Pulitzer, maybe." He smiled, winking at Tony.

"Yeah," Mitch said. He was smiling.

"Hell, Tony would sell the *I* to anybody, given half a chance." Charles watched his brother carefully. He was certain now that the storm had passed. But he did not want to leave it like this. He wanted no false memories. The truth was, the committee would meet. Not now, not perhaps for twenty years; but it would meet. "Mitch, let me talk seriously for a moment. Let me tell you what I think is involved, and what Dad had in mind. The problem is not us, it's the next generation. We simply don't know what's going to happen." He wanted to avoid any mention of Jake Rising. "We all agree that the main objective is to keep the *I* together, in this family, forever. Now take my own family. Dana, you don't know what's going to happen with a girl, who she's going to marry or . . . how she's going to be. What she's going to be like, what she believes in or doesn't believe in."

"Dana's a sweetheart," Tony said.

"We've got to have a mechanism to pass on control, keep it in the family without dispersing the stock in such a way as to foster, uh—"

"Instability," Townsend said.

"Instability," Charles said. "And that's the reason for the committee and the reason you're on it." It did not harm anything to bend the truth, and he'd managed to conceal his own resentment. The truth was, there was no reason at all for Mitch to be on the committee. He, Charles, was the natural choice. But his father and Townsend had seen fit to ignore logic.

Mitch nodded. "With girls, you never know."

"Well." Charles's voice fell a little. "Lee wants to send Dana away to school. She wants to send her east."

"East?" Mitch said.

"East."

"Jesus Christ," Mitch said.

"Lee's got her mind set on it and there's nothing I can do about it. Anyway, Dana goes east. What happens then? You don't know."

"Damn screwballs," Mitch said.

Charles's voice fell again. "Don't I know it. But Lee doesn't like the situation in the schools here. And I guess I can't blame her. She wants Dana to go to college somewhere and doesn't believe she can get in, from here. The high school's barely accredited."

"Though it was good enough for all of us," Mitch said.

Charles said, "It sure was."

"Good enough for—all the kids." Mitch was staring at his shoes.

Charles looked at him and could see the sadness coming again. But he had said what he had to say; nothing of importance was concealed now. "Look, Mitch." Charles went to him and put his arm around Mitch's shoulders. The older man turned away, trying to hide his tears; next to him, Charles looked very small and years younger. "Mitch, I think it's entirely appropriate for you to take Dad's office. It's what he would've wanted and it's what I want. You move in there tomorrow, lock, stock and barrel . . . Let's have one more drink."

"The army," Mitch began.

"No," Charles said.

"If—"

"—no, no." He took his brother's arm and led him to the liquor cabinet. It had happened when he mentioned Dana's name and the high school. He knew what Mitch was about to say and he didn't want to chase that hare again. Late at night, drinking heavily, Mitch believed that if he had reenlisted at the outbreak of the Korean War, Frank would have been saved. "Spared." It was not a belief that Charles or anyone else could shake. Mitch believed it and would always believe it. He believed it for the same reasons that he believed he was responsible for Charles's success. Charles had always, as he said, had it easy because he'd had protection; he'd always had someone to back him up. First his older brother; next his father. Charles had never had to go it alone.

Mitch stood quietly to one side while Charles made the drinks. He

said, "We're not going to change anything." It was part statement, part
question.

Charles shook his head. "No."

"The politics remain the same."

"Down the line," Charles said.

"We have our instructions," Tony said, smiling.

"And damned good instructions they are," Townsend said.

Charles clinked glasses with Mitch. He said, "To the old man." The
others rose and repeated, "To the old man." For a moment conversation was general. Then Mitch turned to his brother. "What about that
thing we were talking about on Sunday. That development, the shopping center. Kerrigan—"

"It's settled," Charles said.

"It'll go through?"

"Like a greased pig," Charles said.

Mitch turned to Townsend, frowning doubtfully. "Dad didn't think
it was such a good idea. What do you think?"

"I think at the end he was reconciled," Townsend said softly. "I
think he wanted to move ahead."

Mitch shook his head. "Dad—"

"Hell, that's something else," Charles said cheerfully. "That's business. Something else altogether. Let's talk for a minute about the
newspaper and the policy. The *editorial* policy. Politics. The serious
stuff." He looked at Mitch. "We're going to have two damn tough
races next year."

"You're sure about the development?" Mitch asked.

"Yes, for Christ's sake." Charles was suddenly weary, tired of Mitch
and his damned resentment. Tired of Townsend and his lawyer's talk.
Tired of *talk*. Tired of this family, of which he was now the head. But
he smiled at Mitch and continued. "Two damn tough races—" He hesitated, trying to remember what they were. Who was running and for
which offices. Townsend quickly intervened, naming the races and the
probable candidates. They stood there around the liquor cabinet talking county politics, the conversation gradually taken over by Mitch
and Elliott Townsend.

She had stayed back among the coats, out of sight, not moving. She'd heard everything and her heart went out to Mitch Rising. She was shocked hearing his voice; he sounded broken. Because of his bulk and hearty manner she had always thought of him as strong, inside as well as out. This family business, she saw it suddenly as a live thing; a thing with a life of its own, a history and geography independent of the family that owned it. These men sounded to her as if they were dedicating their lives to it, as to an ideal of some kind, marrying it as if it were a woman or a religion. All of them were marrying it but each would receive different pieces of it in return.

They spoke of her, Dana, as mysterious. They did not know what she would "believe in." *You don't always know what's going to happen with a girl.* It stunned her and she almost laughed out loud. With joy, not scorn. She had always believed that they knew absolutely; it was a secret they had and would not share. It was an astonishing admission, one her father never would've made if he'd known she was listening. But surely he spoke the truth: they really didn't know. The conversation made that clear. They were frightened of the East Coast, the edge of America, these men of the interior. They really didn't know what she would or could become. They didn't know any more than she did. Dana had always believed that they had a kind of superior knowledge, withheld from her as a matter of course; they knew her future in a visceral way and did not choose to reveal it. Therefore she believed her life was foreordained and she fought this knowledge, searching for contrary evidence in the books she read. But not all the evidence was contrary and none of it was conclusive. She assumed she was "in a line" as her brother had been. She leaned against the coats, smiling widely, warm in the tiny vestibule. It was true after all, life could be a series of surprises; it could be *shaped*, like a painting or a novel. The future suddenly opened before her, a vast and gorgeous country. Dement would always have a claim on her, the place of her birth and the source of her earliest memories; the location of the family and its business, the *I*. But that was all it had: a claim. It was not a destination, it was a starting place.

Carefully she opened the door, then slammed it hard. She walked down the hall to the library, rubbing her hands. They were all standing, talking beside the liquor cabinet, a little tight, even Elliott Townsend. She stood in the doorway, looking at them, four older men. Her father motioned her in and put his arm around her waist and kissed her on the cheek. He smelled of whiskey and she wrinkled her nose. She said, Yes, she would have a ginger ale; then to Mitch Rising, Yes, her schoolwork was coming along fine. She had an urge to take out her silver cigarette case but did not.

Tony said kindly, "I hear you're going east to school."

She nodded. Yes, it looked like it.

"It's a great opportunity." Then, in a low voice, glancing at the others, he added, "And it's about time." He looked at her, smiling. "Where is it?"

Dana was surprised; Tony Rising was not often free with his opinions. She said, "We're going to look at three or four of them. In Connecticut and . . . Massachusetts." The names sounded foreign to her; she might have been saying "England" or "Italy."

"You're the first one in the family to go away like that," Tony said. "Except of course for Mitch and his travels were a little different. At the command of the United States government." Tony walked off then, toward the window.

"Damned East," Mitch Rising said.

She looked at him innocently. "What's wrong with the East, Uncle Mitch?"

"Screwballs," he said. "Damned liberals."

Her father said, "Now Mitch."

"'S true," he said.

Her father looked at her. "We're not even sure, definitely, that she's going yet. You're sure you want to go?"

She shrugged; yes and no.

"You know," he said quickly, "nothing's signed and sealed. It's just in the idea stage—"

"I'd like to try it," she said.

"Well, sure."

"If it doesn't work—"

"Sure," he said.

"Nothing ventured, nothing gained."

"That's what your mother says," he said.

Charles Rising turned away; he would say no more. He did not want to interfere with his wife and would never form an alliance against her. It was a guiding principle of his life that parents were on one side of the street and children on the other. When that principle was compromised chaos followed. But his expression was anxious and as he backed away from the conversation she felt suddenly sorry for him. It was true, she would change; her father wouldn't like the change, whatever it was. Any change represented a threat. Her mother did not see it the same way, believing that blood was thicker than any other single thing in life. Her mother did not see it as change, she saw it as improvement. Perhaps she saw Dana as a missionary leading Dement out of the wilderness. In any event, her mother was bound and determined and it was important that Dana not show too much enthusiasm. The talk drifted away from her; they were discussing some political matter. She filled her glass again with ginger ale and stood listening for five minutes. Then she slipped out of the room and ran upstairs. She could hear her mother in the kitchen. She hid the cigarette case among the things on the top shelf of her closet and flopped down on the bed, reaching for the phonograph. In a minute the sound of the blues washed over her. She turned the volume low. Then she picked up *Lie Down in Darkness*, opening it at the marker. Immediately she felt the damp heat and brilliant colors of the South, and the sharp anticipation of tragedy. Then she was in New York City, burning in the summer's scarlet heat; Peyton Loftis whirling to her own destruction. Dana was quickly captured by the novel and did not hear the angry voices of the men downstairs. They had resumed the argument.

September, 1960

SHE SAID to him, Sometimes on Sundays I went riding with my grandfather.

My father dropped me off at the old man's house on Oak Street, and we'd spend an hour with the Chicago *Tribune* funnies. Tim Tyler's Luck, the Katzenjammer Kids. My grandfather would put me in his lap, big as a pillow, and then he would read, beginning always with Tim Tyler. The old man smelled of cigars and something else and only later did I understand that the "something else" was brandy, and that was surprising because I'd never seen him drunk. I was told later that he took a pony of brandy every morning before breakfast and it was the death of his wife, my grandmother, but there was nothing she could do about it. It was in that living room reading the funnies after lunch that I heard of the attack on Pearl Harbor and the end of the war in Europe. When my brother Frank was killed we all went instantly to my grandfather's house; that parlor. I came to believe that all events, wonderful or terrible, found their way to Oak Street, sooner or later.

After the funnies we would go to the crossing at Blue Lake and watch the trains. Just that, nothing else. The old man sat behind the wheel of his Cadillac smoking a cigar and consulting his pocket watch. Five minutes, he'd say; then four minutes. Then we would open the windows and wait with great expectations. At last we heard the whistle and the ground would begin to rumble. The old man smiled and flicked an ash out the window. I'd climb into his lap (I was six at this time, the time I am remembering) and we would wait together for the train, a slow freight bound for Chicago. The heavy engine came round the bend, drawing behind it a hundred cars; the most we ever counted was a hundred and sixty-seven cars, the majority carrying coal. The old man waved at the engineer, who would wave back. I remember him saying, "I worked as a gandy dancer for a summer once." And shaking his head, "Never again." We'd sit in the car feeling the rumble of the train and it was like putting a vibrator to your entire body, the rails bending under the great wheels. I imagined the goods, coal, furniture, soybeans, fruit, on the way to Chicago; all goods were destined for Chicago as all great events ended in Grandpa's parlor. Presently the caboose would round the bend, its red lantern swinging from the grillwork, two bored trainmen playing cards inside. We'd wave, the trainmen would wave back, and my grandpa would laugh, "Dana, those are contented men. Pinochle beside a warm stove." Then he'd fire the engine of the Cadillac and we'd move off toward town, bound for the newspaper. He always had an appointment after lunch on Sunday.

We'd park in the alley, though there were plenty of places on the street. I remember the slow procession through all the departments, the pressroom, composing, classified advertising, and finally the third floor and the old man's corner office. He strode through the place like an emperor, proprietorship in every look and gesture. I couldn't imagine anyone owning the *Intelligencer* but Amos Rising. Not my own father or my uncles, any of them. He was like Duvalier, President for Life. The old man made his way through the building as if it were his own house, the vestibule here, the parlor there; here a wife, there a son. Finally we were in the office and he would sit in his leather desk chair, feet firmly on the floor. It was a small office. In the corner was a hat rack with a pearl-gray fedora hanging from the topmost arm; I never saw him wear the hat but it was always there. He was waiting for "a man." When the man came, he said, I should remain where I was. But quiet, very quiet, "still as a mouse." But if you're smart, he said to me that day, talking to me as if I were an adult, you'll listen. Listen hard, you might learn something of value—this last said kindly, accompanied by a pat on the head. Then Grandpa would open his desk drawer, taking from it a memo of some kind; he left the drawer open. I leaned over his shoulder, my arm light and small against his back, and looked into the drawer. Ah, what treasures! Two deputy sheriff's badges, enough pencils for a school, political buttons, a zillion paper clips, a brass letter opener, a magnifying glass, a wristwatch, two cigarette lighters, a stale cigar, a bottle of aspirin, a key ring with a dozen heavy keys, a beer-bottle opener, paperweights, metal rulers, a tiny Bible, faded photographs—what else?—a pair of eyeglasses with one lens missing, rubber bands, a gold coin, a line of type—and at the rear of the drawer, a revolver. Chrome-plated, it was a snub-nosed .32 Smith & Wesson, hammerless, loaded. Beside it was a small box of cartridges, unspeakably lethal in appearance; a small box, tightly packed with heavy slugs. My hand moved to the rear of the drawer, drawn to the gun like a fly to a fire; I think it was the surprise. The surprise of seeing it there. I could feel his eyes on me, could feel the grin even before it came, and felt finally the small pressure on my arm. Then my grandfather's big hairy hand reaching beyond my own, bringing the revolver from its place, expertly breaking the breech and emptying the bullets, then handing it to me, watching me while I took it awkwardly in my small hands, turning it, looking at it, then pointing it into the drawer, as if there were an enemy there, hiding among the pencils and paper clips and files. I remember him saying, "That's right, Dana. Never point a gun at anyone, even in fun." I had the gun in both hands, it was so slippery and hard to hold. I wondered—why? Why this gun in the drawer? But I never asked him. It was wonderful having the gun as a mystery, a secret shared between us. (And I knew I was one up on my brother, the old man's supposed favorite.) It was another legend to spin around this old man, a man who kept a revolver in his desk drawer. I suppose just the way I held the thing, looking at it as if it were a talisman, he knew I'd never say anything about it. Even then at the age of six I loved him for his trust. My grandfather never needed to warn, This is our secret. They were all our secrets. No one would ever know about the revolver and the box of shells. (You're the first person I ever told about it; you're in on the secret now.) God knows what my mother would've thought if she'd known. I'd try to guess what would make him use the revolver, and decided that it could only be a threat to the newspaper. To the newspaper or to himself, either way the same thing; the same threat. That time I remember hearing a noise downstairs in the building and the old man quietly closing the drawer and telling me to go sit down quietly and listen. He closed the drawer, the treasure sliding slowly out of sight. He winked at me as he closed and locked the drawer.

The man came into the office and was introduced to me. He made a fuss. "What a pretty girl, how are you young lady," and all that. Then he looked inquiringly at Amos. I looked at him, too, expecting to be dismissed. But the old man said nothing, just motioned the man to the big visitor's chair. I'd sit stone silent and listen, and for years I thought that somehow I would never be an adult; never understand what adults said to each other. I could not understand the conversations my grandfather "held." What were they about? The words escaped me, the men talked without finishing sentences. There were names, first names, last names, nicknames, and episodes. Frequent laughter and expletives; the talk was often rough, and just listening to it I knew I was being ushered into a strange and wonderful society. Then, inexorably, the visitor would begin to move forward on his chair. His hands went out in front of him, palms up; he smiled with his mouth, but there would be no laughter. There would be a new smell in the air. My grandfather's face would darken, and silence fall upon it. His gray eyes became opaque. As the visitor moved forward, my grandfather would move backward. They were like two saplings caught in the same wind, the one bending toward the other, the distance constant. Amos moved farther back in his chair, the chair tilting and hitting the desk (the desk was jammed up to the wall and Amos had his back to it when he talked to visitors). Then I understood. The visitor wanted something. He wanted something of Amos's or something that belonged to someone else that Amos could get for him. (Once I asked him what it was that these men wanted, all of them seemed to want something, and the old man just laughed and laughed and replied at last, "My autograph.") I did not understand the words but I understood the motion—the wind of desire that blew both men, the one forward and the other backward. At length the visitor would leave, and while he would appear confident and cheerful I understood in some strange way that nothing had been decided and that the visitor was . . . dissatisfied. The visitor's hat was in his hand and then it would be on his head; nod, smile, exit. And my grandfather, leaning forward now, watching the visitor disappear in a hurry down the stairs. Grandpa would wait for the first floor door to close (you could hear them just barely, the double doors into the street clicking and sighing), and then he would smile widely and bring me into his lap again. Come on, Dana! Let's go have an ice-cream soda. We would leave the office, that huge old man and me, both of us grinning, as close as we would ever be. We'd stride on down to the drugstore and I'd have a chocolate soda and Grandpa would have a Green River. The owner would always ask after Grandmother. After a while he and the old man would fall to talking about "the situation"—whatever it happened to be at the time, an upcoming election, a matter before the city council, the weather, business downtown, a local scandal, whatever it was that was turning time in Dement.

You see, he believed that the newspaper was the public memory. It was narrative, chronicle, journal, biography, obituary, fable, parable and myth—all of those. But mostly memory, without which he believed no civilization could proceed. Much later I realized that he was truly a man of words, and that required a leap of the imagination because there was nothing "literary" about him. He was not an intellectual and had no use for intellectuals; his personal philosophy, such as it was, came from his own experience and a highly selective reading from his shelf of the Harvard Classics. Some of those old-time editors, they were well-educated men, reading Fowler for pleasure and corresponding with Mencken and acquiring fancy editions of the Lake Poets. Not Amos Rising. He read the *Tribune* and the *Reader's Digest* and occasionally *Time,* though he hated Luce for what Luce did to Taft. No, he was a newspaper editor; just that. And I believe that somewhere in a region of his mind he hated "the news." The news brought uncertainty and disorder to his life and to the life of the community; it threatened the sanity and tranquility of both. He loved the process, the reporting and layout and editing; the smell of the ink and the roar of the press. In that way he resembled a great general who hated war. Editing was one thing; the news was something else. It was not benign or indifferent; it did not exist to be published whole, in toto, but to be weighed and edited. The news was like gold, its value depended on the assay; sometimes it wasn't gold at all but pyrite. Amos Rising, obsessed by his own memory, was the assay-master of Dement, the man who determined the value of the various lumps of metal placed before him. Unedited news was a calamity, for without editing a reader had no context by which to judge it, and no means of knowing its truth or falsehood or durability. An unedited newspaper was a delusion, a carnival sideshow of freaks and shell games, all of it chaotic and hysterical. It gave altogether the wrong impression of life, which to my grandfather was not a random affair. For all those reasons and more, at the end of his life the old man despised television—television, he believed, was the ultimate lie, a lie so devilish that one was at a loss to grapple with it. He sat in helpless rage, watching the defeat of Taft, the greatest Republican since Lincoln, the general and "goddamned Dewey" engineering a public humiliation. Television supplied no context. It did not disclose immorality, it displayed only the surfaces of things: a smoke-filled hall, weary delegates, confusing floor fights, and the appearance of triumph—the appearance concealing the reality. Television had no sense of history. *The camera had no memory.* My father said once that the old man did not believe his own eyes, but what he meant was that he did not believe his own eyes when they were seeing through another's eyes.

Now this will be hard for you to understand. Your milieu is a different milieu altogether. The dress of the *I* was essentially nineteenth century. There was a single photograph on page one, a concession, in the middle 1940s, to a circulation manager who diffidently suggested that the paper ought to become more modern; even the *Tribune* had a cartoon on One. The circulation manager theorized that readers would not be alarmed at photographs from the various theaters of war. The old man did not like it but he yielded, knowing that the strength of the newspaper was in its numbers. A newspaper had to be read to be influential. But he wanted nothing to detract from the *words*, the twelve-pica columns of gray type. He wanted people to read, and to put as much effort into the reading as he put into the editing. It was through the printed word that the people would find their silhouette, the profile of their dreams and nightmares. And this was not chaos! There were occasions when the people had to be protected and on those occasions bizarre and unpalatable (literally inedible) facts were withheld. These facts were not altered, they were concealed. A sex crime too gruesome to describe outside the confines of the firehouse or the Elks Club was suppressed altogether—out of respect for the girl and her family, and for younger readers, and for the town's sense of itself. When the state's attorney was discovered with a five-figure bank account he was asked to resign and when he refused the *Intelligencer* simply stopped printing his name. A protégé of my grandfather's, he'd been told that his future was unlimited—that is to say, he could go as far as the U.S. Congress or the governor's mansion. It was as if he'd ceased to exist. When the primary election came, the *I* gave over its columns to the state's attorney's opponent. There were a few readers who thought the incumbent had died and they had somehow missed the obituary. Poor Carl, they said. Then the rumors began. There was a late-night auto accident, a fall in a tavern, a scuffle on the golf course, a separation from his wife with hints of sexual misconduct. It was assumed the *I* was protecting the state's attorney out of a sense of political loyalty, and that was partly true. But that state's attorney was finished and he knew it and when he tried to sue for peace the old man threw him out of the office, muttering about abuses of the public trust. But no hint of scandal appeared in the pages of the newspaper because it would have undermined confidence in the existing order—not least in the old man himself, mentor to the discredited state's attorney. And how had this peccadillo been discovered? Harry Bohn, the banker, had told my father and my father told Amos. Grandpa at first refused to believe it and the banker was obliged to open his books late one night for the editor's personal inspection. At midnight the three of them stood in Harry Bohn's office while Amos went over the deposit slips and the mounting totals. There were photostats of checks received, and they were all drawn on Chicago banks, which infuriated the old man and drained whatever reservoir of sympathy he had. The next day, without explanation, he told the managing editor: "Carl's name is out. Until I say it's in, which I never will until the son of a bitch is dead." Thus did Carl Brady vanish from Dement.

But understand me this. The *I* was not *Pravada*. Private scandal and public mischief received a hearing. My grandfather did not want his readers to be misled into thinking Dement was utopia. Dement was a tough little town, everyone knew that, and he had his own credibility to maintain. He held a mirror to the town and like any mirror it was imperfect, there were foggy spots and holes, and of course the mirror had a frame. Such scandal and mischief as were reported were reported in such a way as to appear isolated; isolated incidents that in no way blackened the reputation of the town or of the man who ran it, namely, Amos Rising. He was protecting what he believed was the town's essential goodness, call it symmetry. It was a frequent accusation that the *I* protected the business community; no businessman was ever arrested for drunken driving, or sued for divorce, or brawled in taverns, or went bankrupt. Amos Rising, if he were asked (which he never was), would have agreed that it was true. He did protect the businessmen, lifeblood of any community, *but he protected the others, too.* No group deserved a bad name—not the Negroes, or the Eastern Europeans, or the Jews, or the businessmen. So there were occasional mentions, a cutting here, a wife-beating there, drunkenness somewhere else, along with honors, awards, and success. However, I am not certain that the NAACP or the ADL would give you the same version of Amos Rising's journalism.

The truth was, he believed that the people were violent—violent beyond anyone's worst imaginings. He believed that at any moment violence might erupt. Any spark could ignite it and he was determined that that spark find no kindling in the pages of the *Intelligencer.* He and his friend Elliott Townsend, they were frightened to the soles of their shoes. The law was fragile and capricious, descended as it was from the frontier. They decided to present the world as it was, mostly. The world was hard and breaks were not evenly distributed. But the world was essentially fair even if life was essentially unfair; in any case, it was as it was. The key to controlling it was information. The darker impulses must not be allowed free rein for in that direction lay disorder and anarchy, conceivably a revolution of some kind. Elliott Townsend had a phrase for it: "A free field, and no favor." My grandfather believed that Dement provided the structure for a peaceful life, so long as it was allowed to develop on its own. The principles were sound enough. The old man believed in his heart that his edited version of reality *was* the truth—a higher truth perhaps, but the truth nevertheless. It agreed with the aspirations of the people. This was something he knew in his bones. Unfortunately his boys, my father and my Uncle Mitch and my Uncle Tony, did not understand the situation as he did. They thought they could release the town's energies in the name of growth. They thought that progress would come with growth. Progress essentially meant a better life; it meant more money in people's pockets. The old man was not educated, in fact he had never finished high school, but he knew that growth could not be controlled. Growth was willy-nilly, that was its essence. Amos believed that it was natural for the town to stay as it was, a place in relative stasis. He believed he could stop the clocks. His sons proposed to speed them up. They did not know or care where the new energy would lead them and the town. Amos knew that when he was gone they would not know how to contain it—indeed, worse thought, they did not realize that it would have to be contained. That was the old man's nightmare.

And it was the reason he spent so much time with my brother. He wanted Frank to see it clearly and from the beginning, see it as he had seen it as a boy sitting around the coal stove in his father's blacksmith shop, listening to his father and his father's friends talk about the town—a hamlet then, lawless, a hard-drinking, brawling place, in no way benign. That was the history of Dement: The French threw the Indians out, then the Indians threw the French out, finally the Anglo-Saxons threw the Indians out for good—slaughtered them to a man. Until well after the Civil War a woman was not safe on the streets. The local doctor was a drunkard and a charlatan who permitted Amos's mother to die alone and unattended. The place seemed to him a volcano of passion—mostly hatred. He had been strong enough to make his own way, but he had had to fight and kick to do it. He wanted his own understanding of the facts to seep into Frank's consciousness. He believed that Frank was my father's natural successor as my father was his. Hard to say how much of it Frank took in. The old man was appalled when my brother enlisted for Korea. He simply couldn't understand it, a war half a world away. But Frank had listened to my Uncle Mitch and thought it was . . . right that he go. And go he did, following some untypical strain of idealism. I think he was clinging to the same idealism when he died, was killed, but it was only with a fingernail. I think he would have come back from there hard as nails. I don't think the old man fully understood that what interested Frank was technology: the process, not the product. At any event, with Frank no longer around the old man turned briefly to me. He would take me to lunch in the same way he took me to watch the trains when I was six or eight. But it could never work out. I could never tell him that I understood absolutely what he was fighting and why. He scared me to death most of the time. And of course I was the wrong sex. Thank God. I am very lucky in many ways, and possibly I am luckiest in that way . . .

You understand that most of this is inferred. He would never explain it as I have explained it. The life of the family conformed to the columns of the newspaper. Its range was narrow. One understood that out there somewhere was disorder and chaos, but it remained unspoken. Heat meant fire so the heat was unrecognized, and in some ways it was like growing up in a convent or monastery; turbulence was elsewhere. And it was another reason why he hated television and movies. My uncle told me this story: The last day of the 1952 convention, listening to Eisenhower's acceptance speech, Amos shuddered at an awful thought. What if newspapers were blacksmith shops and television motorcars? What if by 1970 there were no newspapers, there were only millions of television sets, all of them broadcasting lies. What if every event in the country were filmed at the moment it was happening and displayed on the instant, without editing. An endless flow of disconnected incidents, now here, now there, episodes of every shape and color, a daily panorama of disorder without an assay of weight. No context. No memory. Of course he did not believe it would ever happen, or so he told my uncle. Television was a fad that would fade. The people would at last return to their newspapers, snug.

I remember very well the day I told my father that I was not returning to Dement after graduation from Holyoke. It was Christmas vacation of my senior year. I told my mother in the morning and then went down to the office to tell him, trembling. For some reason I felt it was better to get it over with in the office. I gave all the reasons you might expect me to give, except the real one. The truth was, I was infatuated with the East; if I had gone to Stanford, it would have been the West. But it was the East, old Connecticut towns, New York, new friends. I thought I could slip into the city like a character out of "Manhattan Tower." So I told him I had a good chance for a good job, which was not true, and that in any case it would only be temporary, and of course that wasn't true either. No more than a year at most, I said, and then I would return to Dement. The reaction was predictable: he was dead set against it and called my mother right then on the telephone. She was very diplomatic and agreed with him that of course it was a screwball idea and that was the very reason he should let me do it, "to let her get it out of her system." I knew then that I had won. At the end of the interview with my father my Uncle Mitch came in. I think it embarrassed my father, he did not want Mitch or anyone else interfering in his family. But Mitch only listened, shaking his head. Then he turned to my father and said, "Dad would never approve of this. Never. He would turn over in his grave." And my father, strangely, smiled. "I guess he would," my father said.

Amos Rising, always there. I am twenty-three now and really remember him only vaguely. I remember him very well physically, the busy eyebrows and the big belly, but less well in other ways. There are isolated incidents, the train and the contents of the desk drawer, but not the whole life—or the whole man. Seven years dead now, he's forgotten by everyone except the old-timers. In the memories of the old-timers he'll live forever, a permanent standard of conscience. And of course they believe "the *I* has never been the same since." So if you want to know why the Midwest is as it is, its landlocked sense of inferiority and rejection coupled with an equally strong sense of virtue and destiny, you could do worse than study the editors of its newspapers and the geography and climate they live with, the one even and the other extreme. That motionless, level, fertile place; nothing round, no curves; mature, not ripe . . .

He asked, "Did it?"

"Did what?"

"Did the revolution come to Dement?"

She laughed and said, "No, of course not. Not if you mean workers heaving paving stones at Sheriff Haight's tanks. But it isn't the same, either. It isn't any better, I don't think. I'm not as close there now . . . as I was."

"It's a wonderful story. Would your father tell it the same way?"

"No," Dana said. "I don't know how he'd tell it. Not that way, though. My father is not an introspective man, never was. Everyone in my family is one of a kind." She laughed. "Unlike other families, of course."

He was silent a moment, lost in his own thoughts. "I can't imagine it, growing up inside a newspaper family. It means the family lives every day with the news, getting it, writing it, printing it. Or *not* printing it. Literally living off the news, as an army lives off the land—"

Dana smiled. She did not remember it that way. She remembered sitting at dinner, listening to her parents talk, and then the ringing of the telephone. A sour look passing between her father and mother, and her father rising to answer the phone. And his return to the table; someone wanted a story kept out of the newspaper. A divorce, usually, or an arrest for drunken driving. They had tried to telephone Amos and he was unavailable so they called his son. *I know your father would never approve publication of a purely private matter such as this* ... Her mother shaking her head. Her brother asking, Who is it? What happened? And the subject changed.

He said, "When you think about it, it isn't so different from New York. Allen Dulles or somebody calls up an editor of the *Times* and asks him to withhold a piece of information. 'It would not be in the national interest to publish this.' And the editor always says, 'Of course.' Just like your father with the drunken driver."

"Except Daddy sometimes said no."

"Well, it would have to be truly in the national interest," he said with a smile.

"Is that true? What Dulles does?" She was surprised, she'd never heard of that.

"Sure," he said.

"And they'd withhold?"

"Of course they'd withhold." He moved his legs languidly, stretching them in the grass. "My God, if it's a question of national security. It's a question of the country. Editors are patriotic, like most other people."

"I guess so," she said.

"So." He looked at her, nudging her foot with his own. "So you've followed in the old man's footsteps after all, it's very heartwarming—"

"I have *not*," she said, indignant.

"Well, what do you call what you're doing?"

"Not that," Dana said. She sat up straight. "Not by a long shot. What I do is completely different, my own work. I'm not electing anybody to anything and wouldn't if I could. The farthest thing from my mind, nothing farther. I would never get involved in anything like that, never."

"Um," he said.

She said, "You're way off on that."

"Yes," he said.

"It so happens I don't believe in patterns in families."

"No," he said. "One can see that. Of course not. Everyone in your family is one of a kind, unique . . ." He held up a two-inch-thick pile of paper, long sheets secured by a metal clasp. "What do we call this?"

"I edit books," she said. "Now I am editing your book, to the extent that you will let me. That has nothing to do with what he did, nothing at all."

McGee stretched his legs again. "I see."

"I am not a newspaper editor or publisher," she said evenly. "I work for a book publisher, from whom I take orders. I am not interested in running the city of New York. Withholding military secrets. Even in selecting the next state's attorney. I edit books. Fiction, except for you. For you I've made an exception. Noah said to me, 'We're in a lot of trouble with the McGee. The old fella is confused, needs help—'"

"Who, me?"

"'—needs help with the organization. Too much between the lines,' Noah says. Needs help in leading the reader. Making sense." She began to laugh. "Of his distinguished career."

He rolled over on his stomach and put a blade of grass in her mouth. "I sort of touched a nerve there, didn't I?" He watched her smile and shrug. Then he touched her forehead, drawing his finger down to the tip of her nose. "You've really done a job on that thing." He pointed to the manuscript lying between them. "Really, I mean that. I didn't know what I was doing. I'm not a writer."

She nodded, pleased, and took his hand. Then she said what she always said, "All the material was there."

"Between the lines."

"Some of it's still between the lines."

"Mn," he said.

"We're going to have to bring some of it up to the surface. More is between the lines than ought to be. And some of it isn't even between the lines." She sat up, facing him now, brushing her hair back in a nervous gesture. "It's going to hurt the book. And it's not going to do you much good either."

"Mn," he said.

"Mn, yourself."

"Well, I know it and it can't be helped." He smiled at her, looking up into her eyes. "I will take my basic text from our distinguished man of letters, Mr. Amos Rising. It's an edited reality and it can't be any other way."

"Why did you want to write it in the first place? I mean want to so badly." She asked the question softly, hoping its softness would lull him into a direct answer.

He thought a moment. "Because I thought there was enough interesting stuff. And I could hint at the other. I just wanted to get it down, even as hints. I guess," he said, touching her arm. "I wanted something on paper, even something imperfect or anyway not quite whole. Because it's all coming out someday, in some form, and I want my own record."

"Even hedged."

"Even hedged," he said. "It's better than no record at all."

"What's there is tantalizing."

He lit a cigarette and pulled the wine bottle from the cooler and filled both their glasses. "Yeah."

"I mean *really* tantalizing."

"Well then?"

"It'll sell like crazy to your people. People who have a real interest and understanding. But it won't sell generally and a lot of ordinary readers are going to be, frankly, baffled."

"But you'll publish."

"Oh sure," she said. "It's publishable, more than publishable. In the first place it's literate, which most memoirs aren't. And commercially, your name guarantees a certain sale. As I say, to people who have a professional interest and I suppose there's a *small*"—she smiled—"general public. Ike's hotshot boy ambassador."

"*Wunderkind*, please."

She sipped the wine, cold on her tongue. "Right. And we could get lucky. Some book-review editor might assign the thing to someone

who *can* read between the lines. A little guesswork here and there."
She made a face; that part of the business did not interest her. "But I
don't think so. You see, what's here . . . the raw material. If you'd just
fill in the blanks a little, just a couple of blanks." She looked at him,
knowing she was losing her point. "A little more about Hungary. Just a
bit more information about Albania. Perhaps not quite so much about
the agricultural failures in—when was it?"

"Nineteen fifty-seven."

"Yes."

"Very important, the point being—"

"No doubt. But you understand. This is just a reader's opinion. My
guess is that the U–2 is worth more than a long footnote. Perhaps—
two footnotes? The second one could explain the first one."

He began to laugh. "Mn."

"But-it-can't-be-done."

"No," he said.

"This-is-highly-classified-material-which-might-damage-the-na-
tional-interest."

"Well put."

"Well, it could have been a barn-burner." She clinked glasses with
him. "A book of the month, the whole kit and caboodle." Then, "You
said it'll all come out someday and you want your own record. Why
do you want your own record?"

"Oh," he said. "For you. For me."

"Your kids?"

"Them, too," he said.

"Will you tell me about it sometime?"

He nodded. Yes.

"But not for a while."

He shook his head. She hated to let it get away but she had no
choice. He wasn't yielding any more today than he yielded yesterday
or last week. She believed in her heart he was making a mistake; he
was too cautious and circumspect. He still thought of himself as a
diplomat. She could only guess at his reasons, though instinctively she

sympathized with him. That was her trouble; she always saw all sides to all questions. And God knows she understood the principle of edited reality and keeping chaos at bay. She understood the impulse to protect the center at all costs. But it was disastrous for an author to begin his career with a compromise. Of course he wasn't an author in the strict sense of the word; he was a lawyer who had become a diplomat and was now a lawyer again. She touched his cheek, then ran her hand over his temples. "You're going to be prematurely bald."

"We all are, the entire family. All McGees. It's a pattern. An inherited characteristic. All McGees are alike."

"Oh," she said. "Balls."

"Yes, as a matter of fact. Those as well."

She said quickly, "I wish you'd come back with me, just this weekend. You can make an excuse. Just two days, we'd be back on Monday."

"Can't," he said. "The land's too flat."

"You could use some flatland."

"Gives me claustrophobia."

"And Belgrade didn't?"

He thought, You kid too much. He said, "No, in Belgrade it was the jitters." He looked at her hair, pale red where the sun's rays hit it, and at her fine legs and ankles, and the thin gold chain around her right ankle. He lifted it with his fingernail and scratched her ankle and she put her arms around his neck, pulling him to her. She muttered, "It isn't such a bad feeling." He didn't know what she meant, what idea she had in mind. She said, "The jitters." She rolled over on top of him, her arms strong around his neck. She smelled of grass and sweat and tasted of wine. He tickled her back with a long blade of grass and she moved closer to him, shuddering against him. He slipped his hands inside her bikini, her bottom warm and slippery to his touch. She unhooked her bra and let it fall away, then knelt above him. He kissed the inside of her thighs and she sighed, moving, leaning over him now, her long hair covering his face. He kissed the underside of her breasts and she craned her neck, breathing hard.

Behind him the grass of the lawn gave way to sand, green suddenly to white, and the blue of the ocean beyond. A man and a woman were strolling at the edge of the surf, arm in arm, laughing; their heads moved in harmony. He kissed her again, one eye on the couple walking on the beach. He wished they would turn toward the lawn, though they would be unable to see him and Dana. He and Dana were below the low rise where the lawn met the sand and of course there was the castle. This most extraordinary castle, there was nothing else like it in the world anywhere. It had four turrets and a crenellated battlement and a moat, though the moat was dry. Any architect would be impressed by the irregular fenestration, the openings alternately round and square. They had tried for water, and had dug the moat two feet deep; but water could not be found at that depth. He reached over his shoulder and put his finger through one of the round windows. She moved to look, then stretched and put her own finger through the adjoining window. Her naked breasts touched the grass, her suntanned skin smooth and alive against the green. The pads of their fingers touched and then she began to scratch him lightly with her nail. She concentrated as hard as she was able, watching their two fingers touching. Gently they widened the windows until they each had two fingers inside. Four fingers astride and moving. She thought it was a just-bearable agony, and after a moment they both began to laugh. Then she moved away from him and lay on her back, eyes closed. He kissed her closed eyes and she moved the palm of her hand lightly on his back. Her loose hair was spread out in a fan on the grass, a sunburst matching her bikini.

He looked at her and touched her mouth, as slippery as porcelain. The wind was freshening and her skin was no longer wet. But her body had not lost its tension. The breeze swept the blond hairs on her forearm, ruffling them. Her eyes were turned slightly away from him, aimed over his shoulder at the sea. The beach was deserted now and he could see small whitecaps and a sloop farther out. She rose slowly and extended a hand to him. His breath caught, muscles everywhere contracting and sinking slightly, awed by her flowering vitality. A swim before dinner, she said. A swim together. She pulled him up and they walked around the sand castle and down the dune to the water.

THE BEACH HOUSE belonged to his father. They'd used it every weekend for a month, driving out from the city on Friday night and returning on Sunday. It was remote, a three-room cottage with an incongruous patch of lawn leading to the dunes and the beach. Arriving at last light they'd immediately race to the sea and swim together, washing away all traces of New York City. Then she'd cook dinner, usually wearing nothing but her bikini bottom, and they'd dine on the deck, watching the stars and each other and making every kind of love with words and gestures. At those times she would tell him everything about herself, her life came tumbling every which way from her memory and he would listen, rapt. He could draw anything from her; she loved confiding in him, a man who invited confidence, his eyes never wavering and his emotions always at perfect pitch. Telling her own stories, she found herself funnier than she ever thought she could be, and forgiving. Talking to him, she began to understand her family; who they were and who she was and what they all believed in. They would straddle the bench at the edge of the deck, facing each other; finishing a story she would begin to laugh and put her hands on his face, watch him smile and say something wry, and they would collapse into each other. Then she wanted to swallow him up, have him inside her forever, his body filling her inside, warming and consoling and loving only her.

Later, in the big bedroom, windows open to the sea, they would lie naked in the darkness and explore each other. She was not experienced with men and had never before loved a man in stillness without limits of time or circumstance. They were unhurried in the beach house, talking and making love often until dawn; then rushing from the room across the sand to the water, golden at sunrise. Things surprised her: She had been in some way blind and insensible, her emotions guarded. She felt herself open wide. The first night she touched him she was as-tonished, smiling first, then laughing softly with delight. She had thought always of men's dimensions, their size. But touching him she did not think of that at all. She had turned to him and whispered, "It's so heavy." And he too had laughed; no woman had ever expressed it to him that way before.

She supposed he invited confidence because he withheld so much himself. She found him mysterious in the best possible way, the result (she was sure) of New England reserve and a disorderly childhood and the career he had chosen. She could not imagine him discussing her with anyone, any more than he discussed himself. What they had was private between them. She believed her life was secure with him, like a rare book with a bibliophile or a painting with a connoisseur. And he desired her. In her life she had not known passionate love. He desired her with a ferocity that frightened her until she equaled it. She was enchanted, discovering this man by inches as she discovered herself.

In many ways they were worlds apart. His father was a New York lawyer. His mother had died when he was five; there were no memories of her. McGee lived in Boston, around the corner from his wife and their three children; he and the wife were separated. She told him if he went overseas for Eisenhower she would leave him, and she was true to her word. In New York on weekends, he would stay with Dana in her apartment and they would explore the city together. The man she'd been seeing before McGee took her to plays and art exhibits and she'd come to know and appreciate the city's cultural life. A Beethoven quartet gave as much pleasure as "Milenberg Joys." McGee had little taste for the theater and none for music. Instead he took her to the fights when there was a good one or to the movies, usually a foreign-language import. It surprised her that he liked the fights and after the first one she found she didn't mind them. The ambience was hot and colorful and exciting to her. McGee was wonderful to be with and New York all she had imagined. They always went to Shor's after the fight to watch the Broadway sports and their women. McGee said he was not "in love with" violence but understood the various techniques of boxing, and enjoyed watching professionals.

Once each weekend they would dine with McGee's father. She knew she would never forget their first meeting, her own nervousness and the corner table at a currently fashionable restaurant. Harold McGee was a small restless man who relaxed after drinks. It would take a minimum of three drinks before dinner and wine during dinner and a liqueur after dinner before he would truly relax and tell stories. Relaxed, he was a wonderful raconteur. The first night they'd met he'd turned to Dana and said that sometimes after dinner, after the drinks and the wine and the calvados, he'd talk—indiscreetly. "I have never been discreet in front of my son," he'd said. "And now he tells me that you're both . . . close. Going together, whatever you people call it. We used to call it 'Walking Out,' but I suppose no one says that anymore. I am not discreet in front of my son and I don't propose to be discreet in front of you. But I must know that none of my stories will come back to me, ever." Dana looked at him over the candlelight and silver, noticing the wine waiter hovering in the background, and said yes in a pro forma way. But Harold McGee was not satisfied. "I don't trust the press, never have. It has to be a real promise, as if under oath." Then he looked at his son for confirmation. McGee said, "She's not in the press, Dad. Dana works for a book publisher." He said, "Same thing." The wine waiter continued to hover. Then McGee turned to her and said, "He's serious. Better do it." Dana turned to him and raised her right hand. She said, "Yes he said yes and again yes." Harold McGee laughed loudly and the waiter filled their glasses and retreated. McGee turned to his father. "That's—" And Harold McGee roared, "I know what the hell it's from. I did some work on that case, more'n thirty years ago." He turned to Dana. "He thinks the only thing I understand is alimony and child support and hiring private dicks to peek into key-holes. Jesus!" She had begun to laugh and now he looked at her approvingly, eyes narrowing. He said, "'Stately, plump Buck Mulligan—'" He faltered and she said, "'. . . came from the stairhead, bearing a bowl of lather . . .'" He finished, "'. . . on which a mirror and a razor lay crossed.'" He turned to his son. "This one's all right. Definitely trustworthy." Then he went on to tell the story of his latest client, a mélange of sexual promiscuity and financial misconduct. It was the account of a woman who had divorced one man to marry another and of her daughter by her first husband who had fallen in love with the second. The second husband now lived in the south of France with the daughter, beyond the reach of the authorities, and Harold McGee's apparent objective was to find a way to lure him back to the United States. The husband had departed for Europe with a substantial portion of his wife's fortune, along with the teenager. The story in the hands of Harold McGee was rich and ribald and Dana laughed without stopping, though it was an appalling story. He stopped talking suddenly, indicating that the story was finished. Then she got it. They were both smiling privately and she leaned across the table to the older man. "Okay," she said, "tell me the other side." Harold McGee looked at her and nodded, chuckling. Dana leaned back, waiting. "Of course there is another side. I have never encountered a situation where there wasn't." Dana and McGee listened attentively as his father turned all the facts around. The truth was, the wife was not entirely sane—as the courts of the state of New York would define insanity, were they asked—and there was some evidence to show that she wanted her daughter seduced, and wanted her seduced by her second husband, the stepfather. All of which did not *excuse,* but it helped to explain. In any case, those facts were the responsibility of defendant's counsel, and there were ways and means to frustrate that gentleman.

Dana learned later that this man and his son were fascinated by contradiction and paradox. They loved to pin facts to walls, as an entomologist would pin an insect; turn the fact this way and that, measuring its length and breadth, its weight and size—discovering in the process that it was not a fact at all but a circumstance. Harold McGee believed that there was no story so simple that its corollary could not be found and by "corollary" he meant "contradiction," equally persuasive. In Harold McGee's world there were no blacks and whites, only grays, and he fancied he could argue either side of any case with equal skill and authority. He thought that he had three-hundred-sixty-degree vision and that was what fascinated Dana about him; she thought she did, too. Late that evening he announced quietly, "I'm a litigator. That's what I do. I litigate. Love to litigate and lucky for me I almost never lose. That's because I understand the other side of the story so well. I am always prepared and of course that is nine-tenths of the law, preparation. I have an instinct for both the poison and the antidote. That"—he was speaking to Dana now, his words slurring a little but entirely amiable and cogent—"is the kiss of death for a judge but a mighty advantage for a litigator. Also," he said, "I worry for them. That's what they pay me to do, worry. They pay me well to worry well and I'm the best worrier in New York. I got a call the other day from a client who was upset with some aspect of her case. I was very patient over the telephone but I didn't know what she was talking about. I listened and was very sympathetic, and then I hung up and called my associate. I had to ask my associate who was doing the worrying on this case, him or me. Turned out he was and he said he was worrying about it two hours of every day, two hundred dollars a day worth of worry and everything was coming along fine, for me to relax, he was worrying the hell out of his case—"

His voice had begun to wither and grow melancholy, and at length she looked at him fondly. "You ought to be writing the memoirs, not him. I'll get you a contract, top dollar, anytime you want."

Harold McGee was silent a moment. Then he said to his son, "You didn't tell me."

"Just a few things on paper," McGee said casually.

"Huh," he said. "What things?"

"A kind of diary." McGee glanced at Dana and quickly shook his head.

"That's a good idea, son. That's the best idea you've had in years." He turned to Dana, very serious now. "Is he telling everything?"

She knew she was in the middle of something, some family business, but didn't know what it was. "It's a very nice book," she said.

He continued to stare at her. He put his glass down and nodded. "I figured. He's got quite a story. He's one of the few people who can tell it properly, but he won't. He won't tell it *all,* he thinks he owes those bastards something; why I don't know. If the shoe was on the other foot—" He snapped his fingers and lapsed into silence.

"No," she said. She was trying to salvage something. The old man had touched her with his obvious concern, but her first loyalty was to McGee. "Look, please. I'm sorry. I shouldn't have said anything, but I didn't know—" She reached over and touched his hand. She wanted to support McGee. "Really, it's a fine book."

"You editing this book?"

She nodded. "Yes."

He said, "Well, that's something."

She shook her head; that was harsh of him. "Honestly—"

"Could be," the older man said. "It *could* be, definitely. But won't be. He knows why but he won't say." Harold McGee motioned for the waiter to bring them more calvados. He was looking back and forth from Dana to his son. He said to her, "You press him. He won't like it, but you press him anyway. He'll be sorry if he doesn't publish what he's got, and he's got quite a lot. Things that surprised even me and I don't surprise easily. Not that this crowd would listen to any of it."

She was completely mystified now. At that time she'd only known McGee a month and had read the manuscript twice. She had made suggestions about its organization and he was now rewriting. "What crowd?"

"The government."

"You mean the administration? Eisenhower?"

"Any of them," he said roughly. "They're all the same. It's all the same government. Some names change, some slogans. Different emphasis, different style. But it's the same people. Now or in November, same difference. Worked for FDR myself in the mid-thirties. Worked two years for him and then came back here. Now that was a change. But there hasn't been one since and won't be for another twenty years. Government is like the New York Bar. That doesn't change either, new fads, new fashions, new men, same policies. The center does not change. Sometimes the edges change a little." He smiled suddenly. "I've been severe, and forgive me." He lifted his glass first to her, and then to his son. "Apologies from the litigator. Who loves both wisely and too well but talks too damn much."

McGee had said nothing during this, had sat with his pony of calvados and his cigarette, his eyes and attention elsewhere. He had ceased to listen after his father's first comments. These were familiar; he'd heard them many times before. He was sorry that Dana had to be caught up in it, but she'd brought that on herself. Obviously enchanted by the old man, as they all were. His arguments were unassailable as always, except his father did not know everything. They had not had the same experience; his father had not grieved. He did not know the hard facts of the cold war, and Dana knew even less than his father. He looked up then and caught his father's salute and grinned. He was a hell of a man wherever he was, but he thought he knew everything; and he didn't. "Tell us," McGee said softly, "about Witsell versus Witsell." Harold McGee laughed and drained his glass and was off, a new excursion. Witsell versus Witsell, a litigation of unusual complexity, a large bed of money contested by two small voluptuaries. A thin layer of smarm . . .

Dana sipped her drink, listening. She loved watching them. There seemed to be no distance between them at all; they could have been brothers, the old brother and the young one. She guessed Harold McGee's age at a few years beyond sixty; McGee was thirty-six. They seemed to understand each other completely. The older man's apology came as naturally as breathing, and was accepted the same way. There were no secrets between them, except apparently the facts of McGee's diplomatic service. The father seemed to want the son to understand everything he understood: the way of the world. The world was a passionate place. Understand the passions and you understand the place. More difficult than it sounds, he'd said. There was no fact that could not be stood on its head, no act that did not have at least two causes and two results. He admitted he was a cynic. In this business, how could I be anything else? McGee had told her he loved his father—"I love him and like him both," he'd said, "even though we all know he's a little nuts and that makes him a pain in the ass, sometimes." He'd always been a little nuts, even when his wife was alive, and of course they'd been separated for years when she died. That had set up an emotional chain that was not ended even now. Harold McGee had been seeing a psychiatrist for twenty years, the same psychiatrist; he said he tithed to the psychiatrist as a monk tithed to the church or an actor to Equity. His euphemism for the thrice-weekly appointments: "I'm going to see my agent." Dana told McGee that she loved just being around them, listening to them, watching them together. They did not surprise easily, either of them. She felt that by contrast her own world was closed; there was so little light. But they traveled from different beginnings: she loved surprise, embraced it and savored it when it came. Her world had been very closed before he came into it. He'd said with a smile, My father thought you were young, too young. He called you the Very Young Miss Rising. He thought you were too young for me but that was before he met you.

You were both new to me, she'd said.

Well, the life we've led. It's different—

From mine, she'd said.

From Dement, he'd replied.

Now they were driving from the beach house to New York. It was Sunday night and the traffic was heavy. She moved up close against him and put her hand inside his shirt. She closed her eyes and listened to him hum, then sing. It was the song about the million-dollar baby in the five-and-dime.

She said, "When are you going back to Boston?"

"Tomorrow."

"I wish you weren't."

"Next weekend. I'll be back next weekend."

"That's no good," she said glumly.

He said, "We're putting a trust together, the most complicated . . . What's no good?"

"I'm going home to see my family."

"Damn," he said.

"It would be all right if you'd come."

He shook his head. "Next week is going to be a monster, and I'm going to work on the manuscript, too. Though it won't be the same without you there."

"Don't forget to water the plants," she said. "Please?"

"Maybe I'll stay with Harold."

"No," she said. "Don't do that. Just water the plants."

"Okay."

She said, "I love you."

His arm tightened around her. "I'll come to Dement with you the next time."

"I love you anyway." They were on the Fifty-ninth Street bridge, the big convertible rattling over the pavement. The city rose, twinkling and gorgeous all around them. She flung her head back, the wind catching her hair and blowing it every way. "Look at that." She touched the manuscript in her lap. "Look at that wonderful city."

He smiled. "I love you too," he said.

2.

MY GOD he looks awful, Charles thought. He took his feet off the desk and leaned forward, peering across the room. He looks sick, puffy in the face and dark, his manner distracted. No spark to him, his grin hesitant and insincere. Not a good time for it to happen but he was one of those men, perhaps, who did not have good luck. The voice droned on: . . . *I believe that we have the secret for progress. We know the way to progress and I think first of all that our own record proves that we know the way . . .*

Blah-blah-blah, Charles Rising said to himself. Best thing you bastards can do is keep out of our way, if it isn't too much trouble. I've seen him a lot better than this, Charles Rising thought. He was a hell of a lot better in Washington a year ago but of course that was private, just forty men in a room. The thing that came through, and came through clear as a bell, was that he was trained. Trained all his life for it, he had the experience. He understood *work*. You could look at him and see that. He came from nothing, his people were dirt poor but he managed college and law school. Still, he was a remote man, his antecedents obscure. His career had been a solo, ever since law school. The voice said, *I know what it means to be poor. I know what it means to see people who are unemployed.* Charles Rising smiled. That was better, give them a little red meat, let them know who you are as opposed to the other fellow. It was smart politics, or it used to be smart. Now it was hard to tell; this was a strange year. Politicians seemed to believe that "me too" would get them elected. And that thing in the corner had as much to do with it as anything, that box. Hard to know what a fellow was really made of through the box. At the Washington reception you could watch him up close and listen, too; the surroundings were intimate, though of course his office went where he did. Difficult to separate the man from the office. However, this one had seen hard times and his courage couldn't be questioned. The determination was visible around his mouth and in his eyes, hidden and bright as polished stones below the heavy brows. Not a man to be pushed around, by the Reds or by anyone else; the unions or the minorities. God knows he'd proven his anti-Communist credentials a hundred times over, there were no worries on that score. He was clean. But he had an odd personality, dark without being in any way threatening. Odd thing, Charles thought, you felt a little sorry for him; felt sorry about his background and his awkwardness and evident desire to please. In Washington he'd mingled with them, publishers and their wives, a glass of tonic water in his hand, and he'd been ill at ease. Later Charles described it to Dana, who said she knew what he meant. She said there was something accidental about him; there was nothing intrinsic. Dana was biased of course, but there was a little something in what she said. Charles stood up and moved closer to the television set. Now one of the reporters was asking Kennedy a question: . . . *the vice-president in his campaign has said that you are naive and at times immature. He has raised the question of leadership. On this issue, why do you think*

people should vote for you rather than for the vice-president? Charles listened
to the answer, though he was preoccupied with the man. There was a
fascinating and dangerous quality to Kennedy. He was ten years
younger than Charles, but they were men of the same generation.
They were men of the twentieth century though their outlooks
were opposite. Kennedy had more in common with Dana, who was
twenty years younger, than he did with Charles. His lean build, his
clothes, his hair; he was too young, not seasoned in any way. He carried authority but it was a strange kind of authority. He reminded
Charles of a southern newspaper publisher he knew. He'd see him
from time to time at the ANPA. This newspaper publisher wore English clothes; once he appeared at the Banshee Luncheon in a tweed
coat with patches at the elbows, as if he couldn't be bothered to wear
a suit like the rest of them. A soft southern accent and a stiff back and
teetotal, a man sought after for panels and committees, he spoke fre-
quently on the necessity for a free press and his statements were always long, "eloquent," and condescending . . . Charles realized
suddenly that he was a little afraid of Kennedy and what he might do.
He was not a predictable man and his background was mysterious.
The old man had had something to do with the liquor business and
with the movies. Not a man to get into a quarrel with; he wouldn't respect the rules. He wasn't as tough as Nixon, that was the truth of it,
but he was more ruthless. He flouted convention and seemed to have
contempt for those who didn't. That trait probably came from the old
man, rich as Croesus, a man who'd buy the White House with no regrets. There would not be the slightest twinge of guilt, no understanding that it was not an office for sale. You fought hard but you
fought fair. Ike had and so had Adlai Stevenson, give him that. There
was something about Kennedy that suggested mockery and disre-
spect. Was that it? Charles looked at him and thought that in a way
Kennedy was European. He carried with him an air of English country houses or Mediterranean beaches or some rich man's club in Paris
or London, a dozen men sitting around a table . . . laughing. Women,
there'd been talk in that area; not the kind of women who hung

around the Waldorf at the convention, but friends; friends' *wives*. Charles snorted. Maybe this Kennedy was trying to prove Marx right after all. Charles Rising did not like Easterners, particularly Easterners of that sort, rich men who sucked up to poor men. When the taxes came to pay for it all, it would be the businessman who got soaked. Those others, their money would be hidden away in places the IRS could not look. Or would not look, if Kennedy became President. It came down to privilege by birth and Charles despised it. They, that class of people, excused themselves and the very poor—and the hell with everybody else. If Kennedy didn't like society's rules (and he apparently didn't, from the evidence), he'd remake them without a moment's hesitation. And he'd remake them from the White House, Lincoln's place.

Charles listened to John F. Kennedy: *. . . I think Mr. Nixon is an effective leader of his party. I hope he would grant me the same. The question before us is: Which point of view and which party do we want to lead the United States . . .* Charles shook his head. In a subtle way, Kennedy had managed to gain the upper hand. He, the opposition, had contrived to endorse Nixon. Kennedy had flattered his opponent, thereby putting him on the defensive. He had established himself as the heavier man. Get him now, Charles Rising said aloud. He wanted Nixon to move in close, Nixon was damned good at the counter-thrust. He'd proved that many times. Nixon said, *I have no comment.*

Charles moved back in disbelief. *Oh for Christ's sake,* he said aloud. *Oh Jesus Christ.* No comment, good God. He looked more closely at the screen. The vice-president was sweating. But he couldn't let Kennedy get away with that. What was he trying to say? Thanks for the plug? Oh goddam, Charles thought, this is a disaster. Only a fool would permit himself to be placed in that position. When you had an opponent who would be tough you never mentioned that opponent's name. Never. That was the policy great editors followed and it had never failed, hardly ever. Now here was Nixon agreeing to debate— whatever the hell that was, this television theatrical was certainly not a debate as he understood the word—his challenger. Now another reporter was putting a question to the vice-president: . . . *would you tell us please, specifically what major proposals you have made in the last eight years that have been adopted by the administration?* And the vice-president replied, *It would be rather difficult to cover them in eight and—two and a half minutes* . . . He had been about to say eight *years.* Charles listened to the rest of the answer. It was lame. Something about his trips abroad. Part of the problem was the goddamned reporters. All of them were in Kennedy's camp, that much was obvious. They thought that if they kissed Kennedy's ass that would make them big in Washington. There was a new word, all of them were using it. "Access." This was a new theory of journalism: that to report Washington scandals you had to have access to the White House. Jesus Christ. The White House was the *problem,* or would be if Kennedy won the election. He listened to Nixon and shook his head. The Republican was spooked, that was clear enough. He looked at Nixon and sympathized with him, wishing he'd draw back, recede a little, remember what he was now. Whatever his life had been, however many wounds he had, now he was vice-president of the United States. Charles reached into the ice bucket and placed two cubes in his highball glass and refilled it with Scotch. He looked away, staring for a moment at the photograph of his father. He stared at it, lost in thought. When he turned back to the television set, the senator was speaking.

. . . *I think freedom will conquer. If we fail—if we fail to move ahead, if we fail to develop sufficient military and economic and social strength here in this country, then I think that the tide could begin to run against us, and I don't want historians ten years from now to say, these were the years when the tide ran out for the United States. I want them to say, these were the years when the tide came in, these were the years when the United States started to move again. That's the question before the American people and only you can decide what you want, what you want the country to be, what you want to do with the future. I think we're ready to move and it is to that great task, if we are successful, that we will address ourselves.*

Charles found himself listening closely. It was true that Kennedy had a theme and Nixon did not. Nixon didn't understand that the issue was Kennedy. Or perhaps he did understand it and didn't have the courage to press an attack. But he was on the defensive now. At that moment Charles understood that Kennedy would be successful. He would be successful because the nation was restless and (thanks to him) unsure of itself, and therefore prepared to believe the worst. Except in the Midwest. The Midwest had a memory, its line of sight as clear and far as the land itself.

He was no longer listening to the voices. A depression had settled over him like fog, he could feel fog in every recess of his mind. Poor benighted Nixon; he'd never match Kennedy's promise. He was dark and Kennedy was light and the voters for certain would choose light. The truth was, both of them were trying to mobilize the population. But Kennedy was worse than Nixon; he was a Socialist no less than Roosevelt. Neither of them knew what could happen when populations were mobilized. At least Nixon was not part of the East Coast apparatus, the Ivy League and the social workers and government bureaucrats, all of them arrayed against the people. One way or another all of them fed off the government, resentful of those who didn't; who only paid the taxes. Damned Kennedy had never done a day's work in his life, had never held a *job*. It had all come so easy to him, he assumed it came as easy to everyone else. Ahhh Christ, he thought; there'd be a war for sure. The Democrats always managed a war. If there wasn't a real war they'd invent one. There'd be a war just as soon as people understood that Kennedy could not deliver what he'd promised to deliver. He didn't understand human nature. Lincoln did. Lincoln was a man of the interior; he'd understood the heart of the country. There were no photographs of Lincoln grinning. How could there be? Life was nothing to smile about, if you knew human nature as Lincoln knew it. Life was not kind.

Charles rose and began to pace his office, moving deliberately to the door and back again. He looked at his watch. Dana was due soon. She'd insisted on hiring a car and driving the distance from the airport. He did not like to think of her driving at night but she'd insisted. He had not seen her for six months and did not understand her life in New

York any better than he understood the damned election. Maybe she could explain Kennedy's attraction; she lived in his country.

SHE CAME over the rise of a hill and could see Dement's glow on the horizon. There was little traffic and she was driving swiftly, passing when she could. Her headlights bore a tunnel into the darkness; she was only vaguely conscious of woods, secondary roads, billboards and farmhouses slipping by. She was thinking of her father and his insistence that she come for the weekend, and then she was thinking about McGee and her job. She was in a wonderful mood, loving the details of publishing, from typescript to fair copy to galleys and page proofs and finally the book itself. She knew McGee's book was better for her editing; he tended to write institutional prose, thick with Latinisms. However, she had lost more points than she had won on substance; he refused to tell the full story. He would not even tell it privately, to her. From the beginning she had seen the book whole in a way that he had not. She saw it as a narrative, his story and not a diplomatic history. During the furious editing sessions at the beach house and her apartment he yielded bits and pieces of his life abroad, amused (he alleged) that she thought anyone would care; but he was careful to disclose nothing more of importance. She'd selected the title, *Ambassador's Journal,* and the subtitle, *The Cold War in Eastern Europe, 1955–1959.* He regarded the title almost with indifference, concerning himself with the content only. She loved all of it, the editing and the publishing, because at the end of it there was a *book,* a book people would buy and read and that if it were good enough would remain in great libraries forever. Of course this particular book: she had managed to fall in love with its author. Editors did not as a rule fall in love with authors; mostly they fought and ended up enemies. But there had been no pride-of-authorship problems with McGee, probably because he did not see himself as an author; he saw himself as a diplomat and lawyer, though he was hard as iron when he made his mind up. This far and no farther. "That's the end of it, Dana," he'd said. "That's all I'm going to say about it so let's end it. Now." She'd begun to protest again, then saw the look in his eye and understood he was serious; he would go no farther. She'd said, "Okay, you win. Allen Dulles can tell the rest in *his* memoirs." McGee had nodded and grunted sarcastically, "Huh-uh." Then he handed her a sheet of paper, one line of type. *For my associates, for my children, and for D.* The dedication. She'd cried at that; nothing that had happened to her in her life had touched her more; it was completely unexpected.

She guessed that after all it came down to the results. She believed that books were noble, even imperfect books. They disclosed what they had to disclose, at cost and at pain. The more the cost and the greater the pain the finer the book. She believed it as an article of faith: *nothing should be withheld.* An author's freedom was not a right but a duty, whether composing *Ulysses* or *Mein Kampf.* Books were like oxygen, necessary to life. There were bad books as there was bad air but one did not always know in advance. So the principle was to publish; publish as much as it was possible to publish, and a masterpiece would reveal itself. Sitting in her tiny cell of an office she had been forced to reject manuscripts, but she was always gentle with their authors—too gentle, according to Noah. Well, she thought, perhaps. But in the catalog of human follies gentleness was not the worst. It was not a felony or one of the seven deadlies so, she told Noah, if it was all right with him she would continue to be gentle with those who wrote unpublishable manuscripts. And one fine day years hence she would get another "Ambassador's Journal" from McGee, the real journal; nothing concealed or withheld. She believed that at some date in the future men like McGee would find it necessary to disclose what they'd heard and seen, and it would surely be an heroic interval . . .

It was raining softly now. At a definite moment she knew she'd crossed the county line. The darkness softened and the land became familiar and she knew she was home or close to home, in any case occupying her own territory. Now, ten minutes from the city, she recognized the landmarks. A stoplight, a billboard, a crossroads, a roadhouse—she saw these at the edges of her vision. There were no lights at all now and she shot into the shallow miles-wide depression leading to Dement. The narrow highway cut through the prairie and an occasional wood, fallen leaves clinging damply to the highway; the liquid woods hung on the edges of her headlights, thick and obscure, trees' branches like veins of the body. She imagined birds and animals moving in the darkness, a swarm of life hidden in the woods, invisible in the ground fog that clung to the cold earth like a blanket. At this time of year there would be a variety of life moving at night, owls, deer, groundhogs, blacksnakes. She knew the region but it frightened her at night in this rented car, the sky black and leaking rain. She turned the radio on and as quickly turned it off, swerving to avoid a branch in the middle of the road. The trees formed a canopy over her now; it was as if she were driving through a tunnel, the walls of the tunnel under pressure from the rain and blackness. Then she was in open country again, and heedless of the wet pavement she put the accelerator to the floor, and the car leaped ahead.

Approaching Dement's outskirts she slowed. Ten years ago you entered the city in darkness; now it was bright as day with neon and flashing lights. There was a tangle of cars by the side of the road and rotating red lights; an accident. Traffic slowed to a crawl. There were two police cars and an ambulance in attendance. One sedan was skewed across the road, leaking water and gasoline, its hood yawning; the other car was on its side in the ditch. A woman was sitting on the pavement, her face in her hands; the police were shouting at each other and presently one of them walked slowly over to the woman and said something. Easing past the confusion at five miles an hour Dana saw that someone still sat in the front seat of the car on its side, a motionless person, head slumped on the dashboard. Traffic crept so people could see the accident. She averted her eyes and drove on, though through her rear-vision mirror she could see the head on the dashboard, watched by half a dozen curious passersby. Now she came upon businesses, a discount house, a liquor store between a gas station and a steakhouse, a drive-in movie and a motel and another steak-house. It reminded her of a stretch of Queens Boulevard and astonished her. She thought suddenly, It's a different night. Night has been changed. Night now is exactly like day. Ten years ago night was dark, stores were closed and locked and it would not occur to anyone to "cruise." She supposed that before long stores would be open twenty-four hours, there would be no minute of the day when you could not spend money, if you had a mind to spend money. She passed a bill-board and laughed out loud.

The Dement Intelligencer
SERVING DEMENT COUNTY

This billboard was flaking at the edges and tucked between a hamburger stand and a tiny church, the church prettily whitewashed and demure in the glare.

She paused at a red light and beside her an engine roared. She looked across into the eyes of two grinning teenagers. She gunned her own engine and they smiled and the driver rolled down the window and shouted something. Without hearing what he said she smiled and shook her head. The boy smiled and the two cars raced off, bound now for the center of town. She slowed as she turned into Blake Street, to night from day. Here in the center it was dark except for the streetlights. The buildings, department stores and offices above the stores, were as she remembered them. It was silent in the center; there were few cars and no pedestrians. As she drove slowly down Blake Street she saw that there were a few vacant stores in each block. The courthouse and the monument were not lit. She thought it was like moving back ten years in time; things in the center were as they had been. She passed the bank and the largest department store and the lawyers' building. On the second floor was Elliott Townsend's office, announced in gold letters:

TOWNSEND AND RISING
ATTORNEYS AT LAW

That was her cousin, Jake Rising, Elliott Townsend's new law partner. A single light was burning in the office; doubtless Jake working late. She moved on. The glow from the streetlights cast queer shadows, the town seemed to her—empty, a ghost town. There was no activity, no automobiles or people or blinking lights or sound. No, she thought, it was by no means a handsome town; it was a nineteenth-century mill town, the buildings undistinguished, false fronts concealing nothing. The store windows were laden with goods but many of the windows were dirty and the goods seemed placed there almost as an afterthought. The silence was disconcerting to her, and suddenly, remembering the face slumped on the dashboard of the wrecked car, she shuddered. Dana pulled into a parking place across from the newspaper building and sat a moment, motionless, watching the deserted street. She shook her head and got out of the car and walked into the *I.* The street door was not locked and she went quickly to the third floor.

She saw her father before he saw her. He was bent over some papers on his desk.

"Stop the presses," she said.

"Dana!" Charles smiled broadly and came around his desk and embraced her. "You got here all right."

"I did," she said. "It's not that long a drive, and the plane was a little early—"

"Gosh," he said. "It's good to see you."

"It's nice to be home." She noticed the television set in the corner and remembered the debate, cursing herself that she'd not listened to it. She'd forgotten completely about it. "How was it? The debate."

"You didn't hear it? Nixon blew it, I'm afraid. Blew it sky-high."

"Kennedy was good?" She tried to keep the enthusiasm from her voice.

"Terrible," her father said. "Just awful. But Nixon was worse. Nixon looked worse. It wasn't what he said but how he said it and how he looked. Kennedy spooked him. But maybe he was sick."

"That bad?" She took off her coat and hung it on the rack.

"Worse," he said sourly. "Death warmed over. And as you know, I'm a Republican."

"There have been rumors to that effect," she said with a smile.

"Do you want a little drink?" Dana nodded and he went to the liquor cabinet. "Scotch?" She nodded again. The liquor cabinet was a new addition to his office. It was a well-stocked cabinet with bottles and glasses and an ice bucket. "You look wonderful. So grown up, I can hardly believe it." He poured the drinks. "Well, what's up?"

She sat in the chair next to the television set, pulling off her gloves slowly, finger by finger. She glanced quickly around the office. Nothing had changed in eighteen months. Same photographs on the walls, same furnishings, except for the liquor cabinet. She thought her father looked older. "Town has changed," she said, "since I was here last. It really has changed." He nodded, his back to her. "Except for downtown. Downtown's no different. And I saw that Jake's got his shingle out."

Her father grunted, she could not tell whether in simple acknowledgment or disapproval. Then the telephone rang and he turned to answer it. She sat looking at the front page of the *I*, the paper lying on the secretary's desk. She hardly read it anymore though it was sent to her in New York. She read the *Times* and the *Herald Tribune* now. The *I* arrived two days late. It was amazing, the paper had not changed since her grandfather's day, its appearance replicated each day, an echo. The nameplate, one photograph above the fold (she could remember when there had been no photographs at all on page one), the big black line below the nameplate, CANDIDATES PREPARE FOR DEBATE, with the photograph of Richard Nixon climbing out of an automobile in the Loop, grinning and waving. She smiled. There were no photographs of the Democrat. There were ten stories on One, eight of them local; it was still a reader's newspaper.

". . . you have him talk to Elliott Townsend," her father was saying. "Elliott's handling that for the estate and I'm certain the price will be a fair one. The rest of it we can handle from here . . ."

She liked the office. It was strictly functional, the big safe in the corner, the heavy desk with the old Royal on a typewriter stand next to it. A water carafe and glasses rested on the table along the wall back of the desk.

". . . Harry Bohn says there will be no problem with the financing and as for the zoning, there will be no difficulty there, either. But we need a commitment from the construction boys. We're out on a limb and we don't want to be sawn off, so next spring is ground-breaking . . . Well, you talk to them and call me and I'll call Bohn. Fine, Irish. And we'll see you in a couple days? Fine." He put the phone down and clapped his hands together and faced her. "So."

She nodded at the telephone. "Business?"

"Guy wants to locate his plant here but there are some zoning problems. Or were. There aren't anymore. One thousand people employed, half of them locals. This lousy economy, it'll mean a lot to us. Especially if your friend Kennedy is elected President, which I devoutly hope he won't be."

"Was Nixon really bad?"

"Awful," Charles said. "You know—" He paused, wondering whether to continue. He did not want to get into a political discussion, an argument, with his daughter, not now, her first night home. And he most especially did not want to confess his doubts about the vice-president, poor square peg. "—it wouldn't surprise me if he lost. It wouldn't surprise me at all."

"But the *I* will support Nixon."

"Oh sure," her father said. "More experienced. The other one's dangerous." She did not reply to that. "Hell," he said suddenly. "They're both good men. I don't like Kennedy and don't trust him but I suppose the country can survive him. Survived Truman, I suppose we can survive Kennedy."

"Don't let Grandfather hear you say that."

He laughed. "God, no. For him, the sun rose and set on the Republicans. But times change. You know, the truth is"—he leaned forward, resting his elbows on the desk—"it doesn't make the difference now that it did. We used to think that if there was a Democrat in the court-house here, the sky would fall. Well, there is and it hasn't. The truth is, they're all alike. Politicians. They've either got their hand in the till or in your pocket, one or the other . . . "

"You don't think Kennedy's different?"

"Hell, no," he said.

"But he's another generation—"

"He's *my* generation," Charles said.

"Well," she began doubtfully.

"He's only nine years younger than I am. Too damned young, if you want the truth." Odd, Nixon was the same generation; but one did not think of Nixon in those terms.

She looked at him and smiled. "That's funny, you're right so far as age is concerned. Funny, I've thought of him as closer to my age, though he isn't really, now that I think about it."

He said, "Tell me about you. You look—fine. What's new in New York? When are you coming home?"

She said, "I'm editing a really fascinating book." She watched him rise and move to the liquor cabinet. "A man who was an ambassador for the past four years. You'd recognize the name, McGee. He's writ-ten a kind of journal of his work in Eastern Europe, the bloc coun-tries." He was fussing with the ice tray, his back to her. "Some of the things that happened in the bloc in the past three or four years." He'd freed the ice and was dropping cubes into his glass. "A remarkable man. He's out of government now and lives in Boston. He's a lawyer." Her father poured Scotch and added a splash of water. He'd gained weight and stood at the cabinet with his shoulders bowed. She was re-minded of the photograph, her and her father and grandfather. He did not look so much like Amos now. She thought, He looks old.

"I'll be damned," he said, his back still to her.

She wondered if he'd heard a single word and concluded that he'd heard everything, and understood almost nothing. Not that she'd been very helpful in that regard. There was silence between them and she added, "He's separated from his wife."

Her father shook his head. "I don't know why it is that people can't keep their marriages together."

She said, "I don't think they liked each other very much."

"Well, then they shouldn't've gotten married. Or they should have worked it out. That's what people do. I suppose there are children."

"Three," she said.

He said, "The poor children."

She had not met the children. She knew them only through McGee's conversation. "Yes," she said.

"What was his name? McGee?" She nodded. "Don't know the name," he said firmly.

"Well," she said, definitely irritated now. "Of course he's concerned with foreign affairs."

He went back to his desk and sat down. "Your mother and I are thinking about going to New York the first of the year."

"Fine," she said.

"It's not settled yet."

"I'd like it. You could see my apartment. Maybe we could all have dinner together."

He looked at her. "Your mother of course is very disturbed about the apartment. She's been disturbed for a year, though of course she wouldn't say anything to you about it."

"Um," Dana said.

"She's worried about your safety."

"I'm perfectly safe," Dana said.

"She worries and so do I." He said, "I think it's the greatest mistake I ever made, letting you go there. I don't know what the hell I was thinking of, there isn't any telling what might happen. It's dangerous in New York, the people—. A young girl alone in an apartment."

"Not always," she murmured.

But he had not heard her. She listened to him talk about New York and its perilous culture, and her attention wandered and finally slipped free altogether. She was walking with McGee down Fifth Avenue to the Plaza, the day gorgeous with sunlight and syncopated, cab horns and the click of high heels on the pavement. The afternoon sun slanted down Fifty-ninth Street like a river of gold, and they stopped to look in the window at Tiffany. There was an owl with ruby eyes and a fox with a diamond nose. She felt his pressure on her arm, and turned to him and they both smiled and leaned against each other, looking at Tiffany's animals in their glass and velvet zoo . . .

"—she wishes so badly you'd come home . . . "

They'd strolled slowly up the street and into the Sherry Netherland for a drink and he'd excused himself and was gone it seemed like forever and when he returned he handed her a tiny box wrapped with silver paper. Inside was the owl and she'd thrown her arms around his neck and kissed him fiercely and conversation in the bar died, and she felt envied by the entire world.

"—and you haven't written very much, and that distresses her . . . "

"Daddy," she said. "I have a job."

"Well, of course if that's more important."

"Than what?"

"Your mother's happiness," he said. They sat in silence a moment. At last Dana rose and stood behind the secretary's desk, her shoulders against the wall. Her father looked at her from his big leather chair.

She said, "I've been bad about writing."

"We can talk about it later."

She nodded gratefully. "What's new with you? The *I* looks the same, maybe a little fatter."

"We're having a hell of a year," he said. "I get an offer every month."

She looked at him blankly. "An offer for what?"

"To buy the *I.*" Charles was enjoying himself now, talking business. "One very interesting proposal."

"*Buy* it?"

"Buy it," her father repeated. "What's wrong with that?"

"Nothing at all," Dana said hastily. She could not conceive of the *I* being sold. "Who wants to buy it?"

"An attorney."

"What would a lawyer know about running a newspaper?" She thought at once of Harold McGee. She could not imagine him in Amos Rising's chair.

Charles said patiently, "I think, Dana, that this attorney is acting for someone else. He is the point man."

"Oh."

"The attorney is a nominee." He stared thoughtfully into his glass. "Acting for downstate fellas. I know the lawyer, played golf with him a few times."

"How can you sell the newspaper without knowing who you're going to sell it to?"

He sighed. "Of course you don't, Dana. That isn't the way it works. Do you want to know how it works? Are you interested in the way things work? It doesn't have anything to do with Eastern Europe but it's interesting in its small way." He paused, avoiding her gaze. His eyes were fastened on the ceiling, his hands locked behind his head. Then he turned to look at her, seated now and casual in her high heels and tailored suit and jewelry and careless curly hair. She looked—"smart," he supposed that was the word. He had told no one about the offer, not even Elliott Townsend, but he thought about it every morning when he drove to work and every evening when he drove home. He thought he might as well tell his daughter, this smart-looking woman who sat now in his office; it would be no different from telling a stranger. She had not replied to him, and he correctly interpreted her silence as a rebuke. He said, "What I'm supposed to do is get in touch with the attorney. I tell him I'm not interested in selling the *I* unless the price is X dollars. Twice what I'd take, way more than they'd pay. He tells me my price is way out of line but he'll talk to his principals. Won't do any good, he says, but he'll talk to them anyway. Then a month later I get another call from him—a call, not a letter—and he tells me he's going to be in Chicago having lunch with a guy and would I like to have lunch with him. I say that by an odd coincidence I'm going to be in Chicago myself that day, so I'd be glad to have lunch with him. And the guy he's got with him is a guy who's a little closer to the action. A guy who's authorized to speak for the principals, but only so far. Attorney asks me if I'd mind bringing last year's audit with me and I tell him, 'Hell no, the audit's private.' But I have most of the numbers in my head, any number he's likely to be interested in I have in my memory."

Charles paused, amused at his own narration; his daughter was listening carefully, saying nothing. "So I get to Chicago and lo and behold there's my old friend Butler. Butler is an auditor of newspapers, a sort of independent accountant and tax consultant. Good man. Butler's got a pretty good idea of the value of the *I*, with or without the audit. We have a nice lunch; the attorney pays. Butler tells me he'll be in Dement in a month or so and maybe he'll bring some fellas with him. I know who his clients are so already I've narrowed down the possibilities. He says that he knows some guys who like to tour newspaper plants and would I give them lunch in my office. I tell him that my office is not a restaurant but I'll be glad to pop for soup at the country club. Fine, he says. I ask him if these fellas have names. He says they do but he doesn't want to spoil any surprise by revealing them. This is all bushwa, if I pressed Butler he would tell me; but I know who they are already. Anyhow the mouthpiece is out of it by now and Butler is the guy putting the deal together. A month goes by and I get a call from Butler and sure enough he's got a couple of guys with him and could they come up to see me tomorrow. And when they arrive I find it's my old friend Harold Dows and his kid, who own the morning in McLean and the afternoon in Berlin; the kid's still in high school but he goes everywhere with his old man. Nice kid. The Dowses have got their mechanical man and their circulation man with them. They'll get together with their opposite numbers at the *I* ostensibly for the purpose of picking up any fresh tricks we might have. That happens all the time, newspaper publishers stick together. After lunch it'll just be the four of us, the Dowses and Butler on one side of the table and me on the other. They'll offer me a deal, after first looking at the audit and talking privately with their circulation and mechanical men. Of course they'll already have a damn good idea of the value of the *I*. I'll look at them and say, 'Not a chance.' They'll laugh and offer me another deal, the same deal only more complicated; it'll sound better but it'll be the same deal. I'll tell them thanks but no thanks and it's been nice seeing you but I'm not in the charity business. Then they'll get serious, and so will I. And what we'll finally get down to is cash and an exchange of stock, and a payout spread over maybe five years to avoid some taxes. Our family will get cash and maybe thirty percent of stock in Dows Communications, Inc. And they'll have a hell of a deal because the *I* kicks over more cash than Berlin and McLean put together. Jonah swallows the whale. The profits aren't as large as Berlin and McLean because that's the way I choose to run this place. But they could be. Dows and Butler have sense enough to know that and they're already salivating over the possibilities. The profits *could* be three times what they are. And with Dows and Butler in charge, you can bet your booties they would be." Charles was silent a moment, his eyes again on the ceiling. "The bastards."

"And that's the way it would go."

"Would go, sure."

She looked at her father. "But won't."

He shrugged. "No."

Dana smiled. "I'm glad to hear that." Charles looked at her strangely. "Tell me, though. How would Dows and Butler turn over three times as much profit?"

He said, "It would be Butler. Butler would sit in McLean applying his own monthly audit, and each department would have a budget not to be exceeded. And when a guy got sick or had family trouble they'd say the hell with him and cut him loose. No matter that he's been with you since before the war and you've known his wife since grade school. They'd say the hell with him. Then they'd close down the pension program, which they're entitled to do because it's a company-funded program. And then they'd really start to trim. They'd make a deal with the unions and cut editorial by maybe twenty, twenty-five percent. Freeze salaries. Eliminate expense accounts. There'd be centralized purchasing and you couldn't buy a paper clip without clearing it through Butler. And before you know it, the *I* looks like that sheet Dows runs in Berlin." He hesitated. "And of course Mitch and Tony would be retired."

"What happens to you?"

"A sweet deal. I go on the board, representing the family. It's done to signal continuity, but they've got me outvoted eight to one. Maybe I could force another seat, Townsend if he were younger, or Mitch." He smiled. "Even you. So that means instead of being outvoted eight to one I'd be outvoted seven to two. If they were smart, they'd try to keep me on as publisher. A front man to deal with the big advertisers and developers. But that wouldn't be so good for me because I'd have to go to Butler for my paper clips. A nightmare. And I'll tell you where the crunch would come. I'd try to get contracts for our key people, Desmond and the others; those who are part of the family. And I can tell you what the answer to that would be. Harold Dows and his kid would look me in the eye and say, 'Why would we want to break up the Yankees?' Dows would say, 'There'll be no changes at the *I*. You have my solemn word.' And that and a dime would buy me a phone call." Charles laughed. "You want a nightmare, you've got it." He lapsed into silence.

"What's Dows like?"

Charles shrugged and waved his hand vaguely. "He's all right."

"You don't like him much?"

"No. He's a loudmouth. Chases after women." Then, "He tried to buy me out a year ago. I said no and he said he'd be back. And so he is. This new deal just came up a week ago."

"The way you explain it, it's like selling a family."

He said, "That's close enough."

"How much do you think you could get for it?"

"Hell," he said. "That's not the point. That doesn't have anything to do with it at all." He rose and walked slowly to the cabinet and refilled his glass with Scotch and ice. Then he went to the window. "You'd turn this town over to people who have no interest in it or knowledge of it. People who have no interest in the way the town goes or whether it goes. Your grandfather was wrong about a lot of things but he was right about that. They'd sit there"—he indicated his own chair—"and use the paper as a license to print money. And by God they'd do it, too, and to hell with the"—he groped for a word—"spirit. A newspaper isn't a shoe store or a movie theater, to be sold at will and to hell with the consequences. It doesn't matter a damn who owns a shoe store. It matters a hell of a lot who owns the newspaper because nothing happens in Dement that the *I* doesn't want to happen. I mean the important things, the developments and the new industries and highways. Or new streetlights for downtown or a tax break for a guy who's going to build a plant employing a thousand people. You're too young, you wouldn't remember the hassle over the Reilly property . . ." She listened to him and thought to herself that he was far removed from myth, her grandfather's pursuit; the public memory. Now the *I* was the catalyst for change, her father leading the revolution that his father had feared with all his heart. ". . . best thing that ever happened to this town. Our Rubicon, we finally broke the eastern boundary. There wasn't anything that would have happened if the Reilly had fallen through. Bill Eurich and I and lucky Harry Bohn put it across—"

"What's happened to Mr. Bohn? Why 'lucky' Mr. Bohn?"

"He sold off a piece of his bank. It's a hell of a deal, though of course he can't run it like the corner grocery anymore. The loans've got to be justified—"

"Who bought it?"

"There're some guys who own four or five banks. They've got a pretty good piece of Harry now and they'll have more before the end of the year. It was one of those"—he shrugged—"either/or deals. I think he should've waited. He sold low, considering the potential; I don't think Harry understands the future. But he needed capital badly and that's one thing these guys have got. Good thing about it was, Bill Eurich put together the deal. But Harry's not used to taking orders from anybody and he's having a tough time right now."

"That's terrible, if *they're* in control—"

"It could be," he said. "But isn't. Eurich will keep them in line. So far, we've managed to keep things steady. You need two things for control. You need the newspaper and you need the bank. Lose either one and the game's lost."

She smiled. "I thought all you needed was the newspaper."

"That was what my father thought. And he was wrong."

She said, "I was appalled at the look of downtown. It's falling apart."

"It's not that bad," he said defensively. "In recent years the boom has been on the edges, east and west. Business has been stagnant downtown." He shrugged as if to say, What can you expect?

"Shopping communities," she said.

"Of course."

"A shopping *center.*" She thought, It isn't a community. It is something else, not a community. "It's interesting, you made the decision to develop the bog and it changed the town forever. Suddenly opportunity was on the outskirts, the periphery. Money followed and downtown began to decay. Why? Because you and Harry Bohn and the others decided that the future was east."

He smiled broadly. "Exactly."

"But the place is dead at the center."

"Because they didn't hold on to it."

Dana leaned forward. "What?"

There was a long silence before her father replied. "Guys are waiting to take it away from you. You've got to be smart enough and tough enough to hold on to it, and you've got to have a reason to. A damned good reason, something you believe in yourself. The guys downtown didn't care enough. There are other ways of getting it away from you than buying it. Anything can be taken, *anything.*" Charles began to move restlessly around the perimeter of the room. "That's one reason why a newspaper's got to be profitable. Money is strength. Your grandfather, a great newspaperman, didn't understand the balance sheet. Didn't understand because he didn't have to. It was all different then. The time Capone's people tried to move in and buy the *I,* and then failing that considered setting up a rival newspaper. Do you know they couldn't get a single advertiser to trade with them? Not one. They couldn't give their advertising away, literally they couldn't give it away, and believe me they tried. That was the kind of loyalty there was then. Dad didn't even have to push hard. He just said to a few guys, 'Do this for me.' They knew the loyalty was reciprocal and abolute. That was when most every business in this town was owned by a single guy or a single family or two guys who were partners. Every man in this town decided to stick by Amos Rising, no questions asked. There was no need for telephone calls to the home office in New York asking for instructions. Damn shame, in a way." Charles said, "We *had* to grow." His voice was almost pleading now. "There wasn't any choice in the matter. Bill Eurich was the right man at the right time. Some of them still don't see that, they don't understand that Eurich was in the best interests of the town. It was Eurich or stagnation." He looked away. "Most of the old-timers are dead. And their businesses are either marginal or sold to the chains. Old-line families have drifted apart, one or two of the boys killed in the war, like Frank. Others drifted away or didn't hang on. Some were incompetent. The family tradition isn't there anymore, so you've got to deal with the tradition that is there. Growth. The family business isn't a way of life now, where the family served the business and was served by it." He looked at her. "It's different owning something than managing it."

She said, "You wouldn't ever sell."

Charles said, "I don't know." Then, "It's damned complicated."

"Because of Frank?"

"Partly," he said.

"And Grandpa."

"Grandpa?"

"His memory."

Charles smiled bleakly. "Actually, I was not thinking of your grandfather's memory. However, it is true that a tradition is not"—he smiled—"fungible. This is a family business. Like your friend Kennedy. Their business is politics. Ours is newspapers. It's exactly like that." He looked down at his daughter. "I was thinking of you, actually."

She stared back at him. "In what way?"

"All this," he said. "It was Amos Rising's. Built from scratch. Now it's mine. Someday it'll be yours. That has to mean something, that line. Even to you it has to mean something." Dana said nothing; there was no answer she felt able to give. He said, "Your children."

"But *Dad*—"

"That's what I'm looking to now, the next generation. Listen to me. If there's no one to leave it to, why not sell? What's the point otherwise? I look down the road and I don't see anything there. I wouldn't mind spending part of each winter on the golf course in Phoenix, with my friends. I could do that right now, I'm in a financial position to do it. More than do it . . . But I can't leave the newspaper hanging, and it's all I think about day and night. I mean by that, I don't want to leave it hanging. There isn't anyone here besides me who's capable."

"What about Jake?"

"No," he said without elaboration. Then, "He's tied up with Elliott now. He's a lawyer and that's apparently what he wants. Anyway it's a family business and no one outside the family knows how it's run. Look," he said suddenly. "The truth is, it's my business. And it's not like other businesses, the board of directors doesn't matter, the stockholders don't matter. That's the way Dad and I set it up. It's not a— what did Khrushchev call that thing at the UN?"

Dana said, "Troika."

"It's not a troika."

"Well, Tony—"

"Tony," he said scornfully.

"Or Mitch—"

"—is too old. I don't understand it, I've got half a dozen friends, their sons have all gone into the business. Damn fine boys, doing well, taking the reins. But my son is dead. What happens when I'm gone, is what I want to know?"

"Dad—"

"That goddamned war."

"Oh Dad," she began.

"The goddamned politicians and their wars."

"Dad—"

"I wish you'd come home, Dana. You here, settled, married—" He looked at her. It seemed to him at that moment that all the beauty of the world was within his grasp. His boy was dead but his girl was alive and she had it in her power to revive and refresh him. He had not really objected when she went to New York; he knew that Dement was a small town and not to everyone's taste. But he hoped in his heart that she would return and the family would again be whole, or nearly whole; the line would be restored. He wanted her home and married and he wanted grandchildren; a son-in-law to advise and a grandson, or two grandsons to take with him to the office on Saturday mornings. "All I've done," he said, "I've done for the family."

She turned away, exasperated. It seemed to her that he wanted her *life*. She was to turn over her life to him, that was what he wanted. But she was unable to give it. He was right, people wanted to take it away from you. And you had to resist them with your whole heart. She said, "I can't." And added, hating herself, "Now."

"—provided for you," he said, "your mother, Mitch, Tony, their families. The employees here, we employ eighty-five people. Known most of them for twenty years, longer. What the hell? Why can't you?"

She said, "You love the *I*. It's your life, you've spent your life at it—"

"Is it?"

"Of course, what you've just said."

"That's what everyone says. It's what your mother says and she isn't very often wrong." He said, "What is there to show for it? You're in New York living alone. Don't see you from one year to the next. I bet you don't even read the *I*. Bet you don't even know we're going to have a new courthouse, we'll tear down the old one. An eight-million-dollar structure, it'll revive downtown . . ." He was rambling now, the point lost. "Who cares? The town succeeds or it doesn't succeed. We publish a million lines of advertising or we don't. Paper's good or bad. What's the point if the family's not together to share it? It's all a vacuum. If you're not around. Frank—"

"No," she said, pleading now.

"—is dead, and I can't help that." He began to pace the room again, moving around to the secretary's desk. He sat heavily in her small swivel chair, staring at the drink in front of him, the change from tycoon to martyr complete. "I'm working my tail off for strangers."

That wasn't true either, she thought. Why would he say that? Her *father?* Her heart went out to him, and she leaned across the secretary's desk and touched his hand. Blood was the gulf that lay before them and it could not be bridged, perhaps because they were on the same side of it. She said, "You can't base your life on other people."

He looked at her. "You can't?"

"I don't think so," she said.

"I always thought you could." He turned away then. "I don't think you know anything about it," he said thickly.

"I'm sorry," she said.

He nodded. "It's all right."

She leaned closer to him; her hand was now on his forearm. "You know, I love what I do. I'm very good at it. So they tell me." He looked at her blankly, not understanding the reference. Good at what? "I've got a real career, I like it. I like doing what I do and I've got to be in New York to do it. I'm only twenty-three, this book I'm editing now—"

"The one you mentioned."

"That one. It's going to be good. The author—"

"Um," he said.

"It means a lot to me." She shook his arm a little, waiting for an acknowledgment; a word, any word of approval.

"I don't know much about books and authors," he said. "I'm just a poor newspaper publisher."

She literally had to grit her teeth to prevent an outburst. She said, "It's all right."

"I don't live in New York. Don't know what goes on there. Always lived here, it's always been good enough for Risings. Dement, we've lived here for four generations."

Oh, she thought, *shit*. "Well, you're missing quite a lot," she said evenly. She wanted to leave now, to end this conversation.

"You've done a swell job, apparently," he said. "But your place is here. Your mother." He took a last swallow of his drink and rose. "The trouble began when we sent you away to school."

"Could be." She smiled sadly.

"Your mother—" he began.

"She'll be waiting for us, let's go home." She handed him his hat and coat and they moved out the door.

"—her idea."

She nodded. Yes.

He said, "I was thinking of this. I want you to come on the board of directors of the *I.*" He held the door for them as they left the building. "You wouldn't have to do anything. It would be a good thing for the company." He turned away, opening the passenger's door of her car. "For me."

She said, "I'll drive."

"Just come back once a year—"

She put the car in gear and accelerated. Was that what this was about? "Of course," she said.

He smiled hopefully. "It would be a help."

She heard something new in his voice, something that had not been there before, and she was on her guard. "How would it be a help?"

"This way and that way," he said carelessly. "Who knows?" Then, "In case I decided to sell the *I* to Dows. Then I'll need some backup." He was silent a moment as the car moved onto the highway, back the way she had come. "Hell," he said. "I'd just like it, that's all. You on the board."

"Well," she said. "I'm very flattered."

They were on the strip now. It seemed bright as day. She looked for evidence of the accident but could find none. The memory of it had stuck with her. The damaged cars were gone, and there were no police or medical men. She described the accident to her father, the flashing lights, the confusion, the woman sitting on the pavement, the figure in the other car, the head on the dashboard . . . As she talked her hand went inside her raincoat, absently caressing the little owl anchored to her lapel.

"You're driving too fast," her father said.

3.

TWO NIGHTS LATER there were friends in for drinks. Her uncles and their wives and Elliott Townsend and the banker, Bohn, and Bill Eurich and her cousin Jake. She loved watching these large and self-confident men, dominating the room with their booming voices. And the wives: fresh, pink/wives; serene as hens. The men were prosperous on the outside, dark suits and gold watches and heavy rings on their fingers. The one who had not changed at all was Elliott Townsend, in his eighties now. Dana took the old lawyer's arm, leaning against him. He reminded her of old Amos, same cigary smell, same bulk, same flat accent and stubborn mouth. They were talking business, the new courthouse and the two new banks, the possibility of a spur off the proposed Interstate, another shopping center to the west, a park downtown, and an airstrip if federal money could be found. This friend had prospered, that one had gone broke, another one was on the edge—of success or failure, it was hard to tell which. Listening to it she marveled again at how intimate the town was. The businessmen of Dement were linked by commerce, by property bought and sold and services exchanged. They shared the same lawyers and bankers and doctors, and read the same newspaper. They drove Buicks, and took their vacations at the Spa or in northern Wisconsin or in Fort Lauderdale, and believed in God—without thinking very much about it or needing to go to church to prove it. And she marveled too that

the names had not changed. There were Risings and Townsends and
Bohns and Haights and Reillys; and of course now there was Eurich.
She watched Bill Eurich talk to her mother, telling a joke, laughing; in-
disputably a man at ease, a quieter man than Mitch or her father or the
banker. She turned to Townsend. "How's Marge Reilly?"

"Poor Marge," Harry Bohn began.

"—is fine," Townsend said firmly. "A fine woman in all ways. There
are those who say the clerk's office is less efficient than it used to be
but of course there's twice as much work as there used to be. I never
have any trouble. I send Jake over there for something and he's back
with the goods in thirty minutes."

"Some of the newer lawyers complain a little," Bohn said.

"And last time they tried to run someone against her. But he withdrew so she's unopposed as usual. There is nothing wrong with Marge
Reilly. She's been clerk now for almost thirty years. Knows where all
the bodies are buried."

"The younger fellas complain a little about that, too," Harry Bohn
said. They were talking to each other now, and she was surprised that
their differences were so close to the surface. There was a pause then
and she wanted to ask about her cousin Jake but did not know how to
frame the question. However, Townsend guessed what was in her
mind and told her that he was doing very well. He seemed to have a
flair, though of course it would take time for him to acquire judgment.
Judgment came only with experience and hard work. He said that
Jake's father, Tony, was very pleased with his decision to practice law.
"Very pleased indeed," Townsend said.

"I thought that Tony would want him in the paper," Dana said. "He
worked for the *I* every summer of his life."

"Didn't," Townsend said.

She said, "Surprising."

He said, "Not too."

"Well," Bohn said. "It's odd in that here is a flourishing business, a
family business, and a boy decides to pass it up. It's quite unusual.
Most of the family businesses in Dement, insurance, law, the larger

stores, the sons follow the fathers. That's the way it's been done, though I agree there are exceptions." He named three or four businesses, fathers and sons. "I thought it a bit strange."

"Jake likes the law?"

"Doing very well," Elliott Townsend said.

She did not believe that answered the question, so she returned to the other. "And Tony—"

"I think, Dana." He looked around. Tony and Jake were with the others, clustered around the television set, silent. He lowered his voice. "It could be that Tony felt it would be wiser for Jake to strike out on his own. I don't believe that Tony has the, ah, *commitment* to the newspaper that your father has or Mitch has." He put his hands up, fingers spread. "Don't misunderstand me. His loyalty and affection are complete. But Tony has always been rather an odd man out, and since Amos died—" He cocked his head. "I believe that he was not eager that Jake follow the same path into the newspaper. Well, it's only guesswork, of course."

She thought, Guesswork, my eye. "Makes complete sense to me," she said.

The old lawyer looked at her, smiling slightly. "I thought it might."

"Yes," Bohn said, mystified at the turn the conversation had taken. He knew Tony only slightly and did not know Jake at all.

"It happens sometimes," she said.

Townsend nodded. "True."

"Damned shame," Bohn said.

Townsend said, "Sometimes."

"Well, that's what businesses are there for," the banker said. "You know that better than anyone, Elliott."

"No," Townsend said. "*You* should. But you forgot."

"Don't remind me," Bohn said.

"Well," Townsend said, not letting go. "You should've known, dammit. They tell me your new partners gave you a hard time on the bond deal."

Bohn sighed. "But it went through, Elliott. The point is, it went through. Only difference is, you've got to go to the head office and make a pitch to those apes. Stand there like a clerk. They always say yes, but sometimes they say no. Sometimes they say no just to let you know who's in charge, who's got forty-nine and who's got fifty-one percent. They do that from time to time just to throw a note over the wall—"

Dana had turned away, distracted by the television set. The women had moved toward it and now surrounded it. The men were looking over the shoulders of the women. Now she and the lawyer and Harry Bohn moved close, looking between the women to watch the screen, and listen to the conversation.

". . . thinks her father is no different from any other father in this block. It is slightly different because every other father isn't in Alaska one day and California the next. She saw someone with a . . . button the other day and was amazed to see them wearing a picture of Daddy but she thought it was completely natural, that she loves her father so much that everyone should wear his picture. Would you like to see her?"

"Oh, I'd like to very much," Charles Collingwood said. "Are you sure it's all right for us to intrude on the young lady?"

Jacqueline Kennedy said, "Well, we will see, Charles. Keep your fingers crossed."

Charles Collingwood said, "Hello, Caroline."

"Can you say hello?" Jacqueline Kennedy asked her daughter.

"Hello," Caroline Kennedy said.

"Here," her mother said, "do you want to sit up in bed with me?"

"Oh, isn't she a darling," Charles Collingwood said.

"Now look at the three bears," said the mother.

"What is the dolly's name?" asked the daughter.

"All right," Jacqueline Kennedy said. "What is the dolly's name?"

Caroline Kennedy said, "I didn't name her yet."

"You didn't name her yet?" Jacqueline Kennedy said.

"No," Caroline Kennedy stated.

"When are you going to name her?" Jacqueline Kennedy inquired.

"Is that her favorite?" Charles Collingwood asked, referring to the dolly belonging to the candidate's daughter.

"It is her favorite as of this minute," the mother replied.

"Oh!" cried Charles Collingwood. "Just like all little girls."

Oh sweet Jesus Christ, Charles Rising muttered. *This is a goddamned outrage.* Charles Collingwood! Caroline Kennedy and her dolls! He had met Collingwood once at a seminar at the ANPA or the AP managing editors, one or the other, and he had seemed to be a stand-up guy. A fine war correspondent and a great storyteller. Charles had heard him for years on the radio, he and Murrow and Sevareid and the others, Lowell Thomas, Fulton Lewis, Jr. What was Charles Collingwood doing interviewing a child? He'd interviewed Hitler, Churchill . . . *Oh, isn't she a darling,* Charles mimicked. The men laughed but Lee glared at him. Shhhh, his wife said. He turned to her, irritated. He saw with amazement that his wife was smiling softly at the screen. She looked as if she were about to cry. He walked stiffly to the bar.

"Isn't she sweet," Lee said. The others murmured agreement and Charles, pouring whiskey, had to agree that she was. Most three-year-old girls were.

"Just darling," Tony's wife said. "Look at those curls! Isn't it a riot?"

"It's a riot," Charles said. "Would someone tell me what this program is called?"

"*Shhhh,*" Lee said. "It's called *Person to Person.* In a minute, Kennedy himself is coming on. Then you can get the anger out of your system."

Charles looked at the others. All of them were staring at the set with fixed grins. Kennedy "himself." What the Christ did that mean? Who did she think he was, God? Charles Rising groaned audibly and turned toward the screen again.

". . . we will go and join him now," Jacqueline Kennedy said.

"Oh, that will be a treat for him," Charles Collingwood said.

"Shall we go see Daddy?" the mother asked.

"Yes," Caroline Kennedy said.

"Can you take us to the parlor?" the mother asked.

"Yes," Caroline Kennedy said.

"And we will go see Daddy?" the mother asked.

"Yes," Caroline Kennedy said.

Charles Rising looked at his wife. Her hand was at her mouth and her eyes were shining. Emily Bohn and his brother Tony's wife were standing poised, their heads to one side, as if they were witnessing a christening or some other religious event. It was Mitch's wife Sheila who stared at the screen in sullen fury; everything there was out of reach. Charles watched the others. They were enchanted by the ambiance, the pretty young mother, the golden-haired daughter, the house in Georgetown with its antiques and quiet paintings and tasteful appointments, and Jacqueline Kennedy looking cool and self-possessed. It was Collingwood, usually so smooth, who seemed nervous and ill at ease. Charles looked at her and tried to imagine her as a president's wife. Too young, he thought. He looked at his wife again. Kennedy "himself" was on the screen now, talking to Collingwood. The newsman seemed more relaxed now, talking man to man with the candidate. His manner said, Now we can get down to real business, the women are out of the way. But the deference was still there. Then Kennedy was talking about the primaries, the four years of campaigning, his own family, his father and grandfather "in" politics. Well, this would do it, Charles thought. The son of a bitch would win the election. Nothing could prevent it. Lee Rising was smiling through tears; Sheila Rising was watching with narrowed, envious eyes. Dana was looking at him, grinning widely. She nodded at Sheila and at the television screen and then she shrugged and levered her fist, thumb down. Charles laughed out loud; at that moment, he could have kissed his daughter.

Lee said, "She has wonderful taste."

"Wonderful," Sheila Rising said, her anger barely disguised.

"The house, the way it looks. She has the background for it."

No, Charles thought. He has the background. Rum-running and the films and a crooked mayor of Boston . . . Charles imagined suddenly that all over America, wherever television sets were on, damp-eyed women were saying that Kennedy's wife Jacqueline had the background—whatever that meant—to be a president's wife. Shit, he thought. Nixon didn't have a chance, poor bastard. And Pat Nixon, as gracious a lady—*lady*, quiet, kept to the background. There wasn't a woman in the room who would vote for John F. Kennedy, thank God. They had not yet come to that. But they would not mind if he was elected because he had her, the stylish Jacqueline. And that was what won or lost elections, not minding if the other man won.

"Pretty soupy, isn't it?" Dana whispered into his ear. He put his arm around her and sighed and shook his head. Kennedy was telling Charles Collingwood about his service on the Senate Rackets Committee and how "uncomfortable" the hearings had made Jimmy Hoffa.

"What *is* this, Dana?" He was genuinely puzzled, it was as if he were watching a commercial for the Democratic campaign. "Isn't there a law—"

She laughed, quietly because the others were attentive to the program. "No, Daddy. No laws. They're doing the same thing with Nixon in a few weeks."

"But Nixon can't match—" He did not finish the sentence. He wanted to say that it wasn't equal, that Nixon couldn't match the house and the furnishings and the infant daughter and the young wife, all of them "attractive." Pat Nixon could not draw tears from an otherwise sensible woman living in the Midwest. "It makes me laugh, look at your mother!" Lee Rising had moved forward on the edge of her seat and was staring at the screen, listening carefully.

"Look at your friend Eurich."

Charles turned. Bill Eurich was leaning against the bookcase watching. He held his glass under his chin and his eyes were narrow and alive, his mouth parted in a slight smile. He was watching it all with the impartiality of a camera, and while he watched he listened and there was a kind of hush around him, like a man witnessing aerialists or magicians. He looked at Charles and winked, then returned to the screen. Charles thought there must be something there; Irish didn't waste his time, and Irish was truly *listening,* and listening with respect.

Elliott Townsend was at his elbow. "About the bond issue," he said. "One word before we break up—"

"Did you watch that?"

The lawyer turned back to the screen. "Part of it," he said.

"Doesn't it make you mad as hell?"

"No," he said. "Why should it?"

"It's crap like this that wins elections," Charles said heatedly. He lowered his voice when the women turned toward him, fingers to their lips.

"Hell, boy," Townsend said. "Nobody watches television."

Dana turned toward him, incredulous. "Nobody watches television?"

"Of course not, it's a boob tube." Then the lawyer took her father into a corner. She could barely hear his slow, logical voice explaining something to do with a bond issue. She could sense her father's impatience. She watched the screen. The child had returned and conversation ceased in the Rising library. Even the lawyer and her father turned reluctantly toward the television set. She listened, half amused, half fascinated.

". . . hello, there's Caroline," Charles Collingwood said.

"Hi, Caroline," her father said.

"Do you want Daddy to read you a story?" Jacqueline Kennedy said.

"Come on over," Senator Kennedy said.

"Read these stories to you?" her mother asked. "All right, which one do you want him to read?"

"That one," Caroline Kennedy said.

"What's 'that one'?" Charles Collingwood asked. "Looks like a good one."

"What is the name of that one?" Jacqueline Kennedy inquired.

"That is 'Turkish Fairy Tales,'" John F. Kennedy said. "Do you want to come up here and we'll read it?"

Dana heard her father groan and mutter something obscene under his breath. There was a chorus of *shhhhhs* from the davenport. But her father and Townsend were looking again at the screen, as were the women and her two uncles and her cousin and the Bohns and Bill Eurich, whose narrow eyes were missing nothing. Her mother was literally rapt in front of the screen, fascinated with the transaction. The room was dead silent except for her father and the lawyer, who had pulled away to the far corner of the room. On the screen Charles Collingwood was making his farewells. *Very good of you,* he was saying, *to let us come by and call on you today.* Everyone was smiling, the people on the screen and the people in the room. Then a commercial replaced Charles Collingwood and conversation began to build again. The women were talking about Jacqueline Kennedy's clothes and the furnishings of the house in Georgetown. No, they agreed, they did not like the senator's politics or the party he belonged to. But they all liked his wife and his daughter and his surroundings. And God knows he was a handsome man, probably too handsome for his own good. Bill Eurich stood in the background, saying nothing but listening carefully; his drink, lukewarm now, was forgotten in his hand. Above the female voices she heard Mitch talking to Harry Bohn. She heard the words "labor unions," "balanced budget," "socialists," and finally "goddamned menace." Suddenly she wished that McGee were there, McGee who knew some of the senator's men and had given money to the campaign even though he was a Republican. All of this would be new to McGee and she wondered how he would react to it.

"How are you, Dana?"

It was Jake, handing her a drink. She thanked him and said she was fine. He gestured in the direction of her father and Elliott Townsend and said, "I don't think they cared much for the TV program."

She said, "It doesn't matter anyhow."

"Why not?"

She said, "No one watches television. That's what Elliott said, 'Nobody watches television.'" She shook her head, laughing.

"He really said that?"

"He said it."

"Well, as you can see. Everyone here is just as much in touch as they always were."

"Looks like it," she said.

He leaned close to her. "I may vote for him."

"Shhh," she said. "Don't let them hear you." Then, "How's the law?"

"Hard work."

"What are you doing? Corporate?"

"Almost entirely. All the businesses around here, the head office may be in New York but they find they need local counsel." He smiled. "We've seen to that." He looked over his shoulder at the old lawyer in conversation with Charles Rising. "Of course Elliott handles most of the *I*'s legal stuff. We need a third man, actually. If we wanted to, we could add six men. There's enough work for six but Elliott wants to keep it small. Tidy." He sighed and drank. "Close."

"Jake," she said. "I'm surprised you didn't go into the paper." He shrugged and his eyes moved away, and then back to her. "Though it was probably for the best."

"Why do you say that?"

She didn't know why she said it; it seemed the thing to say. She looked at him and smiled. "There's an awful lot of family in that business."

"That's what it's there for," he said. "But what with one thing and another my dad didn't think it would be a good idea. Of course he didn't insist. You know Dad. But it seemed to mean quite a lot to him, that I practice law. And Elliott's almost family. Close enough anyhow."

This was all new to her and she did not reply for a moment. Jake was so earnest, towering over her now; she noticed he was dressed in corporate gray. She asked, "Why?"

"He thought I'd get frozen out. In a word."

"Well—"

"He didn't want me to devote my life to something and then get frozen out."

She felt his hostility and moved back a step. "What'll happen to the *I*, then?"

"I don't know. You tell me. That's for your father to decide, he's the one with control. It's his candy store. Is it ever."

"All right then. I'll put it another way. What do you suppose he'll do? When the time comes to do something."

Jake said, "Nobody knows."

"I suppose they don't."

"Frank was the logical one . . ."

She listened to him talk about Frank and wondered if anybody had ever thought of her brother as anything other than an heir. It was possible that he had been an excellent soldier; the letter from his commanding officer indicated that he was. Though of course he had been frightened. Perhaps he had been fantastic in bed, though he was only eighteen when he went to Korea and might not've known. But men knew. Even inexperienced men knew that. She said, "Yes," when he finished.

"But I'll tell you this," Jake said. "He ought to make some decision soon, and let it be known. Because people are nervous. There's been so much movement in the town, there are only a few things that are continuous, if you know what I mean. Townsend is continuous; Marge Reilly is continuous; and the *I* is continuous. Bohn's bank was continuous but it isn't any longer. There's talk he's on his way out. Between Mrs. Reilly and Elliott and your father the town somehow gets run. Though sometimes I'm not sure who's running who. Whether they're running the town or whether the town's running them. They've completely neglected the political picture, Elliott's too busy and out of touch and your father doesn't care. Never has cared, politics has always bored him. But now there's a new cast of characters, some good, some bad. Somebody ought to be paying attention and nobody is. The state's attorney is a thief—"

She put her arm on his shoulder. He had begun to talk faster and faster. "The state's attorney has always been a thief."

"Well, that's not true."

"It's true," she said.

"You really are different," he said suddenly. He stepped back and looked at her at arm's length. "My parents always said you were the different one in the family. You always had an opinion about everything and that opinion was always different from anyone else's. Always, even when you were little. What do you know about Dement state's attorneys?"

"Well, I grew up here, for one thing." She motioned to the corner where her father and Townsend were deep in conversation. "I have ears. Eyes."

"Well, they haven't 'always been crooked.' Our grandfather saw to that. And the one we have now is crooked as a stick and no one's prepared to do anything about it because of course he's a nice guy, they always are, and because he's been helpful in other ways." Jake paused and looked at her, waiting for a reply of some kind. She heard the women on the davenport, talking now of food. Mitch and the banker were at the liquor cabinet. She said finally, "What do you mean, 'different'?"

He said, "In a minute. The thing is. They believe everything is under control, the way it's always been. They think it's just the same, only bigger. That's what they think but they're wrong." He turned away. "The truth is, it's falling apart."

"Jake, the town has always been rough. It's a tough little town, always has been—"

"Do you see him?" He nodded at Eurich, who had moved now to Mitch's elbow, listening. He had put down his drink and was smoking a cigar. Dana could not help thinking there was an insolence about him; the cigar's fumes filled the room, evidence of his silent presence. "He owns half the land around here now, or options on it which amount to the same thing. And he has a piece of Joe Steppe's construction company. Offices in half a dozen towns, you never know where he is. Funny, when he needed a lawyer he didn't come to Elliott. Elliott was the logical man but he never came near Elliott. He uses Jimmy Kerrigan, the judge's son. Jimmy is"—Jake fluttered his fingers—"a very clever young lawyer. Look at him, he's like a Buddha, doesn't say much. Doesn't say anything when he doesn't have to, and yet he's the man to see now. He's the way into Harry's bank, and there isn't a project in this town that doesn't bear his mark, one way or another—" He said softly, "And it surprised us when he turned up on a list of big contributors to the Democratic campaign."

"Oh, *Jake,*" she said. It annoyed her; she thought Jake Rising was beyond that. Then suddenly he gripped her arm.

"You're not reading me," he said grimly. "I don't give a crap about his politics, except look at him. The pillar of the Republican establishment. I just think it's damned odd, that's all. But we all know what it is, it's influence. And he's got it. He's going to get the spur off the Interstate and your father's been working at that for five years, without success. Bill Eurich got it. Now isn't it just a little bit strange and puzzling, don't you think he'd be more comfortable with the Republicans? I do. But he isn't. Who is Bill Eurich and what is he doing here and who are his principals? You can ask your old man. Maybe he knows." He let go of her arm and was silent a moment. "What I meant about the other: you've always done exactly what you wanted to do. And in every case that collided with—people here. What are you trying to prove?"

"You're making me sound better all the time," she said lightly. She had not completely understood what he'd said about Eurich.

"That's what I mean," he said.

"There isn't much I can do about it now," she said.

Jake said, "I thought you'd like to know how it was around here."

"Yes," she said.

"It isn't all terrific."

"I can see that."

"The rest of the family, we think you have a good effect on your father. A positive effect. Sometimes he's a little hard for the rest of us to—get through to, you understand? It's good that you're back, Dana."

She said, "I'm leaving tomorrow."

"Maybe you could arrange to get back more often. The point's this. We're all concerned about the *I*. It's family, it's *Rising*. And we're all tied up with it, in a lot of ways including income, my father's income, Mitch's, your father's, mine up to a point, yours—"

"Not mine," she said quickly.

"You know," he said. "You could just change your name and be done with it. Select a new identity, there would be a hell of a lot of them to choose from. Then you wouldn't have to fight it, and us." He pointed across the room at Eurich. "You're just as much a stranger here as he is."

She said, "What I do with my life is my business." She looked at him, his old-young face, his tired eyes, the gray suit. He was only four years older than she was but he looked much older. It would be hard for a stranger to place his age. But he seemed to see the town in a different way and that surprised her.

He said, "You're welcome to it. What I'm trying to say to you now is that it's important the paper stay inside the family."

"Why wouldn't it?"

Jake looked at her a long moment. "Rumors," he said quietly. "A rumor a day. I don't believe any of them but in this town . . . There are too many rumors, there's talk your father might sell—"

"Where do the rumors come from?"

He stepped back, moving his shoulders. "All over. They come from all over. Is he tired of it?" She shook her head. "Frank's dead, you're in New York—"

"I wouldn't worry about it."

"But I do worry about it. So do my mother and father and so do other . . . elements in town. Who are worried." He drained his glass and smiled mechanically and left her without another word. She stood by the window a moment, allowing herself to settle. She refused to show any emotion at all with Jake Rising. She lit a cigarette and wandered over to her father and Elliott Townsend. Her father put his arm around her while he listened to the lawyer. It was legal language and she did not understand it. She moved away from them and walked to the davenport where the women were sitting. The women were discussing a specialty shop that had just opened but stopped when she sat down. Sheila Rising asked her about New York and she began to tell them, general details about her job and the location of her apartment and the expense of living in the city. They listened politely but with reserve and Dana finished quickly and excused herself and said good night. She shook hands with all of them, Bill Eurich last.

He said, "What did you think of the program?"

She smiled. "It won't hurt him."

He smiled back. No, it wouldn't hurt him at all.

"What did you think?"

"I thought it was new," Bill Eurich said.

"A novelty," she said.

"No," he said, very seriously. "Not a novelty. An invention."

"Successful," she said, moving away into the hall.

He took a long pull on his cigar. "Very." Then, calling after her. "You going to vote for him, Dana?"

She turned back; there was just Eurich standing in the door. She said, "Yes."

He smiled. "I thought so. He'll win, too, despite—" He shifted his eyes to indicate the others, out of sight. She did not reply, and at that moment she quite definitely disliked Bill Eurich.

Her room was unchanged from the time she was a teenager; there were the same stuffed animals and pictures and a few recordings and books. She stood looking out the window into the yard, thinking about her family; her mother and father and her uncles and aunts and Jake, and the thing that bound them together, the *I*. Then she went to her closet and reached among the things on the top shelf, searching for the silver cigarette case. She rummaged for a few seconds but it was not there. Then her fingernail touched metal and she brought it out and opened it carefully; one of the hinges was broken. It held a single Lucky Strike, years old now. The tobacco dribbled out its end like sawdust from a rotten log. She stood looking at it, wishing that she had not taken her best blues records to New York. She wished that McGee was there with her. No, that was not it at all. She wished that she were with him, in her own apartment. Lying naked in bed, listening to music; away from this town and this family and their tangled fortunes. Damn, she thought. Damn Jake Rising.

THE NEXT MORNING she said good-bye to her mother. Her father had already left for his office. Her mother was worried about the drive to Chicago and Dana told her not to worry. She said she would worry anyway. Dana said she would be back, probably next summer; in the meantime, they should come to New York. She said, Dad said that you might and we could all have dinner together. And we two could have lunch and see a show, she said to her mother, who nodded with tears in her eyes. Dana was standing on the front stoop looking through the door to the living room, everything in sharp relief as she always remembered it, vases and end tables and the beige rug. She kissed her mother on the cheek and her mother gave her a little hug. A nice visit, she said. Then Dana moved closer to her and put her arm around her shoulders. Her mother asked, please, that she stay, only one more day. Dana answered, truthfully, that she'd been allowed only four days' holiday. She had to get back to work. Now she tried to make up for that in some way. They stood together a moment, silent, and her mother tried to smile but failed and at last turned away, disguising her tears. Dana held her close, but there was no more to be said. She promised to call her soon; would call tonight when she got back to the apartment; would call her next week as well. Her mother nodded, Fine. And please write. Dana said, I love to get the news, know what's going on . . . Her mother gave her a sharp look and said, So do we. We don't understand your life in New York, is there some man? Dana looked away; she had not told her mother about McGee. McGee was too complicated; the situation was. She embraced her mother and said it was a wonderful visit. Then something caught her eye; it was the newspaper lying in the driveway. They'd delivered it yesterday afternoon, as they delivered it every afternoon, even though her father always brought a copy home from the office. She picked it up and said suddenly, "I'm going with a man called McGee."

"Oh," her mother said, brightening. "McGee?"

"McGee," she said. "I'm editing a book he's written, a kind of a memoir, though he's not actually an author. He's a lawyer."

"Isn't that nice," her mother said.

"He lives in Boston," Dana said.

"Well, dear—" Her mother kissed her again. Suddenly she seemed anxious that Dana leave.

"He was an ambassador."

"Oh," she said. "An ambassador."

"Yes, a roving ambassador." That would mean nothing to her mother. She said, "He quit last year."

"Oh," she said. "Well." Her mother turned away, distressed. "An ambassador," she said again. "Well, how old—"

Dana smiled. "About thirty-five."

"That's very young to have such a position." She touched Dana's hand, a tentative gesture. "He must be quite—something."

"He is," she said proudly. "Maybe you recognize the name, his name was in the papers quite a bit two years ago." She watched her mother shake her head slowly. No, the name was not familiar to her though of course she was not generally *au courant* with—embassies.

"Well," she said. "Dana—"

"We're just going together now, it isn't any more serious than that. But I thought you'd be happy knowing."

Lee Rising was listening carefully and the words "going together" and "any more serious than that" had an electric effect. At once she was certain that her daughter was seriously involved with an older man from another world, and that world was in no way familiar. She said, "Boston."

Dana looked at her mother and suddenly wanted to tell her about McGee, everything about him; and their life together. They had been close once and could be again. It had been her mother who had forced the issue with her father and sent her east to school, and her mother who had not opposed her when she went to work in New York. This solid woman, a woman without guile or pretension, fiercely loyal; loyal to her, to her father. She had always wanted the best for Dana, always. And if that ran head-on into something else, the something else would have to yield. She blurted, "Mother, he's married but has been separated for a year, more than a year actually."

Lee Rising said, "Oh, Dana."

She shook her head. "There's nothing clandestine about it—"

Nothing clandestine? "Dana, a married man—"

"He was married when he was twenty, it was a mistake—"

"It's always a—mistake."

"Well, it does happen."

"And I suppose there are children," she said stiffly.

Dana closed her eyes, hearing her father's voice. Their voices, her parents', were the same voices. No difference in tone or timbre. She nodded. Yes, there were children.

Lee Rising turned away, her foot on the front step. "Dana, what can I say?" Dana said nothing, knowing now that she had made a ghastly mistake. How could she have done it? Not known, not *remembered*, that there were two worlds, her world and her parents' world; how foolish for her to think that they could be in any way bridged. But she felt small now and unclean, not for what she had done but for what she had said, and the look in her mother's eyes.

"I shouldn't've said anything. I'm sorry."

"No, you should not've," her mother said. "What are we going to do now?" Her face was still turned away.

Dana said nothing and handed the *I* to her mother. She took it and looked at it sadly, turning it in her hands, and then tucked it under her arm. Dana waited a moment then smiled sadly and moved off to her car. She stopped at the sound of her mother's voice. Then she listened.

"When your father and I were first married, it couldn't've been more than a couple of months, a friend asked me to serve on the hospital board. I was flattered, your brother wasn't born yet and I was a young woman with a lot of energy and a feeling I should . . . contribute. Something. I almost agreed on the spot—what possible objection could there be?—but then told my friend I'd have to check with Charles first. Some small voice told me to do that, and thank God. Your father told me that of course if I really wanted to do it, if it were a matter of life and death, it would be all right. He would support me in anything I really wanted to do but *his* father felt very strongly that no family member should be involved in any community activity. He insisted it was harmful to the newspaper. A family member on the board of the hospital or the Red Cross or the Boy Scouts or any orphanage or service club would signal the community that the newspaper endorsed it and it was therefore protected. That was the reason your father never joined Kiwanis or Rotary. It would compromise the integrity of the *I.* I asked your father if he believed it, and he admitted that he did. It seemed to me a silly rule and I argued with Charles. I said that there was a difference, I held no position on the newspaper. I hurt him with that remark and he didn't reply. Then he said again that if it were really something I had to do, well . . ." She paused and looked away. "So of course I didn't join the hospital board. I didn't 'have' to do it and I didn't want to do it badly enough to make an issue out of it. It didn't seem so very important, in the light of your father's concern. Instead I became involved with the church." She smiled suddenly, moving her locked hands. "For some reason your grandfather did not believe church membership compromised anything; God was neutral. That is what I have done for thirty years, run the bazaar to raise money for the First Presbyterian Church of Dement. Twice a month for thirty years Horace Greismann and I have met for tea; planning the bazaar. This is a church that no one in our family cares about. Your father attends when there's a wedding or a funeral. Neither you nor your brother showed any interest. It's an odd little community, Dement. We're conservative people here. Law-abiding, slow to change, free of scandal. We don't divorce and our personal lives, we keep to ourselves. And we are not religious in any formal sense. I've spent thirty *years* of my life raising money for a new church building. I've given myself, gotten Charles to give, run the bazaar. The bank account grows and grows, and the church membership declines; it has declined every year for the past five. And it will decline again this year. How do you like that?" She smiled sadly and moved across the driveway to the front step. Then she looked back at Dana, who had not moved at all. "But we care about our reputations. That was what your father was saying to me thirty years ago about the newspaper. Its reputation was more important than anything I might want to do, however innocent or innocuous it might seem. That's all there is, Dana. Reputation. Yours, your father's, mine, the newspaper's. It's all one. It's indivisible."

"Mother—" Dana began.

"Write me," her mother said.

Dana looked once more at her mother, then moved to the steps. Her mother leaned down to kiss her briefly, then stepped back. Dana withdrew toward her car, waved once, and slipped behind the wheel. She left her mother standing in the open doorway, holding yesterday's newspaper and angrily blinking back tears. Dana drove out of the driveway and for no reason at all turned right, away from town. She had time to kill; she'd promised to stop at the office to say good-bye to her father, but her plane did not leave until five. She began to cry then, smelling the fall air and noticing the trees and their brittle leaves, just beginning to turn. The day was warm, almost sultry. My God, she thought, all of that, bottled up for so long. Wrong, she was so wrong; what a waste. But there was something splendid about it too; a splendid sufferance and strong sorrow. Well, she thought, what did you expect? A pat on the back and a hearty "Well Done!"? No, she did not expect that. She expected that somehow her mother's excitement would match her own. No, the truth was she wanted to *tell*. They kept asking her about her life . . . It was what happened with parents when you spoke what you felt, without editing your emotions. Damn, she said aloud. She was passing a new housing development, a cluster of split-level houses surrounded by a chain-link fence. A mile beyond that, a crew was narrowing the highway. Suddenly she knew exactly where she was going. She made an illegal U-turn and retraced her route, past her parent's house toward the center of town.

The cemetery was set back from the road, seen through a grove of high elms. A ragged privet hedge marked its boundary and beyond was farmland. She parked her car and walked through the entrance, touching an ancient wrought-iron gate that hung drunkenly from rusty hinges. Black paint flaked at the touch of her fingers. Grave-stones and marble obelisks spread out before her, the silhouette of a miniature city. She stood very still for a moment, then began to stroll down the path, taking her time, feeling the warmth of the sun, dry leaves crunching underfoot. This was the best time in Dement, early autumn, the earth going to rest and the aroma of burning in the air, fallen leaves everywhere. The dry air touched her skin, McGee's touch, and she stopped and breathed deeply, raising her face to the sky. Then she resumed her search, though she believed she knew the exact spot; she would know it when she saw it. The cemetery was empty, with only a few fresh flowers to indicate that there were occasional vis-itors. Here and there an American flag was placed next to a grave-stone. Some of the names she recognized, fewer than she believed she would. Most of them were family plots, Reilly, Haight, Evans. She smiled; Aces Evans had his own polished obelisk. If there were any wit left in the world it would be decorated with an inside straight—but there was just the name, and the dates of birth and death, and a tat-tered corsage, looking like something left over from a dance. She said a brief prayer for the repose of the soul of Aces Evans and moved on to the farthest corner of the Garden of Faith.

At least it was not gaudy, she thought. A solid block of granite was not gaudy. It said simply,

RISING

"LORD, I BELIEVE."

with two smaller headstones,

AMOS	/	JOSEPHINE
1868–1953	/	1870–1950

and room for half a dozen more. Room for all of them, all living Risings. Generations yet unborn would have to find another Garden of Faith; this one was filled. She stood back from the big stone, staring at it, staring at its legend, and then she was laughing and crying at the same time. *Lord, I believe;* Stanley should have said it to Livingstone. She turned away, lifting her eyes to the prairie beyond the hedge. The land was soft and fallow and there was a farmhouse and dark woods in the distance. She could see movement around the farmhouse, a woman carrying eggs in a basket followed by two barking dogs. She moved off a few yards, scuffing along the path, then turned back, staring at the headstones. Amos, Jo. She lit a cigarette and leaned against a marble monument, looking at the dates: 1868, 1870; only two years' difference in their ages. She understood suddenly that her history, the history of the family, ended with Amos Rising. Or began with him, one or the other. He stood like a closed door to the past. There was nothing before him and everything that came after was too close; so close you could touch it. Touch it, and him too. Somewhere back of him were men and women who'd managed to leave no trace of themselves. They were ghosts. No letters or drawings or artifacts of any kind, only obscure genes; a vaguely prominent nose, a certain set of the shoulders. And long life. Physical characteristics. A thousand generations, vanished. Perhaps—who knew?—there were pharaohs in the family, Carolingian kings, sensual popes, gallant crusaders, ancestral castles on the Rhine or palaces beside Venetian canals. Doubtless most of them had been people of the interior; she thought of them as living on the slopes of mountains, inland, wary of coasts and islands. Somewhere there had been an interruption or collective loss of memory because nothing whatever was known, or would ever be known. Amos had disclosed nothing. She wondered about Jo. She had come to Dement as a young girl from Indiana. Somewhere in Indiana, no one was certain where it was; her grandmother had never spoken of it. Her mother's parents were dead and while there were living relations they were scattered and no longer kept in touch. Her mother, too, was circumspect. Amos cast a dark shadow over all of them, and substituted something else.

In place of family traditions or history, an intimate dramatis personae, or heirlooms, legacies or birthrights—they had a newspaper. The newspaper was all those things, family business, carrying with it rights and responsibilities and patterns of conduct. The men stood "in a line," prepared to serve the business and be served by it. It was similar to the military or the clergy: you took certain orders and abided by the rules, though the code of conduct was different . . . She shuddered; thank heaven that Amos's *I* was exactly like the military and the clergy, a masculine order. No females admitted, but they wanted you in the gallery, for sure. They wanted your attention and concern. Women: perhaps they thought of them as maidens in the tower, waiting for rescue, or with picnic lunches and parasols on the slopes of Antietam or waiting for the ships to return to New Bedford. If they ever did return. In any case, wanted; necessary; they wanted you around, waiting. They wanted appreciation for their sacrifices. "I'm doing it for you." And they were certain they were, on those occasions when they could assemble no other plausible explanation for their actions. When they were tired or dispirited or frightened, late at night. *You must be strong,* her father had said, *or they'll take it away from you.*

She thought, *Not likely.*

She dropped her cigarette and ground it underfoot. Harsh, that was harsh; too harsh. This was her only family, though she often had difficulty distinguishing between the family and the business. The business hovered over all of them, like a great umbrella, protecting them from rain and sunshine alike. She could see the pain and uncertainty in her father's eyes. He did not know what would happen to the *I*, and all of it was his responsibility; he had to provide for its future and he did not know how. His son was dead and he never accepted that. All his hopes were pinned on his son, and that son had been dead nine years. His daughter had drifted away from him, living now in New York; sleeping with a married man. He did not understand her life, *could* not understand it given the terms of his own. Dana could not solve his problem, no; but her presence was in some way valuable to him. She was there. She cared. It mattered to her, what happened to the *I* and therefore to the family and its history, past and future. She could explain this to no one else: it represented their very existence, the essence of their lives.

And the man in the grave. He still cast a shadow. It was dim, but it was there; more within the family than within the town now. Well, why not? She smiled suddenly, remembering that her grandfather had once described the family business, from Ford to the corner grocer, as the Bulwark of the American Economy. She laughed out loud. Perhaps he was right after all. An economy could be wonderful if you owned one of its bulwarks, living permanently on a rampart . . . She moved away from the Rising graves, walking slowly through the stones back to the ancient gate. She noticed other names, Brandon, Ashcroft. The Ashcrofts had been friends of her grandparents. Ella Ashcroft had been her grandfather's special friend. Her memory moved, and was still. She walked quickly now, she wanted to be on the road. If she hurried she might make an earlier plane; she could be in New York by eight o'clock. She took off her raincoat as she hurried through the light mist that had gathered around the cemetery. Her father would be waiting for her, and once she said good-bye she'd be free again.

4.

THEY WERE drinking cognac from huge balloon glasses. McGee was describing trusts and they were laughing, one riotous table in the corner of a quiet restaurant. Trusts: serpentine documents whose words resembled the stones of the great wall of China. They were immovable, clogged, words piled upon words, clauses, subclauses, codicils, subcodicils, capital letters for each Noun. Unbreakable trusts. Trusts put together like chain mail, the words themselves resembling free verse. McGee was serious but his father was light. Harold McGee recited, describing each line with his forefinger, like an orchestra conductor:

> The Trustee shall distribute
> to each of said Issue
> Upon reaching the age of 21 years
> His or Her share of the Principal, Interest
> and/or Income
> of the Trust!
> The Remainder shall continue
> In Trust for the Benefit of
> My Children
> Until such Time as they all have reached the
> Age
> Of 21 years.

Dana laughed and Harold McGee leaned back in his chair. It's all code, he said; a gigantic cipher, to which the family attorney alone holds the key. He said, "It's nonsense of course. I apprenticed to a man who thought the trust the noblest creation of the law. Sublime. He told me once, 'The trust is to the law as the Sistine Chapel is to wall decoration.' And." He leaned across the table, pointing the balloon glass at Dana. "'The preservation of a family business through the mechanism of a trust.'" He put the glass on the table and dipped his forefinger, a passable imitation of Michelangelo's Adam. "'Is the moment of creation.'" Then he looked at his son, and at Dana. "He believes that, sees some sort of poetry or drama in it."

"That's true," McGee said.

"Give me a messy divorce any day."

Dana said, "You're Daumier. He's Michelangelo."

Harold McGee laughed and turned to his son. "You've been a fool. You could've come into my firm, not those Boston idiots. We need a good trust man. It would be a pretty satisfactory fee-split, now that I think about it. A fresh will follows a fresh divorce as the day follows the night. And nine times out of ten the testator, newly sad but newly wise, has concluded that the only way to preserve the fortune is to lock it up, so to speak."

"I finished a trust last week," McGee said. "Remarkable document, if I do say so myself." He mentioned a great name and the business associated with it. "My trust will preserve that fortune *forever,* if the children are prudent—"

"Hah!" Harold McGee blurted. *"Naïf!* The children are never prudent." He wagged his finger at his son. "No trust can prevent profligacy after three generations, you're damn lucky if you can hold it together for two. Unless of course you establish a foundation whose officers have no connection with the family and are superhumanly wise, Solomons all. You can retain some of the swag through a foundation but the cure is often worse than the disease. Because the money is not in the family's control. To the family's benefit, but benefit is not control, alas. That's a pity but on the other hand the money is still there. It is not in the federal treasury, which is the important thing—"

She glanced at McGee. He was distracted and not listening carefully. He had been distracted all evening, and now she put her hand on his, locking fingers. He looked at her and smiled. She said, "Well, *naïf.* Tell me about imprudent children." But he said he had to make a telephone call, excused himself, and left the table.

Harold McGee watched him go. Then he said, "My son is a very serious young man. More serious than I am. Believes in things I don't, anymore. Do you know how serious he is? Dana," he said. "You take your time. He needs a period of recovery." Their eyes met and she shook her head.

"I believe he's completely over that marriage, he doesn't think about her anymore—"

"I don't mean the marriage. I mean Europe. Tough time for him. I think you're the best thing that's happened to him in a long time. A very long time—"

She smiled at the older man.

He said, "I mean it."

"I know you do. It surprises me," she said. "The life he's led, what he's done, where he's been. To slip back so easily into the life of a Boston lawyer. I can't believe it'll last."

"It won't," Harold McGee said.

"He's really a superb diplomat."

The older man laughed quietly, toying with the balloon glass in front of him. "How do you know that?"

She said, "Instinct."

"It's true of course. I don't know where he got it, certainly not from me. But he has a way of putting himself in the other man's shoes, not in order to seek an advantage as a lawyer would, but to understand the—what?—mental process. As a priest would. He'd never make a litigator but he's probably the best back-room man in the business. Law or diplomacy. The thing about my son that no one's ever understood is that he's extremely shy. No one understands it because of the way he looks. He's tall and good-looking and appears to be self-assured. But he isn't." Harold McGee paused for a moment, rocking the balloon glass in his fingers. "Worries me."

"Shyness. It's not an unattractive quality."

"By no means."

"Well, then—"

"It leads him to believe that others know a hell of a lot more than they actually do. He has a knack for understanding the motives of other people. That's what it is, you know, *motive*. Once he understands he begins to sympathize, and then to believe. I guess I wish he had a firmer center of gravity of his own, because sooner or later—"

"Maybe that *is* his center of gravity."

"Maybe."

She said, "I love him, you know."

He smiled broadly and a witty remark came to his tongue, and mercifully remained there, unspoken. Harold McGee was not accustomed to the directness of this girl. It was a quality that enchanted him and puzzled him at the same time. He said, "How did you ever manage to escape the Middle West? Just how did you manage that?"

"You don't like the Midwest?"

"I don't know it."

"Well, it wasn't easy."

"You won't take it amiss if I say there's still something very—"

She began to laugh. "And I've worked so hard to overcome it."

He said, "I didn't mean—"

"This outfit, it's from Peck and Peck. This little pin, McGee got it for me at Tiffany. And now you tell me it's all for nothing, and I'm straight out of J. C. Penney."

He said, "Touché."

"I guess I'm doomed. What is it, the accent?"

"Seriously," he said. "How did you manage it?"

"My family thought it would be temporary. I knew it wouldn't be but it didn't seem wise to disclose that little fact. After Mount Holyoke I didn't want to go back; it was as simple as that. I wanted out and I was determined to get out and if it had come down to it I suppose I would've just *left*. Lit out like Huck Finn. No note."

Harold McGee looked at her a long moment. "Huck Finn," he said, "did not 'light out.' He contrived his own murder. A counterfeit murder, then dealt himself a new identity."

"Yeah," she said. "I know."

Then McGee was back, smiling, looking at them both, realizing then that he'd interrupted.

"Good thing you're back," Harold McGee said. "I'm about to fall for this enchantress. The Very Young Miss Rising. From Mount Holyoke."

McGee smiled. "What brought this on?"

She said, "We were talking about trusts."

"Of various kinds," Harold McGee said.

McGee turned to Dana. "Have you ever heard him on the subject of family businesses?" She shook her head. "Go on," he said to his father. "Give her the full treatment."

"You're the trust man," Harold McGee said.

McGee looked at Dana and laughed, his first genuine show of amusement all evening. He said quietly, "My father believes that they tend to break up after the third generation. He says—"

"It's not exactly new or original," Harold McGee said. "Sometimes it's merely a question of blood, the grandson of the founder seldom has the tenacity and . . . grit. The business is the founder's *life*. To the son it's a challenge. To the grandson it's a property. He doesn't want it enough to devote his life to keeping it, so it disintegrates. And of course by the third generation families commence to quarrel. One branch is always richer than another and that brings resentment, both ways. The chairman finds he is spending more time negotiating with relatives than he is running the business and when that happens the business is in trouble. One tends a business like a garden: care for the flowers and the weeds and understand where the fertilizer goes and what happened the year before; prepare for flood and prepare for drought. If the chairman is shrewd, he'll mix up the people under him, a rapid turnover so no one knows the business as well as he. That's the key to it, and of course he has the old family retainers to deal with and sooner or later they'll want a piece of the business. But the arrangements are difficult because nine times out of ten into the third generation the stock is split a half-dozen ways with no one in absolute control. Tamper with one block of stock and you affect the relationship of the others, each to each. Even a percentage point here and there can affect—not the ownership of the business but the psychology of ownership, which is just as important. A company which has been run on attention to detail and a loyalty *to the business itself* becomes a business matter pure and simple. The esprit goes to hell. It becomes a business like any other. Understand: The founder and his immediate successor serve the company because they do not distinguish between the company and themselves. Identical egos. Not so the grandson, two generations removed. The grandson—"

"Or granddaughter," Dana said.

"Or granddaughter. Looks at the mess, the quarreling family, each member with his percentage, and says the hell with it. This chap, call him the head of the family, decides it's too much trouble and sells the family interest. It's usually a simple enough matter to round up fifty-one percent among a fractious family, when the object is to sell the business at top dollar. He gets a seat on the board and a title and something to do and it signals continuity. Especially when there is no continuity. Everyone else gets money and an exchange of stock, and if you do that in the right way you can generate quite a lot of capital and *avoid federal income taxes.*"

"I had a feeling you were coming to that," Dana said.

"Mn," Harold McGee said. He paused for a moment, lost in thought. The balloon glass rested against his lips. Then he smiled from behind the glass; the lecture was almost over. "But if the point is to keep the business, then you've got to risk it into the third generation. Give somebody complete control. Keep it through the third generation intact, functioning, solvent and harmonious, and you can keep it forever. You couldn't kill it with an ax. Into the fourth generation an instinct for survival overcomes all other instincts. Family quarrels recede. The business again becomes identified with the family, or that part of it which is in control. By the fourth generation new blood has supplanted the old. The founder is no more than a memory, more honored in the breach. That's why to seal everything away in a trust is a mistake. It's a straitjacket and more than that it's unnatural because it doesn't allow for the craziness—"

"What do you mean," Dana said. "Craziness."

"People," Harold McGee said. "Heirs particularly."

"Trusts are too remote," she said.

"That may be," McGee said. "But they do—preserve. That's what they're devised for, preservation. They—"

"Taxidermy," Harold McGee said.

"Do you think it's a good thing?"

McGee said, "I do. I don't like to leave things to chance. I believe that all acts have consequences, and that's why I think it's best to define the acts as precisely as you can. Somebody worked like hell and made a load of money and if someone hires me to protect the money, forever if need be, that's what I'll do. You can't allow one profligate to destroy a family." He looked at his father. "And that's the consequence of what you're suggesting."

"It's a risk," Harold McGee acknowledged. "You never really know."

"Then you agree," Dana said.

"Dana, I don't know," the older man said. "I don't know what's good or bad. I only know the system. I'm a lawyer. I work within the law. I know the statutes. I advise my clients on these statutes, what can be done and what can't. I am not on the bench. I argue before it but I am not on it. I am retained as an advocate. I litigate. I do the best I know how. I work hard, my opponent works hard. Usually I win. I have occasionally been bested in a divorce action. Not often. In any case, I work inside a courtroom before a jury." He looked at her with large eyes.

She said slowly, "What do you believe in?"

His smile began before he spoke. "Thorough preparation," he said softly.

McGee laughed and she smiled in spite of herself. She was restless and irritated; she felt that somehow these eastern lawyers could reach into Dement and find a way to pry the *I* loose. "It'll never happen in my family," she said.

"Oh," the lawyer said. "Never, never say 'never.'" He turned to his son. "It distresses me, you've got to talk some sense to this daughter of the prairie."

"She's got plenty of sense," McGee said.

"But if it ever happens," Dana said. "Happens in some way I can't foresee. I'll want you to represent me."

"Only handle divorces," he said lightly. He signaled for the check and leaned toward her. "Before I go. What's happening with the book?"

McGee looked away. "Let's not talk about that."

"Now, now," she said.

"I mean it," McGee said.

She ignored him and leaned toward the older man. "Fine. We'll have galleys in a month and if we do our job right it's going to be very handsome. Dust jacket's being prepared now. You're going to be very proud."

"I'm glad to hear it," he said. McGee was silent.

"And one final thing for you. Who are you supporting?"

The lawyer grinned. "Can't you guess?"

"I guess I can," Dana said.

"Trouble is, that family of his and his own record. It requires a certain leap of faith."

"Um," she said.

"And something about him puts people off, particularly in your part of the country. I hope they come around."

"I agree with that," Dana said. "He's made one big mistake. He's got to get Ike into it. That's been his problem. He's got to wrap himself around the war hero, Father Figure—"

Harold McGee looked at his son and then at her, and laughed. "I'm talking about Kennedy, Dana."

"Kennedy?"

The litigator smiled widely and drained the balloon. "My dear, you've got a lot to learn about the smart money." Then he signed the check and left them, explaining that he had to be at the office early the

next morning. When he shook hands with his son he winked. Take
her to the Plaza, he said. She'll like the Plaza. Then he kissed Dana and
ambled off, distributing money as he went: cash for the wine waiter,
cash for the maître d', cash for the hatcheck girl. They all followed
Harold McGee to the door, summoned him a cab, wished him well,
bade him a pleasant evening, all the while expressing desires to see him
again very soon.

McGee watched him go, smiling.

She said, "Sometimes he does go on."

"Well, that's Dad. Nobody like him."

She asked, "The Plaza?"

"Not on your life," he said. "*He* likes the Plaza. It's his special place,
he knows the waiters, one in particular. His special man, Mister Hopkins. I don't think we need Mister Hopkins to guide us through this
particular evening." He said, "He always took my mother to tea at the
Plaza. And *her* mother. He used to go there during Prohibition and
they'd give him setups and he'd mix his own drinks from a silver flask
he carried in his coat. It's one of my earliest memories. I must have
been about six. He's been going to the Plaza for more than forty years
and it makes him reminisce. He's very good at reminiscing, don't you
think?" McGee looked around the small candlelit room. They were
the last to leave. He said, "The White Horse."

She reached over and brushed back a lock of hair that had fallen
over his forehead. "Sure."

"It won't be crowded this late."

She said, "Let's go."

They hailed a cab and were flung back into its hard cushions as the
car shot down Fifth Avenue. Dana loved the speed and recklessness of
driving in a cab at night in New York City. On New York streets at
night, the cab windows down, she heard music in the breeze. They
sped eight, nine blocks at a time, then slid through a yellow light and
came to rest at the next red, the car bouncing on the asphalt, the avenue sloping now. She kissed him and he put his hand on the back of
her neck, pressing lightly. He murmured something, the last words

catching in his throat, and she kissed him again. She wanted never to part from him. She would float down Fifth Avenue to Greenwich Village forever with him, not watched. The cab swaying, his hand in hers, her hair touching his cheek, she looked at the nights behind apartment windows and imagined romantic lives and spontaneous laughter, laughter crashing against the windows like so many insects. She imagined them both in bed or in the shower in the morning or at the dinner table, he leaning over in the candlelight, kissing her on impulse. Their lives would be run on impulse. He shifted his arm and she kissed him again. His eyes popped open and she winked at him, waiting for his smile and smiling back: smiling for him only, her emotion thick and full. She burrowed into his chest. The cab lurched forward and they were thrown back. *Easy,* she called out, laughing. *Sorry lady,* the driver muttered.

Now they were in Greenwich Village, moving slowly through the bright, crowded streets. She thought of New York as a city of escapees. One slipped into the city's life like a suit of clothes off the rack, disappearing into the anonymous throngs. You could experiment with different voices and there were no accusers nearby who cared if you were different now, or had invented new personalities, or dreamed. They arranged themselves at the end of the long bar, wedging between two solitary drinkers. They ordered ale, which arrived in white china mugs. Standing at the end of the bar, they looked dreamily at each other through cigarette smoke. His arm was around her waist, her hand touching his elbow, both of them leaning into the worn and polished wood, making wet circles with their mugs. The room was crowded, men and women at the bar and at tables, their voices rising in intense crescendo. He took off his tie and stuffed it in his jacket pocket. She rumpled his hair affectionately and murmured into his ear, smiling delightedly. A blast of laughter from the corner was followed by loud argument near the door, the sounds in heavy counterpoint. At a table behind them three men in shirtsleeves and a woman in a mackintosh were gravely discussing Billie Holliday, her death a year ago. Dead surely of an overdose of drugs, probably morphine. Dana dipped her head, a gesture of sorrow. *O-o-o*, one of them sang, *What a little moonlight can do-o-o*. Drinkers in the immediate vicinity were silent a moment, remembering; then the talk resumed. The woman in the mackintosh began to cry, burying her face in her hands; she said the singer's name again and again, talking through her fingers. She lifted her head and looked imploringly at her companions, her face wet. *She's dead!* The men stopped singing and all three nodded in solemn agreement. The bartender and the waiters floated through all this, imperturbable as bishops, the china mugs filled, emptied, and filled again. The door swung on its hinges, admitting new arrivals: esoteric cries of greeting, arms around necks, kisses, shouted exchanges of information. The four at the table stared silently at each other; there was nothing left to say about Billie Holliday. At a table along the wall a man sat with his head in his arms, peacefully sleeping, a girl's hand on his knee. He was a well-dressed man with a soft red face, one hand in his jacket pocket as if he had reached for a cigarette before dozing off. The girl was talking to a second man, often nodding at the one asleep; their heads wagged in commiseration for the sleeping man, evidently in distress. She removed her hand from his knee long enough to light a Gauloise, then replaced it.

Dana touched McGee's arm and said she loved the White Horse Tavern, she could spend her life in it. He nodded, still tense but more comfortable now with his tie off and a relationship established with the bartender. He'd left his money on the bar and when they finished an ale he'd push their mugs forward. The bartender filled them automatically and took his payment from the stack of bills and coins. She looked over his left shoulder and began to smile: *Look at that.* In the corner a rumpled man stood, apparently intending to address the group at large. He paused, assembling his thoughts, and then began to fall. Friends on either side caught him but he was dead weight and crashed to the floor like a heavy tree, bringing smaller trees with him. Glasses and mugs fell with the table and then everyone laughed as the table was righted and the rumpled man seated again, semiconscious but grinning.

"Christ," McGee said. "It's a zoo."

She said, "I love it."

A glass crashed behind them. "It's late. Why aren't they home in bed?"

"With their 'jammies on?"

"Right." He pushed their mugs toward the bartender and leaned close to her, blocking out the noise. "Dana, we have a problem."

"Not now," she said. "Tell me about it later." It would have something to do with his father; McGee was so silent and preoccupied during dinner. He worried unreasonably about his father's health. She squeezed his arm and smiled, loving being with him in the White Horse. He looked as if he belonged, older than most of them standing at the bar. "Your dad's fine, I've never seen him in better—"

"Not about him," he said slowly.

"—form." There was embarrassment in his voice. Its tone was serious and she looked into his unsmiling eyes and saw them shift; he did not want to look at her. His face was thinner than ever and drawn, and his mouth was set.

"Look," he began. She was silent, holding her breath. Her eyes were wide and bright as stars and he had a fierce desire to take her by the arm and leave; have done with the noise. He smiled apologetically. "There's a problem with the book," he said.

Her eyes closed for a second, then opened, laughing. She'd thought—she didn't know what to think. But she'd been frightened and now she was amused. The *book*. "Don't worry, it's going to be fine."

"Well, I don't think so." He leaned closer to her, avoiding a new arrival at the bar. The noise had subsided and was now a gentle roar.

"Hey." She put her hand on his cheek. "Don't worry about it." He looked so stricken that she had to smile. "I'm watching it every step of the way and if I get stymied there's Noah and he's never stymied."

"The book's off," he said.

She let her hand drop to his shoulder. "Off?" Her voice rose. "How can it be off? It's at the printer's, we'll have galleys—"

"Not anymore," he said miserably.

"Lamb," she said. "Please. Explain."

"There are problems."

"Problems," she said. The noise receded; she was concentrating on him totally. Nothing so far made any sense to her.

"There are problems with the—material."

"So? That can be fixed. Anyway, it isn't true. There aren't any problems with the material. We've gone over the manuscript together and agreed. Two weeks ago we agreed." She smiled. "We signed in blood, remember?"

"I feel terrible about it."

"Look," she began.

"Really, more for you than for me. You've worked like a Trojan, you've worked your head off."

"Perhaps you'd better tell me what these problems are." This was all so unlike him. She had never seen him nervous in this way.

"I had a visit while you were in Dement. Two men who had read the manuscript and had objections to it." He leaned closer to her, talking into her ear; his hands moved on the bar. "Two colleagues, erstwhile colleagues, good friends. Really." He looked at her, anxious that she believe the truth of what he was about to say. "Really, excellent men. But they'd obtained a copy of the manuscript. Or, to be more precise about it, someone had—I believe they said 'furnished' them a copy."

"Lamb—"

"It doesn't matter who it was," he said quickly. "That's the least of it, and it doesn't matter. They're friends and colleagues and I respect their views." He took an envelope from his coat pocket, looking at her out of the corners of his eyes. Numbers were written on the back of the envelope. "There are specific objections to the third chapter, parts of the fourth, the last half of the fifth and the first half of the sixth, all of the ninth, and the epilogue." He put the envelope, numbers down, on the bar.

"But that *is* the book. The third, fourth, fifth—"

He nodded. "That's correct."

"These men," she began.

"—were very polite and very firm."

"And you're taking their *word*." She stopped and moved back from him, looking at him now in profile. "Lamb, it's not their book. They don't have any right to stop publication, or suggest revisions, or anything else. This is a book, yours, not a government pamphlet. The government has no interest here." She shook her head and took a long draft of ale. "They have no right—"

"They're solid people," he said stubbornly. "Doing their job. It's important to them—"

"What kind of 'solid people' try to stop a person, a *friend* according to you, from publishing his book? A book containing his own experiences. It's your life, not theirs. Your work."

Her voice had risen and he put a finger to her lips. He said, "It was not unexpected. Though they were very quick about it. I had a feeling that they'd seen the manuscript in earlier drafts and were hoping I'd change my mind and not publish. Decide that on my own, without their having to interfere."

"Who showed them the manuscript?"

He shook his head. "I don't know. Honestly."

"Someone at my office?"

"Presumably."

"It's theft."

He shrugged. "Technically—"

"I don't think they can do it," she said flatly. "It's up to the author and the publisher. Actually, it's in our hands now. It's the decision of the publisher."

He ignored that and lit a cigarette. Then he put his hands flat on the bar. "Sweetheart, let me explain something."

"You're defending them. Why are you defending them?"

"Well, yes I am. Up to a point."

"McCarthyites—"

He laughed at that. *"McCarthyites?* Oh, God no. No, really. Understand that, if you understand nothing else. These are good people, people about as far from Joe McCarthy as you could imagine. They fought McCarthy while the rest of the government was kissing his ass, and fought him with great skill. Sweeney and Caull are not yahoos—"

"Sweeney and who?"

"Never mind the names." He looked at her severely. His composure had returned now and he stood at ease at the bar. Then he said formally, "There are no more dedicated civil servants in the American government."

"All right," she said calmly. "Did these two dedicated civil servants explain why? What is wrong with the book?"

"Well," he said. "They do not hold me at fault. Or you either."

"How wonderful for us," she said.

He said, "We can skip the sarcasm." HIs voice softened then. "I'm sorry about everything. I didn't know how to tell you. I'm sorry as hell about it."

"Lamb," she said. "What is objectionable? There is nothing in the journal that can in any way be construed as a criticism of the government. You are completely dispassionate in your reporting, scrupulous—as I've said—to a fault." She watched his head wag and knew that somehow she'd missed a beat.

"It's not the government. It's not a question of politics. It's *policy.*"

"Policy," she said dully.

"Nothing is spelled out in the journal. Everything is between the lines, right? But anyone who understands the area will know that there's quite a lot of sensitive material. You understand?" He watched her nod. "I didn't think it was as obvious as it apparently is. It seemed to me to be no more than hints, more knowledgeable than material that had appeared in the press, but not really . . . *more,* uh. They convinced me that it was simply not in the national interest at this time, an election, a new administration—"

"I thought you said it had nothing to do with politics."

"Doesn't," he said confidently. "But nothing occurs in a vacuum. Eastern Europe doesn't occur in a vacuum. Events happen against a political backdrop."

"Yes," she said.

"So there we are."

"No," she said. "Not yet. You agree with them?" He nodded. "You're satisfied?" He nodded again. "Well," she said. "And I'm not to know exactly what this material is? I don't know what to say. What can I say, I'm so disappointed. I guess your father was right after all, I don't understand about the smart money. I suppose that's what it is. I love that book. Loved working with you, loved seeing it grow." She picked up her mug and set it down again. "Ah, shoot," she said.

"Look," he said softly. He knew now that it was almost over and that she had taken it well. "Look, Sweeney has already talked to Noah—"

She jerked backward as if struck. "He has done *what?*"

"Talked to Noah," McGee said. "You're out of it entirely, in the clear. It's Noah's decision."

"It is *not* Noah's decision. I am editor of that book and the decision, if any, is mine."

"Dana, I didn't mean—"

"Talked to *Noah?*" She paused and shook her head, as if coming awake from sleep. "And what did Noah say?"

"He agreed, of course."

"Agreed not to publish."

"Certainly. Noah's an experienced man. He understood the problem. Actually, he told Sweeney he didn't want to know the details. Would rather not know them. Not that Sweeney would have given him any. Noah's a stand-up guy, he was grateful to be warned. Christ, nobody wants to make a mistake like that—"

"No," she said.

"We're all Americans," he said.

She looked at him incredulously. "I want to understand this in the simplest terms. Your Sweeney went to Noah. He asked Noah not to publish because it would harm American . . . interests."

"American *security*," McGee said.

"And Noah agreed. Just like that." She snapped her fingers under his chin. "He didn't ask to see the evidence. Didn't ask questions. Didn't cross-check. Didn't probe. Just listened to Sweeney and said yes. Is that right?"

"That's essentially correct," McGree said. He was going to add that Sweeney had offered a generous settlement, to defray expenses. And Noah had turned him down, saying it wasn't necessary. Noah said he was happy to cooperate, one gentleman to another . . . But there was no reason to tell Dana, so McGree remained silent.

She said, "Incredible."

"Of course Sweeney told him that I was in full agreement. Noah knew that we knew what we were talking about. We are the authorities in this area, not him. The point is this. Sweeney has no reason to lie. No more reason than I do. What's the percentage there? It's genuine, a true bill. My God, why would I want to sabotage my own book? As for Noah, it was a fine, public-spirited decision—"

"You mean, he was happy to get rid of it."

"No," McGee lied.

"And you? Are you happy?"

"Happy and sad both. Happy to've done the right thing; sad to've lost the book. I hate losing the book because the book brought us together. That's more important than a book or any other single thing. Dana, you know I'm a professional—"

She wondered, a professional what? "Well, in that case—"

"But it's a decision that has already been made." He touched the owl on her lapel and smiled.

She turned away, feeling physically sick. Behind them the man in shirtsleeves began to sing the Billie Holliday song. He was off-key and someone hissed. Noise rose around them; loud voices mixed with the singing. Someone proposed a toast to Billie Holliday, dead in the service of her race; martyred Billie. A fat man stood on a table and began to speak but the words made no sense. She leaned toward McGee, her next words were lost in the din. ". . . love me?" He bent forward to hear. The bartender moved professionally to fill the empty mugs. Behind them the woman in the mackintosh began to cry again, little tears sliding down her cheeks. McGee said, ". . . adore you." Another toast, and more applause. The fat man quoted a line from *The White Negro*, identifying author and page. A glass smashed and the bartender looked up, angry. McGee turned and shook his head, irritated by the noise and violence. The door flew open and a party of four arrived, the men in black tie and the women in gowns. The women were clutching sequined handbags. Someone hooted and the four beat a retreat, backing out the door, one of the men already looking for a cab that would return them uptown. Dana stared into the mug of ale and began softly to cry. The man began to sing again, still off-key. Someone yelled *Shut up!* to renewed applause. Dana remembered Billie Holliday, her suicidal voice and its heartbreaking rhythm. The bartender raised his arms and shouted. The noise fell. McGee said, "Hey." She was standing half turned away from him, angry at her emotions. Now she came around and focused on his face, blurred through her tears; his hair had fallen down over his forehead and he looked stricken. But when he put out his hands she danced back from the bar.

She said, "Didn't you feel anything?"

"Yes," he said softly. "Yes, believe that."

"Did it break your heart?"

"Yes," he lied. He would have given anything if it had broken his heart, but the truth was it hadn't. He had had misgivings and the misgivings had been proven correct.

"It's broken my heart."

"Sweetheart, don't." Those close by were beginning to look at them.

"Why not?" She took a long drink of ale. "Why not?"

"It wasn't the greatest book in the world, really."

Oh, she thought, starting to cry again. Oh, that isn't the point. She said, "It was to me. How could you not've told me? How *could* you not tell me?"

"I didn't know," he said.

"But you said, 'not unexpected.' You said that you'd expected them, Sweeney and the other one."

"I tried not to think about it," he said. Then, smiling: "I fell in love with my editor. Please," he said. "Don't cry." Others were beginning to definitely notice them now, and had pulled away from their place at the bar.

"It deserved life," she said.

"Yes," he said soothingly.

"You should've told me, a hint, just a hint to let me know that something like this—"

"Yes," he said.

"You let me down," she said, "and you didn't have to."

He moved closer to her and put his arm around her shoulder. Half a dozen people were listening to them. "I didn't know it in that way," he said lamely.

"It wasn't serious to you," she said.

"Sweetheart," he began. Then he looked at the bartender and said, "Double Scotch. And another ale."

"Sweeney," she said. "Apeneck Sweeney." Then, "What was the name of the other one?"

He said, "Johnson."

"Mister Johnson," she said. "Apeneck Sweeney and Mister Johnson, the gentlemen from national security. How nice to meet you. What can we do for you today? What books can we burn? Any facts we can suppress for you? What—why are you smiling?"

He shook his head in amusement, rubbing his finger along the side of his nose. "Well, you've come closer than you know. Everyone calls Sweeney 'Neck.'" He took a long swallow of Scotch.

"And Johnson? What do they call Mister Johnson?"

"Johnny," he said.

"Is that his real name?"

McGee looked at her. "No," he said.

She was staring into the mirror at the back of the bar, looking at her reflection and his: a young woman in a raincoat, a thin man in a gray suit. Both of them good-looking; they would be admired anywhere they went. What a good-looking couple. They were no longer being overheard; the place was quiet now, and conversation muted. Then she saw a middle-aged man at the opposite end of the bar, where it curved. The face was familiar to her but she could not place it. He stood ramrod straight, a military posture, a man with a lean face and hooded eyes and tight mouth. Dana tried to picture him in a uniform of some kind. She had seen his face in a hundred newspaper photographs, but still no name came to her.

". . . go to bed," he was saying.

"What?" She looked at him apologetically. All the emotion had gone out of her.

"Let's go home," he said gently.

"All right."

He drained the glass. "What can I say? I'm afraid you're involved with a man who has a past, and not a very satisfactory past."

She had stopped crying. It was over for the moment. It was over until she could think about it alone, and then it would start again. The information had come to her too quickly. She said, "I know."

"I'll make you scrambled eggs at home."

"You will? I'd like that."

"I'll bet you don't have any eggs."

"There's an all-night deli—" She laughed suddenly and looked away. Apeneck Sweeney. What was she involved with, an advanced class in Amer. Lit.? No, it was not that. The middle-aged man was staring at her.

He said, "Eggs and some beer."

"Okey-doke."

He said, "I love you," meaning it.

She said, "Me, too."

They prepared to leave. There were only a few people remaining in the White Horse Tavern. She felt drained and heavy, and her eyes ached. She knew her eyes were red. The bartender scooped up the money and wished them a nice night. McGee nodded curtly. When they were at the door, Dana stopped to button her raincoat. She said, "Look around casually. You'll see a man at the end of the bar. I've been trying to place him but I can't. Who is he?"

McGee snorted. "I wondered if you'd notice him, and remember the face."

"Who is he?"

"That's Alger Hiss," McGee said.

Dana snapped around, facing the mirror again. Alger Hiss was chatting with the bartender. She started to giggle. Face to face with the Antichrist. How many times had his name been taken in vain over the dinner table in Dement? The symbol of Roosevelt's misrule, the triumph of the Ivy League and the Socialist rich. The East. She sighed and finished buttoning her coat and they moved out of the White Horse and into the street. McGee was silent and his face was dark. She turned back to look through the window. It was like staring at a television set with the sound off. The place seemed to vibrate but no noise was heard in the street. The bartender was fussing with the cash register and talking to a new arrival, doubtless a regular. The windows were steamed and the atmosphere inside was thick with tobacco. She leaned against McGee and he took her and held her a long moment. He tucked her head into his shoulder and they leaned against the window, cheek to cheek in the darkness. She could hear traffic on Fifth Avenue, an automobile horn and the whine of an ambulance. A man and a woman walked quickly by, giving them a wide berth. She took out a cigarette and lit it and gave it to him, and saw that he was trembling. They shared the cigarette walking down the dark street toward Fifth Avenue. She didn't see the man in the doorway, only glimpsed his arm as he reached out of the darkness to seize her shoulder. Suddenly McGee grabbed her and thrust her roughly aside and with a growl turned toward the man in the doorway. He'd hurt her when he grabbed her and she cried out, staggering to the curb. But McGee wasn't looking at her at all, he was shuffling into the doorway. She saw him hit the other one once in the stomach and once in the face. The man in the doorway tried to run but McGee had him trapped. He was small and had his hands up, trying to protect himself. McGee hit him a third time and a fourth, heavy, graceless blows. Then he began to slap him as hard as he could. The man in the doorway was doubled over now, both men were panting. McGee grunted each time he hit him. McGee wouldn't stop. She could see blood on the other one's face. He tried to get out of the doorway but McGee blocked him. She hadn't said anything but stood on the curb in horror and astonishment. Then she rushed to McGee and put her hands on his back, pulling at his gray suit. *No,* she said; *no.* The other one was on his knees now, defenseless; he flailed at McGee once or twice but the blows didn't land. McGee was crouched now, hitting him at will. He turned around then, facing her, his hands up. His eyes were blazing and for a moment she thought he would hit her. Then, as quickly, his hands were down and she was in his arms. *No,* she said again, and began to pull him away. They looked back at the man in the doorway, conscious and beginning to rise. McGee turned toward him, but she pulled his arm. *No,* she said. *It's enough.* He stood there a moment, bewildered. Across the street half a dozen people watched silently. *Come on,* she said. And they began to run up the street, turning left there. They ran down the alley and onto another narrow street. They ran for five minutes until they came out on Fifth Avenue, out of breath and sweating. They paused in front of a store window and he looked at himself in the glass, buttoning his coat and straightening his tie, and brushing his hair back. ". . . incredibly stupid," he muttered. She was silent, watching him in the glass. Finally he turned toward her. "Are you all right?"

"I'm all right," she said.

He smiled at her. "I'm sorry." Then, "I can't imagine what was in my mind, where I thought I was—"

She whispered, "What?"

He appeared not to hear her. His head was bent forward, staring at the sparkling sidewalk. He shook his head again. "Impossible."

She pressed his arm. "What?"

"I saw that guy—" He shrugged. "I boxed in college," he said apologetically. "All that talk in the White Horse. Explanations, excuses. I hated doing that to you." He shrugged helplessly. "Let's forget it." So they began to walk up Fifth Avenue, bound for her apartment. They walked slowly, in step, touching shoulders. She hooked her arm through his and they moved loosely through the midnight crowds of the upper Village, then out of the lights and the people until they were alone again on the broad avenue.

"The whole business," he said without preamble. "I'm an adult, not unfamiliar with the government. I can't imagine what was in my mind, why I didn't submit it through the ordinary channels. There are procedures for that, always have been."

"Will you tell me," she said softly. "What you did over there."

He said, "I did double duty. Don't ask."

"You wore a cloak and carried a dagger."

"Sometimes I wore a cloak."

"Yes," she said.

"And sometimes I didn't."

"I like thinking of you in a cloak," she said. She thought she would try to pry it out of him. He'd refused to talk about it before and this was the first flat answer she'd had. The truth was, she had no idea what he'd done. He had a double life and one part of it was concealed. He'd done double duty in the cold war. It did seem to her the slightest bit—tempting, just that. She knew no details, though she had guessed at a few, not knowing if she was right or wrong.

"The truth is." His voice and manner were serious now; he was the familiar McGee. "It seemed to me quite mild, what I wrote. When I apologized to them and told them that, they agreed with me. It was quite mild and unexceptional, unless you knew the full picture. Then it wasn't mild at all, it was dynamite. I didn't know the full picture. Still don't. They understand that, there are no hard feelings." He paused, thinking. In darkness now, surrounded by small gray buildings with signs in Hebrew and Slavic, he took her hand and squeezed it, reminded suddenly of evenings in Belgrade. There was a particular café overlooking the Sava, with a Turkish ruin nearby. He and Caull sometimes met there for a beer in the evenings. He usually had an escort and so did Caull, and of course both of them were normally followed by someone, Yugoslav or Soviet or German. He and Caull always took a table near the sidewalk and in ten minutes half a dozen men were in the café, all of them reading newspapers or having their shoes shined or otherwise appearing conspicuously inconspicuous. He and Caull didn't talk much, except to notice a girl from time to time. At that time, the end of his tour, he was fearfully depressed and drinking too much and there didn't seem to be anything of value to say, to Caull or to anyone else.

She said, "It must have been. All of it. Very difficult."

He smiled. "Sorry, nothing very spooky. I was a rather high-level courier, nothing much more than that. A mailman." He lowered his voice and shortened his stride to match hers. "I'll tell you something." His voice was so low she could barely hear it. "I spent three years on and off in the bloc. I'd never met people like that before. I mean the people I was working with. We're isolated in America, we don't understand what's happening elsewhere. The rest of the world is a mystery to us, and I suppose it's just as well; we don't solve mysteries very well. We are not, as a people, deft." He said, "That's why I wrote what I did, to lift the curtain a little and let light in. Do you know how Trotsky described Europe? 'A system of cages in a provincial zoo.' Our assets in Europe . . ." He paused to smile. "Sorry, that's jargon. I mean the people I dealt with. I didn't know there existed men and women with that order of—courage. Intelligence and sensitivity and raw passion. A *passion* for freedom, the things others have without thinking about them; freedom to love. They were patriots and spent their lives underground, as patriots have to do . . ." He shook his head, walking faster now; it was difficult for Dana to keep up. "All of it by inches.

They didn't want utopia, knowing in a fatalistic way that there wasn't any; they just wanted to loosen the chains. They saw themselves living in a cage within a cage and they were right. So they fought like hell, struggled, risked everything—wives, families, husbands, children—themselves. Many of them died. *Died*. They wanted it so much they'd die for it. And we helped them die. Dana, you have to *see* them, their faces. Touch them. You need to talk to them personally, or watch them die yourself." He knew then that he had gone too far and fell silent. Then, "I would do nothing to jeopardize those people. They live in permanent jeopardy anyway. That's why Sweeney just had to nudge me a little. He and the . . . other one had only to say, 'Don't do it.' They knew that was all they had to do. God damn us."

She nodded. "I understand."

"Please," he said, tears in his eyes.

He was close to her; she could feel his hot whiskey breath. "I don't know anything about it," she said.

He put his arm around her shoulder. "Dana." Then, after a moment: "It isn't the Europe you read about in the brochures."

"Darling McGee." They halted in a doorway and kissed in the shadows for a long moment. She pressed against him, her hands on his chest, kissing his neck, his cheeks, his eyes. His eyes were wet and his face grim.

"Home," she whispered.

"Gets to me sometimes."

She said, "I'm glad you told me."

"I hate it." He stood with his hands plunged into his coat pockets, desolate now. "It's so damned sad."

"I know," she said.

"We let them down. That's what we did. We put them up there on tiptoe." His voice was metallic, his body rigid. "We put them up there on tiptoe and then we didn't kiss them. We kicked them in the balls instead."

She traced a line down his cheek. "Oh, McGee. It's over now."

He nodded. "Indeed."

"Let's go," she said gently.

"Do you suppose it's true? That the death of one god is the death of all?"

She shook her head. "No."

"Christ," he said thickly. "Those years. It was all so crazy."

"McGee," she said, her forehead against his chest. He stood like a statue, arms at his sides, his eyes faraway. They stood in a dark doorway, as close as they had ever been or ever would be. He had opened to her suddenly and fully, a door swinging on a hinge, and she had passed through. She felt she was fully inside him now. She took him by the arm and they walked into the middle of Fifth Avenue to call a cab. She leaned against him, caressing his stomach; she had never loved him so much. He smiled suddenly and kissed her on the forehead, his lips just brushing her skin. She began to hum, pulling her skirt above her knees, her feet tapping on the asphalt. They were in semidarkness though lights were all around them. The street was empty and skyscrapers towered above them, soaring into the Manhattan night. He flung his arms wide and she came to him, hanging on his neck with all the strength she had.

Oh, she said, *I love you.* She began to whisper to him but she couldn't get the words out. He laughed and swung her around, her skirt flaring. She said, Home now? Right now, he said. Presently a Yellow slid up to them. A weary moonfaced man looked at them holding hands in the middle of Fifth Avenue and grinning. But they behaved correctly climbing into the rear seat. They were correct leaving the cab and correct in the elevator ascending to her apartment. She gave him the key to open her door and noticed then the condition of his hands, raw and torn along the knuckles. There was blood on his shirt. She kissed each knuckle in turn, standing in front of her open door. She would get warm water, iodine, some bandages. But he picked her up instead and carried her into the room. He said to her, We're never going to talk about that again. Not ever. She said without thinking, All right. But first the warm water and iodine . . .

It's nothing, he said.

Autumn, 1973

THEY MAINTAINED HIM in a cocoon of comforters and placed him by the window, so he could see the big tree and the cornfield. It was a mistake, and instantly recognized as a mistake. The cornfield had been with him nearly all his life and looking at it now his memory was provoked. The future was—limited. So he concentrated now on the past, staring at the oak and the cornfield with bad eyes. The colors and the lines merged and blurred and what he saw resembled a painting; the kind of painting that he had always hated. He saw daubs of color that merged at the horizon, all of it split by the large tree. But one used what one had. That was what he had so he used it, and when McMann and young Bohn came to him with the proposal to buy the cornfield of course he said no. He said no at the end rather than at the beginning because he wanted to hear the details. He'd kept them tied up for a month, looking forward to the meetings; it was something to do, a transaction to occupy his time. They wanted the cornfield for a block of apartments and they had to explain to him about a condominium, what it was and how it worked. "An entirely new concept," they said, and he had grasped it right away. It wasn't new at all but it was clever and in the end he had said no. McMann and young Bohn were exasperated. He caught the look that passed between them; it was a look that said, Senile Old Fart. They looked at him closely and he knew they were measuring his life span. How long would he last? How long could they afford to wait? At last McMann suggested that he give them an option and set a purchase price, closing to take place after—"in case anything happens to you." Townsend said, "You mean, when I kick the bucket." McMann said, "That's it, Mr. Townsend. In the meantime, you've use of the option money." He'd croaked, "Go to hell." And the three of them had laughed.

But it wouldn't've made any difference if they'd placed him in a different chair. If he'd been looking front, to the street, it would have been that—that street, those houses, trees between them—provoking his memory. He possessed ninety-five years of history now, *owned* it as one owns a security or a dwelling. The mortgage was paid up, though many of the rooms of this dwelling were dark. He found his mind worked only in bursts. There were times, he thought, when he was no better than a vegetable, a desiccated potato, wrinkled and juiceless. He shifted his eyes then, to the bookcase—he supposed he'd read five thousand books in his life, over and above the law books—and the burgonet. This was the three-combed burgonet, said to be Florentine, crafted in the middle of the sixteenth century. A fine century, the sixteenth; there was much to be said for the autonomy of cities, Venice, Genoa. In the sixteenth century there was adventure and stability, though the world was shifting west; west and north. The movement was always west, whether in the old world or the new. Men followed the sun. The burgonet was doubtless a fake; the Field Museum was unable to authenticate it. But he liked looking at it, this piece of armor, protection for the skull but graceful too. There was a panache at its base . . .

He was always tired now. He could feel the spirit draining from him, each day more difficult than the last. "Difficult"—he meant complicated. He could not concentrate on more than one thing at a time. He could feel himself withdraw, as if his brain and soul were contracting; he felt there was distance now between his center and the surface of his skin. It took time for his thoughts to compose themselves and find voice. They seemed to do that on their own motion; there was no way for him to force it. He measured the distance between his brain and his lips in miles. And what he thought and what he said were often different. A sentence would begin with one thought and end with another, somehow acquiring a life of its own as it made its way from the interior of his soul outward to the world. The late afternoon was best, the time of least resistance. He was not apprehensive then and could think and talk with relative speed and security. A glass of Scotch helped; he could feel it in his stomach, radiating upward and outward. In the afternoons he thought about women. He had always been a man of conservative habits; his memory was not a seraglio. He believed in some region of his mind that women were superior of soul, their emotions deeper and more profound. They were capable of inspiration. They gave life! He and Amos, they had never mistreated women. Of course all women were not identical. His own mother was an angel, bless her. One was never entirely secure with women; often they departed without warning. It was not always deliberate. His own mother was merely walking off to town, before the storm. Charles's Dana had not intended to leave the family for good; it was something that had happened at random. It was necessary sometimes to hold them close or they would fly away somewhere. It was necessary to be very good to them. His memory picked away, meandering back a half century and more. There had been a widow in Dement, that was shortly after the Great War. He laughed suddenly. And the suffragette who'd come to him for legal advice and stayed the night. A political woman, he'd forgotten her name . . . Then it came, a source of continual embarrassment. His mind began to spin. His sexual urges were uncontrollable, though his penis never moved. Imagining the most outrageous couplings, working back into his memory and improving on it; but nothing moved. Hot behind the eyes he would wait for Mrs. Haines to leave and then he would give himself over to his thoughts. It was absolutely mandatory that Mrs. Haines leave. He thought her ugly as sin. She reminded him of an awful portrait by that Spaniard Communist: two noses, a hole in her head, almond eyes. His emotion became so strong sometimes he thought he could not stand it. But then it crested and receded like any tide, leaving him weak and morose; he felt himself pitiable. God, he hated being old.

In the late afternoon he was less self-conscious, less aware of his reedy legs and his slow voice and the skin that gathered around his cheeks and neck like a cowl. He was fine when he forgot about his appearance and concentrated on his thoughts, and occasionally he could tell that his visitor was amazed at his lucidity, and could imagine what would be said about him later—"Old Elliott, clear as a bell yesterday afternoon . . ." When he forgot about the small pains, the pains so persistent and ubiquitous that he could not determine their source, they were no longer there. He could become interested in something else and not feel the pains, but it only happened for short distances; when something truly interested him he could turn away from himself and his infirmities. Oh Lord, he thought, what a horror it is to be old and sick with only one emotion ahead of him. Just one experience remaining. His only possession was his memory, which he guarded now like a treasure. In the afternoons, sitting in the armchair, listening to Mrs. Haines puttering in the kitchen, he would stare into the cornfield and think about a specific. Then he would try to recall everything about it. At the end his thoughts would become vague and discontinuous, and he'd move a generation in a split second, realizing that he was misremembering; names and faces would blur. He'd try to summon them back but realize that he'd tired himself. His brain would become tired exactly as his body had long ago exhausted itself. He supposed that he had very few virile blood cells remaining. There were only enough for an hour of thought, and everything then lost its color and shape and lapsed into an amorphous gray, disconnected words and images: the paintings he despised. Then he would nap and waken long enough for a light supper, something nutritious. Mrs. Haines was both practical nurse and nutritionist. How wonderful it was to dine on food that was nutritious, vitamins balanced as carefully as the accounts of a corporation. Then Mrs. Haines would wheel him into the parlor, which was now his bedroom. She would undress him and put him to bed. Before sleep came he could hear the television set in the next room, muffled voices and laughter and bursts of music. Mrs. Haines never made a sound herself. She sat silently in front of the television, giving it her undivided attention. If he had a last wish on earth it would be to take a baseball bat to the television screen. He laughed, though no sound came from his lips; well, that was one wish, though

not the final wish. He would save the final wish for himself, a positive
thought for the night. He fell asleep dreaming about a young girl with
yellow hair and slender legs, a girl he had seen once on a stage in a theater on the west side of the city of Chicago.

Mrs. Haines handed him his whiskey and he thanked her. She asked
him if there was anything else she could get for him and he shook his
head, as he always did. No, nothing else. Then he turned and said that
he would like some cheese and crackers. He would like some small
snack with his drink. She smiled her nurse's smile and remarked that
we were certainly feeling better, weren't we, and that was one sure
sign, a healthy appetite. A blunt retort came to the edge of his lips but
he forced it back. He merely smiled and said, Yes, he was feeling fine
today and would feel even better if he could have some cheese and
crackers—

"To munch," she said. "You want a munchie with your cocktail?"

He smiled politely. If he shot her between the eyes would they
prosecute him, an old man of ninety-five? The insanity plea would
surely prevail and they would never jail a sick man. He could outlast
them, take the case to SCOTUS and by the time it reached the docket
in Washington he would be dead anyway—

"I can make a cheese dip," she said.

"I believe," he said, "there is a small wedge of Camembert cheese
in the icebox and some saltines somewhere."

"Well, I'll look," she said doubtfully.

"You can leave the bottle here," he replied. She looked at him
strangely. "Not for me, Mrs. Haines. As you know, a single *drink* is my
limit. It's for Charles Rising, who is coming by in fifteen minutes and I
would not like him to starve to death or die of thirst while he is my
guest—"

When she went into the kitchen he poured another finger of
Scotch into his glass. It was true, he felt good, better than he had in
some time. He could not remember when he felt entirely fit; could
not remember how that *felt*. So it was enough to allow that it was the
best he'd felt that week. He'd told Charles to come at fifteen minutes

after five; he thought then he would be at his best. He wanted to be entirely alert and responsive because Charles wanted to talk business, and over the telephone he'd sounded subdued.

There were one or two things he had to say to Charles, and now he tried to work the phrases around in his mind. Charles had a low boiling point sometimes and did not take criticism well. But this was important and he felt he had the right to intervene. His fortunes and the fortunes of the Risings had been entwined for more than sixty years; when he spoke to Charles it was like speaking to his own son. No one had more right than he to speak when he saw mischief. It was Marge Reilly who drew his attention to the facts when she came to visit on Monday. He'd missed it himself; it must have been one of the days when he skimmed the *I* rather than read it. He had to admit that he no longer followed politics with enthusiasm. Most of the men involved were little more than names to him. In the last ten years there had been a revolution in the party, the older men finally dying or retiring to Florida. The county chairman was young enough to be his grandson. None of the new names—*none* of them—was familiar to him. The new generation had arrived at last, and he did not know who they were or what they stood for.

Marge had begun carefully. "Isn't it a mess?" He replied that it certainly was, how did it look to her? She said, "They'll hound him from office." Then she smiled. "Better sooner than later." He'd nodded vigorously in agreement, though something in Marge's voice caused him to listen carefully. She said, "And locally there's trouble." He'd given her his full attention then and urged her to tell him what was happening. "What's wrong?" he asked, and it was then that he noticed she was truly upset, unable to look him in the eye. She'd waited several moments before replying, and then it all came out.

It was the paper. There was a rumor, and it was nowhere denied, that the *Intelligencer* intended to back Herm Stone for sheriff. And it intended to remain neutral in the state's attorney's race and that would be enough, in a bad year (which the year 1974 was bound to be), to elect the Democrat. She said, "Every time you pick up the paper there's Stone's picture and a story to go with it. The paper looks like a Democratic paper, a paper supporting the Democratic party. No one can understand it. At the courthouse—" She explained that Charles was apparently not attending to business. He'd been very active in promoting the new industrial park and was not watching what they were putting in the paper. "That editor's a Democrat, we managed to find that much out." There was no consultation anymore; she did not feel free to call on Charles. She hadn't seen him in a year and meantime the paper had become more remote than ever. The trouble, of course, was that the Republican had problems. Even if the paper were neutral there'd be trouble . . . He'd looked at her, hating to ask the question; but she understood the look. "It's Callahan. Callahan's the Republican, you might remember the father." He shook his head firmly; he knew no Callahans, had never known a Callahan. "The father had bottle trouble. So does the son."

"How bad?"

"Bad enough," she said. "But Elliott, he's a pretty good sheriff, considering. You know, when he inherited it from Tommy Haight it wasn't exactly—" She paused, then continued. "And he's had some tough family trouble. There was a problem with his father's estate and his wife's been sick. He's been trying to bring up his boys and he hasn't been a great success at it, and he knows it." Marge Reilly looked down at her hands and smiled. Townsend nodded, thinking that nothing changed very much; bottle trouble, family trouble. She said gently, "You do remember Red's father, a big hearty guy."

"He ran a handbook." Yes, he had known him; not well. He could not place him if he walked into the room.

"Well, Red's his son and a *good* man. Just like his father." She smiled dryly. "But he's not J. Edgar Hoover in the law-enforcement department, no doubt about that. But darn it, this is *Dement*, it isn't as if we need Mr. Hoover—"

"I know him now," Townsend said. "The son. I remember old

Callahan took him to the cornroast, the last one that Amos and I gave. That's twenty years ago. He wanted to introduce him around, and did. Wanted him to go into the game, politics."

"Yes," she said. "And everyone liked him, Red." She hesitated, frowning. "But the paper, I don't understand it and none of us understand it. I know it's because Charles isn't paying any attention to the business, and with Mitch gone there's no one member of the family who *cares,* and will pay attention to what's going on. A few of us wanted to get together with Charles last week and he said he couldn't see us until after the holidays and, my goodness, the primary's only ninety days after that—" She sighed. "I'm sure that it's just that he doesn't *see* it, you know, *understand.* Elliott, for the first time *ever* we might have a Democratic sheriff. It just doesn't make any sense."

He said, "You want me to talk to him then."

"Yes, sir," she said crisply. Then she said, "I want you to do what you think would be best. Be right. You know him better than anybody. What do you think?" Townsend could feel himself weakening, the tiredness working its way up his body; he hated it. She said, "It might help, but I don't want you to do anything that's awkward for you." She looked at him, as if trying to calculate in her own mind how much she could say. "A few of the boys have wanted me to come before now. But I've put them off. I thought we could work it out ourselves. Well, we can't and time's flying and I've come to you for help. It's not the first time and it won't be the last."

He smiled thickly, momentarily overcome with emotion. He said, "It's not awkward, Marge. And I think after I talk with him, you should talk with him too. You've got a personal relationship, have had for years. He's reasonable, and my God the last thing he wants is to see anything alien in Dement. He doesn't want to see that." He could feel the fatigue move up his legs. "What's Stone like?"

"Well, he's not anything. Not anything at all. He's very young, wasn't born here, hasn't lived here but five years. He's just someone they've got to file, to fill out their slate, and he figures if he makes a name for himself it'll help his law practice. That's all. See, that's what they're basing his campaign on. He's a lawyer, as if that had anything to do with being a competent sheriff. He doesn't *know* Dement, my God can you imagine what that gang would do if they had the sheriff's department. And of course with Red and his troubles—"

"Is Eurich in this anywhere?"

She looked away. "No, Elliott."

"That's odd, a matter of this kind . . ." He felt himself slipping away for good now.

"Well, Elliott . . ." Did she want to say anything? Bill Eurich had not been much in Dement for three years. He'd moved on to a town farther west; had taken his profits and his connections and was now busy in another small midwestern town, and in the states of Arizona and Florida. His offices remained in numerous midwestern cities. He'd retained his interest in one or two investments in Dement, and of course his memberships on the boards of directors of the bank and the newspaper, but was seldom seen. He'd moved on—like a summer drought, she thought, leaving the land dead and dry, and a dozen very rich men in control of it. He'd promised to make money for his partners and had kept the promise. She couldn't remember exactly where he was now; it was a small, promising town, a more remote Dement near the state line. But he was no longer concerned with Dement politics. She said gently, "Yes, it is odd."

"He's usually very much involved."

"Yes, one way or another." She said, "Well, Elliott. I'm sorry. I've stayed too long." He looked wretched now, his long face thin and drawn and white as paper.

He held up his hand. "I'll call Charles . . . tomorrow."

"Only if you want to."

He smiled. "Want to." He closed his eyes, and when he next spoke the words were badly slurred. "When we fish visting . . . I'll call you."

He was almost asleep and did not hear her reply. But he felt her dry lips on his cheek and the pressure of her hand on his. His mind was still alert but he could not control the fatigue, and was asleep before she left the room.

In the event, he did not have to call Charles Rising. Charles called him. He had been too long a lawyer to let on that he knew the subject at hand. Charles merely reported that he had something of importance to discuss. Townsend said he would be delighted to have a drink with Charles the next day.

The younger man was late, and the old lawyer was sipping his drink and conserving energy. He had taken a bit of cheese and found it hard and cold, refrigerated too long. He tried to relax as thoroughly as he could, sipping whiskey slowly. But he was nicely excited, back in the game now, advising Risings; his special mission. He believed he was not meant to sit idly by on the sidelines; he'd been close to the center too long. He believed himself the last formal link to the past, though half of him was below ground; but still, his memory connected to the frontier. His origins wound back to the town's earliest beginnings. He'd been rehearsing a little speech, much as he used to rehearse summations to the jury, though he had not been in a courtroom for ten years. His counsel was most effective behind the scenes, always had been . . .

"Elliott."

He opened his eyes to see Charles striding toward him, limping slightly. He had not seen him in a month and he looked tired, his face heavy and blurred. "Charlie," he said warmly, extending his left hand. The younger man pulled up a chair and eased himself into it slowly. Mrs. Haines came to the door and smiled benignly. Charles turned and they exchanged greetings. Then she went away.

Charles helped himself to a drink, heavy on the ice, heavy on the Scotch. He sipped it, satisfied, and looked at the old man. "You're looking good."

"Feel good. Feel better than I have in some time."

Charles glanced at the door. "Is she giving you any trouble?"

"Nothing I can't handle," Townsend said.

Charles laughed. "Seriously—"

"Nothing I want that I don't have," Townsend said. "Except maybe ten more years."

"You'll have them. You're too damn tough and mean—"

Townsend snorted. "Well, my head's clear anyway."

"More than I can say," Charles said. "Well, what do you know?"

"Not a hell of a lot," Townsend said. They had opened conversations in that way for thirty years.

"What's happening politically?" The next question, inevitably. Townsend looked at him. That was the opening, all right, except something was missing in Charles's tone. He said, "I understand there are troubles with Callahan's boy."

Charles Rising sipped and nodded. "I heard something about it the other day. Some of the boys in the courthouse are worried, they think the Democrat—what's his name?" Townsend said, Stone. "Stone. They think that Stone may beat him. I don't believe it myself. Hell, Red Callahan's unbeatable in this county. Related to half of it."

"My information is that Red hasn't been a model of deportment." Charles smiled. "Since when have we had a sheriff who was?"

"Stone's a lawyer."

"As bad as that?"

"Maybe worse."

"I'm kidding," Charles said. "I suppose. I suppose you've heard that the *I* isn't doing all it should. That we're giving a free ride to the Democrats."

"I have heard something along that line."

"Christ," Charles said. He shook his head in a gesture of contempt. For a moment Charles Rising was the shadow of his father; the old lawyer had to blink to clear the memory. "You know what that is, Elliott? They want me to do their work for them. They think it's the *I*'s mission to keep them in office. Jesus! They are a collection of the laziest, most bone-idle—" The shadow passed and he was Charles again.

"It was Marge who came to see me."

"Well, Marge is all right."

"More than all right, Charles. She's the greatest friend your family ever had."

"I like Marge."

"Well, it's Marge that's worried."

"What does she want?" he asked slowly.

There was a weariness and caution in Charles's tone that disappointed Townsend. He had never used that tone in speaking of Marge Reilly; Marge was one of those who went way back. Townsend looked away, out the window, trying to compose his thoughts. "They're worried and they've got reason to be worried. They think you're tilting to the other side. They think this is . . . not deliberate. They think you've been so busy with other things that you haven't noticed what that new editor and the others are doing with the newspaper." As dispassionately as he could, Townsend sketched in the facts about Red Callahan. His father and his wife's illness, the difficulties with the children, and of course the other thing . . . As he talked he watched the afternoon sun fall behind the cornfield, the field now a brilliant yellow. Twenty years now since the last cornroast, and suddenly the backyard was alive with old friends. Amos, Tilberg, Steppe, Marge Reilly, all the others, the corn dripping with butter, beer sloshing over the lips of paper cups, loud talk, laughter, he and Amos moving from group to group, a handshake, a reassuring arm around the shoulder. The autumn colors faded and became blurred; the leaves stirred in the autumn air. He talked on, his voice solemn, describing things as they had been. He was speaking now of tradition. But Charles wasn't listening; his eyes were glazed and turned inward. He looked as if he were alone in the room, leaning forward, both hands cupped around the glass. The old lawyer stopped talking, simply ceased at the end of his sentence, and returned immediately to the present moment. There was complete silence and then other sounds came into focus, Mrs. Haines moving around in the kitchen, the clink of a plate, the heavy ticking of the old clock on the mantle.

Charles nodded and rubbed the edge of his highball glass up and down his cheek. His mouth was shaped in a peculiar half-smile. "Well," he said. Townsend did not reply and suddenly he felt afraid, he wished then that he could terminate the interview, send Charles away with a pat on the back and fresh instructions and a promise to meet again next week. He had seen distress too often at a distance in the courtroom not to recognize it when it was three feet away in his own parlor. "Well, well," Charles said again. He had heard every word the lawyer had said and none of it was of any interest to him.

"I guess you've got something else on your mind," Townsend said. He felt foolish, misunderstanding the situation. He did not often do that.

"I guess I have," Charles said.

"And it doesn't have anything to do with politics."

"No, not too much."

"Make me a drink and tell me about it."

Charles Rising took the glass and slowly dumped two cubes of ice in it, neglecting the tongs, and absentmindedly filled it to the brim with whiskey. Then he saw what he'd done and poured part of the liquor back into his own glass. His right hand trembled slightly and he moved to shield his hands from the man in the chair. "We've got to talk about the *I* now," he said. The old lawyer looked at him, puzzled; that was what he *had* been talking about, the *I*, its character and responsibility, and obligations to the community. "We've got to begin the process of succession." He looked at Townsend and added, "Who follows me." Townsend peered more closely at the younger man; it was plain he was holding on with difficulty. He felt a stab of irritation, then brushed it aside. Charles walked to the window and looked out. Dusk was falling quickly. "This time we've got to act."

"It's necessary to do this now," Townsend said. It was half statement, half question. They'd talked about "the succession" for almost twenty years, never to any satisfactory result. They'd talked about it in 1965, the year Mitch died, and again three years later when Lee had a stroke. No solution had presented itself and the meetings always ended in frustration. But Townsend was feeling his way now.

"Yes," Charles said. He coughed and looked away. "I took Lee to the hospital yesterday. Another stroke, a bad one." His eyes began to tear and with his free hand he wiped them dry. "There isn't anything they can do."

"My boy," he said. "I'm so sorry."

"This thing has washed me out."

"Charles." He reached for Charles's hand, caught it, and held on. He could feel Charles's hand shake. His whole body seemed to be trembling. He felt the core of Charles's body move uncontrollably. He looked at the son and saw the father. The set of the shoulders and the nose were identical. He was watching Amos fifty years ago. But now the face was worn and there already seemed an ominous pallor to it. He gave the younger man's hand another squeeze.

"But I'm not here to talk about that," Charles said. "I'm not in a mood to talk medical details, hers or mine either." Townsend nodded sympathetically, but a single phrase repeated itself in his mind. *He's only sixty-three, the youngest son of my oldest friend.* At sixty-three Amos Rising had been at the pinnacle of his life. Charles looked up suddenly and smiled. "Actually, I told them to spare me the details. What's the good of knowing them if you can't fix them?" He sighed and took a long swallow of his drink. He was still looking out the window. "Funny, I've felt it for some time. Lee didn't actually change but I could sense—" He paused. "Something."

"Charles—"

"We don't seem to be a long-lived family," he said. "Maybe Dad used up all the longevity genes. Didn't pass any on to Mitch or me. Frank, now Lee. Me soon, for sure. Maybe Tony got some, but then Tony's been retired since 1935." He laughed quietly and put his drink on the coffee table. "Even this stuff doesn't taste as good as it used to."

"You're young—"

He smiled at the old man. "From *your* mountaintop, sure. Not from mine. No, I can feel it." The old man began to sputter. "Truly, Elliott. I can feel it. I'm *tired*. I feel I've got one last thing to do, and that's to provide for the *I*. I've done my best for Lee and the—others. That's what I'm here for." Then he added, barely audibly, "And that's what I've always been here for."

"Charles," Townsend said. "Charles, men pick up and go on. Life goes on—"

He lifted his chin slightly. "Why?"

Why? Elliott Townsend had clung to life for so long, had fought for it as he had fought for everything he had, that he did not understand the question and had no answer to it. He thought, Because that is what you do. You fight like hell because if you don't it'll be taken away from you. Anything can be taken away if you don't fight. But looking at the younger man he, too, knew that something was wrong. He knew that Charles spoke the truth. He said lamely, "For yourself, your family—"

"Well, there aren't many left, are there?"

Townsend did not want to get into that; they would get nowhere pawing over the past. He began, "You—"

Charles said, "I feel it. I'm drained, washed out by everything. I can feel it in my system, there's an imbalance of some kind. It's as if some part of my body has been starved and is dying. I don't have the re-sources anymore. My account's dry." He picked up his glass and jig-gled the ice in it. "I don't have the *will*. There's something wrong that oughtn't to be wrong and I don't have the stuff to fight it. I fell asleep sitting in Lee's room at the hospital last night. I couldn't fight sleep. I've given part of what I have to her and the rest goes to the *I*. And there won't be anything left over."

In the silence that followed, Townsend felt confounded. But when he looked at Charles he knew that at least part of what he said was true. But if he felt that his family had slipped away from him, there was still the *I* to be served. The *I* existed now as always, as much a part of the Rising family as any living member. "The *I* has been your life," he said.

"Exactly, Elliott." Charles's voice held a note of triumph. "Exactly right. That's what we must put our minds to now. We cannot leave it in limbo. We are going to set it up in such a way that it'll survive for-ever, and I'll tell you now that it's not going to be easy. But we'll work at it all this week if we have to because we've got to establish the line of succession. You're the only one I can talk to about it. I want us to have our minds made up and then we'll go to Marge and ratify what we've decided, as per"—he smiled—"that codicil that has worked so well for so many years. So it's just you and me. Trying to figure out how to save the newspaper. That's the important thing, isn't it?"

"It is. Definitely."

"And we both know that there's only one way to go."

"Wrong approach," the old man said. "There's never just one way. There's always a better way, but never just one way. We'll find there are several ways. Two come to mind immediately. Either you transfer to Tony or you transfer to Dana. Transfer to Tony and it means transferring to Jake. Transfer to Dana and it means—you'll have to tell me what that means." The speech took something out of him and the old man pushed back into his chair. He had not seen Dana in two years. He knew there was a strain between her and her father but did not know the details. He knew that Charles had tried to persuade Dana to return permanently to Dement when Lee had her first stroke and that Dana refused. She stayed six weeks, and then returned to wherever she was living. Townsend had forgotten where.

Charles took the chair directly across from Townsend. "Dana isn't like the rest of us. And she has her own life. Which of course she is entitled to. And she wouldn't know what to do with the *I* if she had it, which she won't." His voice was harsh and he looked away, then back at Townsend. "Tony isn't suitable either, for all the reasons we know so well. Hell, he isn't here half the time. And Jake isn't either. Is he?"

Townsend shook his head sadly. A great disappointment. He had tried to guide the boy, giving him the benefit of more than fifty years at the practice of law. There were just the two of them and he had been generous in the distribution of profits, more than generous . . . But the partnership had not worked and after five years Jake had left. He had his own practice now and was doing extremely well, active in the Bar Association. But he was on the other side of the fence politically, and in other ways.

"As I said," Charles said, "one way to go."

It seemed to Townsend that they were stymied now as they had been stymied for twenty years, though in the beginning Jake was a likely candidate. He said nothing, waiting for Charles to speak.

"We sell the *I*."

"Sell the *I*?" Townsend was horrified. "The *I* can't be *sold*. It's not for sale, it's never been for sale. It's intolerable." His voice trailed away into a rumble. "I won't have it," he said. "It can't be sold."

"Of course it can," Charles said harshly. "It's a piece of property, like any other. A house or a car or a block of stock, or any other thing."

"No," Townsend said.

"All right," Charles said, more softly now. "Of course it's something more. It's a good deal more than a piece of property. But we can't blind ourselves, either." He leaned over and touched the old man on the knee. "We don't have any other way to go. There isn't any other solution."

"Dana—"

"—is a young girl. Who does not live here. She has chosen her own life. And if she hadn't." Charles paused; it was a possibility he considered often, to no satisfactory conclusion. "It wouldn't make any difference, not really. The only thing to commend Dana is that she's a Rising. Supposedly. She has the name, anyway. Or did."

"It means a *lot*," Townsend said.

"Used to," Charles said.

The old lawyer looked at him. Used to? What did he mean, "used to"? It always had, always would. It was inconceivable to him that Charles Rising could even consider selling the *I*. He could not imagine Dement controlled by outsiders, its history written by others. Dement was not a colony, it stood on its own; its principles were its own. For eighty years the Risings had been synonymous with the town. He said, "I could not be a party to a sale. It would break my heart. I tell you that honestly."

Charles nodded, thinking. A truly lovely old man. He'd known him since the first year of his life; loyal as a parent and strong as pig iron.

He said patiently, "Elliott, we can't afford sentiment. It interferes with the hard thinking we've got to do. I understand what you say and I agree with it. And I would act on it if it were possible to do so. But it isn't. And the important thing is that the paper . . . survive. Survive as we have known it. We have put too much into it for too long to see it . . . pissed away. Which it will do if the management is not competent." The younger man turned away briefly, gathering his thoughts. "I'd rather see the *I* go to an outsider and survive than to see it stay in the family and . . . piss away through inattention or damn foolishness."

Townsend said, "Give me a minute to think." The old lawyer had never thought of the newspaper as a thing apart from the family that owned it. It was theirs, as much a part of them as their physical characteristics. If it were owned by others it would cease to be the *Intelligencer.* It would be something else. It would be as if Amos Rising never existed. The old man was fully alert now, as alert as he had been in a year. He felt he was fighting for his own life. "What about Dana?"

"I said it," Charles said. "Dana's different from us."

"In what way? Specifically?" He thought he would pursue it as a lawyer. For the moment he would be careful and dispassionate. He would ask questions to which he already knew the answers, like any good lawyer. He would try to understand as much of Charles's point of view as he could. Then he would find a way out. "We must look beyond the third," he said.

Charles looked up. "The third what?"

"The third generation. Look to Dana's children."

"There's only one. She only had one before that son of a bitch—"

"The father."

"Low-life," Charles said. "She's only nine and her name is not Rising, if that's what's so goddamned important—" He stopped short, and put his hands out. "Forgive me, Elliott. I hate that son of a bitch so. Hated him from the moment I saw him and hated him more when he left Dana. Not that it matters, what I think. Dana apparently doesn't hate him, or didn't the last time I asked her. About four years ago. He isn't one of the subjects we discuss a whole lot."

"A girl," Elliott said.

"Nine years old," Charles said.

"She could have more."

Charles said, "She's thirty-six."

"The same reasoning would apply to Jake," he said carefully. It was not a subject he cared to pursue but it bought time. "Three children, doesn't he?"

"Come on, Elliott."

The old man grunted. "Maybe he'll change."

"He's forty years old. Look. He hates my guts. Yours, too, to be blunt about it. I'm not dealing with him. The hell with it. He's chosen to break up your partnership and go on his own. So he sits down there at Mason's and takes potshots at you, at me, at the I. No. It isn't going to work and you know it isn't going to work."

"Dana," Townsend said. "She's your daughter. Your father's grand-daughter. She has the blood, that's what counts. When the chips are down, she's with you. A Rising, a member of the family. She wouldn't let you down, I know that."

Charles shook his head. "Elliott, she's a girl. A young woman, I guess I should say. Doesn't know anything about the I and doesn't care anything about it. She has her own life, has had it for damn near twenty years. I could as easily hand the paper over to your secretary."

"I like Dana," he said.

Charles smiled. "She was a good girl. An angel."

"Able," Townsend said.

"I don't know about that," Charles said.

"Deserves a chance, Charles," The old man leaned forward, suddenly enthusiastic. "Absolutely. You had your chance." Certainly. That was it. The lawyer was on firmer ground now. He understood what had to be done. "You had your chance, now she deserves hers. You've got good people down there at the newspaper, you've got friends in the business. The details she can learn. Anybody can learn details. The blood. The blood, Charles! The blood will take care of the rest."

Charles shook his head. How could he explain it to the old man?

"I'm not sure, Elliott, that I've made myself completely clear. *She doesn't want it.* She—"

"Have you asked her?"

"Some things you don't have to ask."

"I'd ask," he said.

"Elliott. Do you know what she's doing? Where she is? She is with her daughter and another man living abroad. She is living in Ireland, has been for the past six weeks. That's where she is. When Lee—got sick this morning. Last night. I had to send a cable to Dana. I telephoned but there was no answer. She is living in a place where I have to send a *cable*—" He realized he was almost shouting. "Please," he said. "Understand it. Understand this. Dana is way away from all of us. She doesn't want the *I*. Doesn't want anything to do with it."

"That's screwball," Townsend said. "It—" Suddenly he lost his way; what were they talking about? Was it Amos? No, it was the *I*, its character and responsibility . . . He heard Charles say his name and abruptly his mind cleared. On impulse he reached for his drink. "Screwball," he said. "If she doesn't want the *I*, what does she want?"

"I don't know, Elliott."

"There are people who could help her—"

"I'm damned if I'll give it to her," he said thickly.

"Wait a minute, Charles."

"I'm god*damned* if I will, not that she wants it anyway. Not that she would ever have the slightest thing to do with Dement."

"Now you're saying something else."

Charles stood and walked to the bookcase and peered at the burgonet. He had a very brief memory of an afternoon in the Field Museum, suits of armor and mummies; his nose pressed against the glass of the mummy case. He and Mitch moving through the huge room, he remembered marble walls and lofty ceilings. A nice afternoon, and then the long drive back to Dement, arriving late. His father bundling them quickly off to bed, then sitting in the parlor with Elliott, their voices rumbling. It was Elliott who came up to kiss them good night, accepting their thanks with a smile and a pat on the head . . . He moved to the window and put a fingernail on the glass, the tremor in his hand making a tickatackaticka sound. It was entirely dark now and he stood in shadows by the window, his face partly obscured by the lace curtain, his hands plunged deep in his pants pockets. On the way back to Dement from Chicago they had sung, "Row Your Boat" and other rounds, and stopped for dinner somewhere this side of Aurora. When he spoke his voice came from the darkness. "She's never done a damned thing to earn it. Shit." Then he wheeled around, facing the old lawyer, his words coming quietly and coldly. "The crap I had to take off Dad. It was only for the sake of my mother, I would've packed up." He paused. "He was always amused, 'Charles and his numbers.' When I reorganized the company he thought it was some kind of legerdemain. Some sleight of hand, a minor talent. The balance sheet. Oh, *that,* he'd say as if it were a turd. He never thought it was serious except that it saved the *Intelligencer,* but he never understood that either. I'm sixty-three years old and I still remember it. I remember it like it was yesterday."

"Charles, wait a minute."

"There aren't any silver platters in this world." Then, "There was only one way to do it. He needed me, or said he did, so I . . . honored that. It was the way things worked then. Apparently they don't work that way anymore."

The old man was steady, listening as carefully as he could. He did not entirely understand the last statement, or the one before it. He felt that he was facing a compass swinging on its axis; he wanted to freeze the needle, to face in only one direction at a time. He said, "Yes, but—"

"If you could help, you helped. No question. Tradition, you helped your father as repayment. I suppose it was repayment for his being your father. It was a debt that had to be settled."

"But." Townsend was confused. "But you didn't—"

"Of *course* I did. For Christ's sake, Elliott. You were the one who came down to get me. You remember that? I'm sitting in class and the door opens and you're there. I walk out, close the notebook; we get in your car and we drive back to Dement. We didn't say a word, as I recall. But I can remember sitting in that seat and looking around and seeing you there. Collecting my notes and leaving, the damned classroom silent as a desert."

Townsend nodded slowly. Yes, it was true; he'd somehow managed to forget. It was the most awkward thing he'd done in his life, and he had pushed the memory away, out of sight. "It was a hard thing for me to do. I told your father that he ought to do it himself. It was his responsibility to do it, not mine. He said, 'No. You do it.' So I did. What was the class?"

"Torts. Never forgot that. Second week of classes, and that was that. I'd talked my way into that place, it doesn't even exist anymore. Hell, I don't even know if it was certified. I guess it was. But there wasn't any looking back. 'Your dad needs you now. I've come to take you back to Dement.' I didn't believe it could happen. I hadn't expected it. I had two brothers, they were there; Mitch was working, Tony was working. But that wasn't enough for him. *I* had to be there, too. Be perfectly honest, I suppose I was flattered a little. Dad didn't give out a whole lot of compliments. Flattered and frightened. Frightened of what he would do if I'd refused." Charles looked at the old man, his face still in shadows. But Townsend could feel the slight smile. "So that was the end of that particular ambition. I had an idea that I'd apprentice myself to you, after law school. Townsend and Rising, that was how I saw the firm. I saw you becoming a judge and I saw myself—running things. Well." He shrugged. "I *do* run things, but not from a law office. From a publisher's office, maybe it's the same thing. What the hell, maybe it's all the same."

"I never knew that," Townsend said.

"Well, that was the way it was."

"It meant a lot to your dad—"

"So Jake did what I wanted to do," Charles said. "Went to law school and joined your firm. And I was happy as hell to see it, to tell you the truth; I wasn't eager to have Jake around the plant. I was happy to see him hook up with you and I was happy to see him foul it up. The opportunity you gave him. I was happy both ways." He was unconsciously rubbing the small of his back, bending forward slightly. Then he took a small vial from his pocket and opened it and placed two tablets on his tongue and washed them down with whiskey. "Let me tell you, there isn't anything worse than having a legend for a father. Living or dead, he's still a legend and something that's with you all your life. I watched him die. He died but the shadow didn't die. The shadow won't die until I do and then it'll die for good. I've learned to live with it. That took some time and some doing and now that I've made room for it—" He turned away. "You know, Lee couldn't speak last night. She could barely nod. I'd like to've taken a gun and shot us both—"

"Charles!"

"The truth," he said. He was still rubbing his back.

"Are you in pain?" the old man asked gently.

"No," he said. Then, "You're damned right I'm in pain. But it'll pass in a moment, when the pills take effect."

"Well, sit down then."

"Doesn't help the pain." There was silence between them. Mrs. Haines had apparently gone to her room, for there were no more noises from the kitchen. It was night now and from the street he could hear a car's horn and a squeal of brakes. Teenagers, drag racing. Charles sipped his whiskey and looked at the older man. "So let's get back to business."

"Charles, you were the pride of his life. I can attest to that. It's something I know."

"No, I wasn't." He sat down, cradling the whiskey up against his stomach. "The *I* was the pride of his life, always. As it is the pride of mine, for different reasons. I've used it in different ways, and I suppose it's used me in different ways. But I love it. I love it as much as he did . . ."

Townsend could feel himself slipping again, overwhelmed by memory. He remembered a time, many years ago, when he had followed Amos to the back shop. The makeup man was gone that day and Amos was working the stone, laying type himself. He remembered the care with which he lifted the long metal trays of type, laying them carefully to one side, then returning portions to the stone. He was laying out the editorial page, one eye on the clock, the other on the stone. He worked from the top down, the masthead, and the editorials flush left under the masthead. Solemn black stacks of type, a rule between each column and the next. His fingers worked faster as press time drew near. His fingers caressed the type as if it were skin; the skin of the newspaper. When it came to the letters to the editor he slowed, measuring with his eye. Begin with a short letter, follow with a long one, a long and a short, two longs, ending with a short. There was never a shortage of letters to the editor. He'd step back from it, like a painter examining a canvas, and smile slightly, wiping his hands on a rag near at hand. Then he'd make a change and step back again. "Pretty page," he'd mutter, patting it, then taking the wood block and with sudden violence banging the type into place. Townsend thought Amos Rising's fingers worked as delicately as any surgeon's. Then, reading the reversed type right to left, he scanned the entire page, ordered a proof, and moved away from the stone, arms folded, a big cigar in his teeth, standing still as a statue, waiting for the proof that would confirm his own hasty scrutiny. The stereotypers were waiting impatiently but the old man would not be hurried and no one dared interfere. Finally the pressroom foreman approached him. "We're three minutes late," he said bluntly. Amos looked at him and smiled. "Soon's the proof gets here you can run." The foreman said, "It's your money." And Amos just laughed. The page proof arrived and he stood reading it, his bright eyes dancing along the lines of type. Satisfied, he turned to the foreman, standing easily to one side. "Go," he said, and presently the floor began to tremble from the vibration of the Goss. Watching Amos with the I was like watching a stonecutter with a gem. He said once, "Paper ought to look pretty. Clean and uncluttered and above all *regular*. Orderly. Nervous papers aren't reliable. They naturally reflect the editor and nervous editors aren't reliable." Townsend shook his head and returned again to the present. He said, "You wouldn't sell it."

Charles said, "It would be hard."

"You couldn't do it."

"I could," he said.

"I remember Amos talking about Dana," Townsend said.

"Elliott," Charles said.

"—Amos had faith in her, he believed she had the stuff—" He looked at the younger man and stopped talking. They had already discussed Dana; that subject was closed. He'd skipped time again. "Charles," he said. "Fill that drink for me. I'm sorry, I wandered. You've got to forgive me that. I'm all right now." He watched Charles smile and turn to the cabinet. The image of his old friend bending over the stone was still with him. Amos *loved*. The *I* was a living thing and he loved it with passion; it was *his* . . . He accepted the glass from Charles and consciously straightened himself in the chair. He took a long swallow, the drink burning its way to his stomach; he coughed and opened his eyes wide. Fatigue moved up his legs and he held himself rigid, trying to hold it back.

"All right," Townsend said. "What do you propose."

"We sell."

"Who?"

"Dows," Charles said.

"There have been inquiries?"

"There have. It is a property that any publisher would want. The *I* is a Class A property."

"Price?"

"Complicated, but it would work out well. Cash and an exchange of stock. More cash than stock. They would want me to stay on, but I wouldn't."

The words came with difficulty; he could concentrate on only one thing at a time. "Why not?"

"When it goes, it goes. No strings, and no loose ends. I'm not dancing to any tune Harold Dows plays. I'm too old to play window mannequin."

"Mn," Townsend said. "You talked about it with Tony."

"No."

"Well, it doesn't matter."

"Dows is offering the best price. Berlin and McLean are similar to Dement. Similar size, similar outlook. Of course there have been other offers, always are. We could get more money from the chains. But I don't like chains."

"Harold Dows is not our kind of man."

"No, he isn't. He certainly is not. But his boy is all right and they run a clean operation. I have some confidence in the boy. Most of Harold's time is spent in Florida, he's chairman and his boy is president. Junior does most of the work and makes the major decisions."

"I see." The old man sighed as if it were his last breath. Perhaps by loving her so, Amos had worn her out. No doubt that was it. When he was finished with her, there was nothing left; there wasn't enough nourishment for any man who came after. He'd loved her to death.

"Young Dows wants to come up here, have a talk—"

"Go ahead," Townsend said.

"You mean, commence negotiations."

"Yes, as far as I'm concerned."

Charles reached over and touched the old man on the knee. "Elliott, I'm sorry."

Townsend said nothing; he was moving in and out of sleep now. He raised his hand in a kind of farewell and his eyes blurred. Then all the mist went away and he saw Charles put his drink on the sideboard and move quietly to the kitchen door and say something to Mrs. Haines. Then he looked back but Townsend had closed his eyes. When he heard him in the hall, talking to Mrs. Haines, he let the tears go. He opened his eyes and let them slide down his cheeks, making no sound or movement to signal that he was alive and grieving.

HE STOOD on the porch a moment, breathing deeply. The old man's house was stuffy and smelled of the sickroom, though it contained something of his life, too; his ninety-five years. At the end he had collapsed, poor old guy; but he had been sharp when he needed to be and that was what counted. He understood, bless him; perhaps he was the only one who would. Charles sucked air, wanting the smell of sickness out of his nostrils and off his clothes. The cold night air bit into his cheeks, and he stood motionless a moment, listening to the traffic on the Interstate a mile away; the roar of heavy trucks was distinct. The damp street with its looming Victorian houses was empty and dark, except for the lights of the supermarket at the corner. Television sets flickered behind heavy drawn curtains and somewhere a dog barked. An epoch ago he stood on this porch with his father and then was into the air, on high, his father's big hands around his waist, then tucked into the crook of his arm, legs straddling the big stomach; his father's stubble scratched him and he could smell his cigary breath and clothing, and hear the beating of his heart. His arms went around his father's neck and held, it seemed to him an eternity . . . Charles lit a cigarette and slowly descended the old wooden steps to his own car and drove away.

The hospital was on the other side of Dement. Charles drove recklessly as he always did, jumping lights and barely pausing at stop signs. Downtown was entirely deserted and he drove by the office, wondering if he should stop and ask for messages; he'd asked Dana to wire him via the Associated Press. But he'd given the night deskman Townsend's telephone number and there had been no call. He paused; the guard was watching television in the lobby, the day's paper sprawled across his knees. Charles accelerated up Blake Street toward the courthouse, turned and sped to the hospital. He waved at a cruising patrol car, and the officer waved back.

She was in the intensive-care wing of the hospital, but the doctor agreed to let him come and go as he wished. Charles took the elevator to the second floor and walked down the brightly lit corridor to the nurses' station. One of them went with him to Lee's room, peeked in, and motioned him inside. He removed his hat and coat and sat in the armchair by the window. Lee was motionless in the bed, an intravenous solution dripping into her arm and an array of vials on her bedside table. He was sitting in semidarkness but did not care. He fetched the ashtray from the bureau and put it beside him on the floor. Then he stretched his legs and sat looking at his wife in the bed. The nurse was concerned. She said she could bring a cot into the room, it was no trouble. She said, You look all in. He nodded and thanked her and said he would sit awhile and if he wanted a cot he'd call. The nurse smiled and left.

He was looking at Lee, then he wasn't looking. The door to the corridor was slightly ajar, casting a yellow arrow of light across the floor. He moved the toe of his shoe to the arrow's point and sat staring at it. There were no sounds other than a vague electrical hum. He prayed, his lips moving silently in the darkness. He knew no formal prayers so he said whatever came into his mind, fragments of Scripture that he had heard at weddings and funerals. He recited the Lord's Prayer in its entirety. He did not want his wife to suffer but he did not want her to die, either. There seemed to be no middle ground, according to the information he was given. So he prayed for repose, hers and his own; he prayed for peace and an absence of pain, and then he prayed for a miracle. He moved his shoe as if to erase the arrow's bright point, still staring at her as if hypnotized. He closed his eyes and felt an enormous burden lifted from him; it was as if heavy hands had released his heart. He wanted only to do the right thing, and prayed that he was. It did not occur to him to ask for guidance. He asked instead for sanction. He would talk to her about it and perhaps she could supply some answer or reassurance. They had been married for more than half their lifetimes and understood each other accordingly.

Lee?

She did not move, though he thought he heard her sigh, and he could scarcely see her head on the pillow. He leaned forward, his hands clasped between his knees, his feet crossed at the ankles. He began by describing the conversation with Elliott Townsend. How it had begun and how it proceeded and finally ended with the old man falling asleep in the middle of a sentence, his eyes beginning to glaze and then turn inward and finally close altogether. It had hurt him so;

he wanted to believe that Dad would live forever, that they could live forever together, if only through the shadows of memory. But I was very patient, more patient than I felt, and I explained everything to him. What I didn't explain because I didn't know how was that really everything was different now, the town has changed along with the people. Elliott hasn't been out of that house in a year, he'd be amazed at the changes even in a year. A supermarket at the corner and stoplights. Strange when you think about it how much difference it makes when one structure comes down and another goes up. It changes your perspective and attitude, and the way you think about things. It changes your line of sight. He doesn't know about the town now. It isn't Amos's anymore and very soon it won't be mine, either. It hasn't been his for a very long time. It could have been Frank's but Frank was killed in the war. But nobody wants to hear about that because it happened twenty-two years ago.

Lee, listen.

I have called Dana and expect an answer very soon. I tried to call on the telephone but she was out. We can expect her tonight or tomorrow at the latest, depending on the connections. I know she'll come right away, it's just a question of getting the message to her. She's a good girl, she's always been good as gold. Elliott wanted me to make her my successor at the *I*. Can you imagine that? Dana, who's been away for so many years. A mistaken plan even if Dana wanted the *I*, which of course she doesn't. Nobody seems to, except outsiders. So Elliott and I went though that and I proposed finally that the Dowses buy it. And he agreed, like that. So negotiations will begin by the end of the week and if we're lucky we'll be out of there before the holidays. I can't imagine us living without the *I* but the burden has become unbearable. You understand that, don't you? Dows will do a good job, I know he will. The boy reminds me a little bit of Frankie, he's thirty years old and an expert in computers. That's the way the business is going, computers. There was a time for editors like my dad and a time for businessmen like me and now it's—the computer people. That's what young Dows is, he's sharp as a tack and only thirty. And if you think he isn't smart, listen to this. He told me how he managed to avoid Vietnam and it was very simple. He just went to school! One school after another and they excused him until he was finally too old for the draft. Isn't that incredible? Frankie could have done it, but perhaps the laws were different then; and of course he enlisted. I told young Dows, Thank God. That war was even more stupid than Korea, I guess, though young Dows is alive and Frankie is dead. What sense is there in any of that?

He lit a cigarette, blowing the smoke in a thin thread toward the door, where it dispersed. The odor of tobacco was reassuring to him and he sat silently a moment, smoking.

Lee?

I have had my differences with old Dows, as you know. But I like his son, though his son is not "likable" if you see what I mean. What I will do is provide an orderly transition. That is my assignment. It seems to me that it's always been my assignment, one way or another. I've filled an interregnum. And it has made us rich, I could never have imagined how rich. This piece of prairie is just lucky. The *I* has prospered, Dows is going to howl when I tell him how much he'll have to pay. But it's a bargain at almost any price because what you're selling is the future, and the future is unlimited. The town and the paper are going to grow to infinity, nothing will stop them. And when it happens, it'll be out of our hands; we'll be spectators . . . I wanted to keep it in the family, and I would have done anything to achieve that. You understand, don't you? There wasn't a way to do it that would ensure its survival. You see, that's the only important thing with a family business like the *I*. A *real* family business. That it survives and survives intact. The business is more important than the family that owns it, and you protect it as you would protect one of your own. Whatever they do to it, they can't destroy it entirely. Some part of the family will continue in the newspaper, in exactly the same way that Jefferson or Lincoln is part of the presidency. The only visible reminder will be my father's name at the top of the masthead, Founder. That's in the contract, though I don't know if they'll accept it. I expect that they will. It won't cost them any-

thing to accept it, my guess is that young Dows will read over that provision without a moment's thought.

Mr. Rising?

The door stood ajar now, the nurse silhouetted in it. She bent forward, her hands on her hips. She asked him something, to which he
shook his head.

She said, Please. Get some rest.

He nodded and thanked her and said he would in a moment. He
explained that he'd had a very long day today and would have a long
day tomorrow.

She nodded doubtfully. I'll check back, she said.

Yes, he replied. Do that.

She disappeared, closing the door all the way. He was completely in
darkness now, only the glowing end of his cigarette for light. He bent
forward at the waist, rocking on his elbows, and smiled into the darkness. Old Dows. Old Dows saw what his boy could do and put on his
hat one day and announced his retirement, and went to live in Florida.
He left his boy with complete operating authority, and he had the confidence to do it; and the boy had the good sense to follow the father.
Now he spent most of his time playing golf and chasing women in
Florida, and his boy ran the business for him. Not a bad old age,
Charles thought. Not the worst way to end one's days, Charles said.

No, it was a terrible way. It was murderous.

He began to pray again, the words confused in his mind. He was
disoriented in the darkness, uncertain where his wife's bed was. He
prayed for the family, for Lee and for Dana and finally for himself. He
prayed that they would—*could*—be together at last, all of them in the
house where the children grew up. It would be strange without the *I*
to talk about over the dinner table at night. He longed to return home
and find Dana in her room, listening to her blues music. She used to
listen to blues by the hour, as a young girl. Listen to blues and talk on
the telephone. If the three of them could be together again, if only for
a few months . . . a year, perhaps. It was where they all belonged, Dement. All the sights familiar to them were still there; go out of town

ten miles and nothing had changed. Nothing had changed anyway, the spirit was the same. He stubbed out his cigarette and rose, staggering slightly as he gained his feet. He moved forward, his hands in front of him, and stumbled into the bureau; something crashed to the floor. He was exhausted; the nurse was right. He fumbled along the wall until he came to the door and switched on the overhead light. Then he moved to the bedside of his wife and stood looking at her. There was no movement anywhere. He put his hand in hers but withdrew it at once. Her hand was cold as ice. He felt the chill himself and pulled his suit coat around him. Then he kissed his wife on the forehead, knowing now that she was gone. She and the *I* were both gone, and he would follow shortly. That was the way he had worked it out, a logical progression. He stood beside her bed for many minutes before he called the nurse, who hurried in to search for Lee Rising's pulse and heartbeat. After a moment the nurse relaxed and took her fingers away from Lee's wrist. She touched Charles's arm and smiled and said it was all right. He looked so worn and old, his arm soft to her touch. His wife was still alive. Really, she said, there had been no change at all. Charles closed his eyes and said aloud, Thank God.

2.

THE PASTURE rolled down to the sea in waves, long gentle slopes that ended in a sharp drop to the beach. A footpath wound down through high grass, a lazy traverse moving back on itself through boulders and bunches of wild flowers. Back of the pasture the hills rose a thousand feet, and the clouds boiled over them like steam from a caldron, disappearing when they met the sea air. Above the gray shore and the sea beyond the sky was milky blue.

The beach was deserted always, except on Sundays when people came from church to sit on the sand in their black clothes and feel the heat of the sun. The men shed their suit coats and sat in collarless white shirts and talked among themselves while children chased each other at the edge of the water. There were always one or two old people in each group. The vastness of the beach dwarfed the people: they sat on tawny blankets in groups of six and seven, eating lunch and laughing.

The beach was two miles long, and as wide as any beach Dana had ever seen. At either end the sea cut into the hills, sculpturing the rocks into ragged peaks and long ridged tables. When the sea was calm and the tide switched, the water fluttered back in inch-high wavelets. When it switched again, a few fishermen would come back with it, sculling their dories with slow swings of a single oar. The beach was austere, without ornament of any kind, and despite that an intimate place. She had a game, one of many, calculating the speed of the tide, not in time but in distance, the advance of one wave over another. She'd place small sticks in the sand as measuring rods and watch the water wash beyond them and carry them away. The tide brought bottles and these Myles placed on a shelf and used as targets. They were whiskey bottles, washed clean by the sea. Propped against a rock, they made hard targets for a man pitching stones.

She'd brought two pints of beer to the water's edge and he uncapped them and handed one to her. They walked hand in hand on the soft sand. Two small boats were floating back on the tide and she watched them move, slow as turtles. He was holding her hand very tightly, and now she leaned against him, nestling the back of her head in his neck. He put his arms around her and hugged her; she smelled fresher than the sea. They clung together, watching the boats drift in from the open water. Then they were sitting and facing each other on the rock, her hands on his cheeks, feeling the roughness of his skin; it seemed as rugged as the corduroy coat he wore. She was urging him without thinking. He touched her face and her neck, then kissed her lightly for a long minute, their lips barely touching.

"You're scandalizing the neighborhood," she murmured.

He looked up, over her shoulder, moving a lock of hair with his nose. "They're paying no attention." He saluted the figures in black with the pint bottle, and drank.

"They're fools, then," she said.

"They know all about us."

"And are not interested?"

He shook his head. "They *were*, that first day, you in the bikini—"

"But not anymore?"

"There's a local scandal to occupy them now. They don't want to worry about us, outsiders after all." He stood up and put his arm around her and they walked up the beach. He put the two bottles of beer in his pocket and carried the picnic basket with his free hand. In a moment a nine-year-old girl joined them, dashing over the sand in an awkward run. They turned to meet her and the man picked her up and swung her over his shoulder in a cascade of laughter. Dana stood to one side, watching them—her daughter so tiny and slender, Myles so big and rough in his heavy clothes and bushy hair. The little girl moved in between them as they continued up the beach.

They ate slowly, watching the sea. Then the little girl began to fuss. They joked with her a minute and the man tried to roughhouse, but Cathy was adamant: no jokes, no roughhouse, she wanted to go home, now. She said finally, "I have to go to the bathroom." Dana turned to him with an apologetic smile and a shrug. She would take her back to the house, play with her a little, maybe read her a story; then put her down for a nap, if she'd go. Dana smiled and winked at him. "Back in a while," she said. He watched her run to catch up with the nine-year-old, who was moving away from them up the beach. She put her arm around Cathy's shoulder and said something to her and the little girl slid closer to her and soon they were walking in step up the beach, unmistakably mother and daughter. He watched them enviously until they were out of sight over a dune, and then he finished the beer and closed his eyes.

Myles awakened slowly, his face fuzzy on the beach towel. He had been dreaming of his apartment in Paris, preparing for a party. He was laying out the food and drink and then the doorbell rang. When he opened the door there were a dozen people outside; all of them were vaguely familiar. He stood at the door, tongue-tied. They all pushed past him to get to the bar and he was left holding the door. Then he woke up. He lit a cigarette, lying on his stomach. The beach was deserted, and when he looked at his watch he discovered that he'd been asleep for an hour. He looked over his shoulder but Dana was nowhere in sight. He stood up, trying to remember the identities of the guests in his dream; one of them was his university English teacher, a poet now dead. He walked to the water's edge and tested it with his toe. Cold, as he knew it would be. The memory of the dream faded; he never remembered them for more than five minutes. He touched his toes and jogged in place for a moment, feeling very good after his nap. The sun was still warm and he thought that perhaps the time had come for a swim. Baptism by iceberg: it would be very cold; but it would also be an event, a promise kept. Dana had dared and double-dared and now he would accept the challenge; too bad she was not present to witness it. He walked back to the towel and began to shed clothing, jacket, trousers, shirt, socks. He wore no shorts. Naked, he stood shivering in the sun, feeling a salty breeze on his back. Then he dropped his watch and sprinted for the water. He hit the stones in a dozen strides, stumbled once, and flat-dove into the surf, his body hitting the water with an echoing *slap!* He floated out to sea on his back, dazed, watching the gulls above him, then turning and scrubbing himself in the water, its coldness burning his warm skin. He whooped and struck out to sea in a fast crawl. Buoyant, he porpoised, dipping below the heavy surface and staying there until forced up like a cork. The waves were gentle. He rode them for a yard or two, then watched them go at eye level, moving beyond him. The sun was warm on his face but the cold salt water tightened and freshened his body. His breath came in gasps as he counted strokes, one two three four. Then he turned to face the shore and saw her standing, arms folded, her head cocked to one side. Seeing him, she waved and laughed, gripping her hands above her like a prizefighter. He bolted for shore, his body surging at the sight of her. She stepped back as he broke from the water, coming at her on the run, head down. Running along the waterline she easily outdistanced him and they both began to laugh at the absurd sight of naked Myles and Dana, fully clothed. Finally he tackled her after a zigzag chase up the beach, brought her down panting and laughing—*My God,* she said, *you're freezing.* She began to massage his back, lying on top of him, pummeling him with her hands. He said, *You lose the dare.* His skin began to warm under her touch. She took off her sweater and toweled him with it, until he suddenly turned on his back and took her face in his two hands and kissed her. She floated into him, light as air, loving the taste of him, salty and beery . . . Then he began to shiver with cold. *Come on,* she said finally, *we'll walk up the beach a ways.* He kept her there another moment, then released her and she ran to get his clothes.

They walked along the waterline in bare feet, feeling the cold sea and the breeze, the sand underfoot and the last rays of the afternoon sun. They walked in the opposite direction from the boats, pausing here and there to watch tiny sand crabs burst from the sand and scuttle to high ground. He stooped to pick up a green glass sphere, a fisherman's net buoy, and moved to put it in his pocket. She stopped and opened her pocket for him, guiding his hand with the glass sphere. Their eyes locked on each other, and their fingers touched inside her pocket.

He whispered some words and she returned them. Now they were at the far end of the beach, looking upward at the high hills. There was another footpath that meandered back to their house a mile away. It was a hard climb through rocks to the footpath, and he took her hand when they started up. The sea was flat now, the tide advancing in small even curls. They paused every few steps to look at the sea and the sunset, the sun descending now over America, three thousand miles distant; dusk here, midday there. The boats were home now and the sand and sea were empty. The color of the water changed from light blue to violet as the sun's rays faded. A way off, bumping the horizon, they saw a white light, a small freighter or large private yacht, sailing south. The white light grew brighter as the sunlight failed.

He said, "What a hell of a good time we've had."

"We've always had fun," she said. "Always." She thought, Nearly always. Last winter was not so much fun, nor the preceding fall. They seemed to go in ups and downs; this was an up time. The slow rhythm of Ireland suited them both, long afternoons on the beach, late to bed, late to rise. She thought someday she would buy a house in Ireland and live in it during the summer and fall. New York's turbulence exhausted her and there were times when she needed to escape it fully, to think. There were times when New York oppressed her, as Dement had done; then she became restless and would take her work and leave for a while. But it was a wonderful place to come back to, the closest thing to a home she had. "Myles," she said. "You've been marvelous with Cathy."

"Nice kid," he said. "She needs a man around."

"She's grown dependent, since McGee—"

He said, "To hell with McGee. Never mind McGee."

"Well." She smiled. "He arrives tomorrow to take Cathy for a week, so let's wait before he goes to hell. Let's wait ten days."

He said, "The son of a bitch."

She moved up against him, still smiling. "Forget it, we're the ones having the fun." They moved steadily up the bluff, then over it and the sea was lost to view. They would have the prisoner exchange at Shannon airport the next day. McGee and his wife arriving from London on one plane, and ninety minutes later leaving for the United States with Cathy on another. There would be barely enough time for a cup of coffee, thank God. Shirley would be wearing her smart traveling suit and her tight little smile that said, I-don't-understand-how-you-can-take-that-dear-little-girl-out-of-school-for-a-month, why-didn't-you-take-your-vacation-in-August-like-everybody-else. McGee would be civil enough but would not approve of Cathy's clothes. He would look at her like an *objet d'art* at auction, appraising her for bids. Dana would ask them if they had a nice time in Paris and McGee would reply that they'd had a dynamite time, just dynamite. Then Shirley would ask her how Ireland had been and she would reply—what? Super. She would say, "I have had a super time."

"Do you want me to go with you to the airport tomorrow?"

She smiled; it was not the worst idea she had ever heard. Myles, so big and weathered beside McGee, lean and civilized. They would shake hands cordially, having known each other in the old days; having decided long ago that civility was—easier. Just that. It was easier. It would also give Shirley an uncomfortable moment as a distinct outsider, wondering who Myles was . . . But of course McGee would have told her. She said, "No."

"Why?"

"Awkward," she said.

He looked at her, surprised. "For you? I can't believe that."

"Cathy," she said.

He nodded. "Well, if you change your mind."

They were moving through a tiny glen, the silence oppressive except for the splash of a stream nearby. She was following him, her eyes on the path, her hands plunged deep in her pockets. Maybe it was a good idea, after all. It would be good to have Myles there—

"I'm glad to go with you," he said suddenly.

"I know. We'll see tomorrow." The truth was, she did not want to make a difficult leaving for Cathy. The truth was, there would be a certain uneasiness all around and that would communicate itself to Cathy. The truth was, it would be easier all around if just she and Cathy went. The truth was, she did not want McGee to see Myles now; she did not want to see them together, even for thirty minutes in an airport lounge. She was connected to McGee and would always be connected to him; he had been her route out. It had not been an easy passage after the honeymoon, yet it seemed to her now that the honeymoon lasted years. McGee's drinking grew uncontrollable until he took a cure and quit altogether. But the marriage did not improve. On

a Friday in June in 1969 they were together, as they had been together
for eight years; on Saturday they were not together, except the divorce
took a year and a half. But the marriage ended then, when he moved
out. She saw it coming but was powerless to prevent it; she was exhausted from the earlier preventions. What happened? Shirley happened. Dana'd buried herself in work and tried to ignore the craziness
gathering around her, and she succeeded. Married, she and McGee
never achieved the intimacy of the night on Fifth Avenue. That night
McGee found some part of himself and the discovery was so painful
that he could neither talk about it nor forget it. He never again spoke
of Eastern Europe except once in a speech. He'd been drinking. The
subject was the war and when he spoke his words faltered and he
looked away. From the audience she could see the pain and confusion
on his face. Was the death of one god the death of all? But he collected
himself and finished the speech, to cheers. Dana believed that she reminded him of his days as a soldier in the cold war; she was a living reminder of that failure, and of other failures. There was nothing she
could say or do, no obvious course for her. When a psychiatrist asked
her if she would do anything to get him back she had to answer honestly, "No." So he married Shirley and moved to Washington, where
he would serve various administrations.

Myles said, "Shirley be with him?"

"His letter said she would."

"They probably deserve each other," he said.

She hooked her hand around his belt and said, "Pull. I'm getting
tired." She was following him as they wound upward on the footpath.

"She's not bad looking," Myles said.

"Mn," Dana said.

He turned around, smiling. "Don't you think so?"

She said, "Mouse-brown hair."

"Well," Myles said. "They look alike. And it isn't mouse brown. It's
mouse *gold*."

"They do *not* look alike." Dana was indignant. She believed that
happily married people came to resemble each other. It was true that

Shirley was tall and thin as McGee was, but she had a petulant mouth and pampered skin. She always looked prepared, having spent a sizable portion of her life in clubhouses and cabanas. She said, "They are not alike in any way."

"We ought to give Cathy a good time tonight," he said after a moment's pause. "We can take her to the dog track."

She laughed. That was pure Myles. He'd been trying to get them to see the dogs for two weeks. "Well, she loves animals."

"I'll have to explain to her about the mechanical rabbit," he said solemnly. "But Kelso has offered to go with us, anytime we want. Explain the betting. Kelso owns a dog himself. Kelso knows . . ."

She listened to him explain about Kelso, the local squire. She jerked twice at his belt, wanting to feel the hardness of his body; wanting to feel *him*. He put his hand back of him and she took it and they moved on through the glen, toward the house. This one, she felt comfortable with him; loved him often, though not always. Myles was an itinerant, changing jobs the way other men changed suits. Now he was working for a foundation, well paid for distributing someone else's money. The job had lasted for a year and now she could tell he was ready to move on to something else. Not something new because he'd already done everything—worked for universities, magazines, political candidates, governments foreign and domestic, and once, disastrously, a bank. A job came up and he was incapable of refusing it, believing that life was a series of possibilities and one was obliged to accept whatever came along. "Work is an episode," he'd say when quitting a job. Once he'd written a thriller, not a very good one but commercially successful. He had no desire to write another, any more than McGee would ever write a true memoir.

McGee had gone back to the law firm in Boston and stayed there, satisfied; until "my government" called again, which in due course it did. She still had the original manuscript of McGee's book; he had not even thought to take it when he moved out. What were their names? Sweeney and Johnson. No, Johnson was the alias. She had met Sweeney once by chance: years later she and McGee were flying to

Chicago and Sweeney was in the seat opposite. She was fascinated by him, one of the most strikingly handsome men she had ever seen; he had beautiful manners and looked like a film star. McGee was nervous throughout the flight and she and Sweeney made conversation. She smiled at the memory; he'd tried to pass himself off as a recording executive. When he said it, she laughed out loud and he blushed; McGee merely looked uncomfortable. But *Ambassador's Journal* was never published, and while the reasons—*his* reasons—seemed to her at the time perfect, even noble, they seemed a little less perfect and noble as time went on. In the beginning he refused to publish for the sake of his foreign friends and at the end for his own, and Sweeney's and the others. She believed him absolutely at the time; he'd been irresistible that night in New York. She'd been moved beyond words. But his reasons could not be hers. She believed him and honored him and knew in her heart that he was wrong. He was wrong but could do nothing else and she understood that, too. For herself, *the truth was not poisonous.* The truth was the truth; concealed, it was no better than a lie. So six months later she quit and quickly signed on with another, better publisher. She and Noah avoided each other at parties; they'd not spoken a dozen consecutive words to each other in more than ten years. She could never forgive betrayal, and he could never forgive her knowledge of it. Now Noah was out of publishing altogether and she was doing what she'd always done and loved, she loved it no less now than then. How many books had she edited? More than a hundred now, books of all kinds: fiction, biography, journalism, history. Books threatened to crowd her out of her apartment; they were piled everywhere, books, galleys, manuscripts, *paper.* But still—there was something surrounding her that she could neither name nor understand. She felt herself aloft, out of touch with the common things of her experience. She regretted nothing; there was nothing to regret. But she wished at times that she had not been so—resolute, that she had been willing to pretend a little. Or that the people around her had been more resolute. She did not attract resolute men, with the exception of McGee. And resolute men did not attract her, with the exception of McGee. The resolute men that she knew were cannibals, men of banking or insurance or law or the government, though it was also true that she was on guard. She liked surprise, that was the truth of it. She supposed that was why Myles attracted her so. When she was with him in her apartment or a restaurant, talking about books or about each other, she was entirely herself. She was the woman she had become. Myles was part of her maturity and had no claims on her past. The truth was, he made her laugh. "Work is an episode," whatever that meant. Did nothing last from today to tomorrow? These parts of her life . . . She knew that she clung to her job as something more than a job, a chore she was good at and well paid to do. It was the single thing in her life that was continuous, that and Cathy and the yearly trips to Dement. She had left home fifteen years ago and each time she returned she felt—dread. Returning home, she expected to be presented with bills; long-forgotten debts requiring immediate payment. What these debts were she could not imagine, yet they lay unspoken in every conversation, and in every look or gesture. What had she done that was wicked? She had sought her fortune and found it. Married for love and found love, until her lover decided to love someone else. Live by the sword, die by it. Brother Frank's generous words of two decades past. The trouble was, she had learned no lessons. She was half in love with McGee as she was half connected to her family, and had lost both. She could still go numb at the memory of McGee in the middle of Fifth Avenue, when he'd opened his heart to her; and glow inside remembering her grandfather at his desk, she in his lap peering into the recesses of a desk drawer . . . And tomorrow she would meet an Aer Lingus jet at an unfamiliar airport and hand over her daughter to a stranger. She put her hand around Myles's waist. He was still talking about the dog track. He was the one she depended upon now, and how strange that was; he was the least predictable man she knew. The truth was, he depended upon her just as much. Myles was like the wind, strong one day, weak the next. He was not motivated the way other men were motivated. But he had a distinct silhouette and he enchanted her and he was not a cannibal, and he was what she wanted now. "Myles," she said.

He paused in the middle of a sentence. "What?"

"I like you so much."

"I'm glad to hear it," he said, smiling at her. He was always embarrassed when she said it.

"You're a very fine man."

"Dana, dear—"

"It's true."

"Dana, dear," he said patiently. "People have called me many things in my life—"

"A *very* fine man."

"—nice, amusing, an excellent drinking companion. On occasion, an adequate lover—"

"Myles?"

"They have never called me 'a very fine man.' I am not 'a very fine man.' That implies security, stability, strength, selflessness, success—"

"Myles," she said and suddenly began to cry.

THE CHILD had been put to bed and they were sitting in front of the fire in facing chairs, feet in each other's laps. He was reading the Irish *Times* and she was sewing a button on Cathy's blue coat. Making everything shipshape for Dad, she thought. The coat was a bit threadbare but Cathy liked it and looked cute in it. Perhaps for the occasion she would dress her in organdy, patent leather shoes and a little yellow hat with a ribbon hanging from its brim. White stockings. Gloves. And a curtsy to Shirley, and perhaps a few words of Gaelic. This would be a child who would not speak unless spoken to, a child as good as gold and unfailingly polite. She looked across at Myles, deep into an account of the Troubles. She pushed her foot into his belly and he tickled her instep, not looking up from the newspaper. She giggled and turned back to the button. Then the phone rang.

He watched her disentangle herself from the coat and the chair and his lap and move off to the kitchen. This was an event, he thought; the telephone never rang. Then he returned to his newspaper, stretching in the chair. He could hear nothing from the kitchen; it was a room and a corridor away. Then the door slammed and he heard her feet running down the corridor, and his name twice called. He was half out of his chair and she was in the room, moving blindly toward him, her arms stretched out and fluttering. Her face was red and contorted. Instinctively, he said it was all right; whatever it was, it was all right. Then her arms were around his neck and she was making choking sounds, her body heavy against him. She was limp and he was half supporting her. He eased her to the floor in front of the fire and sat beside her a moment, cradling her in his arms. He was smoothing her hair with the palm of his hand and murmuring to her, it was almost a croon, saying over and over again that it was all right. Then she turned toward him and said, sobbing, that her mother was dead, *dead*. That was her father and her Uncle Tony on the telephone, her father had been with her when she died. Why was her mother in the hospital at all? She had not known about it, she thought her mother was home, as she had always been home. On the telephone her father was not making sense. *Dead,* she said to him. *She died early this morning. She went into the hospital yesterday, they tried to cable us but the cable never got through. That was all Tony could talk about, the cable. My father said he'd been trying all morning, the telephone, the cable.* She looked at him, her face breaking. *My mother's dead, she can't be dead.*

He said firmly, "Wait here. Don't move." Myles ran to the kitchen and poured a tumbler of Scotch and brought it back. She was sitting on the floor, slack, staring at the carpet, her lips moving soundlessly. He forced the glass into her hand and her hand to her mouth. She drank, gagged, and drank again. He took the glass from her. Then she began to tremble and reach out for him again. He took both her hands and knelt beside her and began to talk. He talked so she wouldn't talk, and he could feel her begin to settle and come to rest. Finally he said, not knowing the truth or falsehood of what he was saying, but believing it to be correct, "She had a good life, Dana. A long life—"

"Not long enough!" she cried.

Chastened, he pulled back from her. He said, "I know."

"Not long enough," she said again, and looked away.

"She hadn't been sick?"

"Yes," she said. "She's been . . . not very well . . . for years but there was no—idea . . ."

He moved close to her again, putting both arms around her shoulders. He did not know what to say. "It's better that it's quick," he said.

"Quick, yes," she said after a moment.

"She didn't suffer."

Dana shook her head, silent. She was remembering her mother's face, trying to recall what she had looked like as a young woman.

"It's something," he said.

"My uncle," she said, "doesn't know the score, never did." She recognized that as a phrase of her father's and bit her lip. Over the telephone her father had been confused and distant, almost abrupt. She said, "It was hard to tell what happened. My father was apparently visiting my mother, she had a stroke years ago—" She stopped, then continued. "My uncle kept talking about a cable. We didn't get any cable, did we?" He shook his head. "Well, there was a cable. About my mother. Then when she died they tried to telephone and cable, both." She brought the glass to her lips and drained it. "I'll get drunk," she said.

Myles said, "You could do worse."

She handed him the empty glass. "Please?"

He went into the kitchen and filled the glass again with whiskey, taking a long swallow himself. He lingered a moment, looking into the blackness from the window. Arrangements would have to be made. He would call tonight and try to get Dana on the same flight as McGee and Cathy. Then she could change planes in New York. Christ, he thought, what a thing to happen. It would have to happen while she was here, a continent away. He took another swallow of whiskey and brought the glass back to her. Dana was sitting next to the fire, the child's blue coat in her lap.

"I don't know how happy she was," she said. "In her life." She accepted the glass but did not drink. "My father was so odd on the phone. He just said she was gone and that it was quick and painless and that he hoped I could get back . . . right away. 'The first available aircraft,' was the way he put it. Then he gave the phone to Tony." She took a sip of the whiskey, gripping the glass with both hands. "The town I grew up in, where they lived. Dement." She sighed. "Dement, I don't understand you."

Myles said, "I'm going to try to get you seats tomorrow on McGee's plane. I'll try to book you through from here. You and Cathy. Do you want me to do that?" He spoke very deliberately. She listened and nodded.

"Thank you, Myles."

"Are you all right for a minute?"

"I'm all right."

"I'd better do it now."

"Yes, now."

He looked at her. "I'm so sorry."

"Thank you, Myles."

"Really," he said.

She nodded. "I know."

"It's a hell of a goddamned thing."

"Make the call and then come back to me here."

Twice the line was busy and finally he made a connection. There was a seat available on the Aer Lingus to New York and they would try to confirm connections through to the Midwest. Mrs. McGee would have to check that in the morning. But she was confirmed definitely to New York. He returned to the living room and gave her the information, the flight number and times of arrival and departure. He'd written them on a piece of notepaper. If she would give him the name and address of her uncle, he would cable him.

"I'll do that in New York," she said. "Or tomorrow morning. I'll cable my father then." She added, with a slow smile, "Of all the times. Going on the same darned plane with McGee and Shirley *and* Cathy. Cripes," she said. "That's really the limit. Isn't that the outer limit?"

He smiled. "It's the outer limit."

"Ah, shoot," she said. "Poor mother. Poor lady."

He said, "I'll go back with you, Dana. Let me do that, it's a beast of a trip to take alone. I'd like to, really—"

She shook her head. "I've paid for this place for a week more. You stay, enjoy it. Who knows?" She shrugged. "Maybe I'll fly back myself, after the funeral. Spend the last few days here and then we could go back together." He nodded in agreement, although he knew she would not be back. She said, "I haven't been in Dement in a year. I haven't been very good about visiting. Never have been very good about that. My father didn't like it. We always quarreled." She looked at him suddenly. "You've never met my father, have you? One of his trips to New York?"

He said, "No. I always wanted to."

"He hated McGee."

"That makes him a man of good judgment," Myles said.

"He thought McGee was always trying to put him down."

"Was he?"

"I don't think so. It was just—McGee. His ambassadorial manner." She said, "I wonder what he'll do now." It was not a question to which Dana expected an answer. "Poor man." Then she smiled wistfully. "You remind me a little of him."

He looked at her, amazed. He could not imagine what she meant. "I do?"

"A little," she said softly. "In some ways." Then she laughed. "You and my father are totally. Utterly. Completely different in every way, absolutely."

"But I remind you of him."

"Yes," she said.

"Well—" She was looking at him and then he understood. "Ah," he said. "It's because I'm a very-fine-man, right?"

"Yeah," she said, with a little lilt to her voice.

He looked at her red face and her shining eyes and he thought for a moment that he would weep himself. But he forced a smile. "I knew it was something like that."

She said seriously, "My father did not sound well."

"Dana, that's shock."

"Um," she said. "I suppose. Certainly that's it." She rose, and put out her hand to help him up. "Come on," she said. They went upstairs hand in hand to the big bedroom on the second floor. It was dark and she peeked into Cathy's room to see that she was all right, then went on to their room and began to undress. He turned off the electric heater and flung open the window to the night air and piled comforters on the bed. Gently guiding her beneath the sheets, he turned off the lights. They lay facing each other, burrowed into the bed and themselves. She did not want to talk and they lay there, facing, arms around each other, until sleep finally came.

IT WAS ALMOST dawn when Dana woke and slipped out of bed. Myles stirred and rolled over, muttering indistinctly. His eyes opened and he stared at her, seeing nothing. He frowned, closed his eyes, and was asleep again. She stood looking at him a moment, smiling, and reached down to touch him but at the last moment withdrew her hand. His face was slack and childlike in sleep, only his tangled hair, gray at the temples, and the thick white bristles on his chin betraying his age. She stood quite still a moment longer, shivering in the cold, torn by indecision. She moved closer to the bed, wanting him to waken—dear Myles, there was no one like him. Her hand fluttered above his forehead, then dropped again to her side. No. We are alone, she thought. Alone at the beginning and alone at the end, alone at all the times of darkness. How comforting now to be held by Myles, loved by him, warmed by him, to feel his heavy arms around her back, holding her close, to hear the rumble in his chest when he spoke to her, always in solace and reassurance. But there would come a time when Myles would leave again, chasing a fresh chimera; and she and Cathy would remain. Not cripples, she thought. She touched the pillow, then turned away and began to dress. Cold: the floorboards were like ice under her feet and the chill swept through the house, around her shoulders and belly and legs, pushed by the breeze from the sea. Dressed, she looked at Myles snug in bed; a ship in a safe harbor. She smiled to herself. Why was it that Risings always believed the hardest way to be the best way? For better or worse, she acted in the traditions of the family, inside a narrative that seemed to have been written long ago.

Downstairs, she watched the northern dawn, the starless night change from black to slate gray. Familiar things became visible, the stone walls first, then the dark green of the grass, finally the sea itself, black-green, flecked with white. The sea was lifeless then; she could not imagine life in it. The kitchen brightened, and she turned off the lamp. The tart smell of coffee filled her head and she relaxed, watching the dawn, looking far out to sea, her mind clearing as the definitions changed and became sharper; the soft rise and fall, the light and shade, all of it cold. She pulled on a heavy sweater and a windbreaker for the rain, certain to come at some point in the day, probably before noon. She laced the big shoes, filled the thermos with coffee, and fetched an apple from the dish on the sideboard. She scribbled a note for Myles, then left the house.

Her route was this. Down the road to the town one mile, then through the fields south thirty minutes. That put her within an hour's walk of the summit of Gilles's Mountain. She intended to climb the mountain and with luck make the summit by nine. She would be back at eleven, in plenty of time to catch the airplane at three. Not a difficult climb, Gilles's; it was a rather simple Irish hill, and it was nearby. A winding trail led to the summit and an enormous view. That was the reason she was climbing it, for the view from the summit; for that, and for the exercise it gave her and the chance to breathe fresh air, alone.

By eight the clouds cleared and patches of blue were visible above. She had passed through the town and the fields and was moving upward, the mountain rising in a gentle swell, its slopes green and thick. She vaulted stone walls, following the rise. She had a good stick for support and kept her eyes on the mountain's mass before her, growing as she approached it, and finally dominating her vision. The sea was far behind her now, hidden as she moved into narrow dales, and emerging again when she came onto the heights. The closer she got the more forbidding the mountain: gray and angular, mist draped like a cassock over its shoulders. Halfway up she stumbled on an oratory, its stones tumbled down but still recognizable; a place of worship from the twelfth century or before. She and Myles had climbed Gilles's the week before and he had brought with him a book from the house, and quoted from it. *Da Derga's Hostel.* The women: "White as the snow of one night were her hands . . . dark as the back of a stag-beetle the two eyebrows. Like a shower of pearls were the teeth in her head. Blue as a hyacinth were the eyes. Red as rowanberries the lips. Very high, smooth and soft-white the shoulders. Clear-white and lengthy the fingers. Long were the hands. White as the foam of a wave was the flank, slender, long, tender, smooth, soft as wool. Polished and warm, sleek and white were the two thighs. Round and small, hard and white the two knees . . ." With a roar and crazed laughter Myles had chased her up the mountain and caught her and they had made love on the soft grass beside the path. And remained there for the afternoon. She laughed out loud, remembering it.

The sunlight was hazy but the day was warm. She heard the sound of crickets in the grass, and of wind. It filled her with wonder, sitting alone in an oratory on the side of a mountain in western Ireland, no living thing close at hand, the mass of the mountain spreading out below her like a woman's skirts. She gazed at the hills below her, and the sea beyond that, the water darker than the land, but both of them green and fertile. She saw the village and the road cutting through it, and her own house almost hidden from view, tucked away inside this miniature world. Shading her eyes, she stared at the summit and the way up seemed less forbidding. It was not enormous or menacing, this life-sized hill. The climb was worth it, even if she surrendered where she was. She could forget about the rest of it and go home and still it was worth it. Her shoes with their thick soles made her believe that she was taller than she was and standing on the stones of the oratory she felt huge, a giant. God, Gulliver, looking down at the world.

She was breathing hard and the trail steepened. Often she had to move down the hill in order to get around the outcrops, rocks as big as houses stuck out of the side of the mountain. It unsettled her to look down now; she had never been good with heights. She began to understand what climbers meant when they talked of handling a mountain, working with it rather than against it. The mass became animate and personal, an intimate thing. She was below a large overhanging rock now, slipping sideways to maneuver around it in order to climb again. A quick glance down showed her the mistake: she'd taken a wrong turning at the oratory. No way of knowing that at the time; looking up altered the perspective and therefore the nature of the terrain. Now the oratory seemed very small and oddly positioned; marvelous thing, hindsight. She kept her head into the mountain, working with it, moving sideways until she could move no more. The ledge bumped into a new outcropping: she was at a dead end. If she could get to the next ledge she could get to the summit. But she could barely reach it with her fingertips. Then she saw herself from a distance, from the eyes of the hawks above, and felt the absurdity of it. She was not dangling from ropes or belayed to pitons, swinging on an Alp; she was standing beneath a ledge with sweat dribbling down her back, looking at her bruised palms and puffing like a steam engine.

Two hawks crisscrossed above her, riding wind currents, silent as the mountain itself. She looked straight ahead at the green-veined stone, staring at it the way a fortune-teller stares at the lines in a human palm. She watched the birds from the corners of her eyes, the birds silhouetted blackly against the sky. She thought then that she was beyond her reach and was suddenly frightened.

She had always thought of herself as traveling alone. Now her attendants were two silent hawks, riding the wind. The valuable objective was a ledge, and beyond that an exhilarating view; nothing more. A view from the top of a small hill at the end of a short climb. Hugging the mountain she thought that if she were ten years younger or older she could see the situation in symbols; she'd always dealt harshly with symbols. It would help now to see all this in symbol, mystery or rhyme. She wondered if possibly somewhere her mother was witnessing all this: She saw her, left hand to her mouth in a characteristic gesture. *Don't forget your coat and hat.* A breeze drifted down the mountain slope and dried the sweat on her head. She unstrung her belt and fashioned it into a loop, and belayed the loop on the point of an overhanging rock. But it slipped and kept slipping when she tested it for strength. She reexamined the ledge, rubbing her hands over her thighs, and decided it was serious after all. There was one possible way: If she jumped high she could hope that her hands and forearms caught on the overhang, and then she could haul herself up. She thought about that and glowered at the hawks. She said to them, "Fuck off."

It would be a tragedy to have to go down the way she'd come up, with a long walk ahead of her and nothing to show for it; no reward. The Risings were not like that. What they sought they found, and never looked back. Except her father had spent a lifetime looking back and her own amateur standing in that field was secure. She stood slapping the belt against the side of the mountain, frustrated. The frustrated climber, defeated by gentle Gilles's Mountain. Cousteau frightened by a cod. All those symbols to be overcome, those metaphors and destinies to fulfill. There was something of an Irish saga in it, as related by Myles, fabulous suggestions and overtones of the supernatural. Struggles among heavies. Where was the warrior with seven pupils in one eye, and the eye in the middle of his forehead? The sorceress with thirty-two names (Samon, Sinand, Seisclend, Sodb), Da Derga's hostel with thirty-seven rooms (the room of the Picts, the room of the pipers, the room of Conaire's majordomo), the final bloodletting, dead following dead, "a man for every stone that is now in Carn Lecca." So it was not simply a short walk up a simple hill; it had a magic of its own.

She gathered her nerve and jumped. It was more a dignified hop and in one clumsy motion she was hanging from the ledge, her feet scrambling for a purchase on the stone face of the mountain. She heard the rasp of her shoes and the sound of falling stones, and for one instant she thought she'd fall, had fallen and was even then lying

limp and broken six feet below; but she pulled and hauled herself up
and over the ledge and once there, on top, lay heaving and gasping,
stretched out.

There had to be a reward. She carefully refused to look down,
although her eyes told her to, to see where she'd come from, just one
quick glance over the edge for verification. But she struggled to her
feet and kept moving on. The slope was easier now and she kept her
eyes in front of her. She'd save the view for the summit, with nothing more beyond. Then she'd look down and savor the triumph. It was
a ten-minute walk and she moved slowly and deliberately around the
rocks, her passage suggesting a very old woman climbing a steep flight
of stairs, gripping the balustrade with a heavy hand, head low, pausing every few steps. She made her way thus to the heights and stood
there motionless a moment. Then with an actorish swing of her arm
she turned and looked over the land, a three-hundred-sixty-degree
prospect. Ireland gleamed below her, a dazzling green land, peaceful.
She traced the route from the town, noting the places where she'd
jumped a fence or crossed a road. The stone fences were like veins,
lightly lacing the land together. She could not make out the oratory
at all; all the stone piles looked alike. Perhaps it was hidden altogether. She searched for it a minute, then sat down on a boulder,
exhausted. The land fell away from her, then dipped sharply at the
place the ledge was. With no strength to take in all there was to see
and feel, she simply sat. Then she dozed awhile, slumped on the
boulder, letting her mind go numb. Her head wilted between her
knees. It was not so much, but it was something. She had done what
she intended to do. She had risked, and been true to her life. She had
wanted to get the facts straight in her head, and had done that. She
had wanted to prove herself—capable. Again capable. Prove somehow
that there were no strings on her, that she was chained to no particular destiny; except the one she wanted for herself. And she had not
crawled back into bed with Myles. Her poor mother. How much of
this had she ever known or wanted to know or needed to know?
Dana looked aloft into the milky sky and imagined the dead waiting

there, a sky crowded with dead, dead following dead, one dead "for every stone that is now in Carn Lecca." Her brother and her grandfather and now her mother, and back somewhere the love between her and McGee. All dead. The Dement she had known, dead. Now there was just she and her father, the last of the Risings. Her father with his broken voice and suppressed rage and sorrow. She would go to him now.

Dana looked at her watch. It was late. She drank the last of the coffee and began to move. She set a fast pace down, finding the path and sticking to it, at times running headlong through the heavy grass, the thermos slapping against her leg. She rushed to the center of town, then loped down the road to her house. She never looked back, glad finally to be rid of the mountain and its hawks and oratories and ledges. When she reached the front door Cathy and Myles were there, looking nervous. Cathy ran to her with a cry and she knew then that Myles had told her. Bless him. She comforted her daughter and moved off into the house; she was packed, but it would take her a moment to check everything. She would not be back in Ireland. Just a minute or two, she said; I'll be right along. Then she hurried upstairs with Cathy, wanting to talk with her a little, and explain why they were going home to Dement to be with her grandfather, who needed them both now.

THEY MADE good time, Myles driving. McGee and Shirley were to arrive at one-thirty from Paris, then board the three o'clock Aer Lingus to New York. Dana dreaded everything about the flight and sat staring out the window as Myles sped along the narrow country lanes. She believed she wanted to live in Ireland forever; there was nothing about it that reminded her of the United States. At Shannon he drove directly to the terminal, wheeling the car smartly to a halt at the curb.

He said, "I want to come in with you. And I think I will."

From the rear seat Cathy said, "Why can't Myles come with us?"

He looked at her. "It's popular demand."

"Yes," she said thickly. "Yes, please."

"Excellent," he said.

"I want you there when we meet McGee and that woman." Then she corrected herself. "Shirley."

"I've got to park this car." They all looked around them, as if the car were suddenly an insurmountable obstacle.

"We'll go with you," Dana said. "We're only a few minutes late. They can wait for ten minutes. Do them good, a wait."

Myles turned away into the parking lot and quickly found a space. He fetched the three bags from the trunk and the three of them began to walk to the terminal. When they entered he felt Cathy's hand stiffen in his own and knew that she had seen them. Then he saw them both standing beside the information booth, McGee looking agitated and his wife grim. It was either satisfied or grim, one or the other. Not a bad-looking woman, Myles thought; a little too "done" for his taste; you could hang a sign around her neck—wet paint, don't touch. But a good-looking woman nonetheless, though not so good-looking as Dana; not so alive; not so graceful. She didn't move as provocatively as Dana did, thought she was making a good show now, finding her smile as Cathy and Dana walked slowly toward them. McGee bent at the waist to accept his daughter and Dana and Shirley shook hands. Myles brought up the rear with the suitcases and he could see McGee's jaw muscles tighten as he recognized him. McGee did not, in the strictest sense, "approve" of Myles's presence in the ménage. "Irregular," he had described it to Dana. She was talking in a low voice, and though her shoulders were squared and her head was high, she looked small and vulnerable before them. He saw Cathy turn away and both McGee and Shirley register shock and heard their words, which came in chorus, *I'm so sorry.* McGee's hand went instinctively to Dana's but he offered a brief touch, no more. Dana mumbled a few more words in a low voice and then McGee turned to Myles.

"How are you, good to see you. You know Shirley, Myles?"

Shirley smiled cordially at him and they shook hands. She said, "I think we could all use a drink."

"There's not much time," McGee said doubtfully.

"Nonsense," Shirley said. "There's plenty of time."

Dana said, "I'll go check us in, Cathy and me. You all go to the bar—"

"Of course," McGee said. "You're on the flight, too."

"For the funeral," Dana said. She winked at Cathy and she and Myles walked off. They leaned against the counter while the attendant went through the formalities of checking tickets against passports and collecting the airport tax. Myles kissed her on the cheek and she smiled bleakly. Then she collected her tickets and passport and they turned and slowly walked the length of the terminal.

"What do you think of her now?"

Myles shrugged. "She's all right."

"Stylish," Dana said.

"Yes, that."

"Sexy."

"Not sexy," Myles said.

"Very sexy."

"How the hell would you know?"

"She wears clothes well."

"She wears expensive clothes and does as well as she can with them. Limited equipment."

Dana smiled grimly. "You're saying all the right things. I've never known you to fail to say the right things."

"That is because I always speak the truth," Myles said.

"She pushes him around," Dana said.

Myles looked at her aslant. "Nonsense."

"All right," she said. "Touché." She put her hand in his pocket and made a fist. "Myles, I don't want to go with them on this flight. I don't want to have to talk to them. I want to be by myself for a while. I don't want to make chitchat—"

"I'll explain it to McGee."

"No," she said. "I'll explain it."

"You explain it to her. I'll explain it to him."

She said, "You explain it to her."

"No, she's so sexy I'm afraid my emotions will run away with me and I'll rape her on the barstool."

She punched him in the ribs and laughed. "We're going to say good-bye here."

"No, I want an Irish coffee. And I want that son of a bitch to pay for it." They were approaching the airport bar and she pulled on this pocket. "Hey," she said. "You've been good, you know?" He grunted and walked on a few steps. She said, "I'll see you in New York. Just drop the key to the house off at the agent's, lock the doors—" They were moving relentlessly to the bar; she could see the three of them at a table near the door. No one was talking. "Lamb, please." He turned to look at her and saw she was near tears. He pulled her off to one side and they leaned against the wall, her head on his chest. McGee was watching them from the bar, frowning. He said, "Remember, I'm not going to New York from here. I'm going to London." She said, "Oh," as if she hadn't heard him correctly. He reminded her that he had an interview at the BBC; a promising job, working with an old friend. She smiled and did not let go of him. "Of course," he said, "I might not take it." She said, "You'll take it. You always do." Her voice was muffled and he could not discern its tone. He said, "London doesn't have a lot of appeal for me right now." She nodded sadly. "When are you due back in New York then?" He said briskly, "Not long, before the end of the month for sure. To collect my things. That is, if I take the job. Which I don't think I will." He said, "You take it easy now." She looked at her watch and nodded, then at him, so weather-beaten in his dark corduroy coat and shapeless trousers; his hands looked a size too large. Their eyes locked, slid away, and locked again. They stood silently for a moment and then their arms were around each other and they kissed. Dana, on tiptoe, ran her hand through his hair, tugging a little, her fingers trembling. Then with a whispered word she was gone, through the glass doors, meeting McGee and Shirley and Cathy. McGee was agitated; his coat was over his arm and he was standing, consulting his watch. Dana seemed aware of herself as she sat down quietly and listened to McGee. Then they all rose. Myles watched it for a moment, feeling very much a foreigner; he hated to see her go. He wondered what he would do now, alone in Ireland for a week. He was a man who liked company, the more company the better, except when he and Dana were alone. The prospect of a sedentary holiday in a small town in western Ireland did not amuse him. He knew some journalists in Belfast; perhaps he could go there. Also an old friend in Dublin. He could call the old friend and go there for the weekend. Or say the hell with it and go to London now. Walking to the car he realized she had not told him what to do with it. He supposed she'd rented it at the airport and he could return it there. *Oh hell,* he muttered aloud. She'd said, *I like you so much.* He'd figure out what to do later, in Hanrahan's. There was no better place. There were always one or two soakers in Hanrahan's, ready for talk and drink; there would be no lack of companionship for the remainder of the afternoon. He did not have to be alone after all.

The aircraft was not full. The four of them boarded together, McGee and Cathy leading the way, Dana purposely bringing up the rear. Outside it was raining lightly, "a soft day" as the Irish said. McGee found four seats together and indicated to Dana that she take the single. Cathy could sit next to the window, he could sit next to Cathy, Shirley could sit next to him, and Dana could sit across the aisle. It was like seating a formal dinner, Dana thought. Shirley complained that they were not traveling first class, where the seats were larger and the company more agreeable. McGee replied patiently that first-class seats were expensive and the holiday had already cost him "the crown jewels." Cathy asked for a glass of water. Shirley said that the stewardess would be by in a moment, dear. Why didn't McGee go forward to fetch some magazines, *Time* or *Paris Match* if they had it? Why hadn't he thought to buy a newspaper in the terminal? Cathy said that she was really thirsty *now.* McGee replied that if she wanted a newspaper she could have bought one herself, newsstands were not sexist in their sales policies. They would sell to anyone, male or female. Cathy asked when they were going to get there. Shirley said that it would be about

six and a half hours, dear. McGee tried without success to cross his
long legs, and cursed the narrowness of the space. He said, "Shit."
Shirley said that she would've bought a newspaper if she'd only
thought of it. That was her mistake right there because of course she
couldn't depend on him. Cathy said that the stewardess was just coming down the aisle, would Shirley ask her for a glass of water, please.
Shirley complied and the stewardess smiled and replied that it would
be just a moment, dear. And drinks too, you will have drinks? Shirley
asked. As soon as we are airborne, ma'am, we will be serving drinks
and a meal shortly thereafter. McGee grumbled that the damn seats
were too narrow for his long legs but Aer Lingus was a fine airline, he
liked the Irish accent. Shirley smiled triumphantly and said nothing.
Cathy looked out the window at the rain and wondered when the
plane would leave and her father replied, In a minute, precious. Dana
told them that she wanted to nap for a bit and would return later,
when dinner was served, maybe. McGee grunted. Shirley said that she
had some Dramamine and sleeping pills, if Dana needed either one;
the sleeping pills were prescription and perfectly safe. Thanks no,
Dana said. These trips were such a bore, Shirley said. Indeed, they
were, said Dana. She was standing now. Shirley smiled warmly and
said that after Dana had had her nap they could have a drink together,
pointedly adding that she would join her in the rear, at her seat, where
they could stretch out a bit. How nice, Dana said, and fled to the rear
of the plane.

   She sat in an aisle seat and watched the plane taxi to the end of the
runway, turn abruptly, and heave forward. As they banked steeply over
the airport, she looked for Myles in the little Austin; no sign of him.
She wondered what he would do alone for a week. She doubted he
would stick it out; for sure he'd fly to London or Paris to see friends.
Myles, poor lamb; whenever he began to feel the slightest bit caged he
found a new job. His cage doors slammed like clockwork once a year;
you could set your watch by it. She liked him better than any man she
had ever known, and was in love with him in some region of her heart
and mind; but just now she was content to be alone. She looked

straight up the aisle. The other three were sitting calmly, not speaking, staring straight ahead. Cathy looked to be reading something; she could just see the top of her head between the seats. The stewardess was serving them drinks and McGee leaned over and took both trays, handing one to Shirley. He had changed very little physically, since they'd met thirteen years ago. He still wore his hair short and had not gained a pound, or did not appear to have gained; he remained slim as a pencil and only his sideburns showed white. What was he now? Forty-eight or thereabouts, a boyish middle-aged man. He did not look forty-eight unless you had known him when he was thirty-five. It was strange, the absence of obvious signs of aging, thinning hair, weight, a certain ponderousness, made him ... suspicious. She thought with a smile that he was one of those men who looked older than they looked. It was all there if you'd known him before, in the expression around the eyes, the brittleness of his fingers, the fussiness. It was present in his conversation; he always had an abstracted quality. Now he seemed permanently tuned low, a man of muted volume, very well bred. But Good God he had been a handsome man, there was a time when she could not keep her hands away from him; and vice versa. The physical contrast with Myles was striking, Myles so bulky, lines everywhere, a paunch, muscular arms, thick fingernails, bristling eyebrows, a big smile always. It was like putting a buffalo next to a racehorse.

She watched the Irish coast recede, then disappear altogether as they flew into a cloud. She gave her order to the stewardess, who had finally reached the rear seat. The plane was only half full and Dana had no one next to her. She moved her shoulders irritably, then reached under her shirt and unhooked her bra. It felt more uncomfortable unhooked than hooked so she went into the lavatory to take it off altogether. She took off her shirt and sweater and struck a pose in the mirror. She pivoted to inspect her back, still raw where Myles had scratched her; or bit her, one or the other. But *nicely,* she remembered. Myles was always gentle. Except for that afternoon on the mountain; he had not been very darn gentle then; but she hadn't been particularly gentle either. She stood in the bad light, hands on her hips, and regarded herself. She was in no way sagging, and there were only hints of handles above her hips. She stood up straighter and they disappeared. Flat stomach, smooth neck, good shoulders, no gray. She touched the nipple of her right breast and felt it harden and felt also the beginning of a blush. She bit her lip and smiled at herself in the mirror: she was all there, nothing was missing. Then she turned sideways and threw her shoulders back. There was a red patch on her ribs where the bra had dug into her and she rubbed it now, brushing the underside of her breasts with her fingers; they thickened and rose at her touch and she smiled again. She liked them well enough but wished they were just the slightest bit larger. Every man she had ever known had praised her and reassured her that she was Perfect (and women had always looked at her with admiration) but from the time she was twelve she'd wished for just a little bit more. *Perfect*. Men repeated it like a litany, a public prayer of confidence and celebration. No, her tits had never lacked for attention. Myles told her that he intended for Harvard to receive them for their well-known Tit Bank at the world-famous medical school. This official Bank was a secret closely guarded by the authorities at Cambridge but since he, Myles, was a valued graduate he had "pull" and could assure her that whatever happened to the rest of her body and soul her tits would have eternal life and would in fact be—*cloned*. She was not to worry, he would see to it . . . She began to giggle and the plane gave a lurch, sending her back against the bulkhead. She leaned against it, her head to one side, her thumbs in her trousers, knees apart, remembering her and Myles together on the slope of the mountain, the sudden wonderful violence of it. *Oh damn,* she said softly, aching, her thoughts backstepping in time, the vivid past enclosed by the present; never forgetting the present; the present surrounded her always as the film raced. Deliberately turning away from the mirror she put on her shirt and the sweater over it and put the bra in her handbag, deep and out of sight. Her nipples stood out plainly inside her sweater and she thought that was a shame because no one was there to see them. If

Myles were there he'd make a lewd remark and do his best to excite her, thirty thousand feet above the Atlantic Ocean. It wouldn't take much, she thought. She stood another second looking at herself in the mirror. She heard a voice; the pilot was explaining something. Well, she had always had good coloring; auburn hair, good bones, genuine smile, a slender soft body, and at that moment a flushed face.

She returned to find her drink on the middle seat. When she sat down she noticed the stewardess look back, then quickly front. Probably wondering what had happened to her. Then she saw McGee approaching her, walking slowly down the aisle on the way to the lavatory. She hoped her vibrations were still there. Serve him right.

"You got a drink all right."

"I did."

"I paid for it," he said.

"Well, thanks."

"Dana, I'm truly sorry—"

She held up her hand and for an instant her mind went blank. She crossed her legs. "Thank you."

"Was it sudden?"

"Well, you know." Dana knew she was perspiring; beads of sweat jumped through her skin. "She's been sick for years. But no, there wasn't any warning."

"Well, it's a hell of a thing," he said slowly.

"I want to take Cathy with me, you know. Out there for the funeral."

"Well, Dana, she's only nine."

"I believe that children should know the bad with the good," Dana said rapidly. "They should witness funerals as well as weddings. That's what I believe. I've always believed it. Don't fight me on this, please."

"We'd made arrangements." He glanced over her head, out the window.

"Can they be canceled?"

His smile was fleeting. "Nothing's graven in stone."

She said. "No, it isn't." She pushed her knees together with both hands. "It'll only be for a couple of days, my dad hasn't seen her for a year. It'll make things easier for him, perhaps. On the other hand, perhaps not."

"That's what I was thinking, and it might be hard on Cathy—" He leaned over her now, perched on the arm of the seat across the aisle.

"It's something I believe very strongly. I want her with me now. Those arrangements, whatever they are you can cancel them. And please do. I can explain it to Shirley if you don't want to." She was being sharper than she wanted. She knew he would not, in the end, refuse her. But she didn't want to argue with him. Really, she didn't want to talk to him at all.

He said, "All right, Dana. Under protest."

She shrugged. Her head was beginning to ache and she took a swallow of her drink. "I'll let you know from Dement when she'll be back. It'll be ten days at the most."

"I don't want to quarrel with you Dana," he said stiffly. "It's so good to see Cathy again, she seems to have had a pleasant enough time with you." He looked at her with his dry eyes and bland smile.

"And Myles," she said.

"Myles, too," he said.

She said, "They're great friends." She put her shoulders back against the seat and patted her stomach.

"Is that right?" he asked coolly.

"Yes, they went—swimming. Every day." Then she said, "They built sand castles together." She was laying waste to everything now and enjoying it. She watched him nod slowly and noticed that his knuckles were white, gripping the seat in front of her.

"Well, they must have had fun then."

"We all did," she said, leaning away from him. "Me. And Cathy. And Myles."

He looked straight at her then, as grim as she had ever seen him. Suddenly she felt ashamed and turned away, though the expression on her face did not change. He leaned down and said in her ear, "When did you decide to be such a bitch?" Then he stood up and straightened his tie and went on to the lavatory.

She slumped in her seat and looked out the window. She was no longer perspiring and her hands were still. The clouds were below them now and the plane seemed to float through the atmosphere; there was no sensation of speed. She took a swallow of her drink and held the glass at arm's length to reassure herself that she was steady. She decided that she felt both better and worse for all that. She heard the lavatory door open and felt him brush her arm as he moved up the aisle, no backward glances. She could not suppress it, and why should she; she had a connection with him. She could not destroy it, no matter what she did. They had had a child together but the connection went beyond that. No one could ever know her as he knew her. He had a part of her and would always have it. She had come to him fresh, had opened herself in a way that she never would, never *could,* ever again. She would have given her life for him. Those bright, fresh, crowded hours—they had behaved like spendthrifts; there was no end to anything. It was a time when all promises were kept. She looked at his angular body, settling in between his wife and daughter. She had known every turn and crevice in that body. Now she could hardly remember it at all. There was a long ragged scar, but was it on the right or left thigh? She had known everything there was to know about him and she supposed that somewhere in her memory she had it still. She did not care for him as a man now and was surely not in love with him. But the connection remained, similar to the connection with her own family. Her grandfather, her parents; the parent that was dead as well as the parent that was alive. She watched him turn to his daughter and smile and the smile stirred her because he was the first man she had ever truly *watched*—move a certain way, speak, and smile. She saw Cathy tilt her head and laugh. There was a Rising look to her. There in the nine-year-old were parts of her grandfather, her parents, herself. She had her mother's shy look around the eyes and the way she held her hands when standing. Dana smiled. It wasn't true that all promises were dead; some were and some were not. There was always a new promise to be made and kept; the world was full of promises. They were still laughing, father and daughter. She felt wretched, she should have asked McGee about his father. She hadn't seen Harold

McGee in five years; he was retired now and living somewhere on Long Island. Maybe he was living in the beach house, that funny sanctuary, that place they'd both loved so. She swallowed her drink in a gulp and closed her eyes. She breathed very carefully. One, she said, two, three; she said, four. The surge came from behind her eyes and she fought it back. One, two, three. She saw her mother's face as she had been as a young woman, a determined woman who stood at the center, holding things together, a woman of no little strength and purpose. Too young. Surely too young to die. She squeezed her lips together and felt the pressure recede, and then disappear. She'd won; it was gone now. She breathed out, a long sigh. Her eyes popped open.

"Goody!" Shirley McGee, gray eyes bright as stars, sat down beside her. "Now we can have our little chitchat," she said, and began to talk about her husband.

3.

DANA PULLED into the driveway and stopped at once, her head resting on the steering wheel. She turned off the engine and watched a flight of blackbirds approach from the field and settle in the big oaks, each bird releasing a memory, their cries like tolling bells. She opened the door and got out of the car, her head fuzzy from lack of sleep and the long hours of concentration. She scuffed through the wet leaves on the lawn, the leaves clinging to her shoes. The air was stale and damp but she breathed deeply, walking away from the car. The high trees were dark and forbidding in the failing light but at the top of the driveway the house looked cheerful. The porch light was on and from a distance she thought she could see movement behind the curtains. But the kitchen was dark and empty. She pulled her coat around her and walked to the stand of oaks, the place where she went to smoke cigarettes as a teenager, and dream of jazz bands and voyages and feasts. The blackbirds flew off into the field, screeching; in the distance was a house that had not been there a year ago. She turned away, facing her own house now, the stone birdbath and the cast-iron love seat in the foreground, the shrubs flanking the driveway, and on the second floor the window to her own room, the cloister from which she had viewed the world. She smiled sadly, home at last. She began to move up the lawn toward the house and the front door swung open, the inside light silhouetting her father. He was motionless in the doorway and she walked toward him up the lawn and still he did not move. His hands were at his sides and he looked to his left and right, and then saw her car at the end of the driveway. "Dad?" She walked more quickly now and he came out of the doorway and onto the front steps. His head jerked upward then and he came carefully down the steps and across the driveway, his shoes crunching the gravel. His walk was unsteady and still he did not seem to hear her, though he was only a few yards away now. He wore no coat and his shirt was unbuttoned, his tie at half-mast. He was looking at her directly now and his face broke open in a crooked smile. She ran the last few yards and they embraced on the wet lawn in front of the cars. His skin felt feverish, as if he'd been wrapped in a blanket. They stood there swaying a moment, close, then turned and walked into the house, arms around each other's waists. Inside they embraced again and she began to cry. He comforted her with his arms and helped her off with her coat. She turned to look into the kitchen but it was dark, and when she looked up the hall stairs she saw the second floor was dark, too. There were fresh flowers in the hall and in the living room. Her Uncle Tony stood as they entered the living room, and the old wall clock chimed six.

"My God," she said. "I left Cathy in the car."

"Cathy's *here?*" Charles Rising turned away in confusion.

Dana nodded. "In the car. I left it at the end of the driveway." She laughed apologetically. "I'll go get her."

"Oh Dana," he said. "You should not've brought her, it's no thing for a child—"

"Dad, she's almost ten years old."

"Yes, that's what I mean, she's just a little thing."

But Dana was already out of the room and opening the front door. She strode briskly down the driveway to her car. Cathy was still sleeping, curled up in the front seat. Dana drove the car to the front door and gently prodded her daughter. "We're here," she said as the child wakened slowly. "Sleepy?" She nodded. "We'll get you right into bed. But first we'll say hello to Grandpa and Uncle Tony. You remember Uncle Tony?" Cathy nodded sleepily. "We'll leave the bags until later. You can go up and have a nap and then come down for dinner if you want to." They got out of the car together and saw both men standing on the stoop. Cathy ran to her grandfather and he scooped her up. Dana thought he looked hardly strong enough to lift her, but she came off the ground easily and put her arms around Charles Rising's neck. The four of them went into the house and Dana took Cathy straight up to her old room. She needed no urging to go straight to sleep. She was asleep again when her head touched the pillow. Dana kissed her on the cheek and went into the bathroom to put a cold towel on her face and brush her teeth. The room had not changed; it retained a little-girl look and smelled vaguely of stale cologne. Dana stood wearily at the basin. She had not slept at all the night before, they were late arriving in New York. Of course there had been no sleep on the airplane, Mrs. Shirley McGee had seen to that. She stood for a moment with the wet washcloth on her face, then went on downstairs. Both men were talking quietly in front of the fire. They rose when she entered the room.

She took Tony's chair and moved it closer to the fireplace, explaining about the flight. McGee and Shirley at Shannon and the late arrival at Kennedy, an overheated motel room until seven a.m., the delay of the flight's departure until nine. The only comfort she had was Cathy, who was an excellent traveler; not a word of complaint from her. But it had been an exhausting two days, though she supposed nothing compared to Dement.

Her father shrugged, his eyes on the fire. He said, "We tried to cable you, telephone. When Lee went into the hospital at first. No answer on the phone and no answer to the cable."

She said, "We didn't get any cable, Dad."

"I suppose they aren't very efficient over there."

She said, "No."

"Well," he said. "She had a seizure on—" He looked at Tony, who said, *Friday; it was Friday.* "Friday, early in the afternoon. We called an ambulance and I went with her to the hospital. Stayed there most of the night, then went to see Elliott Townsend Saturday afternoon. I guess I got back to the hospital around eight. They said she'd had a fairly comfortable day but she was still in a coma. But I hadn't felt good about her all day. She looked—sick. Sicker than before but the doctors were hopeful." He paused and looked at his hands, for a moment lost in thought. "The hospital's improved quite a bit in the last few years, it isn't what it was. It's better. Better doctors, though you'd be surprised how many are foreign-born. Indians, Orientals. Well," he said. "I returned about eight. Elliott and I had had a long talk and I was tired. I just sat for a while and then I guess I fell asleep. I woke up and went to sit by her bed, you know; hold her hand. And she looked to me then as if she'd gone." He was still staring at the fire, talking now as if to himself. Dana put her hand on his arm and he covered it with his own hand. "I was very alarmed and called the nurse who did— whatever they do. Checked her pulse, her heart. She told me that Lee was all right. No change in her condition. I remember she looked closely at the I-V and some other gadget they had hooked up. I don't know about these things. The nurse." He paused and swallowed hard. "Insisted that I go next door and rest myself. The room next door was empty. They added a new wing to it, you know, and there are about eighty more beds than when you were around here. It's really a very fine hospital, as fine as any in the state."

"Dad," she said. "We can talk about this later."

"No," he said calmly. "So I went next door. I didn't want to go, you understand, but the nurse insisted. And I must confess that I was tired, maybe as tired as I've ever been in my life. I haven't felt so red-hot lately, so I permitted myself to be taken next door. But I couldn't sleep. Have you ever been so tired you couldn't sleep? My mind wouldn't stop working, it was as if there were people inside my brain who wouldn't stop talking. I felt like covering my ears, and I remember that I did; but it didn't help any. The talk went on and on as if there was a meeting going on inside, everyone talking at once. I don't know, maybe I was dreaming." He stopped again and opened his mouth; she could hear his tongue snap. She pressed his arm but he appeared not to notice. He said, "Strangers' voices. So after a little I got up again and wandered out into the corridor to the nurses' station to get a glass of water. I must've been quite a sight because the nurse insisted I go back and wanted to give me a sleeping pill. But I said I was allergic; sleeping pills upset my stomach. I remember, we were talking in whispers at the nurses' station. She finally got me to admit that I wasn't allergic. She told me they were doing everything they could for Lee but that I had to be strong, too. Then she led me back to her room and we looked in and I remember—" He looked away and his hand moved away from hers and settled on his knee. His body was rigid, as if made of iron. She looked at Tony, alarmed, but Tony shook his head. It was a gesture that said, Let him talk. "Somehow the needle had worked loose in her arm. I don't know, maybe she had a convulsion. But the nurse quickly went in and closed the door, leaving me in the corridor. Hospital corridors have a strange light at night, did you ever notice it? You don't know where the light is coming from. Well, there was a wheelchair in the corridor and I just sat down on it. And of course then I couldn't help thinking about the time Dad was in the hospital. It was in the old part of the hospital of course, the walls and floors built of wood. Damn place was a firetrap and of course they use it as a storehouse or something now. This new place, it's steel and concrete and the floors are covered with a sort of rubber. Rubber linoleum."

"Sterile," she said.

"Um?" He looked at her pleasantly.

"Sterile. Antiseptic."

"Yes," he said. "That, too."

She said, "Not *warm*."

"No. So." He looked around the room, as if to get his bearings. It was a room that had not changed in twenty years, all the things in it familiar to them both; the books and pictures and bric-a-brac. His eyes rested on a photograph of his father, then he was staring at the fire again. "She came out of the room, a nice, capable woman. This nurse. She said that Lee was all right but that she was going to call the doctor. Meanwhile, I was not to go in. I was to go to the room next door. She was very firm about that, though of course I could've overruled her. Rising money helped build that hospital, and of course . . . Do you think I should have overruled her?"

Dana shook her head. No.

Tony said, "No, Charlie. You did what you could."

"Yes," he said. "Well. I did go next door. She was leading me like a child and talking. I had all those damned voices and her, too." He smiled unexpectedly and they all laughed as if a great joke had been made.

Dana said, "Poor Daddy."

"But it was what the nurse said to do."

"Of, of course," she said hastily. "Of *course.*"

"But the nurse doesn't know the family."

Tony said firmly, "You did the right thing."

"She didn't understand that the family always stuck together. *Always.*" He'd lost the thread of his story and looked at Dana, puzzled. The silence grew.

"The nurse," she said gently.

"Oh yes, I'm not sure that she understood what Lee expected."

Tony said, "She was doing what was for the best, medically."

"Yes, she called the doctor." He nodded sharply and began to talk in rapid bursts. "I went with her to the nurses' station though of course I couldn't hear what they were saying on the telephone. She spoke with the receiver right up to her teeth, like this." He put his fist to his mouth. "But at the end I heard her say, Thank you, doctor, and give me a big bright smile. Then the two of us walked on down to the room next to Lee's. I didn't notice it as she was walking but she had two sleeping pills and a glass of water with her. She gave me some pa-

jamas, one of those darned *smocks* they wear. Flimsy white things.
Made me get into it and then made me get into bed. She was very polite but very determined. I took both pills and swallowed them down
with water and I can tell you the nurse looked relieved."

Dana winked at Tony. "She didn't want *two* patients, Daddy."

"No, she didn't want two. One was enough."

Dana said, "So you fell asleep at last."

He shook his head. "Not right away. I told her that I was allergic to
sleeping pills. That wasn't true, I'm not allergic to anything. What is
true is that they don't have a big effect on me, never did. They *work* of
course, but it takes time for them to work."

"Just like Dad," Tony said.

"Exactly," Charles said. "Exactly like Dad."

"Takes more than a couple damn pills to put a Rising down."

"Much more," Charles said. "Much more. Do you remember?" He
reached over and tapped Tony's knee, almost cheerful now. "Do you
remember, the pills the old man was taking, at the end?" He smiled
and shook his head. "Damn hospital room looked like a pharmacist's,
the blue pill, the green pill, the yellow pill. Anyway—"

"They don't work on me either," Dana said.

"You don't take sleeping pills?" her father asked.

"Once or twice," she said.

"You're too young to take sleeping pills."

She smiled at him and touched his arm reassuringly. "I don't take
them very often. Hardly ever."

He said, "Good. That's good." Then, "Anyway, I could hear her go
off down the hall and the corridor was silent. I could feel myself begin
to relax, ohhhh I was tired. Tired everywhere. My *bones* were tired.
But I got up and opened the door and looked out and there was no
one in sight. The corridor was absolutely empty. I felt like some criminal, skulking around without the authority to do so. I tiptoed into the
hall and went next door to look in on Lee. I just wanted to make *sure,*
you know. I just wanted to *know.*" He looked at them both in turn, to
assure himself that they were listening and understanding. "—to *know*

that she was really all right, not that I suspected anything. The nurse was nice as could be, and competent. But you know the way they sometimes are in hospitals, they don't want you to know everything. I guess they think you aren't capable of understanding it. All professional people are like that, doctors as well as lawyers. They think they've got some secret—"

"And they don't at all," Dana said.

"And they don't at all. But the sheet was pulled up over her face and she was dead."

Dana groaned and put her hand over her eyes; a thickness settled on her chest and she felt the tears coming. Her chest began to heave and the bottom went out of her stomach and she put her head between her knees. Tears were coming from between her fingers. She felt arms go around her back and was grateful for them. In a moment she heard herself through the roaring in her ears. Hands were holding her shoulders together like bookends. She opened her eyes and took her hands away and her tears dropped to the carpet. She turned her cheek to touch the hand on her shoulder and saw a huge signet ring. Tony's. It was Tony holding her. She looked to the other side and saw her father sitting as before, staring straight ahead, his fingers just touching his mouth. She began to count, one, two, three, four. She patted Tony's hand and it went away, resting now on her back. He handed her a handkerchief and she wiped her eyes and blew her nose. Her father looked at her then and put his hand on her knee and gently squeezed it. His own eyes were glittering and his smile was cracked. She kissed his hand and looked at him. He moved closer to her then, and spoke into her ear, almost whispering.

"The nurse didn't know."

"No," she said brokenly.

"You see, if I'd been with her—"

Dana said, "No, Dad."

"If I'd been with her. There." He shrugged as if to say to all the world, *Well, then, it would have been all right.*

She said, "Daddy."

He said, "She didn't know the family, you see." He was still whispering and she had difficulty understanding him. Tony was standing in front of them and she looked at him for guidance. He made a motion with his hands, half helpless, half encouraging. She said, "Dad."

"I must've blanked out for a while. Something happened. I don't know. I stayed with her as long as I could. I went back to the chair I was sitting in before. I stayed with her as long as I could stay awake, and then I went back to my own room. I didn't think it was right—" It was as if he'd sustained a defeat. "I went back to my own room, I don't know how late it was. I didn't look at my watch." He paused; this seemed to him an immensely important fact. "It was after midnight surely, but not yet dawn. Perhaps it was two o'clock in the morning." He nodded, satisfied now that his time estimate was correct. "The drugs were taking hold of me then, to a fare-thee-well. And I climbed into bed and went to sleep. The next morning Doc Nelson woke me and told me the news. I didn't let on that I knew already, I didn't see any point to that. That was Sunday morning, around nine o'clock."

"That was when you called me, Charlie."

"I called Tony then, and of course we phoned you. You were back from wherever you'd been because you answered the phone. No. We tried in the morning and couldn't get you and then again an hour later. And of course we'd cabled. We finally got you about four o'clock, our time."

"We'd been—out," Dana said.

"Yes, that's what we guessed. And there was no one else in your house."

"No, there wasn't."

"Charlie," Tony said softly. "Dana didn't know—"

"I'm here now, Daddy," she said.

He said, "Thank God." Then he turned away again, toward the fire. "Why didn't they tell me at the time? She was dead in the next room and they didn't tell me. The nurse must have told the doctor when she went down to telephone. She was already dead then, and I wasn't told."

Tony and Dana were silent, looking at each other. Finally she said, "Just what you said before, Dad. They don't understand about Risings. They just didn't know."

Tony nodded. "They're fools."

"I guess so," Charles Rising said. He continued to stare at the fire.

"Dana?" Tony said, "The funeral's tomorrow. Privately, only the family." She nodded. "Only a graveside service, nothing at the church." She nodded again. "That was what your father wanted and he knew you'd agree."

"Yes, that's what Mom would've wanted."

"It won't be fancy," he said. "That's what your father thought, and I agree."

She said, "Well," looking down at her hands.

Tony said, "It'll be private."

Then her father stood, rising slowly. He stood blinking in the light. "The nurse didn't understand that we take care of our own in this family, we always have since my father's day. She didn't understand that, that nurse. That's all there *is*—" His voice trailed away and he began to move aimlessly around the room, touching things. "That's all a life counts for, the connection to other lives." Dana looked at him, nodding in agreement; encouraging him. "Your own," he said. "Having your own, living with them, dying with them. Keeping what's yours, knowing what it is and keeping it. What's yours alone, your spirit and flesh and blood. That above all." He was still in motion, now behind her, wandering to the window. "Keeping it and having the strength to keep it, until your strength gives out. Keeping love." He looked at them both with his glittering eyes. "Until it gives out which it always does and then someone takes it away from you."

Tony shook his head. "You did everything you possibly could, Charlie."

"Nobody does," he said.

"It's a changed world, it isn't the same." Tony went on in that vein for a moment but his brother wasn't listening, and at the end he knew that.

"It's a rotten life," Charles Rising said, walking stiffly across the carpet to the liquor cabinet. He stood fiddling with a bottle. "It's the rottenest life that ever was."

"Oh, Dad," Dana began.

"But I will survive it," he said.

SHE FIXED bacon and eggs for him but he only picked at his plate. Everything was over now. He seemed to grow stronger after the funeral, which he had not permitted Cathy to attend. Too sad for children, he said; they'll find out about all this soon enough. Besides, it would break his heart to see her there, next to the open grave. Dana resisted but finally gave in. She didn't have the heart to argue with him, though for a moment she wanted to force it. He had been distant with her, not cold or unkind, simply distant. She wanted to believe they could speak openly with each other, but he was inhabiting another world altogether. It was a world that could not be reached by normal means. So she waited in the overwhelmingly silent house, the house that she had known her entire life; the house whose every detail showed the hand of her mother. He looked like a stranger in it, traveling from room to room like someone lost or unfamiliar with its design. The night before they had stayed up late, reminiscing a little, then playing a game of backgammon—he'd found the backgammon board in a closet and suggested a game. The last time he'd played was twenty years before when on a vacation with Your Mother somewhere. A cruise, he thought it was a cruise. They played two games and then he lost interest. She turned on the television set but that did not hold him either. At length he had gone to bed, abruptly rising and leaving the room until her voice brought him back. With an apologetic smile he returned and kissed her on both cheeks and wished her a pleasant night, then with the same vacant gait moved out of the room and up the stairs to bed. From the top step she heard him call her name and she went to the hallway to see what he wanted. "It was a nice service, wasn't it?" His tone was that of a man asking a question to which he required a specific answer. He peered down at her from the second-floor balustrade. She replied, Yes it was; a beautiful service. He said that he thought so, too, but wanted to make sure. She said she agreed with him completely, it was very beautiful. He nodded and smiled at her and went off to bed. Now, the next morning, he was sitting at the kitchen table, staring at his cup of coffee. She had tried to make conversation, mentioning articles on the front page of the *Tribune*. But he was not interested in the scandal in Washington. One scandal was no different from another. Then, suddenly, he shook his head as if to clear it. He massaged his neck and opened his eyes wide and looked at her, as if seeing her for the first time. He poured fresh coffee in his cup and lit a cigarette and offered her one.

"Dana?" He looked at her a long minute, carefully weighing his words. He fussed with his coffee cup a moment and then he said, "I'm going to sell the *I*."

His tone had changed then; he seemed crisp and decisive. But she could not tell if he were serious. She said, "Oh, Dad. It's so soon—"

"Meeting with the fella today."

"*Today?*"

"Talked to him yesterday, he'll be here today with his lawyer. Elliott has gone over the papers. I'm meeting him in my office at eleven o'clock this morning. You're invited, if you want to come."

"Oh, Dad—"

"I've been thinking about it for some time, before your mother—" He pursed his lips and turned away. "I've been thinking about it for a year or more. I remember, I once mentioned it to you; years ago. Remember?" He smiled. "No one thought I was serious. But I was serious. Then and now."

She leaned forward, her two hands touching his. "What was that," she said quietly, "that you said the other night about keeping what was yours?" She felt that she had no right to ask him not to do it, or to plead with him in any way. But she saw it as a last act. Without the *I*, the family would cease to exist. She said, "What will you do? I can't imagine you without your office at the *I*, going to it every day. You, Tony, Mr. Townsend."

"They want me to stay on the board."

"But—" She paused to collect her thoughts. She saw he was smiling at her. "But you wouldn't *own* it, it wouldn't be yours anymore. How could you watch others, outsiders, run the *I*. They want you down there as window dressing, I remember once you told me—"

"That's why I'm not going to do it," he said evenly.

"Who are the—buyers?"

"A family from downstate, Dows. They already own two newspapers and a television and a radio station, and I think they've got the cable license in a couple of towns. Solid people, run a good outfit. There's the old man, he's a little older than I am; and his boy. His son runs it, a nice boy; you'd like him, maybe. He's a regular genius with computers, he understands the business the way it is now. He"—her father laughed with genuine amusement—"kicked his old man upstairs. Old Harold was glad enough to go, too. Boy runs the paper more efficiently, more profitably, than he ever did. The boy'll be the one negotiating, he and the accountant, Butler. Smart as a whip, a good team."

"The father isn't active anymore?"

"He lives in Florida and chases women half his age."

She smiled, imagining a squat man in huge bathing trunks chasing teenagers on the beach at Fort Lauderdale. "And his son is a computer man."

He nodded. "Computers."

"I thought," she said, "the *I* was a newspaper, not a calculating machine."

He smiled sardonically at her and she quickly looked away. He said, "That's because you haven't been around and don't know. Maybe that's not how they run the New York *Times* or—publications in Dublin, Ireland, if there are any. But what runs modern newspapers now are computers and you'd better know the language. You've got to know your apples and young Dows does."

The archaic phrase brought a smile to her lips. "Well, I don't know what to say."

He shrugged. "No reason to say anything."

"I'm sorry about it."

"So'm I."

"Tony's in agreement?"

"Not entirely," he said. "But Tony's not in a position to do anything about it."

"It's a shame. But I understand." Then she remembered something, it was only half formed in her memory. "Wasn't there a clause in Grandpa's will, a committee of some sort—"

He nodded. "Three people. Elliott, Marge Reilly, and Mitch. When Mitch died, I replaced him. All I needed was Townsend and I've got him. Truth is, that codicil never would've stood up anyway . . ." As he talked she looked into the yard, where Cathy was playing. She saw her daughter standing alone under the big oaks at the edge of the lawn, watching something. Suddenly the little girl clapped her hands and a squirrel scampered up the tree. She saw the gardener raking leaves at the far end of the lawn. ". . . my hand was forced, really." He said, "There isn't anybody around to take over when I'm gone. I'm the last of the line. I have to see that the *I* survives, that's my responsibility. Always has been. Now with your mother gone, Frank gone, you in New York or wherever you live now or in the future . . ." He pushed the coffee cup away, jostling it, and she noticed that his hand was shaking, though his voice was steady and definite. "Elliott wanted me to hand it to you, lock, stock and barrel. He said, 'She's got the blood.' And I refused to do that, the *I* is no place for a caretaker, though I believe you'd've done well enough, maybe, if you'd stayed here. I didn't think I'd be doing you any service, that's the long and short of it." He looked at her briefly. "So I'm going to take the money and run. Part of it'll be yours, in time you'll be rich."

She made a gesture of dismissal with her hand. "Run where?"

"Not sure yet. Florida maybe. I've got friends in every damn town on the west coast of Florida. Hell, maybe I'll buy a condominium next to Harold Dows and chase women with him."

She rose and went to him. "Anything you want to do is all right with me. Anything at all. And I suppose you're right about the caretaker. I've never been able to understand legacies. Maybe I've always felt that females were excused from those." She spoke to him very softly now. "When a woman declares her independence it's usually total."

He patted her hand, his fingers dry and warm. The vacant look had returned to his eyes. "A thing like the *I*, it's either a curse or a salvation. Sometimes both at once." The telephone rang and he rose to answer it. He seemed about to say something else, then turned away. "Maybe I'll go to Tucson. Phoenix."

"Phoenix?"

He answered the telephone and put his hand over the receiver. "Nice golf courses both places." He listened for a moment, then handed the phone to her. "For you, overseas. It's a call from Europe somewhere, it sounded like a man." He handed her the telephone as if it were something diseased and went to the kitchen window, where he stood with his back to her, hands in his pockets.

She took the telephone gingerly, watching her father at the window. *Why now?* she thought. *Why did he have to call now?* But when she heard Myles's voice she was happy. He was calling from London; one day alone in the west of Ireland was more than enough. The house was very empty. He missed her terribly, did she miss him? Yes, she said; very much. How was everything in Dement? It was all right, she said; very, very sad. But better now. She intended to stay for a while, a week; perhaps longer, depending . . . She wished he were there with her, she said in a low voice. Well, he replied, the job was still uncertain but he didn't think he'd take it. The deal wasn't what he thought it was, and London was a long way away. He'd be back in New York by the end of next week, would she be back by then? She said she thought she would, depending. He said that everyone missed her in London. He named three friends with a brief account of their adventures. She said it was wonderful to hear his voice but it must be costing a fortune. Ha-ha, he said; he was calling from the newsroom of the BBC; their dime, not his. She laughed; it was characteristic Myles. All right then, he said, he'd meet her at the apartment at five the following Friday. He'd call next week to check. Oh Myles, she said; yes, absolutely. And thank you for calling, lamb. There was dead air between them for a moment. Then he asked her how Cathy was and she said, Fine. He said, Did you mean what you said a moment ago? Of course, she said. I wish I was there, too, he said. But we'll meet on Friday. Yes, she said, yes. It's four in the afternoon here, he said, and I didn't sleep last night because I'm under very considerable sexual tension . . . She began to laugh . . . and it's causing insomnia. What about you? he asked. Are you having insomnia? She glanced at her father. This was not the time for coocoo talk. She said yes, she was, but she had to go now. He said that talking to her made him feel better. Then he told her he adored her and hung up. She shook her head, staring at the buzzing receiver. When she turned around she saw her father was no longer at the window. She found him in the hallway in his hat and coat, his hand on the door-knob. He was ready if she was. She said, Fine, got her coat, and they walked silently to the car for the ten-minute drive to the newspaper building. She waved to Cathy, who was tagging along behind the gardener. Cathy ran to meet them. Where were they going? Dana said that Grandpa had a meeting and they'd be gone about one hour. Cathy wanted to come but Dana shook her head firmly, *No*. What was the meeting about, she asked. Charles said, "I'm going to sell the *I*, sweetheart." The child looked blankly at Dana; she had no idea what her grandfather was talking about. Dana said, "We'll be back in an hour," and moved off with her father. Cathy called to her before she'd gone a dozen steps and she returned to the little girl. Dana bent her head so she could hear her daughter's whispered question. "I don't understand what Grandpa means. You can't sell an eye." Dana smiled sadly and kissed her on the cheek. Cathy Rising McGee did not know the name of the newspaper. Dana said, "I'll tell you about it when we get back. Grandpa means he's selling his newspaper." The little girl laughed and said that in that case she was glad to stay home, with Bert the gardener. Dana kissed her again and rejoined her father.

She said to him, "That was my friend from Ireland on the phone. He's in London now and just wanted to call."

"That was very thoughtful of him."

"He's a very nice man," Dana said. She looked at her father, smiling. "A bachelor."

"A European?"

"Chinese," she said. "Russian father, Chinese mother. French grandparents. A Spanish aunt." She looked at him, grinning.

"Well," he said. "As long as he's not *Red* Chinese—"

She laughed and put her hand over his, resting on the seat. "What did Marge say?"

"Well, Marge." He shook his head. "Marge thought it was a betrayal. I've delivered the town into the hands of the enemy, to hear her tell it. Normally I wouldn't've listened to that sort of thing. Who is she to tell me what to do? But Marge is entitled. She had a right, she was a member of the committee. So I listened politely and then I hung up." He smiled bleakly. "But it wasn't very damn pleasant for me."

Dana said, "No." They were driving now. Dement's outskirts looked no different than they had the last time she was home, or the time before that. Growth had ceased and the general shabbiness was now a year older. Ashes to ashes, she thought. In a hundred years the plastic would sink into the swamp, the old Reilly Bog would win after all. They passed the billboard,

The Dement Intelligencer
SERVING DEMENT COUNTY

and she noticed that it had a fresh coat of paint.

She said, "Doesn't Mr. Bohn live in Phoenix?"

"Harry Bohn has a place there, bought it when he sold the bank to Bill Eurich's friends. And Bill has a condominium there. He's quite a fella, has moved on to another town. Has operations in three states and his son is now a partner. He'll be taking over in another couple of years. Bill Eurich made a fortune by getting guys together. That's all he ever did. Well, he's been urging me to get out, retire. He and Bohn and I can play golf all day."

They were passing an automobile graveyard. She did not want to talk about Bill Eurich. She pointed at the graveyard. "When did that happen?"

Charles smiled. "You know who owns that now? You may not remember because he died a number of years ago. Aces Evans's boy."

She laughed out loud. "The poker game."

"Good memory," he said.

She asked, "How do they do it now? Is it still the poker game, or is it done some other way? Manila envelopes? Numbered Swiss accounts?"

Her father shrugged. "You know, it's the damnedest thing. I don't know. I don't *know* how they do it now. Probably the same way. The ante's bigger, is all. It's been a long time since I checked. A hell of a long time." He thought a minute. "Probably too long."

In downtown Dement there were a few solitary shoppers, mostly elderly people walking in twos and threes. The town's heart looked more deserted than ever; it might have been a Sunday morning except there were no church bells. Charles parked the car and turned to face her. "Did Cathy know what I meant when I said I was selling the *I?*"

She hesitated, then smiled. He was owed the truth. "She said you couldn't sell an eye. 'I don't understand what Grandpa's saying,' she said."

Charles nodded, still looking at his daughter. "Isn't it the craziest thing?"

Dana looked away. It was indeed.

He said, "My earliest memories—"

She turned to face him. "I know. Mine, too."

He shook his head. "Not to know the *I.* Not to *know* it . . . Well," he said, "I suppose Cathy has other memories."

"Who knows? Maybe they're better."

"Better?" He smiled widely then. "Impossible!" Then he was out of the car and moving confidently across the street, Dana in his wake, turning the heavy revolving doors and walking quickly through the building. She shook hands and chatted with several of the older employees while her father looked on, jiggling coins in his pocket and grinning. A few of the employees she had known all her life. Half of those who had served as pallbearers at her grandfather's funeral were still at the paper.

In his office she asked him, "Does anyone know?"

He shook his head. "But they will as soon as Dows and Butler walk through the door. This place, they could never keep a secret. They can smell a newspaperman a mile away."

"What are they going to think?"

"It'll be upsetting as hell at first. But then they'll get used to it, like any death."

"And Tony knows."

"Sure. He didn't like it but there wasn't much he could do about it. So he's selling too. It's a sale of one hundred percent of the stock. Dows wouldn't want it any other way."

She sat in the visitor's chair while he read the mail. She picked up yesterday's *Intelligencer* and leafed through it, stopping at the editorial page. She wondered if they'd keep the Rising name on the masthead. They probably would, for a while. Then one day it would be gone and it would take some time for people to notice. It would make no difference anyway.

Then two men were at the door, both in overcoats, their manners grave. She said, "Dad?" Charles Rising looked up from his correspondence and waved them inside. He introduced them to her, Harold Dows, Jr., and Victor Butler. He took their coats and hung them on the tree in the corner and asked if he could get them coffee. They shook their heads politely. Harold Dows, Jr., turned to her and said that he understood she lived in New York, and worked for a publishing house. Was that right? It was. She edited books. Butler and her father were exchanging documents. Harold Dows had a manner older than his years, and when he offered his condolences to her his eyes and voice were heavy. His eyes were magnified behind aviator glasses and he wore a conservatively tailored blue suit and striped tie. She thought suddenly that he looked like an aging tennis pro. He seemed to have an easy,

bantering relationship with her father; he paid the older man deference, but it was Dows who was at ease in this office. He sat back in the
armchair, his legs crossed, one foot swinging. He said to her, "The
newspaper business never held any attraction for you? Lady publishers
aren't as rare now as they used to be."

My, she thought, wasn't he up-to-date, young Dows. "I've been
away for fifteen years."

He said, "It's a shame. Editing books, editing newspapers. There's
not a lot of difference."

She glanced at her father, who was following the conversation.
"There's quite a lot of difference, actually."

"Well," he said, "you'll have to explain that to me sometime." He
didn't believe her and didn't care that she knew he didn't believe her.
He gave the impression of having sensed tension between her and her
father. And he was not a man to let an opportunity pass by. A chilly
man, she thought; cold all the way down. He was looking now at
Charles Rising, sitting quietly at his desk, hands folded, a stapled document in front of him. Dows said, "It's the best year you could've
done this, but of course you know that."

"Taxwise, yes," her father said.

"Well, that too," Dows said. "But I wasn't thinking of taxes. I was
thinking of your plant."

"The stuff, most of it, is old but good."

"It's going to have to be replaced," Dows said.

Her father leaned forward. "How soon do you think you can do it?"

"The quicker you get in, the cheaper it is in the long run." He
looked at Dana and smiled. "I'd guess we'll be entirely cold type in two
and a half years. Thank God, most of your composing-room people
are either at retirement or nearing retirement." He smiled at her again.
"That's the nut of it, the new technology will only work if you can get
rid of people. That's what costs money now. It costs money now and
it's going to cost more in the years to come. And salaries are the least
of it, it's the benefits." He looked at her and frowned; he didn't want
to bore her with these business statistics, though there were women in

the business now who understood these complicated matters at least as well as he did. Of course she too was a modern woman who could grasp the numbers and draw the appropriate conclusions. "The moment these papers are signed Vic starts making telephone calls and I take a dozen selected men and send them to school to learn the new language."

She said, "No more back shop."

Dows shook his head happily. "In our plant in McLean we've got Muzak in the back shop. Instead of linotypes we've got Mantovani. It's a paste-up operation, all of it's done with cameras and computers . . ."

Then her father and Dows began to discuss a technical point. She was impressed with his grasp of the language. He was not as secure in it as Dows but he understood it well enough. He rarely discussed the details of the business at home, and she realized suddenly that there were whole regions of his mind crammed with arcane facts and concepts. She looked at Harold Dows, another son-of-the-founder. His father would be proud of him, no doubt. A modern man, at ease in the technological world . . .

"Thought I'd come for the ceremonies." It was Tony, standing in the doorway; she could smell whiskey ten feet away. "Just sit and watch you do it," he said with a smile.

Charles stared at him a moment, then shrugged and waved him to a vacant chair. "You know Harold Dows and Victor Butler?" They both stood and Tony Rising shook hands formally, peering at each man. Then he sat down, next to Dana.

"Thought I ought to be here," he said.

She said, "It's not very interesting."

"Just wait," he said.

They were winding down now and she noticed Butler making lengthy notes. The agreement of sale was in order and they would both initial it. Announcement to come Friday.

Charles looked at the younger man. "You going to keep Bill Eurich on the board?"

"Probably," Dows said.

"He hasn't attended more than three meetings in five years, but he's a valuable man."

"Four meetings," Tony said.

"So they tell me." Dows's eyes shifted. "I expected to see Mr. Townsend here."

"Elliott doesn't move around much," Charles said.

"How old is he now?"

"Ninety-four, ninety-five. Something like that."

Dows looked at Butler. "Charles, this is certainly none of my business. I hesitate even to mention it. But this is a very complicated transaction. I'd want to make certain that everything was understood. I don't believe in surprises. I don't want to be surprised somewhere down the line and I don't want you to be surprised."

"I'll take my chances," Charles said dryly.

Dows held up his hand, *pax*. "So there's just the last item."

Charles shook his head. "It's not going to work."

"Charles, it has to work."

"It'll work," Tony said. "If Charlie's involved in it, it'll work. Take my word."

Charles and Dows ignored him. "Can't," Charles said.

"Let's review again exactly what the requirements are. You stay as chairman of the board, a two-year contract so far as the money is concerned. The money is guaranteed. Obviously if there were severe policy disagreements we would have to make other arrangements. But to tell you the truth I don't think we will have disagreements. Your salary: fifty thousand dollars a year. That's part of the payout. Vic, here, will be chief executive officer and publisher. But we want your firm hand here—"

"Here, here," Tony said, clapping slowly.

"—for guidance. I don't believe we'll be operating the business substantially differently than you did, except for the technical end. And of course we will bring in some of our own people. But you know this town top to bottom and your expertise is—will be—invaluable. I must say to you, it's crucial."

He said, "It's over, Harold. You people own it now, or will when I put pen to paper. It makes no sense for me to hang on. I don't give a crap about the fifty thousand. Fifty thousand or a hundred and fifty thousand makes no difference to me. I'm going to Florida."

"That's all right," Dows said. "You can go to Florida, just so long as you're near a telephone and four times a year return here—at our expense, naturally—and preside at the board meetings. And talk. Spend some time with the merchants and developers, make certain that we're doing our job. Make certain that we haven't caused offense in some way."

"Hell, Charlie—"

"Tony," Charles said patiently. "Hush."

"When are you goan' talk tradition with these assholes? Jesus, Charlie, there's eighty years—"

Charles Rising looked at Dows, and then at Butler. The expression on his face was one of bemusement, as if somehow a harmless madman had wandered into their midst and if they all kept calm, would shortly go away again. "Why not Tony here? Tony'd make a hell of a chairman." Charles grinned but the faces of Dows and Butler were tight, both glaring at Tony.

Tony said, "Wish to hell Mitch were here. Bomb you people—"

Charles began to laugh. "You think that's what the major would do?"

"Christ, yes," Tony said. "Mitch was an asshole, too. Takes one to know one." He took a pint bottle from his pocket and drank from it.

"Now just a minute—" Dows began. Dana looked at him. His son-of-the-founder demeanor was unraveling and he looked frightened. He was unprepared for Tony Rising and his voice began to bluster.

But Charles held up his hand. "Tony," he said. "It's done."

"Firebomb the bastards," he muttered. "Back to the Stone Age."

"Tony—"

"A black day for our father," he said. "You can bet your ass he's up there now, mad. You bastards"—he pointed at Dows and Butler—"better have the insurance up to date on this building, Amos might just throw a lightning bolt at it. Hell, I might do it myself." He capped the bottle, put it in his pocket, and lapsed into silence.

Dows demanded, "What the hell is all this—"

Dana said, "Mantovani in the executive suite."

Charles could not stop grinning. "Well, let's get down to it."

Butler was reviewing his notes and Dows was staring at the ceiling. Dows said at last, "This is all very unfortunate. But the point we were discussing was the board chairmanship. And what I was about to say was that it was good for the town. Good for the newspaper. Charles, you know as well as I do that the *I* is just about the last institution left around here, downtown. Your departure would be like a bugle—"

"Ta-da, ta-*da!*" Tony wailed.

"—to the rest of the people here, sounding retreat." He'd decided that the way to deal with Tony Rising was to ignore him. "We sure as hell don't want that and I can't imagine that you want it either."

Charles thought a moment before replying. Then, to her astonishment, he said, "Do you have any ideas, Dana?"

She had sat numb, listening to all this. Tony, ineffectual and mild his entire life, roaring now like an Old Testament prophet; her father, so humorless where the *I* and his family were concerned, apparently enjoying it. She shook her head. Dows looked at her politely, then turned away; his smile was sardonic. Then she said, "Do you think Junior here is right, a bugle sounding retreat?" Dows's smile vanished.

Charles said, "Maybe."

"Well," she said. "Maybe it's time." She leaned forward, glancing pleasantly at the young man, and then winking at her father. "We've stayed at the party longer than anyone else. Maybe it's time to go."

"Jesus Christ," Tony mumbled.

Charles said again, "Maybe."

"Sharp breaks are not always bad," Dana said.

Tony stood up then, weaving a little, and wandered to the door. They all watched him in silence; he was hypnotic as he slowly made his way across the room. He was completely unpredictable now.

Charles said, "Come on, Tony. Sit down."

He shook his head. "Isn't it the damnedest thing?" He turned away and was silent again. His back was to them all. Dana looked at her father, and at Dows and Butler. Dows leaned forward and began to talk again about the chairmanship. She cut him off in mid-sentence. "What's the damnedest thing?" Tony turned to look at her and when he spoke it was to her alone. "This thing, this *I*. Mitch and I spent our lives serving it and came away with nothing. Your father spent his life serving it and came away with a little more than nothing, though not a lot." Then, without taking his eyes off her, he spoke sharply to Dows. "Don't smile, young man. It's not a question of money, never has been. You can take cash flow and stuff it up your ass for all the good it does. Rest of us never understood it anyway. Charles understood it. So Mitch and I in different ways spent our lives at the side of the old man. And those years were all right, I have no complaints about them; Mitch did, but Mitch is dead. But this thing, good or bad, was all there was. We all lived inside it, like"—he fluttered his hands— "moths inside the cocoon. It was what we had, and at the same time it brought us together and drew us apart. The *I* was like the news itself, ambiguous. Or like the news became, after Amos died. There was no way for Mitch or me to work with your father, there wasn't enough left. So we hung on inside the cocoon long beyond our time. Long after we were entitled to fly away. I ought to hate it, this place, but I don't. I ought to hate your father, too, but I don't. I can't stand to see it go, Dana. I'd rather see it die, killed by greed or incompetence, than live at the hands of—these two. That's the difference between your father and me. He says it's got to live at all costs and I say it's better off dead, exactly like the world it served. It's dead the way monarchies are dead. Sell it off, hell, it's like selling a nation." He stood with his hand on the doorknob, his large watery eyes glaring at them all. "But that's the view from inside the cocoon. The rest of you, you've been outside. No doubt you're doing what's best, Charles. But I hate it. Hate it to death." Then he turned and walked out the door.

Dana could not look at her father or the others. The room was quiet, the only sounds the rustle of paper; Butler was blindly leafing through the document in his lap. Charles Rising was staring at his desk top, his face flushed.

Dows broke the silence. "I think somebody should call a doctor. Medical attention—"

But Charles shook his head sadly, looking at Dana. He seemed to want guidance of some kind but there was nothing for Dana to say. He said finally, "I'll stay if you want me to stay. But it won't do any good. It won't help, it'll hurt. The Risings are no longer part of Dement, what it's become. Bill Eurich'll do you more good than I will. But I'll stay and we'll say no more about any 'voice' for me in policy. You own it and you'll run it and I'll be here for cosmetic reasons only. Let's be entirely clear about that. And I intend to stay on without salary of any kind." Dows looked at him, incredulous. "You've just made yourself a hundred thousand dollars, young Harold. Tell that to your old man, he'll love it. Now I'm going home." He tossed the document across the desk and Butler caught it before it cascaded to the floor. Dana saw her father's scrawled initials on the margins of each page. Before the younger men could collect themselves Charles was out of his chair and putting on his hat and coat and standing by the door. Dows and Butler made hasty good-byes, Dows carefully writing his own initials next to Charles's on the pages and signing on the last page. Then he capped the pen and placed the letter of agreement on the desk. There were a few more words, pleasantries, and then they were gone.

She said, "Why?"

"It doesn't make any difference," he said.

"I know. That's what I mean."

"Tony wasn't all wrong, you know."

She said, "I know."

"Well, it was partly a reaction to him."

"And why no money?"

He smiled and leaned against the open door. "The last capricious act of a careful man. Maybe the only capricious thing I've ever done in my life. But it made it better for me. Easier somehow."

"Sackcloth and ashes?"

"Maybe a little of that."

"You did the right thing," she lied.

"Do you really think so? Tell me honestly."

"I guess I don't know," she said finally.

He smiled at that. "I don't either."

She said, "You can always quit."

"Oh, Dana, no." He began to laugh. "We never quit."

"But Tony was completely right about one thing. Those two are *assholes*."

Her father nodded soberly and closed his eyes. He said nothing for a moment, rubbing the palm of his hand over his chin. Then he made a fist and tapped the door tenderly. When he looked at her he had tears in his eyes. "Doesn't Dows remind you a little of Frank?"

She waited a moment before replying. The evidence on Frank Rising was not in and would never be in. What evidence they had was contradictory. She believed in her heart that Frank Rising was exactly like Harold Dows. She put her arm around her father's waist and kissed him on the cheek. "Yes," she said softly, in reassurance.

SHE LEFT the following Thursday, with Cathy, in the rented car. It was a quiet week; they had gone out to dinner twice and once she'd taken Cathy to a movie. Friday night the telephone rang continually, friends calling to comment on the sale of the newspaper. She took most of the calls, explaining that her father was out or asleep or unavailable, depending on the call. She reminded all of them that he would remain as a member of the board of directors and that seemed to give them comfort. There were very few calls from politicians. Once, she and her father went to her mother's grave for a silent five minutes. Over the week he grew stronger but the vacant look never left him entirely and not once did he and Dana discuss the past. He seemed to want to know about her life and she told him as much as she could; but he didn't understand it, and seemed to disapprove. She mentioned Myles just once more, then did not mention him again.

She promised to return for the Easter holiday and her father agreed that it was a good time, "but we'll see." She invited him to New York for Christmas and he said he might come, "depending." He told her that he'd write her a long letter about the terms of the sale, but in any case she was a rich woman. She tried to be enthusiastic about it, believing that her enthusiasm would please him. But he seemed indifferent and at the end she had to admit that the money didn't matter to her, one way or the other. When she said it out loud, he accepted it, nodding in understanding. They kissed at the door, the distance between them narrower than it had been ever. But then they had always looked out on the same gulf. He asked her one last favor, to drop by—"Just fifteen minutes, no longer"—to see Elliott Townsend. She said that she would. He leaned into the car on the passenger's side and kissed his granddaughter. Then he stepped back, his shoes scraping the gravel. "So long," he said.

She left Cathy in the car, under protest. But the visit would be short and she wanted to be alone with the old man. Mrs. Haines let her in and left her waiting in the hallway while she checked to see if Townsend was awake and prepared for visitors. She heard the rumble of their voices, then him calling for her to come in. She had not seen him in three years and was prepared for a wasted old man. But he had not changed; if anything he was stronger than three years before. Mrs. Haines brought them both a cup of coffee, then left them alone. They looked at each other across a distance of sixty years, saying nothing for a moment. This last visit to Dement, she wanted to make it count.

She said, "Do you intend to live forever?"

He laughed, a dry chuckle like the crackle of a fire. "I might at that. Feel better today than yesterday. Feel better this year than last."

"You look—splendid."

"I know," he said. "Isn't it the damnedest thing?"

She said, "I was with Dad when he had the final meeting with Dows. Did you know that he agreed to stay on for two years? As a member of the board. Chairman."

"He did?"

She said, "Yeah," with that lilt.

"It surprises me. I didn't think he would."

"He said he didn't know why he did."

The old man nodded. "Your father's like that sometimes. He depended on your mother—" She looked at him, her eyes narrowed. "Yes, that and the family. You. Your grandfather. Your brother, when he was alive. More than he thought, I think, and more than was good for him. Me, I haven't had any family for almost fifty years." He was silent and she rose and went to the window. Back of the cornfield she could see the concrete of the Interstate. She'd noticed the new supermarket on the corner and a gas station down the block. It occurred to her suddenly that he was surrounded, he and the five or six other families on the block, all of them old people. They were surrounded by commerce.

"Were you happy when he sold the *I*?" She asked the question tentatively.

"He came here the night your mother died. Before she died, but that night. And we talked about it quite a little. I fought him, I didn't want to see it happen. It seems that everything I have known has been surrendered, one way or another. Everything that Amos and I built, and it was quite a lot, has disappeared. Your father had different ideas, he was a man of his time. I thought Amos's influence would last forever, but it hasn't. It didn't last five years and I can't say whether we're the better for it or not. I don't get around the way I used to. I know the politics've changed. Everything's changed. He and I, the only thing we wanted was to keep the violence away. Make the place safe, and I mean secure. Secure it against the aliens. Amos called them aliens, but he meant outsiders. I guess you'd say now that he wanted things to be predictable. So did I. You know the story about Capone's people, that's a Rising story that will never die. Well, it didn't happen in quite the way we used to tell it. Funny thing, I can't remember anymore what the truth was. So we'll have to live with the yarn, won't we? We live with the stories we make up. Those are the real stories, more real than the originals. The way it really was, that died with Amos." He stopped and looked away, breathing heavily. "Hell yes, I think we were better. Amos and me. But it's like that story. The way it was, that's just my memory."

"Did you hear about Tony?" She watched him shake his head. "You'll pardon my language but Tony called Dows an asshole and then he said the *I* should just die. Die with Risings. It should not, in any case, be sold. He seemed to think that selling it was like selling a nation."

"Tony said that?" The old man was incredulous.

"He said it."

"Tony was your grandfather's favorite."

"He was?"

"And it sounds to me like your grandfather's voice." He smiled then, lost in thought. "Nice to think so anyway. Well. What do you do now?"

"Go back to New York."

"That little girl of yours. Is she all right?"

"She's fine. I've got to get back to her now." Dana stood up.

"And that ex-husband. Is he still around?"

"Still around," Dana said. "But there's a man I go out with—"

"Live with him?"

She laughed; it was an incongruous remark coming from this old man. She said, "Sometimes."

He said grimly, "I thought that's what everybody did."

"Some do," she said. "Some don't."

"Well," he said. "Don't cheat yourself."

She said, "I don't intend to."

"Hang on to it," he said.

"I intend to do that, too."

"Mn," he said.

"But can you give me any advice about my dad?"

He said, "I have no advice." He said slowly, "He sold the *I*. Your mother's gone, nothing is as he knew it. All the familiar things are gone and the future is not as he believed it would be. Though I am not certain he thought much about the future. That may have been part of the trouble, because your father—and me, too—bears some responsibility." He paused then and looked up at her. "We took a lot of things for granted. And now we're a colony with a proconsul like any colony. My *God*, in the Midwest we fought that from the time of the first railroads. Mr. Lincoln fought it. We've lost it for good now, it's over and done with, and in a jiffy it'll be forgotten. But if anyone ever asks you about the *I*, what it was and what it stood for—" He paused again and looked away, past the oak and the field and the highway beyond, a cluttered horizon. "You tell 'em it was the greatest force for reaction since the cold bath."

She laughed out loud, laughed until the tears came. He sat looking at her, smiling a little, his eyes glittering. She leaned down and kissed him on his dry cheek. "Stay close to my father," she said.

He said, "You stay in touch."

"I'll be back," she said.

He nodded. "When?"

"Easter. Next summer for sure."

"I'll be here. He will, too."

"I know you will," she said. "I know it." He closed his eyes, she noticed that she'd been with him fifteen minutes and the vitality had gone out of him as if drawn by a magnet. He said, "Good-bye, Dana." She left the old man then, hurrying from the house to her car, thinking suddenly of Myles and his arrival from Europe. Perhaps she would meet his plane, greet him fresh from Europe and go straight to some familiar place. She fought to think of Myles but the memory of her father kept crowding her and pushing at her; her father kissing Cathy and stepping away from the car, smiling nicely and saying, So long. His sweet smile below the empty eyes; and so much still concealed. This presence in her heart, this hurt; it seemed as much consolation as rebuke. But she also knew that it was the essence of the region. It gave, and it never took away.

In the parlor of the house the old man had already forgotten her visit. He was sitting with his eyes closed, dreaming of a warm day in January on the Nebraska plains, men working in shirtsleeves in the sun and his mother waving good-bye as she walked off down the road to town. The film always stopped there, a frozen frame of a pretty woman in a bonnet and a pleated skirt, her hand raised, standing in a halo of sunlight.

PublicAffairs is a new publishing house and a tribute to the standards, values, and flair of three persons who have served as mentors to countless reporters, writers, editors, and book people of all kinds, including me.

I. F. Stone, proprietor of *I. F. Stone's Weekly*, combined a commitment to the First Amendment with entrepreneurial zeal and reporting skill and became one of the great independent journalists in American history. At the age of eighty, Izzy published *The Trial of Socrates*, which was a national bestseller. He wrote the book after he taught himself ancient Greek.

Benjamin C. Bradlee was for nearly thirty years the charismatic editorial leader of *The Washington Post*. It was Ben who gave the *Post* the range and courage to pursue such historic issues as Watergate. He supported his reporters with a tenacity that made them fearless, and it is no accident that so many became authors of influential, best-selling books.

Robert L. Bernstein, the chief executive of Random House for more than a quarter century, guided one of the nation's premier publishing houses. Bob was personally responsible for many books of political dissent and argument that challenged tyranny around the globe. He is also the founder and was the longtime chair of Human Rights Watch, one of the most respected human rights organizations in the world.

·   ·   ·

For fifty years, the banner of Public Affairs Press was carried by its owner Morris B. Schnapper, who published Gandhi, Nasser, Toynbee, Truman, and about 1,500 other authors. In 1983 Schnapper was described by *The Washington Post* as "a redoubtable gadfly." His legacy will endure in the books to come.

Peter Osnos, *Publisher*

DATE DUE

GAYLORD			PRINTED IN U.S.A.